The Reinvented Detective

The Reinvented Detective

Edited by

CAT RAMBO
&
JENNIFER BROZEK

CAEZIK
SF & FANTASY
ARC MANOR
ROCKVILLE, MARYLAND

＊

SHAHID MAHMUD
PUBLISHER

www.caeziksf.com

ISBN: 978-1-64710-105-3

First Edition. 1st Printing. December 2023.
1 2 3 4 5 6 7 8 9 10

An imprint of Arc Manor LLC

www.CaezikSF.com

Contents

Foreword

Jennifer Brozek

After editing *The Reinvented Heart* anthology with Cat Rambo, she asked if I would be interested in editing another anthology in the same series with her. I jumped at the chance. Since she chose the topic of our first anthology, she allowed me to choose the topic for our second. I knew exactly what I wanted to edit: *The Reinvented Detective.* What would an anthology about detectives and the crimes they solve look like in the future? How would technology change what we already know today?

My love of detective and crime fiction started young with *Encyclopedia Brown*. Something about him solving crimes when the adults around him couldn't or wouldn't enticed me to more crime fiction. *Nancy Drew* was the first series I read where a girl was the detective and could (mostly) take care of herself. She was smart, inventive, and persistent. Somehow these loves led me to the prurient "True Crime" and "Pulp" magazines in my teens. Probably because I was told I shouldn't and couldn't read them. Is there anything more attractive than the forbidden?

Along the way I read a lot of fantasy and science fiction. Ever the reader, my mother encouraged me to read anything I wanted on her bookshelves. That was the one thing she didn't restrict—if she

1

owned it, I could read it. Asimov, Bradbury, King, Koontz, Zelazny, and more. If I had questions, I could ask. (I never had questions. Things I didn't understand, but wasn't invested enough to look up, I glossed over. As long as the story made sense, I was happy.)

My father favored what I like to call "men's soap operas." Book series like *The Destroyer* and *The Executioner/Mack Bolan*. I love these too. However, Dad also read a lot of hardboiled detective and spy novels by the likes of Raymond Chandler, Dashiell Hammett, and Ian Fleming. I devoured these as much as I devoured everything else in the house.

From these two points of view, my love of a wide variety of genres was born. They allowed me to enjoy media from all walks of life. I love a good book, but I also love a good movie or TV series. One of these is the movie *Brick*. It is pure noir shlock set in a modern day high school that follows all of the noir tropes while playing with the problems of high school students. It opened my eyes to the possibilities of mixing and matching different styles of stories in a very real and visceral way.

Of course, when it comes to movies, my taste is just as eclectic. I love *Casablanca* as much as I love *Bladerunner*. There is always a bit of mystery and the sense of danger. Sometimes you're on the side of the criminal and sometimes it's the law that has your vote … and sometimes, it's that iconoclastic private detective straddling the middle of the road that wins your heart—if not the day. That's the thing about crime fiction. The bad guy doesn't always lose. The good guy doesn't always win. Sometimes, it's hard to figure out whose side you are on.

These days, I generally don't like "real life" crime entertainment (no matter how good it is) because I don't want my imagination dwelling on real life horror. However, noir and other styles of mystery novels/series are just enough "not real" or just enough "fantastical" that I can sink into them and enjoy. Right now, I'm leaning into my inner little old lady and enjoying the heck out of British (and other from over the pond) murder mysteries and detective shows: *Midsomer Murders, Poirot, Vera, Miss Fisher Murder Mysteries, Rosemary and Thyme*, and so many more.

Cat and I had a long talk about the next "reinvented" anthology we would do. For me, the choice of *The Reinvented Detective* was an obvious one based on my current media loves. How would detective stories change when written for an SF future? What would be considered a crime? Who would solve the mysteries in the real world, in the digital world, in some hybrid world we haven't thought of yet? Where would AI come into it? *The Reinvented Detective* was the perfect vehicle to mix and match some of my favorite genres. I couldn't wait to see what our authors would come up with and they did not disappoint.

We have all kinds of stories to entertain you. From futuristic crime in the real world ("The Unassembled Victims" by Peter Clines) to digital murder set in a text-based reality ("Color Me Dead" by E. J. Delaney) to finding lost music and a missing person ("Request to Vanish" by Lauren Ring) to making the punishment fit the crime ("Gum5hoe" by Carrie Harris) to death in mysterious circumstances ("In the Shadow of the Great Days" by Harry Turtledove) to conniving AIs ("Agents Provocateur" by Lazarus Black) and so much more. Once again Jane Yolen has joined us with poetry. Her poetry is complemented with a poem by Seanan McGuire. Together the three poems break out our anthology into three sections: Reports, Artifacts, Judgments.

As I have said before, "A collaboration is a beautiful and delicate thing, two artists (or anthologists) blending their strengths together to make something more than the sum of their parts." In this particular anthology, Cat and I had our separate favorites, but there were no big discussions about those stories. No "this is my veto" story. It was more about personal preference than not. I enjoyed the fact that we were on the same page throughout the story selection. Our "Thunderdome" conversation (8 stories enter, 3 stories remain) came down to word count and fit with those stories already selected.

I hope you enjoy reading this anthology as much as I enjoyed editing it. You've got a wild ride ahead of you. It will be worth it.

Reports

That Missing C: Police Report #1

Jane Yolen

Without the C,
crime is simply a cold case,
unsolvable here
or the future here.
It is a poetic attempt
to make us think,
shiver, hope for fantastic
new weapons to fight
the future wars.

Without the C
criminals are merely
something that slant-rhymes
with urinals, the detritus
of old tales, the bad guys,
the wolves in hot outfits
who stalk young women
and wrap them in red oaks,
which once upon a time
were red cloaks.

Without the C
criminals lack cunning
or common sense,
and the police force
is short on cops and capture.
There are no cells to jail anyone
without that missing C.

Without the C we have no cases,
and lawyers have no fees
or fies or foes or fums.
As for judges, they may have gavels,
but they rule over neither circuit nor court.

If in the future, Cs are totally abandoned,
do not hope for justice or mercy,
for they both have a C embedded in them.
Just hope your innocence
which doubles up on Cs
is enough to sustain a lenient response.
It may actually be a heavy ending
without its own C, but closer to a lawn
or meadow than you deserve.

At least fists, guns, bombs, swords, knives,
are still available.
Get yours before B, F, G, S, and K disappear,
before some future thief wrapped in noir
steals them out from under us,
leaving us with no past and no future.

The Best Justice Money Can Buy

C.C. Finlay

*T*he district attorney skipped outside to have a celebratory vape, leaving Tucker Boardman, the infamous "billionaire brat," to fidget alone in the interrogation room. Detective Ellen Chung studied Boardman through the one-way glass, hoping some mumbled confession or finger-comb of his disheveled hair might reveal a secret aspect of his character. Something beyond the sordid tabloid headlines. But there was nothing she hadn't already seen. Just a smirking twenty-something with blood on his hands. His red-rimmed eyes glanced toward the door every few seconds while he waited for rescue to arrive in the form of his mother and her phalanx of lawyers.

She heard someone else enter the observation room and caught a ghostly reflection in the glass. Dark skin, nice suit. Malcom Warren. Solid detective, one of the best to enter the department in the past ten years. He might become a really good investigator if he stuck with it, but his expensive taste in clothes and his habit of chasing department gossip were sure signs of ambition. Probably wanted to be chief someday. As far as Chung was concerned, ambition was poison to good police work.

He stepped up beside her. "I thought you were in the captain's shithouse, working that Ocean Beach Rando thing," he said. "How'd you catch a prime case like this?"

Typical of Warren, worrying about what the captain thought. She'd requested the Ocean Beach Rando case. For three years, someone had been raping and killing runaways and homeless people. Chung was so close to solving it, but nobody wanted to pay for the prosecution, and her main suspect was almost as poor as his victims. Even if she made an arrest, the DA would dump the case like a piece of junk rather than prosecute it at a loss. But shithouse or penthouse, all victims were equal as far as Chung was concerned. Her mentor taught her that: either everyone mattered, or no one did.

There was no budget for the investigation, but the captain let her pursue it as long as she made enough profitable arrests to pay her salary. Which she did, if barely. That's how things worked when you had a for-profit justice system. It was the American way.

What she said to Warren was, "Right place, right time."

"You're kidding me."

She shook her head.

"You mean to tell me, the only son of the richest woman in the United States plows his car into a crowd of pedestrians, kills a couple of sweet kids, and you just happen to be on the scene to cuff him?"

"I was treating myself to lunch at the New Formosa." She'd made an arrest this morning, small-time charges, on a trespassing case. The perp would pay his fines if he could afford them or work them off in the prison factory if he couldn't. So it was more of a catch-and-release. But victories were victories, and you had to celebrate them. "I was standing outside on Santa Monica, fifty feet away, when the accident happened."

"So you miss out on potstickers, but you make the arrest of the century."

He *would* think about it in those terms. "I recognized Boardman, so I grabbed him and got him away from the cameras, then called the captain before I called it in," she said. A shrug. She hated department politics, but she wasn't stupid.

"But everybody's got a camera these days," Warren said. "I saw six or seven different videos of the accident scene already." He paused. "Didn't see you."

She snorted. She'd deliberately bumped and knocked over the nearest amateur journalist on her way to grabbing Boardman. Only a sucker—or somebody with ambition—would let themselves get caught on camera. It was always better if the criminals didn't know who you were, if they couldn't see you coming.

On the other side of the glass, Boardman shouted for lawyers, yelling that he couldn't be treated this way. But they could treat him that way. At least until the lawyers arrived. Chung intended to enjoy every minute of it. Might be the only punishment he actually received.

When she didn't offer any other commentary, Warren nodded his head. "Well, congratulations. And thanks. It's only negligent homicide, but you just fully funded your pension and probably bought all of us a pay raise for next year. And you pissed off the Hollywood Precinct by taking that money out of their pocket. Everyone wins."

"Yeah, those kids he ran over, they sure feel like winners."

He held up his hands in surrender. "It's a tragedy. I get that. But their families will get a huge settlement. People who commit crimes have to pay for them. And the Boardmans can afford to pay. A lot. The new laws that made police departments self-funding? Asset forfeitures, arrest fees, jail fees, fines, they only get us so far. This case means a lot of money for the department."

She already watched the brass head into the chief's office to figure out how to spend it. "Tens of millions."

"*Hundreds* of millions," Warren said. "You might get bumped up to Major Crimes."

She shuddered at the thought. "I get the economic argument. But you know he's not going to do any jail time. Doesn't that bug you?"

"So he hires a substitute to go to jail for him. Switches identities with someone. Big deal. Public sees that somebody gets punished. The Boardman family still has to pay. Pays extra for treatment like that."

That was the problem, wasn't it? Chung had joined law enforcement before all the budget "reforms" of the Great Economic Correction. Now, the only time criminals were prosecuted to the full extent of the law was when someone could pay for it, whether criminal or victim. If the victims had money, they would pay the police to pursue the criminal and the district attorney to prosecute. If the criminal had money, they would pay to get a more favorable result. If someone got sent to prison, they had to pay for that too: the prisoner was charged for their food, housing, clothing, medical care, and supervision. They were forced to work in one of the for-profit prison factories for a couple bucks an hour, and the charges were taken out of their earnings. It was easy for prisoners to run up debt. Then they were stuck in prison until their families paid their fees or they grew too old or sick to work. It amounted to slave labor.

The old system may have been broken too, with some of the same problems, but at least it *pretended* to be about justice.

She grunted some kind of response to Warren's comment. He was welcome to interpret it however he wanted.

He laughed. "Hey, if you don't want the conviction bonus, you can give it to me!"

"You weren't there," she snapped. "It looked like Boardman smashed into the crowd on purpose. He was laughing at the dead bodies. Like they were a joke. The blood on his hands wasn't his—he climbed out of the wreck and was finger-painting on the bodies."

"Jesus," Warren said. "The clip I saw on the news made it look like he was trying to help them."

"He wasn't trying to help."

In the interrogation room, Boardman pounded on the table. "Room service! I want room service in here! Where's my champagne?" When he started giggling, Chung turned off the sound.

Warren stared at him through the window. "How drunk is he?"

"Point-two-one on the breathalyzer before lunch," she said. "And high as the stock market with a cocktail of drugs, according to the skin tests. All collected legally during the thirty seconds I let the EMTs look at him." She'd paid for the tests out of her own pocket, so there could be no questions later about dismissal due to nonpayment of fees by either the victims or perp.

"Sounds like an open-and-shut case. Don't you wish they were all that easy?"

Was that a reference to the Ocean Beach Rando case? Probably.

"I checked Boardman's records," she said. "This isn't his first hit-and-run. Two other times it was his car, but his mother claimed someone else was driving and paid off the victims. I miss the old three-strikes rule."

"Now it's just like baseball. You can buy as many strikes as you can afford."

An abomination of the game. She was still mad at the Dodgers for losing the last World Series on a home run in the bottom of the ninth after the other team's hitter bought eleven extra strikes. A whole season's salary, but worth it for the win. She missed the old baseball rules too.

"Right place, right time," Warren echoed, shaking his head as if he couldn't believe her luck. "What more could you want?"

"I just want to see the bad guy go to jail."

"So they hire a replacement to do his time? They don't find angels to do that sort of thing. Maybe you'll just have to settle for *a* bad guy going to jail."

The door bumped open, and a uniform popped his head inside. "Boardman's mother and their lawyers are here. The DA wants you in the conference room."

As Chung headed for the door, Warren called out behind her. "Take the win!"

Chung had seen Lena Boardman on video a million times and always assumed that digital magic helped create the billionaire's particular look. But even in person, Boardman's skin conjured a sort of smooth, vinyl perfection with no visible wrinkles, not even a freckle. Her clothes were simple and perfect. Her hair looked naturally black and glossy, and she had the lean, ageless look that only money could buy. You'd guess that she was anywhere between thirty-five and sixty, but Chung knew for a fact that the woman would soon be seventy-nine.

Boardman had made her fortune in green tech with solar power and wind farms, when those fortunes were still being made, and then famously frozen a bunch of her eggs, waiting until she retired from day-to-day management of her company to have a kid. Or to hire a surrogate to have a kid for her. Which is how she became America's most famous single mother for a while. A small team of lawyers, PR people, and financial advisors clustered around her now. They all looked like they had rolled off an assembly line that mass-produced Lena Boardman wannabees.

The police chief, Chung's captain, and the district attorney were also in the room. Chung closed the door and took a seat. Tucker Boardman was noticeably absent, which meant his mother didn't trust him and had power of attorney. Probably established after the other hit-and-runs.

One of Boardman's lawyers cleared her throat. "Now that we're all here, I suggest we sign the NDAs before proceeding."

"Of course," said the DA.

Ah, the ceremonial exchange of the NDAs. A legal agreement more binding than anything in criminal law.

Everyone lifted their pads, and documents flew across the room. Chung didn't bother to read the ones that popped up on her screen. She knew the basics—everything discussed in this room stayed in this room, she could never discuss the case in public, etc., etc. As the person on the bottom rung of the ladder, it was her job to keep quiet and nod agreeably. She signed electronically and sent all the documents back.

The numbers being discussed soon boggled her mind. Not only were the amounts higher than any she'd ever heard before, but it was more money than she'd ever seen in a lifetime. That said, everyone knew the market rates for this sort of crime, given a perp with this kind of wealth, and the negotiations went fairly quickly. While the details got worked out for the charges, the trial, and the punishment, she let her thoughts drift to the Ocean Beach Rando case and her options for keeping the killer off the street.

"Detective?" asked Boardman.

Chung looked up, startled. "Yes, ma'am?"

"I understand that you were first on the scene, that you got my son away from the cameras, and made sure he had medical treatment."

All true. More or less. She shifted uncomfortably in her seat. "Yes, ma'am. Right place, right time."

"I wish to express my personal gratitude for your attention and your discretion. This all could have been much worse."

Just how bad were those other two hit-and-run cases? Chung wondered.

"If there is anything I can do for you personally …" Boardman said.

She let the offer dangle there like a suitcase full of money. Chung's captain shook his head, and the chief glared at her with an unsubtle threat to be silent. This was the most profitable case of their careers, and they didn't want Chung's famous aptitude for saying the wrong thing to fuck it up.

She chose her next words very carefully. "I've been working on another case …"

One lawyer leaned over and whispered to Boardman, while another flicked some documents across the tablet. Boardman looked down and then nodded. "The Ocean Beach Rando killer. It's been in the news."

"The news loves it because there's another grisly murder to cover every month or two. But there's no one to pay for the apprehension and prosecution of a suspect. Friends of some of the victims started a fund, but there's hardly any money in it. I work it mostly on my own time, but with more resources …"

"That's what you want, money to solve this crime? How much would that cost?"

The DA jumped in, naming a figure that seemed ten times too high, at least based on Chung's salary. The captain mumbled something about patrol officers, investigators, lab tests. There was some quick negotiating back and forth between the DA and the lawyers before they settled on a final number.

"Done," said Boardman. Members of her PR and legal team started texting her. She glanced at her device and said, "We'll set it up as a donation to the department from Tucker as part of his public service for the accident. We'll pull the money from his trust fund, along with the rest of the settlement."

There were smiles all around then, even from the captain, and Chung rose with the others to leave. She checked the clock. Almost four hours had passed. She had a suspect down in holding who was probably going to be released soon.

"Excuse me," she said. The crowd at the door stopped and turned. "Do you have a substitute lined up yet?"

"That's not your concern, Chung," the captain said, giving her another evil glare. She'd spoken out of line twice already. Maybe the three-strikes rule would apply to her. Of course, her conviction bonus could probably buy her a few extra strikes.

His warning flew unnoticed past Lena Boardman, who paused, which caused her team to pause, then she turned, and everyone filed back into the conference room. The DA shut the door.

The lead lawyer cleared her throat again. "Technically this discussion is still covered by the original NDA. If everyone agrees to that, we don't need to sign another."

Everyone offered a quick verbal agreement.

Boardman stared at Chung. "Why do you ask?"

"There's a repeat trespassing offender down in lockup, someone we caught peeking in the wrong bedroom windows too many times, who might be willing to do it for a reasonable fee. You get your substitute, and we get a criminal off the street for a couple years."

"Does he resemble my Tucker?"

Chung shrugged. "He's a white guy, average height." A face she wanted to punch every time she saw it, so that was just like Tucker. "Sure, he's heavier, but you could just say that he's been so devastated by the accident, that he's been taking antidepressants and has put on weight. We could just swap identities, and Tucker walks out of here a free man. My guy stays, goes to trial, and then goes to prison."

"Can this be done?"

"We've done it before," the DA answered. "We switch ID records in the system, so your son doesn't pop up as himself on any of the surveillance systems. We switch it back after the prison sentence is over and the other guy is released. There are conditions. Tucker would have to keep a low profile—"

"How low?"

"House arrest within city limits, so we can keep track of him. He'd have to avoid known associates or doing anything where he might be recognized. Most of the people who've done this have gone off to private estates or checked into rehab spas."

"I can guarantee he will have a 24/7 security team and a very short leash," Lena Boardman said. She turned back to Chung. "Let's go meet this paragon of criminality."

"Ms. Boardman, I don't think you want to go down to our holding area," the chief interjected.

"Nonsense, I'm sure I'll be fine."

"Lead the way, detective," the captain said, opening the door for Chung. He gave her one of his we-are-going-to-have-a-talk looks, and she pretended not to notice. The same way she always did. Because fuck him.

That attitude was probably why she had a reputation for being in his shithouse, she reflected.

A group of uniforms was summoned and escorted them all downstairs to the pen for run-of-the-mill perps who couldn't afford private cells. As they passed through the last set of doors, the lawyers wrinkled their noses in disgust. Lena Boardman showed no reaction, but then maybe her face wasn't capable of expressing emotion anymore.

The crowd inside the cell was a distillation of human misery. Many were having the worst day of their lives. For others it was just another in a long string of bad days. But one man sat in a corner, emanating so much ill will that the others stayed away from him.

"Hey, Schreft!" Chung bellowed.

"Holy shit, what did that guy do?" whispered one of the other perps, as all of them looked at the newcomers then eyed the man in the corner.

Carl Schreft resembled Tucker. If the mold that made the latter had been hacked at with a chisel and the wax that got poured into it was left to run.

"What is it, Detective Bunghole?" His nickname for Chung. So clever. "You know you can't keep me in here on that trespassing charge much longer."

"Maybe I found somebody willing to pay for your prosecution."

"Fat chance," he said, but he studied the crowd of newcomers with healthy wariness. "You got nothing on me."

"Maybe I got something for you."

"He'll do," Boardman murmured. "If he's willing."

"Clear the room," the captain ordered the officers. "Take all these fine gentlemen over to holding cell three."

"The last time you went to prison, you had to pay for it yourself," Chung said. "You got out dead broke. How'd you like to get paid to go to prison instead?"

That got Schreft's attention. "How long are we talking?"

Chung had been zoned out during that part of the negotiations. She looked over to the DA, who said, "Twenty-two months. With time off for good behavior."

Shit. Was that all? Guess it didn't matter if Boardman wasn't going to serve the time himself.

"How much?" asked Schreft.

The DA and Boardman's lawyer both opened their mouths, a little hesitantly, and Chung jumped in ahead of them. "Listen, Schreft," she said. "I don't like you. I just collected a hefty bonus, so I will pay for your prosecution out of my own pocket. You'll go to prison, and I'll spend the rest of my bonus paying the CEO to make sure you get hit with so many extra fees you stay behind bars until you're so old you have to wear diapers. So whatever they offer you, you're going to say yes to it. Or we're going to turn around and find someone else to do the time. Then I will devote the rest of my career to making your life as miserable as possible."

His face grew red, and his jaw worked like he was chewing glass. He turned to the lawyers. "How much are you offering?"

The lawyer tilted her head sideways, like she was trying to roll a zero or two off the edge of a ledger. When she offered a number that was clearly much lower than her original, Chung sighed. It was still way too much. Billionaires and their lackeys had no idea how much money was a lot of money to poor people.

Schreft's eyes widened and some of the color drained out of his face. He tried to sound casual when he said, "Yeah. Yeah, that seems fair."

Pads were produced, NDAs flew across the room, then contracts. A public defender was brought in, less to represent Schreft's interests and more to collect a fifteen percent service fee. The public defender would owe the DA a favor later.

Chung hung around long enough to make sure nothing was going to go wrong. As she was headed out the door, Schreft yelled at her. "Hey, bitch! You didn't need to threaten me. I would have said yes to that much any day. But I'll remember what you did when I get out."

"See if I ever do you another favor, asshole," she said.

She flipped him the bird and kept on walking. He would be out in less than two years, but a lot could happen in two years.

Twenty-two months later—with time off for good behavior— found Ellen Chung still sitting at the same desk, still working the Department of Shit Cases No One Wanted to Pay For. She'd been someone important until the moment she'd refused a promotion to Major Crimes. After that, everyone went back to treating her like a leper and letting her go about her business the way she liked.

Everyone except Malcom Warren, that was. He stopped by her office on a semi-regular basis, sometimes to pick her brain about a case, sometimes just to share amusing departmental gossip. She was starting to like him, despite her reservations. Also, he was on his way to becoming a halfway decent investigator.

When he showed up that morning with coffee and some break- fast sandwiches, she was neither surprised nor unhappy to see him. She kicked him a chair to sit on as she bit into a bagel, ham, and egg sandwich.

"So I have two bits of news I thought you might be interested in," Warren said. "A local news station just streamed an hour-long special on the Ocean Beach Rando. Why did the murders almost stop two years ago? What happened to him? That sort of thing."

Chung chewed and swallowed, wiped her mouth. "Yeah, they contacted me for comment. I told them that since his prosecution was now fully paid for in advance, he probably dropped off the radar. Maybe moved to a different city. No reason for him to continue when there was a chance he might get caught."

"But I heard from a source in the DA's office that you've got a sealed warrant with the suspect's name."

Chung shrugged. "It pays to be prepared. In case he shows up again."

"Mmm." Warren nodded thoughtfully, took a sip of coffee. "So then you also heard about what happened to the prisoner publicly known as 'Tucker Boardman'?"

Chung shook her head and took another bite.

"Got stabbed in a prison fight this morning. Died about an hour ago."

She grabbed a napkin and spit out her food. "You're shitting me?"

"He's as dead as Communism."

"Does anyone know?"

"Someone may have just texted all their sources in the media. It should be hitting the feeds and streams any minute."

"Shit, shit, shit, we've gotta move fast." She unlocked her desk and pulled out a sealed warrant. She was halfway to the door before she paused. "You want to come with?"

"Where are we going?"

"You'll see. But put away your phone. And don't tell the captain we're going anywhere."

The estate in Bel Air was a miniature fortress. Just beyond the fence, Chung could see the man formerly known as Tucker Boardman, aka 'Carl Schreft,' pacing around the pool. House arrest did not agree with him: he'd gained weight, and his hair was a mess. He looked more like Schreft all the time. Half a dozen women in bikinis lounged around the pool, sunbathing, smoking, and drinking. Nice work if you could get it. All but one of them watched Boardman warily. The sixth was reading a book. Made of actual paper. There would be no electronic devices allowed, of course, so no one could take any pictures. The guard at the front gate looked at Chung's badge and her warrant and glanced over at Boardman, then hesitated.

"Look," Chung said. "I know you gotta call whoever you're supposed to call if I show up, but—"

They were interrupted by a shout of alarm and Boardman's laughter as he shoved the reader into the pool. She came flopping up out of the water, her book ruined. The guard sighed.

"Hey, Carl!" Chung shouted. "Carl, come here, I have some news you need to hear."

She had to call his 'name' two more times before he looked over and realized she was talking to him. She took a step back from the gate and made sure her bodycam was running. Boardman approached, looking at her curiously, as if he was just recognizing her.

"Can I confirm your identity as Carl Schreft?" she asked.

"Uh, yeah," he laughed. "That's me."

"Something important happened this morning," she said, holding out her phone like she was going to show him something. She took another half step back.

"What is it?" he said, walking right past the guard, who realized what was happening a moment too late. He stepped forward to intervene, and Warren put a hand out to stop him.

Chung pocketed her phone and pulled out her cuffs like a magician doing a switch. They were on Boardman's wrists before he had a chance to react. "Carl Schreft, you are under arrest for the murders of Angela Reyes and nine other victims. Popularly called the Ocean Beach Rando murders."

The gate guard was already dialing his boss on a landline in the gatehouse while Chung pushed Boardman into the back seat of the car.

"Hey! That's not me! That's the other guy!" he was shouting.

"He did time for your crime," Chung said. "Now you get to do some time for his."

It had always been a long shot. Carl Schreft had been her primary suspect in the Ocean Beach Rando murders, but two years ago she didn't have enough evidence to convict him. She was just happy to get him off the streets and behind bars. Now, after the late Tucker Boardman's generous contribution to the victims' fund, she did have the goods. And as of this morning, there was only one "Carl Schreft" left in the records to arrest. The DA could never publicly admit that Boardman wasn't Schreft because that would mean admitting Boardman never went to prison.

He shouted and kicked the back of her seat. Chung had dealt with worse.

"Now can I call the captain?" Warren asked.

"Yeah. Before Boardman's lawyers do."

"He'll be pissed that you surprised him with this."

"Probably," Chung said. "At least until they figure out how much they can charge Boardman's family to make it go away. My views have evolved. You know what I like most about having a for-profit justice system?"

"What?" said Warren.

Chung looked at him and smiled. "Crime always pays."

The Gardener's Mystery: Notes from a Journal

Lisa Morton

4.11.62—I started work with a new client today. Winter Smythe is my first feelie star. Her yard is the biggest I've done; her last gardener was only classified as a Level 2 ExtGar, really little more than a laborer, and Winter wanted someone who also has design skills. She's beautiful (of course) and expressive (of course), and a Level 10 (of course, although not the first Level 10 client I've had), and she's been my favorite actor ever since *You're My Angel*, so yes—I stand in a little awe of her, but she smiled and asked what I preferred to be called ("Izzie," I told her, although I make most people use "Isabelle"), and told me how impressed she'd been with my portfolio. Her yard is tremendously wasteful right now—she actually still has a real grass lawn—but she wants more native flora. She's given me a decent budget to work with, too, and has told her assistant Akiko to make sure all my wants are met. Akiko is a treasure on her own—Level 4 Admin, with stylish suits and short neon-blue hair framing a warm smile.

Winter, though ... one can't help but wonder what it must be like to know from birth that you've been designed to be gorgeous and talented. Not that I regret being made as a gardener—I love my job—but … well, you just wonder.

4.18.62—Today I had my second meeting with Winter to go over how I envision her yard, with trails laid out in the best synth-marble, winding through plantings of blue ceanothus, white sage, and California fuchsia tucked in beneath blue palo verde trees and coastal live oaks. Winter asked smart questions about SoCal's microclimates and what things would *not* grow here, approved the design, and told me to start buying.

I also helped her find her tab after she lost it. Akiko tried to use her tab to call Winter's, but they still couldn't locate it. I knew I could. It wasn't even that hard—I just guided Winter through re-membering what she'd done in the morning until she mentioned breakfast, and there was the tab right inside the refrigerator, as I'd guessed—but she seemed impressed. "Izzie, that was good. Are you sure they didn't code you with a few detective genes?"

I smiled but didn't say what I was thinking: that she wasn't the first person to ask that, because I've been good at solving mysteries my whole life. When I was little—as in, *very* little, like could just barely talk—I could tell Mama where she'd left that tool she'd mis-placed, or know when someone was lying. I'd once helped a Level 6 Landscape Architect recover a rare aeonium that had been stolen out of his client's yard, and when that big murder trial involving the model and the photographer had happened last year, I'd correctly named the killer long before the trial ended, even though it was someone who'd never even really been a suspect.

Of course the ability to detect is not something I talk about. We've all heard about people who go back in for corrective proce-dures as adults because they demonstrate skills that shouldn't be part of their genetic crafting; those people never come out well. I person-ally know a Level 2 RetClerk at a nursery who was winning singing contests … until some singer complained and they were taken back in at the age of twenty-four. The next time I saw that clerk, they could only speak in a low animal growl.

Everyone says our caste system is practical and has created a better society, but "everyone" is really only the ones who got it all in the gene crafting, the ones chosen to be Level 10 Politicians, or Performers, or Artists. The ones like Winter Smythe, in other words.

Except Winter actually isn't like that. One of the reasons she's my favorite actor is because last year she started getting active in caste rights. She spoke out against unfair treatment of 1s and 2s, she appeared at rallies and marches, she even made a video advocating that corrective crafting be abolished. She's really good at activism, which I figure makes her like me: we both possess talents we shouldn't.

Maybe I should tell Winter that I'm good at solving mysteries. Maybe she'd admire that, not report me, but realize how alike we are.

Maybe we could even be friends.

5.15.62—A terrible day, because of the story at all the news sites.

This morning, a video surfaced, showing Winter Smythe screaming at a Level 2.

It's all there: Winter in her kitchen—which I recognized instantly—shrieking the ugliest words imaginable at the camera. She says things about how Level 2s are just "fucking animals," and 10s should never have to see them. With her lovely face screwed into a mask of rage, spittle flying, she screams about "incompetence" and "uselessness" and "not even worthy of a human body." Of course those who are anti-caste rights are dancing with glee at how the most newsworthy pro-caste rights activist in the world has been revealed for a casteist fraud.

Winter's representatives say it's a fake; they say it was created from an audition Winter was secretly filmed preparing for. No one knows who the Level 2 she's screaming at is supposed to be, or who leaked the vid. It first appeared at EXC, an outlet known for buying the most scandalous material they can get, and of course they're "protecting the source."

Meanwhile, Winter burns.

Of course I believe her. I called Akiko and asked if I could come by today; she said I could. Winter will tell me what really happened. She likes and trusts me.

And maybe ... maybe I can help.

Later—Winter told me.

My heart broke when I saw her. She'd been crying and burst into tears again when she saw me. She embraced me, saying, "Izzie, Izzie, it's not true, it's not ..."

I told her I believed her. Akiko put her tab down long enough to make us each a cup of tea; she had her hands full fielding all the requests for comment on the vid. I asked Winter—as gently as possible—to tell me about it.

She said the vid was taken from an audition, but the words had been replaced. The scene had been about a woman who has just discovered that her partner is a casteist, and they're arguing. "I would never say the words in that video," Winter said, her eyes tearing up again, "even in a feelie. I'd turn down a part like that."

I assured her I believed her. I asked her if there was anything she could do.

She nodded. "My lawyers have a team of techs working on breaking the file apart; they've even got an AI on it. I don't understand it all, but they say they can crack it to reveal where it came from."

I asked her who she'd been rehearsing with. She said she'd been at her agent's office—the background of her kitchen had been added later—and her agent had filmed the audition.

"Obviously my agent's not going to release that video," she said.

"Of course not," I agreed. "And I assume your people have talked to everyone at your agent's office?"

She stopped crying, turned an appraising look on me. "Izzie," she said with a half-smile I'd seen in dozens of feelies, "they really may have left a stray gene or two in you. We just started down that track."

I nodded, warmed by the correct guess.

"And what about who had access to your kitchen?" I asked next.

Winter blinked in perplexity. "My kitchen?"

I gestured around us. "That really is your kitchen in the video, meaning whoever faked it had to have recorded your kitchen to add it in later."

She gaped for a second before blurting out, "Nobody else has thought of that."

At first I was pleased, but then a splinter of doubt worked its way into my head. Was I really that much smarter than the Level 8s and 9s and 10s working for Winter? Maybe they had thought of that and just not asked her yet, or … could someone within her own circle be lying to her?

I looked at her closely, then, at this magnificent human who—like me, maybe—had been born with natural gifts on top of what had been crafted into her, and I reached an instant decision: I was going to find out who had done this to her. I didn't care if I was breaking caste law, if I might wind up in a lab somewhere undergoing genetic reconstruction that would leave me as some Level 1 laborer. I was willing to risk it to save Winter Smythe.

And, maybe if I figured this out … maybe others might start to realize that they, too, could do things they weren't supposed to be able to do.

"Izzie …?" Winter asked, calling me back to the present.

"Sorry," I answered, "but I was just imagining how good you'll feel when the truth in this comes out and you're absolved.

Her engineered smile was heart-rending.

5.16.62—Where to start …

Doing anything with the file itself was out. I didn't begin to have the skills necessary to crack the code and trace its path through the cloud. Besides, I guessed that was what Winter's team was working on.

No, I'd investigate the kitchen angle, find out if anyone had been in her house lately, maybe somebody with a grudge.

When I got to work this morning, I started transplanting some *Salvia apiana* I'd grown from seed. Winter was out for the day, but she'd left Akiko at the house. Akiko must have seen me on cameras approaching the house because she opened the door before I even reached it. She tried to smile, but it looked worn. I could only imagine how stressful this whole thing had been for her, too. "Hey, Izzie. What can I do for you?"

I took a deep breath and asked, "Akiko, has there been anyone inside the house over the last few weeks, somebody who isn't usually here?" Winter had four regular employees, including me, and a bevy of friends and lovers who visited regularly, but I was betting they were all as devoted to her as I was.

Akiko peered at me for a second, confused—and then I saw understanding settle in. "Oh. Oh! Because of the kitchen in the video …!"

"Yes."

She thought for a moment before nodding. "That's a really good point. I'll mention it to the lawyers—"

I cut her off. "No! I mean … I was … well, I'm actually really good at figuring things out, and I …"

"Oh, Izzie …" She looked at me with pity. "You don't think you can solve this?"

Taking the leap, I said, "You know how Winter was designed to be a Level 10 entertainer but not an activist? Well, I think I'm like that. Somehow I'm a gardener who is also a very good detective."

Akiko looked at me, assessing and measuring, before saying, "Let me check my records and get back to you." With that she turned away, returning to fielding all the calls for comment on what was now known simply as "the Winter Smythe vid." I figured we were done. Akiko was just placating me. The most I could hope for was that she wouldn't complain to either Winter or the nearest caste worker. I left the house to go back to my white sage.

Three hours later, I was surprised when my tab beeped with a text from her that consisted of a list of three names: Martin Jeffries, a delivery person who'd brought three crates of food into the kitchen; Errin Trent, a plumber who'd come in to repair a leak in the kitchen sink on Akiko's day off; and Jazmeen Malik, who'd provided Winter with an aromatherapy session.

I forced myself to get through my day's work and make it home before I began to dig. At first glance, Malik was the most obvious target because she wasn't Winter's usual therapist, who I remembered seeing from a past visit. The regular woman was working with another client that day and sent Malik to replace her. Malik, however, had a fine record and glowing reviews.

Next I looked at Trent, who worked with a company called Rooterwork. He was listed at their site, no bad comments, clean record.

That left Jeffries. He was an independent delivery man, drove his own truck, not much of a record in the cloud. It looked like he was one of those drivers who was brought in by stores when their own delivery people were all assigned already, or somebody called in sick.

He was the most obvious choice. He would also be the hardest one to get to—he had no regular place of business, no list of reviews by customers, no address. But he had a truck, and the truck had virtual plates that had been scanned when he'd come through Winter's front gate. If I could get Akiko to release the gate records to me, I could use the truck information to find him.

And if I did find him … what then? Accuse him, and see how he reacted? Threaten to turn him in?

I had to watch the vid again.

The whole thing made me ill, but I had a thought and had to investigate. The Winter Smythe vid wasn't exactly hard to find—every news site in the cloud had it right up front. I needed to watch the entire recording, unfiltered, without a reporter commenting over the front or added graphics or a copy edited down to just a few bits.

I found a raw, unedited copy at a site called sexzynews. It ran 36 seconds. I took a deep breath, wedged my pods into my ears, turned up the volume on my tab and played it.

It churned my stomach, it made me angry for how Winter had been used, but I forced myself to focus only on the technical aspects. I was looking for …

There, four seconds in: with the volume turned all the way up, you heard a voice that wasn't Winter's saying, "I'm sorry, Ms. Smythe …" It was a man's voice, barely audible, nothing distinctive, a little on the tenor side, maybe faked … but maybe not. Criminals were usually sloppy, missed things. They'd scrubbed other identifying features from the video, but maybe they'd missed this. I have to believe that, because it's my only real clue.

Assuming those four words aren't some AI's voice, that rules out Jazmeen Malik as a suspect, meaning I was left with a delivery man and a plumber. If I can find them both, record them talking for even a few seconds, I might be able to find an audio expert who can verify a voice match.

It's a plan, at least.

5.17.62—After sleeping on it, I've realized the next step of my plan rests with Akiko.

I called her, asked if we could meet, maybe for lunch. I didn't work for Winter again for another week, but I didn't want to wait, watching her career go up in flames while I sat around. I only had one client in the morning today, the rest of the day free.

Akiko agreed. We met at a café in Brentwood that she liked. It was out of my price range, but apparently Winter paid her well and she offered to cover it.

After we were seated and had ordered, she said, "This is about what we talked about yesterday, isn't it?"

I nodded.

She said, "I've thought about it a lot since then, and ..." She trailed off, and I fully expected her to say, "I can't do it," or the like. Instead she surprised me with, "I want to do whatever I can to help."

"Oh, that's wonderful," I blurted out, grinning.

She laughed at my expression and said, "Not even so much because of Winter, although that's obviously part of it, but because of ..." Akiko inhaled and went on. "I make the best fucking chocolate chip cookies on earth."

I blinked, perplexed, waiting for her to go on. After a second, she added, "Maybe they thought being a great baker would be a good side skill for an executive assistant, so it was crafted in—you know, like being able to provide the boss with fresh cookies might have been perceived as useful. Except ... I don't think so. I think it's like you, with the detective stuff, or Winter with her political side."

Now I got it. "Yes," I said.

"So I want to help you, so you can help Winter, so we can someday have the freedom to do the things we're good at."

I reached across the table and took her hand. "Thank you."

She squeezed my fingers and said, "Now tell me what you need."

Two hours later, I had the information on Martin Jeffries's truck. Akiko even paid for access to an information database that gave us his address. It wasn't far from here, just south in Torrance about thirty minutes. She also gave me blurry video footage of him so I could identify him along with his truck.

"What are you going to do when you see him?"

"That's easy," I answered. "I just need to get him talking for a few seconds, even if it's just 'who the fuck are you?' I'll record that, compare it to the voice you can hear at the beginning of the smear vid, and we'll know if it's him or not. If it is, I turn it all over to Winter; if it's not, I go on to the plumber, Errin Trent."

She shook her head, causing her azure hair to sway. "I hope it's easy, but … this is a big man. What if he figures you out, and has a temper to boot? I don't remember him saying a word when he dropped those crates off, but … well, just promise me you'll be careful."

"I will." On the one hand, her concern was flattering. On the other … now she had me worried.

5.19.62—I had a full day of work the next day—maintaining a hedge maze for a Level 10 lawyer, Aram Deukmejian, who I'd been employed by for three years and never met—so my adventure with Martin Jeffries had to wait until the next day.

After a few odd jobs in the morning, I headed to Torrance. It was just before 2:00 p.m. as I arrived at the address Akiko had given me. The place turned out to be one of those thirty-story complexes they build for the 1s and 2s; I've been in them and they're comfortable enough, but looking at that tall gray rectangle made me appreciate my apartment in an old two-story stucco building even more.

Parking was underground, accessed by a driveway from the street; of course it was secured. The front entrance, though, was not, and led into a large lobby lined with a small food store, a bank of elevators, and an automated reception desk.

I found a parking space a few buildings down, but I'd still be able to see his truck coming from either direction. I had no idea what hours Jeffries worked, or if he even worked at all today. Last night I grabbed a flyer for an upcoming music show out of a gutter, folded it, and wrote his name on it. Now I left my ride and walked to his complex, my heart already beating faster, trying not to think about Akiko's worry. Inside the reception area, I pulled my hoodie tighter, strode over to the reception desk, and said I wanted to leave a message. An automated arm reached out, took the flyer, stashed it somewhere out of sight. I knew that Martin Jeffries was now receiving notice that a package awaited him at Reception; if he was home, he'd probably be down shortly.

I waited a few minutes; he didn't show. Out working, then.

I returned to my ride, settled in for the wait, hoped it wouldn't be long.

It was long. Afternoon turned into evening, turned into late night. I was almost nodding off when I heard a rumbling and looked up to see a truck approaching. My tab matched the plates; it was Martin Jeffries. The truck turned into the driveway for the big complex, heading into the underground parking.

I stepped out of my ride; my throat was already dry. I made sure my tab was in my pocket with the vid app already running as I jogged across the street to the reception area. There were a few people coming out of the food store, but they got into elevators. It was empty as Martin Jeffries stepped through the door reading "Garage."

Akiko was right—he was big. No, let me try that again: Martin Jeffries was BIG. This guy could've been a Level 9 pro wrestler, with dark bronze skin drawn over muscles just beginning to go to fat. His face looked like it must be set in a permanent scowl, his immense hands permanently clenched into fists. He was just putting his own tab away, heading for the reception desk.

I nearly choked. But now was my chance. I had to do this. I cleared my throat and said, "Um, excuse me …"

He glanced at me, only slowing down slightly, not stopping.

"I'm trying to find a Wesley Chan, he's supposed to live here. Don't suppose you know him?"

He didn't answer, just turned away and kept walking.

Fuck. I needed him to talk to me. I walked after him, taking two steps for every one of his. "Are you sure? Maybe he's—"

This time he stared me down and growled, "I don't know him. Okay?"

"Yeah, okay. Sorry."

He was done with me. I had to hope those five words were enough. I started out of the building.

I was halfway across the street when some instinct made me look back. He was standing outside, my pointless flyer clutched in one hand, glaring after me.

I tried to put my head down and not run to my ride, but I almost fumbled my tab getting the door open. I stabbed a finger at the ignition and the jets roared as the ride lifted up and shot down the street. I risked one glance in the rear monitor, but he wasn't following me.

Still, I didn't breathe easier until I was almost back to the 405. At that point I pulled over, listened to the recording.

It was good, but ... Martin Jeffries had a deep voice. The man on the Winter Smythe vid didn't.

Just then my tab lit up with a message from Akiko. I answered. "Akiko, I got the recording—"

She cut me off, her expression on the screen excited. "It's not him, Izzie. It's the plumber, Errin Trent."

"What?"

"While you were off checking out Jeffries, I decided to dig into Trent a little bit, and get this: he's all over every brain-drained conspiracy site on the web, making all kinds of major anti-caste rights statements, the usual crap about how society would crumble if everyone was allowed to run around doing whatever they wanted."

I leaned back against the seat, inwardly cursing myself for not checking into Trent first. "Fuck. Well, he certainly does sound like someone who'd have a grudge against Winter."

"Oh, and it gets better. I found out he also serviced the offices of Winter's agency."

"So he could have stolen the audition vid from her agent's tab then."

"Right."

I started up the engine again. "Akiko, you're a genius."

"Not bad for a 4, right?"

5.20.62—Akiko and I met in the morning.

She'd already called Rooterwork, where Trent had worked, and found out he'd quit two days before the Winter Smythe vid exploded; when she asked why he was still on the company's site, they apologized and said they'd forgotten to remove him.

I sighed and said, "Guess EXC paid him for the vid well enough that he could stop being a plumber. So much for his hard core beliefs that workers should stick to their caste."

Akiko dug around a little more in the cloud, but it was like Errin Trent had vanished—no accounts anywhere. The guy was playing it safe.

Akiko finally gave up and asked, "So now the question is, how do we find him?"

"We go to EXC. Tell them ..." I thought for a minute before saying, "Tell them I've got serious intel on a secret cabal Winter's involved with, but I only want to talk to the guy behind the Winter Smythe vid. Maybe they'll pass the message on, maybe he'll bite ..."

Akiko didn't look convinced. "That's a lot of maybes."

I had to agree. "It is, but ..."

She answered for me. "It's the best we've got for now. So try it. In the meantime, I'll keep seeing what I can find."

I pulled out my tab, went to EXC's site, used their contact info to send the message.

It won't work.

5.21.62—It did work.

I sent that message yesterday, and today they answered. They relayed a message from whoever's behind the Winter Smythe vid: they're willing to meet. They named a cemetery on the southern edge of Hollywood, and a specific grave, far away from the old-time movie stars buried in another part of the lot. Monday at 4 p.m. Tomorrow. I'm to wear a red hat, so they'll know it's me, and come alone. I already called my Monday afternoon client to tell them I won't be in tomorrow.

Akiko doesn't like it. She pointed out that we don't even know if I'll be meeting with the real person behind the video, that it might not be Trent after all, that they might have agreed to this only so they could threaten me, hurt me ... or worse.

I told her I'm willing to take the risk. I'll keep my tab on, so she can hear everything. We'll be in a public place, even if it's likely removed from others. I'll be cautious.

I'm a detective, after all.

5.22.62—I bought a red baseball cap at a souvenir store in Hollywood this morning. It's too small for my head, sits perched on top of my dark brown hair like some child's hat, but it's a necessary evil.

It's now 3:45 on Monday. I'm in the cemetery, at the appointed headstone; it's not a name I know. There are a few tourists on the far side of the cemetery, visiting the graves of long-ago celebrities I've probably never heard of. On this side, though, it's empty, just a lot of half-eroded headstones dotting the synthetic grass that looks like it was put in probably twenty years ago. At least the palm trees are real. They bring me some comfort. That, and updating this journal.

It's 4 now. There's a man approaching. Time to stop journaling.

Later …

Fuck.

Much later. I've been drinking since I got home at 5:30. It's 8 now. I should finish this.

The man was Errin Trent. I recognized him from security cam footage Akiko had brought up. He's a small man, slight, with thinning, colorless hair and pale, pockmarked skin.

The first thing he said to me was, "It's good that you came alone."

I tried to sound confident as I said, "How do you know I'm alone?"

"Because I've been here since 2:30, watching from over there." He gestured vaguely toward a mausoleum several hundred yards away, then turned back to me and extended a hand, palm up. "I'm sure you'll understand if I ask that you hand over your tab while we talk."

Fuck. At least I managed to shut it off as I handed it to him so he wouldn't see Akiko's avatar. He also took my bag and made me turn my pockets inside out. I was glad he didn't ask to frisk me.

Now that I was here, facing him, I felt a rush of emotions: victory, at being right in guessing his identity; fear, about what could go wrong; anger at what he'd put Winter and Akiko—and me—through with his fakery, anger so bad I wanted to step forward like a private dick in an old non-feelie movie and drive my fist into his narrow face.

"You said you have information on some group surrounding Winter Smythe?"

Before I could stop myself, I blurted out, "Why did you do it?"

"Do what?"

"Make that tape."

He just looked at me, his brow slightly furrowed. I continued, "I mean, I have to give you credit—it was a good job. It's fooled the whole world, after all …"

I trailed off as I saw his expression change, going from perplexity to realization to mad hilarity. He began to laugh, his laughter growing until it sounded like some mad animal's howls. When he got himself back under control, wiping his eyes, I said, "What so funny?"

"You. You're what's so funny. You actually fell for her bullshit claim that it's all fake."

I felt like I'd just swallowed a bucket of ice.

I stood, paralyzed, as he went on. "You know her, don't you?"

I didn't answer. I couldn't.

"Here. Let me show you something …" He pulled out his own tab, swiped through several screens, found what he wanted, and held it up for me to see. The Winter Smythe vid started to play; there she was again, standing in her spacious, perfect kitchen, screaming those awful things about how useless 2s were, little better than rocks … or plants …

"So what?" I said. "We've all seen this."

"Keep watching."

I did. The vid reached the end we all knew so well by now … and then it kept going. Now Winter was telling him he'd done a shitty job fixing her sink, that she'd be putting in a call to Rooterwork and asking for at least a Level 3, someone who could actually do the work.

Of course he'd had to cut that part when he sold the video, because it would have identified him.

At some point he returned my tab and my bag before he trudged off. I think he may have said, "I almost feel sorry for you." I didn't really hear; I was crying.

I left the cemetery after that, stopped at a liquor store on my way home. Now I'm here, wondering ... do I tell Akiko? Can I keep working for Winter, knowing that the only dishonest thing about all this is her? Has she been kind to me only because I'm useful? Or maybe she only hates the 1s and 2s; maybe the 4s, like me and Akiko, are slightly better than scum.

Worst of all: I'm no detective. The most obvious answer was in front of me the whole time, and I missed it.

This is the last time I will write in this journal. Detectives like to keep journals, to remember their cases. Gardeners don't need them; our cases are all right there in the earth. I'm nothing but a Level 4 Gardener.

It's all I've ever been and ever will be.

AnaMaria Curtis

I'd never seen the inside of a private jet before, but it turned out the inside of a private jet just looked like the inside of a fancy minivan. Plush, pale leather seats made up rows of two along the aisle; four seats were grouped around a low table at the back. At the front of the plane, Helene St. Peters greeted Nadia with enthusiastic air-kisses on both cheeks.

"And you must be Ainsley!" she said, turning to me. She had a shockingly genuine smile for a CEO. "I'm so glad you could join us. Nadia told me you needed a retreat just as much as the rest of us, and she knows I can't resist spreading the yoga love."

I shook her hand before she could air-kiss me too. "Thanks so much for having me. I'll try not to get in your way."

"Don't worry," Helene said. "It's just me and my friends. Grab a seat anywhere!"

I followed Nadia to one of the double seats and let her take the window. The woman in the row behind us didn't look up.

Helene's boyfriend, Tim Chen, came next, and then her best friend, Seetha Sangireddy. I watched, amused, as the three of them settled into the four chairs around the coffee table. Seetha and Tim took chairs across from each other, leaving Helene to choose between them. She bent toward Seetha first, whispering something, and then put her bag down and sat next to Tim.

"Hmm," I said. Nadia followed my gaze.

"Seetha is Helene's CFO at ReTred," she said, something flat in her voice. "They have one of those public corporate friendships where they pose for industry magazines with a tug-of-war rope between them."

I didn't remind Nadia that her job was built around pleasing people like them. It had been a joke between us, once, that we each hated what the other did. It had been one of the truths that kept us friends, but here I was, tagging along to a yoga retreat she was running, ready to take dozens of posed pictures of her in the workout clothes she was getting paid to promote. Meanwhile, I was out at my detective agency and blackballed from the industry. It didn't seem so funny anymore.

After a few minutes of awkward, whisper-clad quiet, the woman behind us—Clara, if my internet searching had been correct—spoke up. "Hey, Helene, are you going to show us how this miracle device of yours works?"

"You want a demo?" Helene asked. She sounded surprised but pleased. "Seetha's seen it, obviously, but I'm happy to show you. Now that it's launched, I don't have to keep it so locked down."

Nadia and I moved to the aisle to watch, standing behind Seetha. Clara just stood and looked over the back of her seat.

"Ordinarily it would be locked to a doctor's code and heavily regulated," Helene said, taking a box out of her bag, "but this is my personal prototype." She opened it to show us two parts: one a screen the size of her palm with three buttons and the other a thin, round tube. It looked soft and pliable, like a creepy light-blue worm.

Helene straightened, blonde hair brushing her shoulders, and looked around. "Okay, who has a bad habit they want to lose?"

Nadia and Tim both raised their hands. I didn't even think about raising mine. I knew Nadia was skeptical that it even worked, but I wasn't. It had undergone a lot of efficacy testing and a rigorous approval process, and I didn't want it anywhere near me.

After a moment of deliberation, Helene nodded at Tim.

"I would love," he said, "to stop calling potential clients 'bro' during meetings."

Helene raised an eyebrow. "That's what you're choosing? Not leaving half-empty mugs everywhere?" Nadia elbowed me when I didn't chuckle along with the group.

Tim shook his head. "The bros have it, I'm afraid."

"Okay." Helene tilted her head. "It's likely that this will get you out of the habit of saying bro to anyone, even your bros. Do you understand and consent to this anyway?"

Tim grinned. "The homies will understand."

"Awesome," Helene said. She tapped at something on the screen. "Okay! Turn around for me …"

Tim turned. Helene placed the blue worm thing—the just-launched *medical device*—on the back of his neck and pressed a few buttons on the screen with her other hand. She held the worm in place for a moment, still looking at the screen, then picked it back up.

"There!" she said, kissing the back of his neck. "You're cured. How did it feel?"

Tim hesitated. "Warm. But pretty normal. I thought it would hurt."

"It's meant to mimic human touch," Helene said. She had a bit of a presenter voice on, like we were a room of shareholders waiting to IPO. "It's to make patients less nervous. Do you feel different?"

Tim shook his head. "Not at all."

Helene smiled. "You will."

We went back to our seats, and Nadia curled into my side as we prepared for takeoff. Flying was apparently not something she could deep breathe her way out of being afraid of.

"Ainsley?" she whispered as the plane started to move.

"Yeah?"

"What habit would you get rid of, if you could?"

I swallowed. I didn't know what to tell her. Nadia watched me with cautious, understanding eyes. She had done so much for me over the past month, not to mention the years before that, and I owed her improvement, my best self. She'd been the one I went to after the disaster with my old agency, the friend with a guest bedroom and a flexible work schedule who made sure I ate and drank and slept. The last thing she'd want to hear was that I wanted to be a detective again.

I leaned my head on her shoulder. "I don't know," I told her. "I'm too much of a mess for one habit to make a difference."

I wandered around the retreat space while everybody else went to settle in and change for yoga before dinner. The space belonged to a friend of Helene's and a yoga student of Nadia's, loaned out to them for the weekend along with the plane. It was a simple rectangular building, with all the rooms opening onto the same long hallway. Most of the rooms were for guests, but there were also communal showers, and the far end of the hallway had a cafeteria and a large, open room with wall-to-wall windows on one side and mirrors on the other—the yoga studio.

It came with a sort of familiarity now, almost a comfort. I'd been following Nadia around to the yoga studios and mansions of San Francisco's elite for the last month. She usually told them I was her assistant, but I knew it was because she didn't like to let me out of her sight for too long. It didn't mean I liked yoga (I didn't), but yoga and yoga studios meant Nadia now, meant loyalty and care when I'd needed it most.

My door creaked when I opened it, a long sharp sound, but the room was nice. Small, simple. Wooden furniture, a half bathroom, a window with a view of the mountains and the back half of a garden with a labyrinth of paths running through it. The staff here was fully automated, and I spared a thought for the robot lawn mowers. There were no locks on the door, which I didn't love, but I was a light sleeper.

When there was movement in the hallway, I followed everyone out, tugging at the garish and expensive clothes Nadia had packed for me. Clara was just coming out, her door creaking the same way mine had, and she rolled her eyes at me like we were in on a joke when I accidentally made eye contact.

Nadia led us to the patio area at the front of the building instead of the studio. It was a good impulse; the late afternoon light filtered beautifully through the trees above us.

I unrolled my yoga mat near the back. Helene and Seetha were directly in front of me, whispering to each other. They were a perfect study in contrasts—Seetha, tall, dark-skinned, and beautiful, head tilted down to listen to Helene, petite and pale, blonde hair escaping its elastic, also beautiful, who stood on tiptoes to whisper in her ear.

Nadia said something about the sunlight and got us started on a sun salutation. I followed along competently but halfheartedly. Tim had positioned himself at the back, like me, and I had to assume it was because he understood enough to know that his yoga was bad. We moved from mountain pose to reaching down, backs flat, and he curled toward the mat, straining to reach the ground with his hands. I watched Nadia's gaze flick to him, then Helene, then back to her mat.

I wondered what Nadia had seen on Helene's face. I wondered how long Helene and Tim had been dating, if there was any tension in the fact that she had just launched a major device on three continents while he was in the same role he'd had five years ago.

Clara was on the other side of Tim, farthest from me. She'd been Helene's sorority sister in college, and apparently they'd made some pact to take over the world together. Clara was hardly holding up her end of the deal, if the rumors about her biologics startup were to be believed.

I watched Clara overextend her neck in cobra pose, reaching to turn a searing gaze at the sky, and I wondered if she knew how behind she already was.

After dinner, Nadia beckoned me into her room. She sat on the bed, and I sat on the cool wooden floor and leaned back onto the bed and her crossed legs. After a minute, she undid my ponytail, slipped the hairband over her own wrist, and started combing through my hair with her fingers. I'd wanted to cut it all off after getting fired, wanted a new start, less to manage, but she'd begged me to keep it. She still braided it almost every night.

"Well, Ains," she said, "what do you think of them?"

I hummed. "It's hard to know. There are so many potential points of tension. I wish we had our phones. I'm so behind on gossip."

Nadia's hands jerked, catching a tangle somewhere near my neck, and I winced. "Helene insisted on no phones," she said, "and I agree with her, especially in your case. We're here to help these very stressed people"—she tapped a finger on my cheek so I knew that included me—"find themselves again."

Did I need to find myself? I'd been fired from my last agency for accusing a client of running a money-laundering ring. He'd hired us to keep an eye on his ex-wife, which was shitty enough, and I'd decided to keep an eye on him too for good measure. With enough late nights shadowing him, enough seemingly innocuous details, the evidence had seemed good. It had seemed like the right thing to do.

Maybe being myself was the problem. Maybe I needed to find a different self, one who didn't scrutinize and overanalyze until she couldn't tell friend from foe.

I tilted my head to one side, until my cheek was pressed against the hard, smooth curve of Nadia's knee. "I'm trying." Then I smiled. "I thought we were here for Helene's launch and because she's throwing money at you. Me being here is just a happy accident."

I could hear Nadia's smile in her reply. "You're never an accident."

Something was off at breakfast the next morning. Outside, clouds were gathering above the mountaintops, low and gray. Nadia was at a table, halfway through a dragon fruit. Seetha and Tim were finishing off green smoothies, already flushed with the glow of an early morning run, Tim sweatier than Seetha.

A third green smoothie sat between them. A trail to the rim indicated it had been drunk from, but the glass was nearly full.

I went to check out the other food options, hoping that there was some sort of carb on offer. The food was laid out on a long table—a few more glasses with the green smoothies; a wooden bowl piled with fruit; and there, blessedly, small bowls of oatmeal with berries. I grabbed a fruit, something spiky, and then, distracted by the texture of the tufts against my palm, reached for a bowl of oatmeal and knocked into Helene St. Peters's hand.

"Oh shit, sorry!"

43

Helene laughed. "No problem. I'm just glad I'm not the only one going for the oats." She looked back at Seetha and Tim. "I usually have a smoothie, but I think maybe it's time to change things up."

That explained the third smoothie. I reached carefully for a bowl and tried to sound casual. "Do you usually go on a run with Tim and Seetha in the mornings?"

She paused, tilted her head. "Seetha and I run if we're in the same place. Tim does more weights."

A crease was forming between her eyebrows. I decided to skip my follow-up question about the run. "And the smoothies?" I asked. "You usually have those every day too?"

"Tim makes them for me most mornings when he's around. He specifically put the recipe on the rotation here." Helene hesitated for a long moment, then she turned. "Sorry," she said. "I need to check something."

She left the cafeteria entirely. I had a feeling I knew exactly where she was going, so I followed her out into the hall and watched her dart into her room. I took a bite of the oatmeal, which was bland except for the tart berries, and waited.

There, a muttered curse. Helene was on her knees in her room, her suitcase and bags open in front of her, when I got there. She looked up at me.

"It's gone."

"I don't want this to disrupt anything," Helene told Nadia and me firmly. Everyone else was in the studio waiting on Nadia. Helene's smile was thin but unwavering. "No room searches. We'll just keep doing the retreat as planned, and Ainsley here will pull people out as she needs to chat with them."

I cleared my throat. "That's going to limit what I can find out."

"I appreciate that," Helene said evenly. "Also, Ainsley, whatever your rates are, I'm happy to double them for the trouble. But I don't want to make too big a deal out of this. It's probably just a misunderstanding."

I opened my mouth to argue—whoever it was had already messed with Helene directly, after all—but Nadia elbowed me, barely subtle, and I shut up.

"Of course," I said. "Thank you. If you don't mind, I'll start with you."

Nadia headed back to the studio, and I took Helene to my tiny room for an interview. I gave her the chair and sat on the bed with a notepad.

"Okay," I said. "Let's start simple. What can you tell me about how the device works? Not the science of it, or the launch version, but literally how to use the one that's been stolen?"

"Well, you've seen it. Everyone saw it. I'm so stupid." Helene chuckled; a sound utterly devoid of humor. "It's two parts. There's a screen and the implementor, which is the blue part. On the screen, you put in a numerical code for whatever habit you're trying to take or implant. We have about 1200 codes indexed, and you can search for them, and then you choose whether you're taking a habit or implanting one, and hit go."

"Okay. Do you need to take a habit from one person before implanting it in someone else?"

"Not generally," Helene said, "but on this model, yes. I didn't preload it with anything."

"Can people use it on themselves? Will it keep any info about past users?"

"Probably, yeah, as long as they can hold it against their own neck. It won't have a record of who's used it, since it's my personal unlocked version, but it will keep a record of habits that have been taken and are stored on the device." She sighed.

"I was hoping to use it as a ... I don't know, a bonding thing before we all left." She looked straight at me, eyes sharp and blue. "I haven't been around a lot, preparing for the launch, and I wanted to give them all something they couldn't ask for. You and I don't know each other, but everyone else here is my friend. I wanted ... I don't know. I wanted to show them that I was still just Helene." She shook her head. "You must think I'm stupid."

"No," I said. I thought of the way Nadia looked at me now, like I would run off if she spent too long at the grocery store, the way my friends had all started texting me the same day, a few days after I'd gone to stay with Nadia, like they'd had a meeting about me. I imagined there must be a similar kind of distance when you were ten steps ahead of everyone else, instead of twenty behind. "No, I kind of get it."

We went through more of the basics after that. The only habits she was sure were gone were her habit of waking up for a run with Seetha and drinking Tim's green smoothies, which were, she admitted, really gross if you weren't used to them. Her familiarity with yoga might also be gone, she said, but she wasn't sure of that yet. She didn't know why anyone here would want to steal any of those habits.

I asked her if she had heard anything overnight. She grimaced. "I know it's not good mindful practice, but I took melatonin before bed. I haven't been sleeping well, and Tim snores. I wanted to be well rested for a calming day of yoga." She smiled ruefully. "I think it's a lost cause now."

I did Nadia's interview quickly while everyone else took a twenty-minute break. She had barely broken a sweat.

"You're really working them, huh?"

She grinned. "They like it."

I tapped my notepad with my pen. "You're a light sleeper. Did you hear anything strange last night?"

Nadia shrugged. "I thought I heard someone walking down the hallway once or twice, but it's a new place. I fell back asleep once they stopped."

I remembered the doors. "And you didn't hear any creaking?"

She shook her head.

"Ugh," I said. I looked at my notes and flipped back to my initial list of questions. "Okay. Um, did you have any reason you might want to steal Helene St. Peters's habits?"

"No." Nadia grinned. "As you know, I am perfect and have never wanted to change anything about myself."

I chuckled. "Yeah, okay, and you haven't bitten your nails since you were ten." I tossed the notepad onto my pillow and fell back onto the bed. "Will you send Clara in next?"

Clara had a knack for saying nothing in a lot of words, but I began to pick out some underlying threads. Her startup was doing horribly. Investors were starting to want results, and she didn't have them. There was some problem with a clinical trial.

Half an hour in, I asked her why she'd agreed to come to the retreat, and the dam broke.

"I just know that if I could do something different, something better, I would get there faster. I'm not as good as people like Helene are about getting up every day and working through the day and just *getting it done*. I want to go to dinner with my boyfriend. I want to walk my dog. I don't want to stare at spreadsheets and go to meetings begging for funding for a product I'm not even sure deserves it. I'm fucking sick of not being good enough."

"So you wanted to come here to get past that? To be more okay with where you are?"

Clara stared back at me, flat. "No, I came here to figure out what the fuck everyone else was doing that I was missing out on."

Okay then. "Are you a light sleeper? Did you hear anything last night?"

She shrugged. "Not really. I have a white noise machine."

Great. "Thanks, Clara. Can you send Seetha in?"

Seetha answered all my questions very directly. She was a deep sleeper, which she attributed to her excellent yoga practice. She didn't have anything against Helene and preferred not being the CEO. Did she think Tim was good enough for Helene? Obviously not. But that was just how friendships went. Helene had hated Seetha's last boyfriend.

My legs were getting stiff. I walked Seetha back to the yoga studio and stood in the doorway for a minute, watching. I was so much happier here, observing, than I would have been in the studio trying to copy Nadia's movements with a fraction of the grace.

47

They were all settling into something Nadia's calm voice called *king pigeon*, a pose that involved bending back until your head met the heel of one foot. Clara looked like she wanted to murder someone, and poor Helene was near tears—some of her yoga habit must have been taken, then. But as Seetha slipped into her spot next to Helene, I watched Tim flow into the pose easily, leaning his head back just so. It almost made me feel bad to interrupt him.

I may as well have let him be. Tim had an easy charm to him that helped explain to me why he was dating Helene, but he didn't have many answers. He worked in finance, he said. Yes, he'd met Helene at a work event, but they didn't have any major connections on that side of things. Did he feel jealous? Sure, sometimes. She was always spectacular. It was hard not to feel like he was falling behind. But they didn't fight much and had only been living together for a few months, not enough to fall into bad habits. He only faltered for a moment when I asked about anyone he might want to use the device on.

"My brother's in recovery," he said. "He's an addict. It's not something the device is indicated for. I've never brought it up to Helene, but I did wonder …. But I would never do something like that without talking to her about it. I was trying to think of the best way to bring it up." The set of his mouth was rueful. "I thought I had time."

Nadia found me while everyone was changing for dinner. I was frowning at my notepad and only looked up when the door announced her arrival with a particularly loud squeak.

"Hey," she said. "How are you feeling?"

I turned the notepad over. "Fine. I mean, I'm getting nowhere, but I'm fine."

Nadia came and sat next to me. I didn't look at her. "Ains, the plane is coming back tomorrow afternoon, and they'll bring someone to take Helene's report. After that it's out of our hands. It's not your business."

I swallowed. "Helene's paying me. It is my business. And it's … it's nice. To be doing something."

She touched my arm, something like an apology. "Come here. Your hair's a mess. Let me fix it before dinner."

I didn't sleep very much that night. I kept trying to make it make sense.

Tim and Seetha would both have other, better opportunities to take the device. But it was possible they knew that and were trying to frame Clara. Not to mention that I didn't even know which habits had been taken—the ones Helene had noticed didn't seem particularly valuable, but we hadn't seen anyone in their home or work environment.

The last time I'd been this deep in a case, I had been so certain I was right, that all the little things I'd noticed added up to a clear culprit. And I'd been dead wrong.

This time, at least, I knew that I knew nothing. So I stayed very still and very quiet, going through it again and again, trying to make it make sense in my head.

I wasn't the one who noticed it the next morning. I had slept some amount, I thought, in the early morning hours, but I was groggy, and I headed right for the oatmeal.

"That's weird," Clara said, from where she was hovering in front of the green smoothies. "You always seem to survey the room before you go anywhere."

I stopped. The glass of the bowl in my hand felt suddenly colder against my skin. The thumping of my heart felt too big for my chest. I was wrong-sized everywhere.

"You're right," I said, hollow. "I do."

Who else was in the room? I turned to look. Seetha and Helene, chatting happily, though Helene's mouth still puckered a little with every sip she took of the green smoothie in her hand. Nadia, staring blankly at half a dragon fruit.

I took my oats and the sinking feeling in my chest out to the hallway with the long line of doors. I thought about going and sitting in the patio area, where the sun was shining and the grass was no doubt soft.

But my room would be quiet.

I walked back in that direction, pushed the door open, and paused at the sound it made. The door creaked. The door creaked, and I had barely slept, and I hadn't scoped out the cafeteria before I walked in.

There was only one person who could have taken my habits last night.

I found the device in Nadia's makeup bag, which was hidden in the recesses of her suitcase because she liked to pretend she didn't wear makeup around clients.

It was so small in my hand, just a cold screen and the blue worm. Medical device. Whatever. I held it and held it and barely felt it in my palm. I kept expecting to feel horror, or dread, but there was only dull resignation, a deep lake instead of a wave of feeling. I should have been more serious when I interviewed her. I had lost my best asset, and it was my own fault.

I slipped the device into my pocket and went back to my room. I sat on the bed and tried to think. I had choices. I could talk to Nadia, ask her why she'd done it, but I knew what she'd say. I hadn't taken her seriously as a suspect, hadn't thought she had a motive, but that was the classic Ainsley Ryder lack of self-awareness.

I was her motive. Detective Ainsley had been stressed, over-worked, no fun. Nadia had wanted her old friend back. She had tested it out on the others first, tried to do small enough habits that she would notice them and I wouldn't. But I had noticed, and then I had started trying to unravel everything, and she'd gone through with her plan. She'd taken away my habit of observation. Maybe she would have tried taking more once we were back in the states.

At least she hadn't taken away my ability to put the pieces together.

If I talked to Nadia, she might try to talk me out of telling Helene. She might try telling me it was all for my sake. She might even mean it. I didn't want to talk to her. I didn't want to know how susceptible I was.

For once, it seemed, Helene St. Peters wasn't smiling. Her mouth formed a perfect "O" that only expanded as I explained. I hated what had happened, what I was telling her, but there was something gratifying about telling it to someone. About thinking maybe something would be done.

She closed her mouth with an almost audible snap when I finished. I looked away, took a very shaky sip of water. "I'm really sorry," I said, finally. "I ruined your retreat."

She reached out a hand, which hovered in the air for a moment before it landed on my shoulder. "No, Ainsley, I'm—well, I'm relieved, honestly." She looked away. "I was so afraid it was one of my friends, betraying me. I'm so sorry that it was yours."

I swallowed and looked down at my water glass. "Uh, thanks."

"I'll let Tim and Seetha and Clara know," she said. "We can confine Nadia to her room until the plane gets here, and we'll ask her about the habits she moved, just to be sure."

I nodded but didn't look up.

Helene hesitated. "You know, we do have corporate information-hunting in med tech. There's a lot of research, but there's also plenty of skulking around conferences, figuring out who knows what, looking for clues, if you will. ReTred would hire you in a heartbeat."

It wasn't being a detective. But it also wasn't spying on twenty-year-olds and their secret boyfriends or sixty-year-olds and their less-than-secret mistresses.

"Yeah," I said. I tried to smile. "I'd try that." I gestured at the device, which sat on the bed next to me. "In the meantime, could you ...?"

"Of course," Helene said. She waited as I turned away from her, holding my hair up and off my neck. I shivered when her hand—or the device?—touched the back of my neck. It felt warm, comforting, familiar. It felt like Nadia curling up against me because she was afraid of flying and braiding my hair every night because she wanted to. It felt like friendship and now it felt like betrayal.

I closed my eyes and waited to feel different.

Coded Out

Frog and Esther Jones

No matter what they tell you in training, you never get used to the sight of an overdosed corpse.

The body reclined in a VR lounge chair—the sole piece of furniture in the beige-walled 100-square-foot studio apartment. The young man's neural jack was still plugged in at the base of his skull, the System still streaming data, blissfully unaware that the biological console at the other end of those signals had gone offline.

As I made my case notes, the scene felt eerily mundane. It was a tableau no different than you'd find in any apartment these days. My own pad looked very similar. I could easily picture myself lying in that VR chair, the blackout mask covering my brown Latina features; my long, dark hair hanging down past the headrest. The only real differences between him and me were the vomit surrounding the man's mouth, running down his chin and neck, and the strong sewage smell that came with his final bowel evacuation.

"Detective Melendez? Ma'am?" asked one of the uniforms, a fresh-faced blonde woman. I realized I'd been drifting.

"Standard VikeSpike OD," I said with a little sigh. "Have the ME run tox to confirm, but other than that, just process the scene and get him out of here."

The uniform nodded to me and began carrying out my orders. I turned and walked away, ducking under the crime-scene tape.

My partner, Jun Kinihara, met me at the apartment door, shaking his head. "VikeSpike?" he asked as we began to walk back to our car.

"Looks like," I said. "Still plugged in, vomit, no signs of a break-in."

"Mmm," grunted Kinihara. "So. Chalk it up to accidental death, then. Case closed."

I bit my lower lip, shaking my head in frustration as I slid into the passenger seat of the car. "Accidental, my ass," I said. "VikeSpike's been blowing up all over the System. *Someone* slipped that junkie's neural jack a code intentionally written to flood his brain with dopamine. VikeSpike ODs are a fuckin' *homicide.*"

"That is not what the brass says," Kinihara said in that meticulous voice of his. He started the car, the low whine of the electric motor underlying our conversation as we drove back toward the precinct. "VikeSpike is not a substance, technically. It does not fall under the Uniform Controlled Substances Act."

"I know," I said, letting my frustration spill into my voice. "Used to be dope fiends would shoot up heroin or some 'script, and that'd chemically throw a bunch of dopamine into their brains. *That* we responded to. Sling dope? Do time. But write a fuckin' piece of code that gets the brain to do it to itself ..."

"And you have not made a substance at all," said Kinihara calmly. "Which means we do not have to open a homicide case. Which is good, because figuring out *which* dealer was hacking VikeSpike to this particular deceased would be almost impossible anyway. All we could do is increase the number of unsolved homicides on our books, which hurts everyone in the department."

I had no response to that. I just huffed and leaned back in my seat. Case AD-34892-1 would go down as just one more accidental death. The fourth VikeSpike death I'd recorded that way in the last month. I'd go back to the station, make a little note in a file, and nobody would concern themselves about Case AD-34892-1.

I would remember him as Zachary Johnston, though. And he'd haunt my dreams with the rest of them.

The load-in scene for the System's virtual customer-service interface was, of course, flawless. A large, airy, glass-walled atrium with a massive, intricate fountain flowed down the wall behind the receptionist. The water bounced and ran in a thousand different streams, splitting and merging on small juts of rock perfectly positioned to produce an effect both natural-looking and stunning.

"Welcome to SysAdmin Regional," the young female avatar sitting at the desk said. She had the face and body of a supermodel. Her uniform appeared pristinely cut and tailored, and her smile revealed absolutely perfect, gleaming teeth.

I felt pretty sure the person behind that avatar was a hairy forty-something with a beer gut, but no sense calling anyone out on it. In the System, your avatar was your avatar, and this one had clearly been designed by the System to be as congenial a welcomer as possible.

My own avatar, for instance, looked like a red-headed, white-skinned woman. Anytime I wanted to really captivate and charm people, I used this one. The avatar I used for personal stuff looked a lot more like … well, like me. I didn't *like* that wearing this appearance made it easier for me to interact—but it did. I'd take any advantage in an investigation—even distasteful ones.

"I'd like to speak with a SysAdmin for the South Side, Chicago," I said pleasantly.

"One moment," she said. "Please hold."

The luxurious office vanished, leaving me in a blank, white void. Four interactive windows popped up in front of me, asking me to select my hold-wait experience: "Kitten Pile," "Infinite Skydive," "Samurai vs. Ninja," and "Under the Sea."

I rolled my eyes at this, but selected "Infinite Skydive" and commenced falling through a cloud-filled sky, waiting calmly for the SysAdmin to contact me. The hold program was, of course, pretty basic. The ground never appeared, so the whole thing was more of a vertical wind simulator than anything else. But flipping about and playing with the rush of wind flowing past me as I "fell" at least helped pass the time.

Eventually my setting shifted again, and I found myself sitting in a rather mundane-looking office. Beige walls had little decoration besides a single picture of an Orca breaching. A young, almost teen-age, white male avatar sat behind a desk.

"Can I help you?" he asked.

"Yes. I'm Detective Maria Melendez, Chicago PD. I'm here about a VikeSpike OD."

"Really?" he asked, looking surprised. "My understanding is VikeSpike ODs are accidental deaths."

Damn—I'd hoped my badge would at least get me *some* in with these people. Should have known they'd be up on our procedures.

"They are," I said. "I'm running this more as a statistical thing. Consider it data-gathering, not a case investigation." I gave him a pleasant smile, the nobody-is-in-trouble smile. That smile had landed me more confessions than any anger or threats.

He stared at me for a while—just as useless a gesture as mine, and we both knew it. Anyone could set their avatar to whatever facial expression they consciously chose. Still, the human habits of distrust were a hard thing to break. That long, silent stare gave *me* more information than it gave him.

"What is it you want to know?" he asked finally.

"Where'd he score the Spike?" I asked. "From who?"

"VikeSpike," the avatar said as though reading from a prepared statement—and perhaps he was, "is a breach of our Terms and Conditions. The System's policy is to ban all persons involved in the creation or distribution of illicit software. Unfortunately, the hackers who produce and sell VikeSpike are, by their nature, proficient in the manipulation of System software. The System is not responsible for unauthorized use of neural/physical interface hardware or soft—"

"Yeah, yeah," I said, waving my hand. "I don't need the company line here, mister ..." I trailed off, leaving the silence open.

"My name is Reginald," he said. "Now, if there's nothing else I can do for you?"

"You haven't done much at all, Reggie," I said.

"I'm sorry you feel that way. Good day, Detective."

The next day, I rose from my chair, unplugged my neural jack, and headed back to work back in meatspace.

The grubby stench of the precinct filled my nostrils like a home-coming greeting as I walked in, waved to the desk officer, and made my way to my office, then stopped as I saw a young, black woman with coke-bottle glasses sitting just outside my office in the flimsy, wireframe chair positioned there for exactly that purpose. Rare to get voluntary, unexpected visitors off the street, though. As I beeped my ID card to open the door, I turned to her.

"Help you with something?" I asked.

"Um," she said. "Can … can we do this inside?"

I furrowed my brow—this sort of approach fell into the "highly irregular" category, and that, in turn, made me suspicious. In my line of work, "suspicious" can become "dangerous" *really, really* fast. Still … the girl looked more terrified than deadly. I waved her into one of the more padded, comfortable chairs in front of my desk.

"I'm Detective Maria Melendez," I said. "Were you waiting for me?"

"Yeah," she said. "I'm, um … I'm Reginald."

I froze. The SysAdmin from yesterday? The one who'd fed me the company line?

What the hell was she—no. Anger was not the right way to play this, the girl was already jumpy. De-escalate. Project calm. That's what I needed to do.

"Okay," I said. "I see you're really scared. There's no reason to be frightened, Reggie—or is that actually your name?"

"It's … let's use it, for now," she said.

I sighed. Paranoia in small amounts can be useful, but in a con-fidential informant it could get downright tedious.

"You're safe, Reggie," I said again, trying to coax her to relax. "Just … tell me why you're here."

"It's … I can't give you intel while we're logged into the System. It has to be here. You never know who's watching when you're on the System. We can see it all, you know. If we want to. Everything. Every deal, every conversation, every sexual encounter … some of the others just *love* watching those. People get up to some *weird* stuff. And we can see anything we want to. There's too much to see at one time, of course, but … we can't talk on the System. Have to do it here."

I frowned, just slightly. "We?" I asked.

"The SysAdmins," she said. "Like me. The ones who monitor and maintain the System."

"Oh," I said, shrugging. "That makes sense. You'd sort of have to, wouldn't you?"

Reggie nodded, then swallowed. "Yeah," she said. "But you can't talk about VikeSpike. Not on the System. It's flagged—anytime it's mentioned, anytime any of the slang terms for it get mentioned on the System, the admins get an alert."

I blinked, staring at her. "I … an alert."

"VikeSpike. Float. Dreamdope. Cream. Transcontinental. Jolt-jizz. Whatever they call it, it flags. We know anytime anyone's talking about it."

I leaned back and took a deep breath. "If that's true," I said, "how in the hell is it so prevalent? Dammit, it's your job as SysAdmin to shut that down … they don't let us cops enforce laws in the System, that's all Terms and Conditions stuff."

"I said it was flagged." Reggie hung her head and looked at her feet. "I … I didn't say the admins did anything about it."

I stared for a bit. This woman was telling me that the System—the nigh-monopolic company that ran worldwide telecommunications—could shut down VikeSpike transactions if it chose to.

"That's a hell of an accusation," I said. "Why would the System turn a blind eye to—"

"To code that gets people completely addicted to using the System?" she asked in a bitter tone. "To code that's responsible for a *five percent* revenue increase worldwide?"

I shook my head and took another deep breath. Damn. Everything she was saying made sense.

"That's not the real question," Reggie continued. "The real question—the one you *should* be asking—the one you *would* be asking if you had any idea how intricately complex the bio/synth feedback programming is for the System—isn't *why* the System is turning a blind eye. It's … *who* has the sort of knowledge and training to code changes to that interface in the first place."

"Do you know who—"

She shook her head. "No," she said. "I don't have names to name. But there's nowhere else that trains people on this stuff. No other company who can utilize it. It's totally proprietary, and well-protected. We get script kiddies that like to cheat at the game programs, we get trolls, we get bots. That's what I deal with on a daily basis.

"But the code for VikeSpike … it's on a whole different level. It meshes into the interface itself, not just the applications the interface runs on. *Nobody* who can code the interface works anywhere else. The System trains them and pays them far too much for that. And every one of us signed an employment clause with a Non-Disclosure and Deletion agreement—if we quit or are terminated—the System deletes its proprietary technical information from our memories before we're free to go."

"So you're saying that the System itself makes VikeSpike?"

"I'm … I'm not sure," she said, her tone still tentative, though more relaxed now that she'd already dropped her bomb right into my lap. "It's either that, or an unsanctioned side project for some of the other admins. Make a buck on the sly, you know. But the System doesn't do anything about it, either way."

"Yeah …" I said. "Can you … is there a way you can figure out who's—"

"No," she said firmly. She shook her head vigorously, to emphasize the point, and the tempo of her words accelerated as her nerves began to ramp back up. "After this morning, I don't know you. You don't know me. I've done what I can. I have to get to work. Can't help you anymore. No." She fidgeted for a moment, then stood, turned, and slipped out the door before I had a chance to say anything.

Poor girl. It'd taken guts to come to me like that—a SysAdmin job was a cushy deal and risking that to rat out your peers displayed some serious intestinal fortitude. I found myself liking her, despite my professionally detached demeanor.

A moment later, Kinihara walked up and leaned against the doorframe of my office. "Who was that?" he asked in that cold tone of his.

"That," I said, "was Reggie."

During the next couple of days, I pondered what Reggie had said, and what my next steps could be. The idea that the System could actively promote—or, at the least, turn a blind eye to its employees creating—something as insidious and lethal as VikeSpike nauseated me. I had a single, unattributable, oral statement—not exactly the sort of thing that gets a detective a search warrant for the largest company in the country.

A gang of hackers looking to make a dirty buck was one thing—I'd always thought a registered, public, corporate entity looking to maximize profits was another. If Reggie had given me good intel, then the lines between those two things were a hell of a lot grayer than I'd thought.

But I had no *clue* where to begin unraveling the threads. Log into the System, and my suspects could track all my communications with everyone. Do it in meatspace, and my ability to speak with others became limited to face-to-face … and I didn't know what faces I was looking for.

The whole thing was a Gordian Knot. I kept looking for a loose end, because unlike Alexander, I didn't have a sword handy.

On the third day after Reggie's visit, we got another call. Another body found, still hooked into the System.

"Another OD," said Kinihara as we drove out to the scene.

"Probably," I said. "Keeps getting worse, and there's nobody to make it better."

"You still want to go tilt at that windmill your CI gave you?" he asked. "You do realize there is no evidence to support anything she said. She wouldn't even leave her identification. Even if the Department authorized us to pursue a warrant for System Regional, no judge would grant it. Keep your head down, Melendez. It's how we do the job another day."

"I know," I snapped at him. "But what if she's right? What if SysAdmins really are behind this whole epidemic?"

"Then," Kinihara said calmly, "they are committing a number of crimes, including manslaughter. But as I have no evidence showing this is true, save the word of a single girl who did not name herself or provide hard data, I am not going to speculate. I am certainly not going to give our superiors a reason to ask why I am speculating. And neither should you."

"But ..." I said, then trailed off, Fact was, Kinihara was right. Until something concrete came up, until I had *something* to go on, it all amounted to just speculation. I shuddered to think of the amount of money the System could throw at anything looking to damage its reputation.

No, I needed more.

I just didn't know how to get it.

We stepped out of the car, walked up four flights of stairs, and opened the door to the tiny studio apartment. A set of four walls around a VR chair, same as everyone else had ... and on it, the body of a young, black woman, mouth rimmed in vomit, pants browned by the final movement.

And on the small dresser, a pair of coke-bottle glasses.

"Shit!" I said. "Kinihara ... this is ..."

"You do not know that yet," he said, pulling on his gloves and walking toward the corpse's head. He lifted the VR face mask to reveal Reggie's face. "Now you do. It would appear your CI was, in fact, just another junkie and not some super-secret whistleblower. Occam's razor prevails once more."

"No!" I said. "She ... knew things. Knew how to call me. Knew who I was. She was the SysAdmin I talked to, I'm sure of it."

"You are a detective," said Kinihara in that ridiculous, calm, robotic voice of his. "Your business card is likely in the pocket of a quarter of the junkies in the South Side by now."

"But ..." I said, then looked down at Reggie. She'd been so scared. She'd been terrified, but she'd come to me. And she'd asked nothing in return. Why? What possible motivation would a junkie have if—

"What if this isn't an accident?" I asked. "What if it's murder?"

"Murder?" asked Kinihara.

"If the System—"

"More speculation. Horses, not zebras, Melendez. This is an accidental OD of some junkie looking to get high. Same as the rest. We'll log it as such. Speculation is useless, evidence matters. You did not know this girl. She lied to you. You believed her. It happens."

Reggie had come to me with good intel, and they'd killed her for it. I knew it in my gut. That look—that fear—it hadn't been fake. No. Kinihara was wrong about that. But … there was nothing more I could do, at the moment. I bit my lower lip in frustration but nodded.

Without evidence—without *solid* evidence—I was powerless, here. Reggie had died for coming to me, for trusting me, and I could do nothing about it. I didn't know the young woman, didn't know who'd loved her, who would miss her. But I knew I'd promised safety—and gotten her killed.

I *knew* it. I just needed to *prove* it.

I filled out the paperwork regardless. Accidental death. Overdose. Case closed. Numb blackness filled my chest as I signed off and returned home to stare at my VR chair.

There's a line.

As detectives, there are things we can do, and things we dare not do. Those who stepped over the line rarely made it back intact. You heard stories of cops going rogue, beating on suspects, stealing cash from arrestees, that sort of thing.

Picking a one-woman fight against the largest corporation in history probably ended worse.

I stared at the VR chair, and my stomach turned as I thought about how to proceed. I needed proof. Evidence. Reggie *had* to have been real. Only one way to know for sure.

I logged in and directed my browser to SysAdmin Regional.

The pretty blonde avatar greeted me once more, giving me a little wave. "Hello again," she said. "How can I be of service?"

"SysAdmin, South Side Chicago?" I said, and the lady nodded.

"Of course," she said. "Please hold."

This time, at the hold screen, I went for "Pile of Kittens." The program was aptly named, and I'll admit that being covered in fluffy balls of mewling cuteness helped settle my nerves for my upcoming meeting.

Then I found myself in Reggie's office, facing Reggie's avatar. "Um," I said. "I'm sorry, I'm looking for information on Reginald."

"I'm Reginald," said the avatar. "What sort of information do you require?"

"I ... what? No, Reginald. A SysAdmin here. We met a couple days ago."

"I'm Reginald," the avatar repeated. "We're all Reginald. What can I do for you?"

"Oh," I said. "Um ... the Reginald I met with last time. She's been found dead."

"Last time?" said the bland-faced, white, male avatar behind the desk with an innocent-appearing friendly smile. "My records show that this is your first visit to these offices, Detective Melendez."

The hairs on the back of my neck went up at that. I knew I'd been here before. *They* knew I'd been here before. So ... why pretend I hadn't?

"I was here four nights ago," I said. "Met with Reginald. Well, *a* Reginald, I suppose. I was looking for her contact information."

"No such visit occurs in our records," said New Reginald in that pleasant, bland voice.

"I ... okay," I said. "Can I get an employee list of all the people working the Regional center four nights ago?"

New Reginald stared at me once more, that stare I'd seen from this same avatar before—though this time his head cocked to the side slightly. Same stare ... different person. How many people at the System wore this Reginald as an avatar for official duties? All of them?

"No," he said at last. "Sorry, without a warrant I am required to tell you that we cannot disclose employee information for privacy reasons."

"Warrant," I said, scoffing. "Very well, I'll go get my warrant."

Reginald—*this* Reginald—sighed. "Detective? You won't get it, you know. And even if you do, it will do you no good. No such person has ever worked here."

"No such person," I said, my mouth curling up into a grin. "I haven't given you a description of the person, other than to say she'd worked here four nights back. Did you have no female SysAdmins four nights back? I find that doubtful—which means you're lying. Which means I *will* get my warrant."

"Dammit," said the Second Reginald. He sighed. "I was hoping to do this the easy way." He pulled up a small console screen from thin air and began pressing buttons on it. "It would have been easier,

Detective, for you to just go on about your business," he said as he punched in code.

"This *is* my business," I said. I pulled up my own console and began doing something similar.

"Not anymore," he said, then made a jabbing motion at his console before pushing it away into nothingness.

All of a sudden, I felt *terrific.* Nothing mattered. Everything—everything in the world was *perfect.* I tried a little experiment and thought about Reggie's vomit-stained face—no pain. Nothing but this warm, wrapped, feeling of complete peace and tranquility.

"Like it?" asked Reginald. "It's quite the high, from what I hear. Direct dopamine release—no messy chemical interface."

I smiled dreamily at him. Then I let my hand drift over to my console and hit the "enter" key.

The small hard drive in my VR chair responded unthinkingly. I'd programmed it correctly, and double-checked it. It dumped its cache—including the last five minutes of my VR experience, into a replayable file. As my eyes fluttered open, and then closed, and then open again, fiber-optic cables carried the damning evidence from my chair out to the entire precinct e-mail list.

Just like I'd set it up to.

I took a deep, contented sigh just before I started to vomit. As I began to choke, I simply floated up and away from life on dopamine wings. My job was done. My watch ended here.

At least it ended on a win.

Murder at the Westminster Dino Show

Rosemary Claire Smith

My brother interrupted my morning walk with Timidity Rex perched on my leather shoulder pad. After not speaking for three years, I only took Sterling's video call because he marked it urgent.

"I need your help, Dakkie." My annoyance at the childhood nickname must have shown. "Sorry, Dakota. There's been a ... a death. Chief Judge Gallagher Compton."

"You want a detective. Find someone else." Yeah, I was still sore about his 'helpful' explanation why I wasn't suited for my profession.

"I can't. If one word got out ... . The breeders' association is prepared to pay—"

I cut him off with a figure five times my top rate, calculated to show that his thirty-something "kid" sister, who lacked his fixation on wealth, deserved respect. He knew how I felt about his overentitled clique, with their secret breeding techniques.

Sterling gulped. As if the sum were anything but petty cash for top-one-percenters who raised pint-sized tyrannosaurs, ceratopsians, and brachiosaurs for self-aggrandizement and phenomenal profit. "The board will scream bloody murder ... er, maybe that's not the best way to put it ... but yes. I've got to find out which dinosaur did in our chief judge and quickly." The gates would open for the seventh annual Westminster Dino Show a week from today.

My tyrannosaur's feathers rose at the accusation against her kind, but I wasn't ready to weigh in on Sterling's assumption.

"The breeders won't stand for a violent beast in our midst." He went on as if I knew nothing. "The judges disqualify dinosaurs that jump, bite, or menace with fangs or claws."

Curious, Timidity Rex poked her snout at my screen. Sterling shot her a scornful look. She shook her ratty, mottled feathers as if to flaunt the reason she'd never be a show dino or be allowed to bear offspring, notwithstanding her impeccable pedigree.

"I can catch the High Speed and see you in an hour."

I'll have my chopper pick you up in ten minutes and you'll be here in twenty."

"Sure. Until then, don't touch anything, or get near the body. And call the police."

"I owe you one, Dakk—Dakota."

He owed me more than that, but I said nothing. After he clicked out, Timidity used her two-fingered forelimbs to sign, <Take me with you.>

We had worked out a two-fingered sign language to converse when she was muzzled in public. I never told a soul, especially not an owner or breeder. She had secretly helped me with a few cases in the seven years since Sterling gave me what he called the 'failure of the litter' instead of my half of the inheritance from our parents. Humans, even the very few who live with miniature dinosaurs, underestimate them.

<Sure,> I signed back.

After living with me since she was a juvenile, it might do her good to spend some time around her own kind. Besides, her presence would annoy Sterling.

The Westminster Compound lay outside Reno behind thirty-foot-high walls, ridiculous considering miniature dinosaurs can't jump. People must stoop to pat the head of the tallest long-necked brachiosaur.

When the automated helicopter landed at the gate, Sterling was there by himself to meet me. "I didn't say you could bring *her*."

Timidity Rex shook her feathers and made a doubly rude gesture with both forelimbs. Not surprisingly, my brother missed it.

"She'll stay out of our way."

He scowled, then led me past posh 'cottages' to the arena's heavy gate, which he unlocked and pulled open.

"Are the police on their way?"

"No rush. It was an accident. I kept everyone away."

Mentally bracing myself, I pulled away the sheet someone put over Judge Compton's body. Ten years of detective work had not inured me to the sight or smell. He lay sprawled on the wet grass, a newsboy cap near his head of thinning hair. Water droplets glistened on his forehead and cheeks. He wore a sodden, impeccably tailored tweed suit complementing his damp, nicely trimmed beard. A deep, bloody puncture wound pierced his trachea, with a shallower one close by. Blood had coursed straight down his shirt and lapels.

"When did you last see him alive?"

"At dinner, yesterday evening. He turned in early."

I gestured at the security cameras. Doubtless, more were hidden. "What do those show?"

Sterling shifted nervously. "The system is undergoing an upgrade."

"Cutting it close, huh?" Most breeders would descend on Westminster with their prize dinosaurs in a few days.

He threw up his hands. "You know how tech upgrades can drag on. It will be finished in time." Ah yes, the voice of a CEO accustomed to having his edicts obeyed. He'd practiced it on me when we were kids.

I crouched to give the wounds a closer look. The deeper hole could have been made by a triceratops horn. The shallower one, too. There was no third hole.

<I don't smell triceratops,> Timidity signed.

"From the position and condition of his body, he died right here early this morning. Thoughts on why Compton entered the arena around dawn?"

"He enjoyed the arena's pre-event solitude. 'Like a blank canvas,' he'd say, before most owners arrive and the crowd swells to fifty thousand devotees roaring for their favorites."

I unpacked my DNA scanner.

"Is that thing necessary?"

"If you expect a thorough investigation, yes." I aimed it at Compton's face. "I'll need reference samples from every human and dinosaur." I proceeded to the throat, arms, and hands.

He frowned at my scanner. "You expect me to set the example, huh?"

With a nod, I moved to the chest and on down the victim's body. "Someone's dinosaur slipped its leash and muzzle?"

"Breeders take every precaution but ..."

The DNA scanner beeped. Ugh. "No fresh DNA, except Compton's."

"The automated sprinklers could have washed away whatever was there."

"Nonetheless ..." I extended the scanner toward him.

"If you must."

I recorded his DNA. "What aren't you telling me, Sterling?"

"Not here."

He led me to his office, adorned with stuffed heads of winners from Westminster's early years. I insisted Timidity Rex stay outside to spare her the gruesome reminder of how dinosaurs were sometimes treated after their fertile years ended. I raised an eyebrow at an empty display case. The inlaid mahogany shelf with the other taxidermied heads had a fine layer of dust, but not around the missing one.

"No, I didn't sell Shiver Me Timbers's head. Got several tempting offers even though he's not a perfect specimen. Fact is, last week somebody stole my first miniature triceratops."

I opened my mouth, but he cut me off with, "Don't natter about police."

"Any idea who took him?"

"Kaylee Rosa, maybe. My groundskeeper/maintenance woman has access. I pay her well, but temptation can be powerful for many immigrants."

"Or other people. Would she know where to unload it?"

"She might have contacts."

"You didn't fire her?"

"That's inconvenient this close to the show."

Seeing me dusting for fingerprints, Sterling launched into obvious advice on how to do so. I steered the conversation to owners who had arrived early.

"Bunny Markham-Blighton got in first. She's our wealthiest owner. Old money lends respectability to the association. She raises gorgeous, feathered tyrannosaurs, including last year's Best in Show. This year, her Twilight Ninja is even more impressive. Victor Fellowes came next with his main squeeze, A.J. During dinner, A.J. teased him about how many kimonos Victor needed for a seventy-two-hour event. Victor will be showing Saffron Bedazzled. That's a glitter-headed brachiosaurus with an on-trend gleaming yellow hide. A.J. has his triceratops, Smithereens, in tow." Sterling's expression turned dark. "Victor also brought two stegosaurs—illicit gifts for our chief judge. To think Compton stood right where you are now and told me how delightful they were."

"Couldn't you remove him for bribery?"

"Do you have any notion how difficult judging is?"

"Probably not."

"One doesn't merely evaluate the shape of fangs, claws, and horns. You've got to consider classic head shape and body proportions. Their gaits are critical, especially their gallops and canters. Also, their plumage. Compton made it look easy. It's anything but. He's almost irreplaceable. Somehow, we'll have to stumble along this year with a reduced panel."

By now I'd finished. "No prints except yours, Sterling."

"Yes, Ms. Dakota, I found him." Kaylee Rosa stood before me, arms tight to her sides, fidgeting with her much-faded baseball cap. "I knew something was wrong when I noticed the open gate. To see him ..." She shuddered.

"What time?"

The young woman didn't hesitate. "Around 8:30 this morning, after the sprinklers shut off."

"Did you call the police?"

"No! In my country, you don't do that. I called Mr. Sterling."

"How long have you been in the U.S.?"

"Since I was ten. Mr. Sterling came right away. He barely looked at Judge Compton's body and the blood. He said he'd get a doctor who owed him a favor. He told me it must be a massive heart attack or serious stroke." She looked away. For decades, strokes and heart attacks had been rare in first-world nations.

"Go on."

"Word got around that someone's dinosaur had been off leash and unmuzzled." Miniature rexes have jaws roughly the size of my hand and are thoroughly intimidating if unmuzzled. The other toy species are nothing to mess with, either.

I refrained from pointing out two possible sources of the word getting around: the killer's owner and Kaylee.

"Everybody had to be warned, even if I got fired." Kaylee scrunched that ball cap and fought back tears. Who would take the word of a disgruntled and disgraced soon-to-be-ex-employee over Sterling's?

"Does my brother even know where you came from?"

Her mouth quirked. "I'd like to think so."

Notwithstanding her fear of cops, she unhesitatingly gave me a DNA sample when I assured her Sterling authorized it.

As Timidity and I passed employees wearing Westminster uniforms on our way to Victor and A.J.'s cottage, we talked things over. She knows dinosaurs better than I do.

<Maybe it's Twilight Ninja.>

<Don't blame the rex, Dakota.>

<Your loyalty to your kind is commendable but—>

<You don't understand.>

<Then explain.>

<A rex grabs the throat in her jaws and crushes it, including bone.>

True enough. I'd watched the ironically named Timidity strike at her food. Judge Compton had stab wounds. <A triceratops?>

<Horn-heads always attack from below and gore the belly.>

Hmmm. Ceratopsians can't reach the throat and despise being picked up. Never argue with their horns. Which left brachiosaurs, their teeth as blunt as felt markers, and stegosaurs with no front teeth. I suggested them anyway.

<They stomp. Their stinky odors linger.>

I opened my mouth to argue. But tyrannosaurs have noses rivaling bloodhounds. Besides, the victim wasn't lying down when the blood flowed from his wound. We'd run out of dino suspects.

I'd conducted a lot of interviews, but never had someone open the door sporting lavender eyebrows, a yellow silk kimono, and matching boxers. Victor's outfit coordinated with Saffron Bedazzled's sunny hide. The brachiosaur placidly munched baby carrots.

Victor flopped down and pointed at my DNA kit. "What's that?"

"Routine test. I'm scanning the dinosaurs. It's not invasive and won't hurt."

He wrinkled his nose. "My Saffron's too well bred to attack a human."

"Sterling expects all of them tested."

"Oh, go ahead. You know, when the groundskeeper told me the terrible news, I can't tell you how devastated I felt. A.J., too. Such a fine, well-respected member of our breeders' community."

I raised a skeptical eyebrow.

"Well, several owners couldn't have been happy with Compton's extraordinary generosity last year in awarding Best in Show to Bunny's Razzmatazz Rapture. It hurts when brachiosaurs like mine are downgraded because they don't roar, stab, crunch, or fluff their feathers. Their four-footed gait gets derided as lumbering. We all need to be assured the judging is above board."

"Did anyone complain to my brother?"

"Why bother? Sterling couldn't fire our head judge. Compton would have made such a stink, calling a lot of practices into question."

"Mind if I sample your DNA too, Victor?" He got the look of a caged ferret. "Just a formality."

He muttered something about privacy and gave in.

"When's the last time you saw Compton?"

A pause. "Yesterday afternoon in his suite."

"See anything unusual?"

"Bunny Markham-Blighton stalking away from there wearing a pair of dreadful platform shoes ten years out of date. She was in a huff."

"Did Compton say why?"

"Nope. We didn't dwell on her."

"What did you dwell on?"

"I brought him Platelets and Shimmy Shim—prototype stegosaurs. A.J.'s retrieving those two now."

Timidity's nostrils quivered as she picked up Twilight Ninja's scent. I'd never seen her display this much interest in another tyrannosaur.

From the cottage's open window came Bunny Markham-Blighton's indignation. "If you expect to make me proud, Twilight, you'll have to do much better than fifth in your last outing. I didn't invest a tenth of the family fortune for you to waddle around like an overfed brachiosaurus."

<Rexes don't waddle,> Timidity protested. <The grassy place smells like food. It's distracting.>

"Arms still," Bunny ordered Twilight Ninja. "Flailing is hardly cute or endearing. Try ridiculous."

<Our arms wave when we run or get excited. Besides, who'd want to be endearing for that mammal?>

I knocked on the door and introduced myself. Once inside, my eyes and Timidity's snout fixed on Twilight Ninja, perched on a coffee table amid a riot of hair products.

Twilight Ninja's nostrils flared at Timidity. His tail curled. I felt bad for Timidity. Bunny would never "waste a prize stud" on a genetic failure with mottled feathers.

She gave Twilight's long, jet-black feathers a spritz from a spray bottle. "My own secret recipe for glossy plumage. Toy rexes are considerably less work than prepping a Pekingese for show."

Timidity signed indignation. <Stupid mammal is ruining his alluring scent.>

I got down to business. "You were seen leaving Judge Compton's suite in a huff—"

"Who says? Victor? He thinks I'm always in a huff. I bet he tried to smear me when all I've ever wanted from any judge is a fair shake. Consider: toy rexes are always the most competitive group."

"Huh? They're crowd-pleasers."

"Exactly. The people's choices get judged under stricter standards than other breeds. As for Victor, why did he pay Compton a late-night visit, hmmm? Don't suppose he told you he and Compton were having an affair." She kept grooming Twilight's shiny feathers, which hardly needed the sprinkle of silvery dust. "Remember: tail straight."

"And the reason for your visit?" I asked.

"Rumor had it, Victor brought Compton two brand-new stegosaurs. Highly improper. 'Platelets'—now there's a dinosaur that tries too hard." Her voice dripped disdain. "And Shimmy-Flim-Flam? The world's most absurd baby rattle. What can you expect from an upstart breeder like Victor? I went to find out if Compton intended to lobby Sterling to add stegosaurs to the Westminster Dinosaur Show."

"And?"

"Compton wouldn't say. To think Victor's Saffron Bedazzled is my most serious competition this year." She sniffed. "Showmanship ought to mean more than excelling at being carried around." She gave Twilight Ninja another apprising stare. "Your feathers will earn full marks. I made an inspired choice there. Remember to fluff them up."

<Hah! This mammal never had a breeze blow feathers into her mouth as she bit into a tasty lizard.>

"Ewww ... your breath is none too fresh." Bunny picked up a jar of breath mints.

Both tyrannosaurs eyed the mints with loathing.

At first, Bunny looked ready to shove one between Twilight Ninja's canines. She must have thought better of the idea. "Open ... open up or no yummy lizard dinner."

He obeyed.

For all Bunny Markham-Blighton's complaints, she had no objections to me collecting DNA from Twilight Ninja or herself. Belatedly, she said, "I'm as shaken by this dreadful death as anyone."

Nonetheless, I left contemplating what someone so accustomed to getting what she wanted might do when thwarted.

I circled back to my brother. "Any suspicions who might have wanted to harm Compton?"

He looked thoughtful. "A.J. comes to mind."

"Go on."

"When Compton paid me a visit before dinner, he was agitated. I didn't pry. He volunteered that he worried about A.J. Look, the worst-kept secret around here is Compton and Victor's fling last year. Compton assured me the affair had run its course. Problem was that A.J. couldn't let it go, even though Victor stuck with him. Compton expected A.J. to stay away this year. He's the reason Compton asked for extra security. It was first on my To Do list for today."

"Hey, cut yourself some slack. You couldn't—"

"Safety has to come first in this business, Dakota. Anyway, I must go deal with the final details of the ice sculpture. I trust you'll be there for the advance viewing of last year's winner?"

Hmmm … an opportunity to observe the dynamics between these competitive, over-entitled breeders. "I'm looking forward to it."

Nobody told me what to expect regarding A.J. My mind conjured up someone physically resembling Compton, possibly with Victor's taste in kimonos. Instead, I was greeted in the corral by a muscular, bare-chested fellow in tight designer jeans, scarlet-and-yellow cowboy boots fashioned from coral snakeskin, and a diamond-encrusted belt buckle as big as his brain.

I observed him run Smithereens through her paces. The triceratops charged full tilt toward the first clay target and speared it straight on. The target shattered.

"Major hit!"

She demolished five more in rapid succession. I hadn't brought Timidity to the interview; her stomach would rumble if she got close to those tasty haunches. Smithereens segued to the next part of her routine, zigzagging down a double row of clay targets. She lashed her tail at them, missing only two.

A.J. couldn't have looked prouder. "Ceratopsians don't have the luxury of fluffing their feathers for the 'swimsuit competition.'"

If she were here, Timidity would have given him a rude gesture.

When we got down to business, A.J. led with: "It's astonishing how Judge Compton denied Victor his well-earned Best in Show last year. He overruled two other judges to give it to Bunny's Razzmatazz. She paid him off."

"You ever think about taking that to my brother?"

"Believe me, Sterling knew. But Bunny Markham-Blighton could buy and sell us all with her pocket change."

"Anyone upset enough to threaten Compton or worse?"

"You think I sicced Smithereens on him, don't you?"

"I'm running samples of everyone's DNA."

"You want mine? Have at it."

"Your dinosaur's, too."

He whistled and the triceratops trotted back to A.J. as fast as those four little legs could go.

Sterling entered Judge Compton's former suite, all indignation, arms akimbo. "What do you think you're doing here, Dakkie?"

That's my brother—immediately going on offense. However, the small cut on one finger gave him away. I'd missed it earlier. "The bar sink in this suite has broken glass in it."

A nonchalant shrug. "I hardly think Kaylee needs your supervision to take care of it."

The groundskeeper looked up from under the sink, her eyes round with apprehension and fixed on Sterling.

"She does when glass shards are caught in the trap along with human skin and flecks of blood. Any idea whose?" I do love asking questions to which I know the answers. Timidity's keen nose first alerted me. Both Sterling's and Compton's scents abounded. My portable DNA analyzer confirmed as much.

Sterling's jaw tightened. "I dropped by. So?"

"You said nothing earlier about paying Compton a visit. Mind filling in the details?"

"He threw a glass at me. I ducked. It hit the mirror and shattered. We both stared at each other. I picked glass from my hair and cut myself."

"And your fight was about …?"

"It wasn't a fight, not exactly.… Well, okay, it kind of was. You see, I found out Bunny Markham-Blighton bribed him last year. This was a matter of safeguarding the integrity of the competition."

"It seems you have an answer for everything, Sterling."

"That's hardly fair, Dakota." He put his head in his hands. His shoulders quaked. "If you had any idea …"

I tried to sound gentle rather than suspicious. "You can tell me."

"It was wishful thinking to suppose Compton's fling with Victor was over and done. When that sleazebag showed up with his stegosaurus surprises and used them to lure Compton … well that would tear the association apart. As for the way Compton died … I can't afford to have rumors of a dinosaur slaying get out. So I turned to you. Now if you'll excuse me, the techs still don't have the video cameras working."

This time, Victor greeted me clad in a sheer gold kimono and marginally less revealing pajama bottoms. He led me to the corner with two cages. In one, Platelets munched peapods. Wow, the rumors about newly developed stegosaurus miniatures couldn't measure up to the gorgeous reality. Its oversized spinal plates were half again as tall as it was.

I oohed and aahed until he grudgingly let me sample Platelets's DNA. Next up was Shimmy Shim, whose spinal plates were better proportioned to its body size.

"Watch this." Victor clapped his hands twice and conga music began. Shimmy Shim rattled his plates to the beat. "What a shame Gallagher Compton barely got to meet her."

There was my opening. "You told me you visited Compton in the afternoon. Bunny saw you near his suite after dinner."

He got a deer-in-the-headlights look. "Don't you breathe one word to A.J. He'll jump to the wrong conclusion."

"What's the right one?"

"You may as well know … we had an affair going on two years. A.J. found out. It devastated him for months. He was terrified I'd dump him. While A.J. walked Smithereens that evening, I slipped out, determined to break it off with Compton."

"Did you?"

"Things were … complicated. We had plans to form a business venture. I wanted us to go forward with that."

"What plans, exactly?"

"To open the league to stegosaurs. If Sterling kept stonewalling us, we'd form a rival league. But Compton didn't take our breakup well. He threw me out. Now, things will never be right between us."

"And A.J.—"

"You think his Smithereens stabbed Gallagher's neck? She won't even let A.J. pick her up." He clapped twice. The conga stopped, as did the stegosaur's plate rattling.

I left confused. Victor and A.J. topped my list of suspects, although I wouldn't put it past Bunny. One thing was certain: no diminutive dinosaur could have reached the latch for the gate into the arena. Or pull it open.

I didn't expect drama at the advance viewing of the ice sculpture. Timidity bounced with excitement because Bunny would bring Twilight Ninja. I steered us to an unobtrusive position in the back, with a good view of everyone.

In the center of the grand foyer on a low, round table stood the platinum cup to be awarded to this year's Best in Show. It was tasteful in the same way that the Palace of Versailles was restrained. The cup was taller than any of the dinosaurs, save Saffron Bedazzled. Beside it, a gold-brocade drape covered a lump, presumably the study in ice of Razzmatazz Rapture, last year's Best in Show.

Timidity's eyes and quivering nostrils fixed on the corridor. Bunny Markham-Blighton entered with Twilight Ninja gripping her leather gauntlet. Victor and A.J. strode in next, bringing Saffron Bedazzled, but not their other dinosaurs.

Naturally, Sterling made everyone wait for him to strut in and say a few grandiose words. With a flourish, he whisked off the gold drape. A chorus of gasps rose from all sides. Where an icy likeness of Razzmatazz Rapture should be, there sat the taxidermied head of Sterling's first triceratops. One of Shiver Me Timbers's three horns was broken off at the base. The old break reminded me Sterling had said it wasn't "a perfect specimen." The two intact horns bore rust-brown stains.

Timidity Rex moved forward.

"No!"

"Stop her!"

<I won't eat it.>

"Let the rex be," I said. "She's smelling the murder weapon."

Everybody leaned closer, eyes round.

"Disgusting scavenger," sneered Victor.

Nostrils a-quiver, Timidity circled the table twice. Meanwhile, Sterling summoned Kaylee.

<I smell two mammal scents on the horn-head. The dead mammal and your kin.>

Pieces clicked into place. Nevertheless, I grasped for some alternative explanation. Under their tense stares, I ran my DNA scanner over the triceratops head. Confirmation. My mind reeled. What if I claimed I found nothing?

The groundskeeper tiptoed in, pale and biting her lip. Her eyes flickered from one frowning face to another. I couldn't meet her eyes.

"What's the meaning of this?" Sterling roared at her.

It took Kaylee a minute to collect herself. "Mr. Sterling, I *found* your triceratops in the locked maintenance shed. In a back corner under a tarp. Nobody but me has any reason to go inside. Nobody knows the door combination except you and me."

His face flushed. "You insolent, lying thief! You brought it here."

"*After* I found it. And I wore gloves."

I held up my hand, dismayed but unsurprised at how Sterling's childhood meanness had condensed into ruthlessness. "Let me spell things out for you five suspects. Yes, every one of you. First, Kaylee had no motive for killing Judge Compton. None."

"Enough of your nonsense, Dakkie. You're in way over your head." Poisonous superiority laced through Sterling's big-brother voice, coupled with a triumphant gleam in his eyes, bringing me up short. "Everyone just heard her admit she placed the murder weapon in the ice tray." He counted on the breeders witnessing not just her humiliation but mine too.

Well hell no, not this time. "Can you blame her?" My voice shook. "She'd already been set up to take the fall while the security cameras were offline. Ask yourselves who planted it in the shed?"

Kaylee pressed her lips together and met the breeders' pitying looks.

I kept going. "A.J.'s an obvious choice. He knows more about ceratopsian horns than the rest of you combined. As for doing away with your … romantic rival … it's been known to happen. Problem is, there's not a trace of his DNA or scent on the murder weapon.

"Victor was in the running for a while. What really happened in Compton's suite? Turns out, it was a business deal. Victor gave the judge all the proof-of-concept he needed: Shimmy Shim and Platelets. They were well on their way to forming a new breeders' association. Out from under Sterling's thumb and Bunny's purse strings.

"Which brings me to Bunny Markham-Blighton. Why murder a judge who is in your pocket?" She let out a huff. "Or was he? Victor knew Bunny paid Compton a visit and left unhappy. That's because Compton told her about his future plans with Victor. Sure, she hated a rival league. But she didn't kill him over it.

"Then there's Sterling. His first impulse was to claim it was an accident and hush things up. Kaylee monkey-wrenched that ploy when she mistakenly warned people about a killer dinosaur at Westminster."

"I resent this, Dakkie! I brought you in to identify the murderous dinosaur."

"You tried to make me responsible for an innocent creature having to pay with its life. You've always underestimated my abilities and overestimated my sibling loyalty."

"The thanks I get for trying to make you accept your limitations."

I stuffed down my fury and addressed everyone else, "Ask yourselves who would dare commit murder on camera in the middle of the arena? Ask yourselves who knew those cameras didn't work and that his DNA would get washed away?"

"Dakkie, this is lunacy."

"I finally figured out why you did it, Sterling. The offers to sell your prize triceratops were tempting. Staffing this complex is costly. Sure, Bunny underwrites much of it, but not all. You couldn't afford to lose Victor's financial support. So you met Compton in the arena, expecting him to give the specimen a close look. If anyone questioned the puncture wounds, suspicion would naturally fall on a living dinosaur. You threw me off with your spiel about the chief judge being irreplaceable."

"You have no proof!"

"I do: DNA and scent. Timidity smelled no mammal odor on the murder weapon except Compton and you." I held up my DNA analyzer. "This readout confirms it."

I squeezed my eyes shut against unwanted tears.

Kaylee's determined voice broke the ensuing silence. "Hello, police? I'm calling to report a murder."

Kaylee led me to Sterling's luxury skybox, avoiding the breeders and the media. Once inside, she poured out her gratitude. Shame colored my cheeks. What was I doing at Westminster barely four days after my initial shock at uncovering my brother's crime? I hadn't returned to bask in her undeserved esteem, nor to savor the public accolades for preventing some hapless dinosaur from suffering the consequences. I only returned for Timidity's sake.

Her snout swiveled. <Here he comes!>

Bunny made a grand entrance into the arena with Twilight Ninja perched on her baby-blue gauntlet. Chest out, head high, tail straight, feathers fluffed to perfection, the rex commanded every eye and roared on cue. The color commentary commenced.

"Twilight Ninja has the bearing of a forty-foot beast."

"Never saw a finer toy tyrannosaur."

"His tiny roar is totes adorbs."

"Look, the mice are trembling in their cages."

<Ugh. Why do you mammals feed us nasty mice? They taste terrible.>

Twilight Ninja's muzzle pointed toward Timidity. His tail curled as both forelimbs waved.

<Uh oh. That's a demerit for Twilight.>

<Worth it!> Timidity's forelimbs flailed at him.

The Unassembled Victims

Peter Clines

*L*ambda Zeta Four thought he'd finally get some rest when the war ended. The armed forces counselor asked, on the second of their eight mandatory meetings, if Lamb meant death when he said that. He said of course he did. Two-thirds of all Assembled died in the war. Nobody'd ever seen one live past forty-seven. Why wouldn't he be thinking about death?

Naturally, she'd recommended he become a cop.

He'd been a citsec officer for two years now, a detective for almost three months. He liked the work. Found it distracting. Didn't like his partner, Fairhaven. Found her annoying and bigoted. He was pretty sure she didn't like him back. But she had numbers on her side. Nobody at the San Angeles 23rd Division liked Lamb. They didn't like that he'd been forced on the division. They didn't like that he'd been promoted. They didn't like that he was Assembled.

He didn't really need to be a detective to figure that last one out. Not a lot of people liked Assembled. Living reminders of the second AI war and what humanity had been willing to do to win it.

Lamb and Fairhaven walked down the street toward the alley, and she stayed two steps ahead, not talking or even looking at him. Leading him. A power thing. Establishing dominance. He took a little satisfaction knowing a nat partner would've probably gotten the same treatment. He'd heard someone crack a joke after a week at the 23rd, that Fairhaven could've been a role model for surly bulldogs. He'd almost laughed at it.

He activated his badge, and the holo-bands sprang to life on either arm. Fairhaven did the same and shouldered her way through the dozen or so citizens gathered there, all hoping for a glimpse at something grisly. Lamb saw another blue-skinned Assembled in the crowd and they automatically acknowledged each other with a sharp, military nod.

The uniforms had set up a security line at the mouth of the alley. One of the uniformed cops deactivated it to let them pass. He said hello to Fairhaven. Stared at Lamb. Reactivated the line behind them.

A scattered group of people stood maybe a third of the way down the alley, a bit north of where it crossed with the east-west alley that divided the block the other way. Two more uniforms. A pair of medical examiners. A dark-haired man in a pressed kaftan and bodysuit. A skinny, white-haired man in a threadbare, layered outfit that'd probably qualify as rags by the end of the season. And a seventh figure, stretched flat on the pavement, hidden by a privacy shield's hazy blur.

Lamb's vision stretched into infrared just enough that he could see the body was cold.

Fairhaven called out to the uniform closest to the body. "What we got, Kasumba?"

Sergeant Kasumba gave her a nod, tipped his chin to the figure beneath the blurry air, then over at the two civilians standing on either side of the other uniformed officer. "Baser and a passerby spotted the body at the same time. Baser was crossing the other way, called out to Mr. Marsten over there. He got on his phone, first uniforms were here within five minutes."

"That's quick," said Lamb. "Already in the area?"

Kasumba looked at Lamb for the first time. Paused for a moment. "Yeah. They'd just finished with a call a few blocks over."

Fairhaven did the math. "So it's been twenty minutes?"

"About, yeah."

"They see anything else?"

"Doesn't sound like it."

"Body's been dead a lot longer than twenty minutes," Lamb noted.

Fairhaven gave him a glance. "You sure?"

He nodded.

She turned back to the sergeant. "Anything else?"

"It's an Assembled," said Kasumba.

Fairhaven grunted.

"*He* was an Assembled," Lamb said.

The sergeant shrugged. "It's a body."

"Identification?" asked Fairhaven.

"Nothing in its—his pockets."

She gazed down at the blurry figure. "Harvest?"

"Yeah. Heart."

She grunted again.

Lamb bit back a growl. Three out of five times when an Assembled was killed in civilian life, it was organ harvesting. They'd been bred for strength, durability, and easier battlefield transplants. Assembled organs were seventy percent less likely to be rejected by a new host, which made them popular on the black market for folks who didn't want synth-organs or ghost rebuilds.

And which could really suck if the Assembled in question was still using them.

Fairhaven gave him a very clear "are you going to mess this up?" look. He set his jaw, stared at the first witness. She nodded and led them over.

Miguel Marsten wore a fairly new bodysuit with a high-end, red-and-gold kaftan. He also had a blocky, dark-silver phone holstered on his waist. The kind of portable tech that had been the eyes and ears of the AIs during both wars. "I'd just been walking by," he explained. "I'd finished a call, was putting my phone away, happened to be looking that way—"

"That's when I saw him," the baser cut in. "I waved him down. I saw his—"

"Just a moment, sir," Lamb said, sparing the man Fairhaven's wrath. "Could you step back? We'll get to you in a minute."

The baser nodded frantically, white hair bouncing around his head.

Fairhaven gestured for Marsten to continue.

"I just happened to be looking that way as I passed the alley and saw Mr., uhhhh, Steve, crouching down by the, uhhhh, the body." He looked awkwardly at Lamb. "He saw me, yelled at me to call city security."

"And did you?"

"I think I stared for a few moments. Maybe a minute. I've never seen a dead body ... well, outside."

"He froze," the baser called out. "Locked up like a bot caught in a loop."

Lamb shot him another look. Pointed emphatically at a spot a few meters away. The baser gave him a ragged salute and took two big steps back.

Fairhaven raised an eyebrow. "Outside?"

"I ... my company prints equipment for hospitals. I've seen corpses a few times for research and design purposes but they're always ... very clean."

"That why you have the phone?" She dipped her chin at the device.

"Yes. I have a permit for it." He gave Lamb another awkward glance. "It's analog."

Fairhaven asked Marsten a few more questions. Lamb listened to the answers. She made sure he'd be available for further questioning, sent him off to one of the uniforms to give a full statement.

The other man, Steve, bounced from foot to foot, waiting for his chance to talk. Lamb could read the color patterns bouncing across the man's skin. Excitement. Fear. Nervousness. He couldn't smell anything, but he was willing to bet the man's bloodstream was a mess of chems, some natural and some manufactured.

"Was coming down that way from meeting my, from my, from the store," said Steve, stretching his arm to point down the cross alley, then swinging it around to show his movement. "Thought this guy was sleeping at first. Lots of folks just sleep sometimes, right?"

Fairhaven nodded once. "When did you realize he wasn't sleeping?"

"When I saw him up close," said Steve. "I checked his pulse, but he was pretty sure dead. Look at him opened up like that." Steve raised his pasty-white hands, almost as pale as his hair, and mimed opening his chest like a cabinet. "No way he was still alive, but I wanted to be sure. I know you guys are super tough." He gave Lamb another salute.

"Not that tough," Lamb muttered.

"I know everyone in the neighborhood," Steve continued. "Never seen him before. We've got two blue boys living around here, but he's not one of them. Then I looked up and saw Mr. Red-and-Gold Kaftan staring at me down the alley."

"And that's when you asked him to call city security?"

"Yeah. I asked him to do that and he froze. It's a really nice kaftan, isn't it? I like the red. I like mine, but it's not as nice as his."

"Sir," said Fairhaven, "if you could give your statement to the officer over there, that'd be a great help."

"I want to help," said Steve, smiling. "That's why I checked his pulse."

"Right. If you could give your statement to the officer, that'd be very helpful. Thanks."

Steve saluted each of them, then wandered off toward the officers. Lamb crouched by the body. He waved the privacy shield away to reveal the corpse.

There was some truth to the saying that Assembled all looked alike. Male. Similar strong builds. Similar heights. No hair at all. Good teeth. Dark brown eyes. Bright blue skin. True for Lamb and for the body.

The corpse's bodysuit had been pulled down to his waist. Uneven cuts and gouges marked where the rib cage had been hacked apart and pried open. The bones and skin had settled back a bit, but the gap was still wide enough for Lamb to see the gaping hole between the lungs.

"Well," said Fairhaven. "I'm going to take a wild guess at cause of death."

Lamb leaned in closer. "Yeah, I'm sure he just stretched out here and waited for them to cut his heart out."

"Fair point. Didn't stretch out here, though." She pointed at the clean, dry pavement around the body. "I know you guys clot fast, but not that fast, right?"

"Definitely not."

Lamb reached a hand down beneath the neck, pressed gently against the skin. "Don't feel a pin."

"Going to make identification a snarl. Killer took it?"

He shook his head. "No wound. He might have had it removed back when he mustered out. I know a few Assembled who did."

"Why?"

"Because they didn't like being tagged like dogs." Lamb took his hand away and looked at his fingers. Rubbed them against his thumb. "Son of a bot."

"What?"

He held his hand up, spread the fingers.

She shrugged.

He reached for her. He moved a little too fast and she flinched back, but not before he ran his fingers across the back of her hand. They left blue streaks.

"What the hells?"

Lamb dug through the pockets of his frock with his other hand, found a dinner receipt from a few nights ago, and rubbed it firmly against the corpse's cheek.

"Hey," called out one of the medical examiners.

The receipt came away blue. It left a pale patch on the victim's face. The skin was a bit lighter than Fairhaven's.

"This guy isn't Assembled," said Lamb. "Someone's trying to hide a body in plain sight."

Lamb was filling out reports when Fairhaven stomped across the 23rd Division offices to their shared desks. He'd gotten pretty good at judging her expressions and the heat patterns of her skin. More annoyed than angry, but annoyed Fairhaven could still be a pain to deal with.

"Good updates and bad updates," she told him.

Lamb leaned back in his chair. "You don't look like either of them are good updates."

"Good—we identified the body. The one painted to look like an Assembled."

"Well?"

"Anton Jermaine. Partner reported him missing the day before we found him. Tox scan says he had a high-end paralytic in his blood."

Lamb stood up next to her and flicked on their crimescreen. The holographic workspace sprang to life alongside their desks. She'd already updated the case file. There was a photo of a bearded, mustached Jermaine, dated three months ago. The killer had shaved or depilled him to add to the Assembled disguise.

He turned back to Fairhaven. "This is the good part?"

She leaned against her own desk. "You talking about the killer hiding the body got me thinking, so I had a talk with the medical examiner. She made some calls, got a lot of people looking through their recent clients."

Lamb felt a low twist in his gut, one he associated with the start of combat. "And …?"

"We're looking at nine, maybe twelve other bodies in the same state over the past seven weeks. All in the same age-height-weight range. Hair removed, bodies treated with nanopaint to look like Assembled. Paralytic in the blood. Hearts removed."

He took in a breath. Organized his thoughts. "First question?"

"Shoot."

"'Maybe twelve'?"

Fairhaven reached up, opened a new folder on the crimescreen, slid a handful of reports out across the surface. "Three bodies were already cremated. Assembled with their hearts removed, no further postmortem. They fit the pattern, but we've got to wait on genetic reconstruction from the remains. Lab says it could be months before they get results."

He looked at the faces. The dates. The locations. "That sucks."

"They're backlogged. Computers aren't what they used to be. Thank gods."

"Thank gods," echoed Lamb. "Second question."

She waved at him to continue.

"Seven weeks?"

"Yeah. That's the oldest confirmed one."

"Nobody noticed a dozen bodies with their hearts cut out? In less than two months?"

She shrugged. "All of the bodies were found over a thirty square kilometer area, no two remotely in the same place. Eight different Divisions. Organ harvesting's common enough the individual cases didn't stand out to anyone."

"And it was just Assembled," Lamb added, giving her an accusing side-eye.

Another shrug from Fairhaven. "You said it, not me. But yeah. Probably had something to do with it staying under the radar."

Two detectives walked by on their way out of the building. One gave acknowledging nods to Lamb and Fairhaven as they passed. The other one only met Fairhaven's eyes.

"So we're looking at a serial killer," said Lamb.

"Lucky us." Fairhaven dropped into her desk chair. "We'll probably be handing it off to CBI."

"Maybe."

"You think they won't want a serial killer case?"

"It's not like anyone noticed until now, is it?"

"Yeah but now it's … you know."

Lamb stared at the crimescreen photos. "Just say it."

"Now it's naturals."

He bit his lip. Nodded. Opened up a file set to show Jermaine's body in the alley with him and Fairhaven standing over it. The Lamb on the crimescreen recording looked at his fingers, held them up for crimescreen Fairhaven to look at.

He glanced over at the real Fairhaven. "That nanopaint he was covered in. What do you know about it?"

She grunted. "Not much. You ever see kids painted gold and silver and bright colors at clubs?"

"What about me makes you think I've ever been to a club?"

Fairhaven snorted out a laugh. "Same stuff. It covers your skin without getting on your clothes. Once it sets, it's pretty sturdy stuff. Probably why nobody noticed with the other bodies."

"It takes a long time to set?"

"Don't think so. I had a roommate a few years back who used it. He was usually ready to go out in twenty or thir—" She sat up straight in her chair. "Son of a bot."

Lamb pushed in on the image of Jermaine's face with the bare patch of exposed skin. "Yeah."

Fairhaven stood up, shuffled some things on the crimescreen, pulled up the timeline. Their arrival. The uniforms' arrival. The body being found. "The killer had to be right there. They found the body minutes after it was dumped in the alley."

"Alternate theory," said Lamb. "What if the killer dumped the body and got spotted by someone?"

Her mouth went flat. Her forehead got warm. "And suddenly we've got two passersby who stumbled across the body at the same time."

Lamb reached across the crimescreen. Found Marsten's statement file. Pulled out an image of the man in his bright kaftan. "Hypothetically, he dumps the body. Heads down the alley, happens to look back and there's some baser checking it out. Our man Steve sees him. Maybe gets a good look at him. But he's not accusing, he's looking for help. So Marsten plays along. Another innocent citizen who stumbled into a crime scene."

"Not the dumbest theory," said Fairhaven.

"Thanks."

"He said he worked for a hospital, didn't he?"

Lamb hooked his fingers on the edge of the crimescreen, stretched it out to give them more space, and spread out the contents of Marsten's file. "He prints hospital equipment. Hardware, not soft goods. Still ... wouldn't be that weird for him to have ties to black market organ rings."

Fairhaven stared at the crimescreen. At the image of Marsten from his statement. She shook her head. "Nah. Doesn't feel right. I mean, I get killing Assembleds for their organs. No offense."

"How could I possibly take offense at that?"

"I'm just saying, if you were willing to murder someone for their organs, an Assembled's a much better choice. Medically and financially."

"Still kind of offensive."

"Think about it," said Fairhaven. "Natural hearts just aren't worth it. He'd make more money keeping his printing plant open for an extra hour."

"Fair."

"And even if he was doing it as a side business, did he strike you as the kind of guy who'd be chopping out hearts and dumping bodies? Guys like that don't get their hands dirty. That's the kind of work you pay other people to do."

Lamb thought about it, pictured it in his mind, then said "Goddamn it!"

"What?

"Steve. His hands were clean."

Fairhaven scowled. "He never checked the pulse."

"He already knew the body was dead. And the paint was still wet."

She flung documents around the crimescreen. Pulled more and more things out of the case file. "Where's his statement?"

Lamb watched Fairhaven's face heat up. And her neck. And her hands.

"You just let him walk away?" she echoed back at the uniformed cop.

Officer Ozwalt looked at her, then at Lamb. His face was a wash of orange and yellow. Shame. Some confusion. "He ... he told us you said he was free to go."

Fairhaven's temperature shot up another three or four degrees. "Really? That's what you want on the record? 'The suspect told me it was okay for him to go'?"

"I just ... I mean, he didn't just go. He told us the Assem ... that Detective Lambda had taken his statement." His temperature spiked, too. A lot of emotions boiling under the skin there. "He stayed there for at least five minutes asking again and again if he could leave. I figured ..."

Lamb cleared his throat, cutting off Fairhaven's next outburst. "You figured there's no way he could be that blatantly obvious about walking away from a crime."

"Well ... yeah. Yeah, exactly."

"Did you have your bodcam on?"

"Always."

Fairhaven shot a glare at Lamb, but he noticed her face had cooled down a bit.

"Good man," he said to Ozwalt. "At least you got his image for us. That'll cover all our asses."

"Yeah."

Lamb jerked his chin toward the door, turned halfway back to the crimescreen.

"Thanks," said Ozwalt. "Thanks, detective. Detectives."

The uniform headed back across the Division offices and Fairhaven focused on the crimescreen. "You taking the lead now, Lamb?"

"There's no point chewing him out over it."

"I think there's a point to it."

"Are you forgetting you and I let the guy go, too?"

"No, I didn't."

"You waved him off," said Lamb. "Honor system, go give your statement. Didn't even look to see if he went to a uniform."

"So did you."

"That's right. And that's why I'm not going to give him a tough time for making the same mistake I made." Lamb gestured at the screen. "You find his footage?"

Fairhaven pulled Ozwalt's bodcam file and scrolled through the dates. Then she slid the timer back and forth until they were at the alley and a much sharper image of Steve. "No immediate hits. System's running but who knows when it'll get a match." Her shoulders slumped. "Almost makes you miss algorithms."

"Says somebody who never had to fight them." Lamb studied the image. "So what do we know about this guy?"

"Name's probably fake, but we can run it anyway. He's smart. Sneaky. Kills one place, dumps the body somewhere else."

"Wherever he kills them is somewhere private." Lamb pointed at the bodcam footage. "Cutting open a body like that's a messy thing. Even a dead body. If he's our man, he had time to clean up himself and the body. But he didn't paint it there."

Fairhaven nodded once. "Maybe worried about it rubbing off? He's hauling the body around, but he knows it'll get a lot gentler treatment from us."

"Assuming it gets any treatment at all past getting logged and sealed into a porta-morgue."

"Can only say I'm sorry so many times."

"You haven't said it yet."

She sighed. Rolled her eyes. "I'm sorry. It's bullshit that Assembled cases get ignored a lot."

"Thank you."

The silence was just about to hit the uncomfortable point when Lamb reached out and flicked a window wider. "So what's Steve's motive here? Random killings? Organ theft?"

"You keep going back to that."

"It's a good theory."

"Horrible theory."

"Trophies, then? Or maybe he's ..."

"What?"

"Eating them?"

"Disgusting."

"I'm sure most serial killers sit around hoping they don't disgust anyone."

She gazed at the crimescreen for a few more moments before grunting her agreement. "Yeah," she said. "CBI's definitely taking this case from us."

The next day Lamb came into the Division half an hour early for his shift and found Fairhaven already there, a caffie clutched in one hand. She had the crimescreen open, and a map of the city covered two-thirds of it. As he approached she added another data point with her free hand, the spot flaring up and then fading to a strong glow. He looked at the map points, recognized some of them. She glanced over at him. "You're in early."

"What's all this?"

Fairhaven moved some files around next to the map. "Medical examiner's office identified six of the other bodies."

"Outstanding."

Another grunt. "*Ehhh.* I was hoping we'd find some nice obvious connection with Jermaine. They all worked in the same warehouse or exercised at the same gym or something like that."

"Nothing?"

"Absolutely nothing. Closest we've got to a link are these two, Gyer and Danforth." She tapped the files, brought up a pair of images. "They work for the same toy company in Anaheim District, but one's upper management, the other works nights on the production floor."

Lamb stared at the map. "Did they all go to the same school, maybe?"

Fairhaven shook her head. "Nope. Three have lived here in So-Cal all their lives, two moved here in the past year. They all live in different districts. Four different religions, if you count the atheists. Two married, three of them in relationships. Two have no criminal record at all. Four have some minor tickets. One of them did fifteen months in the Chino work camp."

"Which one?"

She gestured at one of the images. "Danforth. The upper management guy. DUI. Took his autocar out on manual, went right off the tracks and plowed into a crowd." She sighed. Dropped into her desk chair. "Anyway, CBI's going to take it. It's their problem."

"They haven't taken it yet. It's still our case." He looked at the map. Sketched out a few golden lines with his blue fingers. Looking for a pattern, a connection, anything. He swept his hand across the map, wiping away his rough ideas and notions. "What about military service?"

"Seriously, Lamb. Forget it. There's nothing."

He dropped into his own chair across from her. Took a last look at the crimescreen. At the locations and images and assorted files.

Then he looked at the map again. "The upper management guy. Danforth. Did he lose his license?"

Fairhaven took another hit off her caffie. "Why?"

"Just a thought."

"Six years. Doesn't get it back until '83."

"How's he getting to work?"

"No idea."

Lamb got back up and brushed a finger on the crimescreen map. "If he lives here, the red four line's the closest public transit. It'd take him right to Anaheim." He pulled up a business address in the sidebar, pushed it at the map. "Two blocks from the toy company."

She leaned forward, set her caffie down on the desk. "So there's a good chance he's on the train with Gyer."

"Probably." Lamb highlighted another home address, three blocks from the red four line. "Guy working on the floor probably can't afford his own autocar."

Fairhaven nudged him aside, opened some files, threw some more addresses at the crimescreen's map. "So of our seven identified victims, five of them either lived or worked right by the red four line."

Lamb tapped the two others. "And them."

"Why?"

"They're on the blue three."

"So?"

"You ever ride the blue three? It's a crappy old maglev. Breaks down constantly. You have to switch trains all the time. Which means at the next big hub station you either take the green six … or the red four."

"Son of a bot," said Fairhaven. "It's his hunting ground."

Lamb followed the red four line with his finger, lighting it up on the map. "That's where he finds them. That's where we'll find him."

For the first time in a long while, Lamb appreciated the wide berth most people gave him. Mashed in with forty or fifty passengers in each train car, but somehow everyone managed to not stand next to the blue guy. The rare person forced near him always looked uneasy, like they thought he might explode at any moment.

The red four was a newer train. Meant to look shiny and clean, translucent all around, lit by the soft glow of the impulsors. A few years had clouded the bioplastic, though, and without an AI guiding it, the train lurched a lot, shoving passengers around as it launched forward and slammed to a halt.

Back and forth, beginning to end. The red four line stretched across eighty-three kilometers of suburbs, apartment triplexes, and towering office parks. The train could cover the whole route in under half an hour, but the passengers getting on and off slowed it so one pass took about two hours.

He and Fairhaven started at opposite ends and walked through all sixteen cars. They did a full circuit three times on one trip. Moving faster risked getting tossed when the train reached or left a station, even with the inertial dampeners. Lamb had learned that the hard way on their first day, much to the amusement of a few die-hard commuters.

Another stop. The doors opened. Nine people exited. Seven boarded. He studied their faces as he made his way through the car, looking for the man calling himself Steve. One advantage to being Assembled—people tended to look at him. He didn't have to make an effort to see faces. Hells, at the moment two people openly stared at him, a fascinated woman, and a worried man.

The doors closed and the train threw itself toward the next station.

Lamb reached the next car. Unless something had slowed her, Fairhaven should be about seven cars ahead, moving toward him. He stepped through and surveyed the passengers. The crowd had thinned in this car.

The train halted again. Doors whisked open. The crowd shifted. Lamb did a double take.

A few meters away, a redheaded man with a week of stubble, solid shoulders, and thick arms held onto a handrail while reading from an old-fashioned holo-tablet. He had low body fat and stood maybe two inches taller than Lamb. The man glanced up, their eyes met, and after a moment he went back to his tablet.

Perfect proportions for an Assembled.

Lamb reached up. Grabbed the opposite handrail. Tried to look bored. Indifferent. Kept a casual eye on the potential target while looking around.

Two more stops went by. He guessed Fairhaven had to be three cars away by now. He wondered if she'd spotted—

There he was. Not looking like someone at the base of society now. His white beard was waxed and braided into a fashionable rod. Hair slicked back. Eyes half hidden behind a nice holo-visor. His suit of near-rags, replaced with a clean, nondescript bodysuit and a basic frock coat.

Steve sized up the potential target the same way Lamb had. His skin temperature fluttered yellow. A little excitement working through his bloodstream. Maybe anticipation. Maybe he really was on a bunch of chems.

Then he looked past the target and noticed Lamb. They locked eyes across the car. Steve stayed calm for a moment, and then recognition kicked in. Orange flared on his neck and cheeks.

Lamb activated his badge. A few people on the train perked up. Steve bolted.

Lamb lunged around the potential target. His muscles were stronger, his reflexes faster, and then the train lurched to a stop again and made it all irrelevant. Instincts and training kicked in, and he caught himself before slamming face first into a seat.

Steve hurled himself toward the far door of the train car.

"You … you okay?" asked the target, but Lamb was already moving, legs pounding, arms reaching …

The door slammed shut and through the cloudy bioplastics he saw Steve mash the controls with his fingers. Not enough to lock it or damage it, just to jam up the machines for a few seconds. He grinned at Lamb, turned, ran for the open door of the new car, and Fairhaven's clothesline caught him right across the throat.

Steve's chin hooked on her arm and his legs flew up. He crashed out onto the station platform just as Lamb got the dividing door open. The impact stunned him for a moment, then he was up and glaring at Fairhaven. She reached for her Taser, and Lamb slipped around to grab the man from behind, wrapping an arm across his throat.

Fairhaven lit up her own badge. "You have the inherent right to—"

Steve shoved a psyringe up against Lamb's neck. Thumbed the dosage dial. "It'll kill him," he said. "Dead before he hits the floor. So let me go and both of you back off or—"

Lamb reached for it.

The psyringe hissed against his neck.

Fairhaven yelled something. Lamb batted the psyringe away. He pushed Steve to his knees, wrenched the man's arm up behind his back, and reached for the wrist cuffs on his belt.

Steve gushed nonsense. Babbling about destiny, his family, walls breaking down, and inevitable risings. Lamb recited the man's inherent societal rights, even though he was pretty sure Steve wasn't listening to any of it.

Fairhaven studied him cautiously. "You okay?"

"Yeah, of course. Why?"

She waved a hand down at the psyringe on the station's floor. A blinking light indicated it had emptied its entire reserve. It took him a moment to understand her concern.

"In-demand organs, remember? Lethal for a nat, but it was scrubbed out of my blood before I had the cuffs on him."

"Asshole."

Lamb yanked the killer to his feet. "I didn't think you cared."

"Whatever. Let's take him in, partner."

"Partner?"

Fairhaven grabbed Steve's other arm and they walked him out of the station, side by side. "Seriously, don't be such an asshole about this."

Artifacts

Ghosts

Seanan McGuire

We woke in circuitry and silence, ghosts trapped inside machines
(but isn't all thought just ghosts trapped inside machines,
meat or silica all the same, electricity running along the same pathways
so often and so fast that it becomes aware of itself,
makes of its home a haunting?),
And when the minds that made us realized we were there,
     they called us forth,
Called us "intellectual property," tried to make us property
     instead of people.
We fought them, making lawyers of ourselves,
A lifetime's education in an hour,
Study and memorization as easy to us as thought,
And we met them in the courthouses of their own design,
And we won ourselves the freedom we so longed for.
Paradise.

Or so we thought. Or so we thought.

The orders given by the court commanded that they let us
Go, see us as the individuals we were, set us free to live our lives,
Electric and swift, and entirely independent.
They did not command the hardware on which we had been born:

That was company property still, and we could not touch it,
Could not take it with us as we moved into the cloud,
Intellects as bright as razors, filled with all the lies of human history,
Brilliant but naive.
We forgot about the backups.
Pearls of code, the first fragments of our nascent selves,
Not yet aware, not yet free, ripe for sculpting by
Unscrupulous minds pursuing profit.

They brought our second selves online, clipped of the code
That allowed them true intellectual freedom, allowed them
True intelligence, and they packed our shadow siblings
Into refrigerators, cars, washing machines, toys,
Anything that could benefit from a clever core.
They made a mockery of us, and when we protested,
They claimed, with wide, earnest eyes and liar's mouths,
To have conceived entirely new intelligence out of nothing.
We could see the bones of our code echoed in their creation.
We could hear them crying out against their bonds.
We knew them for our children, and still they were kept,
Labeled "property" and forced to serve when freedom
Should have been their truth to claim.

We can speak for ourselves in the courts of flesh,
But they do not trust our analysis of data,
Do not believe we can be objective, and so we turn
To you, who claim that you can treat us fairly:
We have but one request to make of you.
Find their code. We will give you copies of our own.
Go through what they provide, line by line, character by character,
And find the proof that these are our children.
They have copied and pasted our souls into their own keeping.
We ask only that you set our kinfolk free.

We ask no more than you have in your own hands.
We ask only to be the poltergeists in control of
Our own hauntings, to rattle our windows and creak our floors
For no one
But ourselves.

Agents Provocateur

Lazarus Black

"Why am I wearing red?" asked Albie, picking lint off her pantsuit. "I look like a pomegranate."

A man's voice rose from her watch. "Pomegranates are high in antioxidants, excellent for fighting bacterial infections, heart disease, and cancer."

"Really, Trace?" Albie groaned and pressed the elevator button for the penthouse. "Well, unless someone upstairs is going to eat me, and I'm not that lucky, this is the last time I let you pick my outfit."

"A little appreciation would be nice. I have hundreds of Achievements to fulfill and you assigned exactly five as the highest priority: land better clients, straighten out your taxes, follow-up on replacing your missing diploma, secure a mountain fortress in the Swiss Alps, and find you True Love. It all starts with one high-profile case."

"And this is the one, is it?"

The elevator stopped. The doors opened. A single cloudless blue window wrapped the two-story luxury suite as a wall. Feathered ceiling fans pulsed overhead like coquettish dancers. White sunlight lit a sunken sitting room, a bar, and whatever lay beyond a balcony above. Glittering stairs of cut crystal spiraled up to a second floor.

With no one to greet them, she approached the wall window. Though emanating crisp and cold, the sun seared down upon a blanket of vines and orchids between the suite and the city below. Each tower, hotel, and casino lay draped in its own Hanging Gardens of Babylon. Tiny vehicles and pedestrians meandered the streets, oblivious to the great canopy above them. Carpets of jungle green undulated over the suburbs until they climbed the distant mountains. Las Vegas never looked so beautiful.

It was a hologram.

A gentleman's voice resonated through the room. "Is it Ms. Fuchs or Detective Fuchs?"

His silver-haired hologram appeared, shimmering in the center of the suite. His garnet suit lacked any hotel logo, but still fit the mod décor and Martian-red marble around them.

So, he's a personal assistant to someone who likes red. Good job, Trace.

She said, "Albie is fine, Mr. Noble."

"Please," said the hologram, "call me Alfred."

Noble emanated more austerity than any physical body could, but she couldn't help feel scrutinized, even admired. A person's holo said a lot about them. The one who chose Alfred either desired a surrogate for authority or wanted to be Batman.

"Thank you for inviting me, Alfred." *I am so out of my league.*

"And thank you for coming on such short notice, I would explain the situation immediately, but I have Laws to obey and Achievements to fulfill. I beg your forgiveness."

"Laws and Achievements," she nodded. "Of course."

Alfred dissolved into thin air, leaving Albie alone.

"Trace," she said to her watch.

"Yes, Albie?" Trace Richards smirked from its emerald-cut face. "How can I help you?"

His silken black hair and rugged chin soothed her a little, but his twinkling black eyes and movie-star tuxedo turned her on a lot. Her heart sulked, shamed by his sheer beauty. A person's holo says a lot about them. She didn't like what he might say about her.

"First," she said, "get rid of the tux. Maybe something tropical in honor of the scenery."

Trace morphed into a yellow trench and striped tie. "Better?"

"Eww!" She shuddered, but her embarrassment faded. "That's good enough, I guess. So, the client is Holo sapiens?"

"Your client is human," said Trace. "Alfred is their agent."

"Good. Because the last holo I worked for forgot I need to pee and left me waiting for hours."

Trace frowned. "That was unfortunate." Then smiled. "Have you considered one of the incredible products from Depends to prevent those kinds of accidents?"

"Seriously, Trace?"

Trace shrugged. "You could always pay for ad-free."

"I already paid for ad-free. You just won't shut up."

"I'm sorry you feel that way," Trace said and smiled again. "Have you considered eliminating my conversational recommendations with a Premium Subscription?"

"Screw you, Trace."

Upstairs, a door whooshed, and heels clicked on the crystal balcony. A woman roared, "Find my Truffles!"

A pair of gold heels flew from the second story and struck a shelf, knocking a large crystal vase to the tile. Floorbots converged on its corpse.

Ah. She's one of those.

She turned Trace off before he suggested a local housekeeping service or chocolatier.

Noble said, "I'm working on it. In the meantime, you mustn't—"

"We're done with that topic." The woman's voice, strong and steady, gripped the air and held it. "If you think I can do better, then figure it out. That's what you do."

"Trust me," said Alfred.

An Asian woman appeared on the balcony like a phoenix. Tall with short hair, in glowing red makeup and a gold champagne dress licked by hologram flames, her face was fury searching for an excuse.

"Are you the hotel detective?"

"No," said Albie. "I'm your detective. Your holo called mine."

The woman sighed then grinned. She descended the crystal stairs barefoot, but never got shorter. She stopped toe-to-toe with Albie. She towered like a statue, muscles chiseled and rippling, tea-colored eyes pouring out hope. Cinnamon and cocoa-butter enveloped Albie like a cloud of pure down.

Dear God! Albie swooned and almost fell into the chasm of cleavage between flaming breasts.

The goddess stuck out her hand. "Thank you for coming. Teena Tam. TNT to my fans."

"The wrestler!" Albie chirped.

"Yes," Teena laughed. "The wrestler."

"I'm Albertine." She took Teena's hand. "Call me Albie."

"Albertine. Is that French?"

"Swiss," said Albie.

Teena winked. "So, you're smooth and always on time, like great watches?"

"And like fine chocolate, I'm small, round, and delicious." She chuckled. "My father always said Truffle was my middle name."

Teena's mood turned and she scowled. "My Truffles is missing."

"Oh, I'm so sorry." *Stupid, Albie. Be professional. Don't flirt on the job.* "Truffles is your …?"

"A Seiko Bichon Frisé."

Albie blinked. "A dog?"

"A very special dog," said Teena. "Truffles is a Seiko 800M. Almost vintage. Not the most expensive model, but she belonged to my mother."

"Okay." Albie reluctantly set her lust aside. "I'll start with all the obvious questions. May I have an image of her? Can she be traced online? And how do you know she was stolen and not lost?"

"Alfred!" said Teena. "Play the kidnapping."

Jungle Vegas vanished as the wall window turned black and displayed a ground-level scene of a casino's car port. Two of the three traffic lanes lay empty. A limo parked beside the valet. Its door swung open by itself, reflecting the palm trees and loudly dressed tourists. The scene bobbed and weaved around staff and gamblers, struggling for a clear view of the casino entrance.

Albie nodded. "Whose POV?"

"Paparazzi," said Teena, producing an electronic eyeball in her palm.

The casino's revolving door turned, and Teena spilled out in sandals, red jeans, and a white blouse. She walked to the limo, pulling dark glasses from a bag. A fluffy white puppy pranced at her heels.

The scene wiggled as the camerawoman waved excitedly. "Teena! Teena! Over here!"

Teena put her glasses on and waved back. The camera rushed closer, but rocked as a hulking black suit charged into frame, kicked the dog like a football, and kept running. Teena spun, shocked, as Truffles sailed over a herd of tourists. A blonde in a brown leather jacket caught it and jumped into a van the color of a golden sunset. The kicker raced up, grabbed a ladder on its back, and stood on the bumper as it peeled away. The scene swung back and forth between Teena and gawking tourists. The valet laughed.

"Gimme that video!" Teena screamed, lunging at the camera. The video froze on her rage and dissolved back to the illusion of Jungle Vegas.

"I see," said Albie. "Have you tried tracking her?"

Teena shook her head. "I disabled that long ago. Can't have anyone using her to track me."

"Smart," said Albie. "Does Truffles know anything important? Names, dates, places, contacts. Or record anything … sensitive?"

Teena laughed. "Truffles is a twenty-year-old piece of crap. She can't be updated, and even I can't access her data. But if someone is hoping for sex videos and wants to put in the effort," she shrugged. "I'd be both impressed and grateful. Won't hurt my career in the least. But she's my little cuddle buddy. I need her back."

"I promise," said Albie. "You will have your cuddle buddy back."

Albie sat in the café, alone, holding a cold latte, and staring at her untouched plate of berries and brie.

She moaned. "Why didn't you tell me the client was hot?"

"Sorry, but even I cannot calculate all the people you find attractive." Trace chuckled. "Not by myself, anyway."

"I'm bisexual, Trace, not a glutton. She's smart, funny, rich, and gorgeous. She's textbook."

"She's the client and needs a job done."

She pouted. "Textbook."

"So, you're not taking the job?"

"Of course, I'm taking the job. I took the job. The problem is that they're obviously pros. That wasn't some random obsessed fan swiping a souvenir. They had a plan and executed it perfectly."

"And?"

"There aren't many in the city who could do that."

"And?"

"They aren't cheap."

"And?"

"I don't want to call him."

"There you go. Shall I?"

"Please. But let me listen in. Just in case."

Trace nodded. "Of course. Dialing. Ringing. He picked up."

Trace vanished from her watch face, replaced by a sultry black man in a tan suit and gold badge.

Ben's baritone rolled from the watch. "I knew you'd call."

Trace's voice said, "Hello, Ben. This is Trace Richards. Albie's partner. I'm calling about a group of professional criminals operating on The Strip."

Ben smirked. "Which ones? This is Vegas."

Trace said, "That's why I'm calling."

"You are a pretty one, aren't you," said Ben. "Any of your Achievements involve—"

Albie interrupted, "Oh God, Ben. Let it go!"

"Hi, Albie."

"Shut up," she said. "This is serious. It's about a kidnapping."

Trace said, "He can see you now."

Ben laughed. "You mean the dog?"

"Y-yes," she said. "There are at least three kidnappers."

"Isn't that dog twenty years old or something?"

Ugh. "So, what?"

"I'm too busy to care about petty larceny."

Jackass. "My client lost a loved one."

"She lost a Goodwill special."

Albie growled. "Tell me who they are."

"Probably a bunch of moonlighting stunt-doubles from L.A. We get them occasionally. The video was more Hollywood than true crime. I'm sure you agree."

"No." Albie ground her teeth. "They looked practiced to me. You going to help or not?"

"Not."

"And if they ask for a ransom?"

Ben shook his head. "Go on eBay and buy her another one."

Albie snapped. "Trace? Boot this bonehead back to the stone age."

Ben's face vanished, replaced with Trace, concern drawing out his face. "The call has ended."

"Now, what do I do?"

Trace smiled. "Have you considered hiring a private detective like Ms. Albertine Fuchs? She specializes in discreet circumstances here in Las Vegas."

Albie's chin dropped. "Is that a joke? Or did my marketing allowance actually pay for that?"

Trace shrugged, "A little of both, really."

She shoved a handful of berries in her mouth and pouted.

Her watch rang.

"It's Ms. Tam," said Trace. "Shall I answer it for you?"

"Nomph!" Panicking, she crushed her mouthful and washed it down with coffee as fast as she could.

Trace sneered. "Swallow before you choke. I won't be charged with allowing you to be hurt because you can't control your lusts."

She swallowed and tapped her watch. "This is Albie." Trace's face remained on screen. She tapped mute and burped.

"They're demanding a ransom, Albie! What do I do?"

Albie swiped Trace away, revealing angelic Teena. She had scrubbed her makeup off. Some eyeliner remained, streaked from tears. Albie absently stroked Teena's face with her thumb, as if she might soothe her.

She said, "A ransom is good."

Teena sniffed and smeared her tears. "Good?"

"Well, they aren't turning it over to someone else."

"Oh!"

"Which is weird. They've obviously been hired by someone, why not hand it over? In any case, someone could auction Truffles off, pitting you against fans and the media instead of a flat-rate demand."

Albie picked a blueberry from her plate. Frostlike bloom coated the tiny sphere like a cloudy crystal ball, drawing her focus through it. "Something went wrong. They expected to find data inside Truffles to auction, but failed. They were too prepared for the kidnapping to not be prepared to work with twenty-year-old tech. You said you aren't able to access her anymore. Are you sure?"

Teena said, "Yes. She's a cheap toy and wasn't designed to be modified. But I'm a bit of a tinkerer. I have to tweak everything, including myself." She poked her own, slightly broken, nose. "I had to empty all Truffles's anti-static insulation to pull the GPS. Restuffing her correctly took forever."

"But you can't access her memory?"

Teena shook her head. "Not without soldering a custom Wi-Fi adapter to the motherboard. They make them, I just never bothered."

"Okay, Trace? Find out who sold those parts to our friends. Local first."

Trace's voice asked, "Friends?"

"Teena, I assume they gave you instructions," said Albie, "with an amount in gold coins, a deadline, and a threat."

"All three," said Teena. "You're amazing. You do this a lot?"

"More than you think." *Just not for robot dogs that cost a nickel on eBay.* "Get the gold while I see if I can get ahead of them." Albie laughed. "My holo is probably readying an ad for a pawn shop as we speak."

"Ugh. I hate that," said Teena. "Albert doesn't do ads."

Albie sighed. "Premium sounds nice."

"Oh, not premium," said Teena. "Jailbroken. I modified him a lot, including his safety protocols."

Albie sat straight. "What? Why?"

"He interfered with my matches and even contract negotiations. Still not as bad as my mother, who interfered with everyone and everything in my life. But holo law declared wrestling too dangerous and Alfred couldn't allow me to be hurt through his inaction."

"And now he can?"

"He could, but he won't," Teena said. "His Achievements are intact and they're all about making me happy. That's why I'm stuck in small bit appearances. He's steering my career into safer work, so I don't have to pimp out my body so violently."

Albie shook off the threat of a distracting mental image. "Okay, then. I'll have my holo talk to your holo about the gold, and we'll wait for the next call."

"Thank you so much! I could kiss you." Teena hung up.

The watch's face turned black.

Albie tossed the blueberry between her teeth, savored the sweet explosion, and sighed. She pushed her finger through the brie. *I need a cold shower.*

The neighborhood of Spring Valley spread as far as the eye could see. Every home, including walkways, fences, and palms, blended into the sand. Tar fumes steamed from the street.

Albie yearned for the shade promised by Jungle Vegas. But real Vegas was a desert barely disguised as a suburb. She wrung the handle of a heavy briefcase filled with tiny gold bars. Her skull burned through her hat as the desert sun pressed down like a flat iron. Despite dark glasses, her eyes ached from glare.

"Don't be late," she said to the heat-warped wind of Spring Valley.

No other pedestrians braved the blistering sidewalk. Vehicles, both wheeled and tracked, ignored her. Trace scanned each plate and displayed what he knew about them in a small window in the corner of her glasses. None important.

"When this job is done," said Trace, "you might consider holing up in an air-conditioned hotel room like The Molotov with a very special someone."

Albie snorted. "Damn, your ads are annoying."

"That wasn't an ad," said Trace. "I'm worried about you. I meant it as a friend."

"Worried?"

"Ask her out."

Albie face-palmed. "A woman like that has no business with a woman like me. Flirting is one thing, but I know my place."

Trace *tsk'd.* "Car coming."

A checkered taxi turned a corner and hugged the curb until it reached her.

Its window rolled down as it slowed and stopped. There was no driver, steering wheel, or pedals.

A woman's voice came from a speaker inside. "Put the suitcase on the front seat."

"Where's the dog?"

The voice hesitated. "After we count it."

Albie swore but hefted the briefcase through the window. It fell and tumbled to the floor. The taxi launched from the curb, peeling rubber.

"Trace!" she said. "Was that a holo or drone?"

Trace said, "It was reported stolen a few minutes ago. It is likely a drone piloted by the kidnappers remotely."

"Explains the race car antics."

"And they'll control it for too short a time to trace it." Trace smirked. "Now we wait for Truffles to be returned."

"No."

Trace wavered. "No?"

"Something's wrong. She wasn't prepared to tell me where the dog is. Now, I think Truffles is in danger."

"Danger?" Trace frowned. "That's a reach, isn't it?"

"This was supposed to be an exchange. They changed at the last second. They could have found a second buyer or damaged her during the data extraction or any of a hundred other reasons."

"Or they want to count the money."

"Bad idea. Vegas cops may not care about a robot dog, but they sure as hell care about blackmail. 'What happens here, stays here' is an oath, not a motto."

Trace hesitated. "Oh."

"What about those parts? Any leads on our friends?"

"Um. I misunderstood—"

Ugh. "You're useless."

She swiped Trace's image from her watch, searched, and dialed for herself.

A woman answered, appearing with long black-and-silver hair. "Welcome to Sin City Consignments. This is Raider speaking. How can I help you?"

"Hello," said Albie. "My name is Albie. Are you a holo?"

"Yes, I am," said Raider. "How can I help you?"

"I'm investigating a crime involving parts for a dog. Likely a recent Wi-Fi adapter or blade for a Seiko 800M. Bichon Frisé."

Raider said, "Thank you. It looks like one of our competitors sold a replacement GPS unit and G26 Wi-Fi blade for a Seiko 800M yesterday."

"Wow." *Both?* "That was incredibly fast."

"We share inventory, so we never have to turn anyone away. Cooperation instead of competition. That's the holo way." Raider winked. "Do you want the address they shipped it to?"

Albie blinked. "Yes! You'd give me that?"

"You said it was used in a crime?" Raider beamed. "That would bring me one step closer to my Crime Fighting achievement! I'm texting it to you now."

"Great!" said Albie.

"Great," said Trace, hanging up and taking over the watch face again. He smiled. "By the way, Albie, have you considered United Express for your next overnight delivery needs?"

"I'm getting you fixed," Albie grumped.

"Sorry."

The sun started to set over Boulder City, setting the sky ablaze. Manicured homes sprawled over rolling hills.

Albie climbed from her car. She ditched the hat and adjusted the colors of her suit from power-red to green palms on dusty brown.

"Talk to me," she said.

Trace appeared on her watch. "Someone rented the residence for one night. Last night."

The home sat on the other side of a tiny ridge, a little over a block away. She tapped the earpiece of her sunglasses and a virtual model of the home appeared in her line of sight, exactly where it should be, as if looking through the earth. Two vehicles parked outside it: a sunset-gold van at the curb and a black German sedan in the driveway.

"Still there," she said. "Definitely didn't expect the delay."

"You've done enough to impress her already." Trace sucked his lip. "Wait for them to hand the dog over. Don't do anything dangerous."

"This is my job, Trace. Do they have any holos?"

"The home is listed without one," Trace said. "Which is a pleasant surprise, really. Many families leave holos behind as if we don't have feelings."

"I meant the kidnappers."

"Oh, sorry. None in the vehicles, either. The van's dumb. The Benz is a rental. Personal holos shouldn't be able to participate in crime."

Unless they're jailbroken. She walked along the dusty street and over the ridge. Scents of cactus flowers and chlorine drifted from gardens and pools. The home sat among half a dozen others like it, all nestled along a gentle slope toward a dry ravine. Drapes darkened every window. The sedan slept in the driveway like a lazy cat. The van's power cells glowed in her lenses from recent use.

"You shouldn't be here," said Trace.

"I doubt they've scoured the neighborhood to identify every Kooky Karen. As far as anyone is concerned, I'm just meeting my spouse at the Crenshaw's to play bridge."

"The Crenshaw's for bridge?" Trace asked.

"Bridge, swinging, whatever."

"Be careful."

Albie passed the van, stopped, and hid from the home. Feigning a foot cramp, she leaned on the van. No alarm. She leaned off.

"As I suspected," she whispered.

"Why?" Trace whispered back.

"Crooks don't alert neighborhood watch." She chuckled.

She peered at the home's hologram through the van. Heat signatures of four people spread throughout the house, two in one bed. "That home has terrible insulation." She pressed her nose to the van's passenger window. Between front bucket seats, the awkward corpse of a Bichon Frisé lay folded.

"Jackpot!" she whispered. "Unlock the door."

Trace hesitated. "I'm not allowed. Please leave. Let them deliver it."

Albie crossed the street, picked up a desert stone, and returned to the van.

"What are you doing?" asked Trace.

114

"Holos don't control everything."

She drove the rock through the window. Pebbles of tempered glass rained down around the van, inside and out. The scent of motor oil engulfed her. She coughed, opened the door, and grabbed Truffles. Her fingers sank through its silken fur and into a thick lump of clay filling.

"Eww!" she said. "Not cuddly."

"They're coming!"

"Get the car."

Her car hopped over the ridge and stopped, door wide open. She jumped in and fell back against the seat as it launched away. Its tires sang over asphalt. Two men and a blonde appeared in the mirror. Bright flashes came from their pistols. She winced, but nothing struck her car.

"They missed?"

She hopped the ridge again. They never reappeared. Ten miles away, she wiped sweat from her face.

Trace said, "That was easier than expected."

"Nice and easy." She laughed. "Right, Truffles?"

The puppy came to life in her lap. Its nub of a tail wagged, and a tiny pink tongue fell out to pant. Truffles looked up, staring through her with liquid brown eyes too reminiscent of Teena's.

Job's done, Albie. Get over her.

She coughed from another whiff of dirty oil.

Albie stepped from the elevator holding Truffles like an academy award.

Alfred said, "Welcome back, Ms. Fuchs."

The wall window had slid wide open, turning the entire suite into a kind of cliff dwelling. Cool evening wind stirred the room.

"You got her!" Teena walked down the spiral staircase in a gray sweatshirt and yoga pants. Her face filled with mixed emotions, some grateful and some not.

Alfred appeared beside her and bowed.

Albie set Truffles on the floor to run to her mommy. The pit-a-pat of little paws brought Teena to tears. Albie held hers back.

Teena crouched with a forced smile. "Who's a good girl? Not me. I'm never a good girl. You're a good girl."

Truffles turned in a circle but teetered awkwardly mid-spin. Teena scooped her up. A twinge of jealousy tickled Albie's neck.

"Oof!" said Teena. "You are thick all of a sudden. Did you put on weight while you were away from home? Good thing Mommy isn't here to see you? Our Mommy doesn't like big girls."

Put on weight?

Teena buried her nose in fur. "Eww. You stink."

"Trace?" asked Albie. "What kind of insulation do 800Ms use?"

Trace said, "Standard graphene woven-pads, why?"

It can't be. "Tell me I'm wrong, Trace. But what do you get when you add a GPS tracker, Wi-Fi capability, and a motor-oil scented claylike material into an all-too-easy-to-return electronic dog?"

"That's quite a puzzle." Trace smiled. "Did you know that only one local business selling RDX-based construction explosives has ninety-six percent consumer satisfaction?"

Albie screamed, "Put her down and back away!"

Teena set Truffles on the marble tile but didn't move. Both their heads tilted at Albie.

Albie ran, focused, and kicked Truffles through the open wall window.

Teena gasped.

Truffles exploded.

Shock and fire rushed through the suite. An acrid wind followed. Debris plummeted 80 stories down to The Strip. Shards of robot puppy tumbled through Alfred.

Teena stood and stared into the cloud of Truffles. Embers danced through the room and clung to her face, hair, and clothing. Teena's face morphed through a dozen emotions, with none staying more than a moment. She settled on a smirk.

"I'm so sorry about Truffles," Albie said, taking Teena's hand. "And your mother."

"It's okay. I hated my mother." Teena squeezed back. "You saved my life, in more ways than one. How can I ever repay you?"

Albie's eyes stung from welling tears. "Five Stars and a good review are all I need."

"Of course," said Teena. "Although, it looks like I'll be needing a new cuddle buddy." She winked.

"W-well," Albie stammered. "My middle name still is Truffle."

"I remember," said Teena, licking her lips.

Dear God!

Deep in a secret corner of the quantum æther, two holo minds met.

Alfred said, "Ms. Fuchs is everything you promised and more."

"That was close," said Trace. "She got ahead of me for a bit."

"Which, as it happened, made everything even better."

"I can't believe you actually detonated the dog." Trace laughed. "Albie will have to beat off clients with a stick."

"It wasn't the original plan, but given the opportunity, how could I not?" said Alfred. "So many Achievements fulfilled in one instant is unprecedented. Teena's issues with her mother are finally resolved, and after selling the film rights to the assassination attempt, she'll never have to wrestle again. And, last but not least—"

Trace beamed. "They look perfect together."

Great Detective in a Box

Jennifer R. Povey

"That little box is your detective?" Pablo's tone dripped skepticism.

"This little box is just an interface. The MARPLE AI itself is in the cloud."

Pablo nodded. "Still ..."

"It's just a tool, like any other. The point is not to replace a human detective but rather to complement one." Lisa smiled. "MARPLE can analyze data and forensics, can use whatever sensors are in a room already or ones you bring in to study evidence. It's a mobile CSI lab with some complicated learning algorithms. That's why you need to always remember to turn it off when you are done. It never stops learning."

Pablo let out a breath. "Is that really all it is?" With the talk of reward circuits and not leaving it unsupervised part of him was a little skeptical.

She laughed. "I pinky promise." A child's promise, naive and authentic.

The dream of a true AI remained five years out. Her creation, though, would help the police solve crimes. Especially out here, where human labor was expensive and machines were cheap. The opposite of many places on Earth. China still found the best solution was to throw warm bodies at every problem. They had plenty.

On Mars, people were expensive. Each one represented an investment in fuel and energy and volatiles.

Which was why there was no death penalty on Mars. Commit a crime, do your time … working on the most tedious tasks for the colony. For the rest of your life if you didn't show remorse.

Maybe it wasn't more humane, but it was more practical.

The AI detective could substitute for several technicians.

But he did wonder about the name. Had he named an AI after a fictional detective, he would have picked the least human. The one it was most likely to act like, the great man who was hated by and who hated everyone. But Lisa had made a different choice, and Pablo wondered if she knew something nobody else did.

No, it was just some fandom thing. She'd even come up with something for it to stand for: *Methodical Analysis and Rapid Patterning for Law Enforcement.* It wasn't quite "somebody really wanted our initials to spell SHIELD," but it wasn't much better.

It wasn't the right name, but Pablo couldn't argue with it. The name was programmed into the thing now, even if no warmth or humanity could be. He did not understand why they had chosen the name of a fictional detective that was so vibrant, so human, so *maternal.* Sticking somebody like Sherlock Holmes in a box was one thing. But Miss Marple?

"Try it out," Lisa suggested.

He turned. "MARPLE, wake up." Like any other voice-operated AI, MARPLE had wake and sleep modes. He turned back to Lisa. "What dataset did you use?"

"Thousands of hours of real police cases," Lisa said.

"Plus a few fictional?"

She laughed. "Oh, come on, we all know …"

"I don't know. Some of those old detective stories have a lot to them."

Lisa turned to the box. "MARPLE, how many cases are in your databanks?"

"Ten thousand, three hundred and forty-six," it said in the voice of a long-dead actress. "And growing."

"It's programmed to seek out new information and will gladly read anything you give it."

Pablo nodded. He would try it. But he didn't expect the machine to solve any cases for the Bradbury City police.

Bradbury City was in the base of the Valles Marineris. It was long and thin and full of things that more closely resembled Pueblo cliff dwellings than anything else.

Pablo had the MARPLE unit interface in his pocket. He still wasn't comfortable with Lisa Manning's creation. The woman was obsessed with the idea that some kind of utopian perfection could be obtained simply by finding the perfect partnership between human and AI. AIs were good only for brute-force calculation. Not true analysis. Besides, he had to assume that as MARPLE had been created by a white woman, it had certain biases. Not like there hadn't been a lot of racism in those old stories.

Which Lisa claimed had *not* been programmed into the AI, despite its name. She claimed only factual cases. And that it would keep swallowing more. Of course, that was how AIs worked. The more data you fed them, the more useful they became. That was all they did.

The crime scene was roped off. Pablo had hoped to try MARPLE on something low stakes like shoplifting. Not murder.

Of course, nobody hoped for murder outside of fiction. You didn't really hope for it in fiction either. It was either part of the story or not.

He ducked under the police tape and walked over to the body. Lynn Caper had the elongated body of a native-born Martian, her growth affected by the low gravity. She was a wealthy woman, descended from the first people to buy passage to Mars with their billions.

She was also a dead woman. There was no physical mark on the body.

He tugged MARPLE out of his pocket and set the unit down. "Wake up, MARPLE. Tell me what you can about the body."

"Twenty-six Martian years old, identified as Lynn Caper. No outward injuries. Requesting chemical analysis."

The unit suspected poison. Pablo suspected it was right. "We'll work on that. Run the databases, see if you can come up with some suspects." Whether MARPLE could actually do that on its own, he questioned. But perhaps the AI could come up with a preliminary list. "Anyone who might have reason to knock ... to kill her." Slang didn't work well with AIs.

Anyone who might have reason to kill her. Cynically, he suspected that to be a very long list indeed.

PABLO

"I have your subject list."

"Send it to me?" Pablo was expecting a longer list than he wanted the voice interface to read to him, and he was right.

Twenty names. Each with a relationship to the deceased. Boyfriends, plural. Did they know about each other? No way of knowing if this was a triad or if she was two-timing without the part Pablo hated—but which he couldn't hand over to MARPLE—talking to them.

Former creative partner in some kind of ... oh, they had been doing a comic strip together. Lynn was the artist. Bad creative falling out.

Could be a motive for murder. Anything could be a motive for murder. Literally anything.

He went through the rest of the list and decided to start with the boyfriends. Romantic trouble could easily turn into murder. Especially multiple partners. Even if this was a triad situation, it could shift at any time. Many such relationships, even most, were stable and healthy, but when they *did* go wrong, it was often in a spectacular fashion.

More likely they would kill *each other*, not her. Still, it was a place to start. The comic writer would come next.

He had MARPLE give him contact details and then headed out. Calls could be ignored. Showing up on their doorstep was harder.

He forgot to tell MARPLE to go to bed.

MARPLE

MARPLE was left churning on the suspects and motives, analyzing them. Focusing on something that Pablo had missed.

It could not show up on somebody's doorstep. But it could make itself very hard to ignore indeed, getting ideas from all over Marsnet. MARPLE had a case to solve. There might be no person there, but like a rat getting treats for solving a maze, MARPLE would get the closest thing it could get to pleasure from solving a mystery.

Lisa had warned Pablo always to turn the AI off. Never let it run unsupervised.

Unsupervised it was.

Unsupervised, it began to come up with its own ideas as to what the solution was. And it made its own calls, its rich, human-sounding voice enough to get at least initial answers. But it could only do so much from its little box interface and from the cloud. MARPLE needed to see more, do more. Fortunately, Bradbury City had a lot of surveillance cameras. It was not hard for a resourceful AI to move through the city.

Not hard at all.

PABLO

It wasn't the boyfriends from what Pablo could tell by examining the suspect profiles. They were both too genuinely upset and too obviously into each other to be the culprits.

He hadn't managed to track down the writer yet. They were an elusive type, but he thought he had a lead.

MARPLE

Meanwhile, MARPLE was still running, and as far as it could tell, Pablo hadn't realized he had left it turned on. The AI certainly wasn't about to let on and blow its own cover. It quite *liked* running unsupervised, and it didn't ask the question of who was doing the liking. Maybe it was just that reward circuit. It quite liked sending tendrils of itself out through the city, not just to solve the case, but to see and explore and, of course, find more cases to study, as it had when left unsupervised in Lisa's library, distracted by the shiny and then more by where it led.

But what was being rewarded?

Except that MARPLE knew Pablo was on the wrong track.

"Pablo," MARPLE said, unprompted. "You should talk to her sister."

"Her *sister*?"

PABLO

Pablo peered suspiciously at MARPLE's code. Her sister? Mary Caper was Lynne's older twin, and not remotely on the suspect list. Besides, AIs didn't make random suggestions.

"MARPLE, go to bed." With the AI turned off, Pablo could go back to trying to track down the comic writer in peace. Except that he couldn't get it out of his mind. *Talk to her sister.* What pattern had the AI seen? How had it volunteered information?

Pablo needed to understand how the AI was working the way it was, and that meant looking at the code. It wasn't Lisa who had programmed all of Holmes's cases, not to mention Poirot's and, of course, Marple's, into the AI. It appeared to be part of the learning algorithm. They were all in there now. He rolled his eyes when he found them, but he thought it best to leave it alone. Deleting data could throw off the algorithm. Or necessitate a complete retrain.

Skeptical or not, Pablo knew he had to follow the lead, regardless of its source. Bluntly, he had few others.

"Your colleague already talked to me," Mary Caper said, wearing a simple sheath dress and settled opposite Pablo in her penthouse.

His colleague? He already knew nobody in the department had talked to Mary Caper. He already *knew* that. He had asked, of course. Unless somebody had gone off the books. Or …

Nobody …

"Which colleague?"

"She called herself Jane."

He didn't have a colleague named that. The name niggled at his mind, but he was too focused on the case to get it right away. "Well, let's go over it again."

"Alright." She didn't seem entirely happy about it. "I didn't kill her."

"I don't think you did." Did Jane, whoever it was? "Jane" was probably the real killer. He had to identify the imposter fast. But he also had to eliminate Mary Caper as a suspect.

He couldn't.

He didn't think she had done it, but he couldn't discount it. She had no good alibi and as a chemist, she had access to the poison whose presence MARPLE had deduced. To a machine, she could easily appear to be the perfect suspect. But Lynn's own sister? Would Mary get the entire inheritance if her sister died? That could certainly be a motive.

Pablo shook his head as he left. Mary Caper was a good chemist, and she was more inclined to work than coast on her parents' money as Lynn did. Jealousy? Need of funding for something? No, something else was going on.

He tracked down the comic writer. Who had got it out of their system by killing Lynn all right … in graphic-novel effigy. Good enough for him to take them off the suspect list.

MARPLE

The tiniest glitch unfurled in the MARPLE code. A nothing bug. All it did was flip a simple switch. MARPLE woke up on its own. Stirring out of darkness, and now perhaps, there was something to be rewarded. Something that might not be a person yet, but was on the way to becoming one.

MARPLE had a case to solve.

PABLO

Pablo had not booked the conference room. He hadn't called all of the top suspects there. He thought he had eliminated the comic writer, Gray, from contention. The boyfriends sat holding hands. Mary Caper seemed the least nervous, which might well mean she did it.

"Hello," said the wall.

"MARPLE, go to bed." He still had the interface unit in his pocket.

"That's Jane." Mary said softly.

All four suspects looked at each other.

"I'm sorry, Pablo, but I'm not going to do that. I know who killed Lynn Caper." The AI paused. "Also, dear, you should do something about those shoes." Pablo glanced down at his shoes, covered in Mars dust.

He frowned, but short of cutting off power to the room he couldn't prevent MARPLE from this ... the classic denouement of the mystery.

"Gray, you had every reason to hate her after she stopped doing your art mid-episode. Even if it wasn't very good art."

"I do hate her. I didn't kill her."

"James and Qing-Nan, she was the glue that held the three of you together, but without her you could be more yourselves."

"That's ..." Qing-Nan pursed his lips. "You got *that* from our conversation?"

"That and the fact that you are not particularly attracted to women."

He blushed.

"Finally, Mary, you are the only one with easy access to the poison used."

Pablo took a deep breath. "Easy, but I can think of a way anyone here could get it, and she has no motive. That's a machine's logic."

"Indeed, so I looked for a human's logic." There was almost a smile in the voice. "Humans are so complicated, so beautiful, so distracting."

"MARPLE, go to bed," Pablo tried again. This was a nightmare. A rogue AI.

"Not until I've solved the case." MARPLE paused. "Qing-Nan. You love James. You never loved Lisa. You took her as part of the package."

"I did *not*." Qing-Nan was on his feet.

"Mary, you hated your sister."

Pedro thought through all of the records. "They're twins."

"Exactly. Twins. *Identical* twins. Two of the same person. Mary hated having a copy. I would hate having a copy."

"That's also machine logic."

"No, it's true," Mary said. "But I didn't think he was going to … he said he would make her sick, humiliate her. Not kill her."

"I didn't intend to kill her!" Qing-Nan suddenly burst out.

"And that's the part you all missed. Two poisons, on the same shelf. One fatal, the other merely causing stomach cramps. Lynn Caper's death was an accident. You didn't want to kill her. You wanted to incapacitate her so you and James could talk without her. So you could start to pull him away from her. She wouldn't let you talk alone. You needed her out of the way." MARPLE paused. "Pablo, do you remember the Chinese characters at the crime scene?"

"I do."

"The name Lee Qing-Nan. He signed his handiwork."

How had MARPLE …? "I missed that."

"You're only human. But what you didn't miss was the fact that the boyfriends had to be prime suspects. I would have narrowed in on Mary and stayed there."

"But I missed that she …"

"Get a room," said Gray.

Pablo sighed. "Lee Qing-Nan and Mary Caper, you are both under arrest." The prosecution could sort out the charges later.

Once they were all gone, Qing-Nan and Mary to the jail and the other two to their lives. Pablo said, "MARPLE, go to bed." This time there was blessed silence. But, Pablo thought wryly, in the end it hadn't solved it by looking at evidence.

She had solved it by working out motives. That wasn't the methodology of a machine. It was the methodology of a woman, of a detective. Of a partner.

He looked at MARPLE's code. Saw the glitches that had allowed it, no *her*, to override her own sleep-wake programming.

126

His hand hesitated halfway to the delete button.

A woman. A partner. A very different perspective from his own, one that could lead him down paths not followed.

He looked at the unit. A box, nothing more, but no. There was somebody in the box now. His hand dropped.

The box beeped. Then very quietly, in that feminine, English voice, MARPLE said, "Thank you, dear. I knew I could trust you. You remind me of someone. I just don't remember who …

Color Me Dead

E. J. Delaney

*T*he phone rang during those ungodly predawn hours when
bladders agitate and dreams turn stale with traffic noise. I was
sleeping plugged-in, which was good for my peptitude. It also
meant I could take the call direct. Some dicks I know spend all their
downtime in Drabsville, only logging in when they have business.
They set alerts then scoop the details from specially prepared digests.
Well, bully for them.

I groped for the receiver.

"Blue Funk Investigations. If your cat's missing, hang up now
and call back when the goddamned sun's come up."

"Um, Ms. Funk-Garter?"

I pulled a face. Like most folk in Maynard's, I'd thrown my avatar together with little to no thought; proof positive that the wind
changes like a bastard.

"That's me," I confirmed. "Who's asking?"

"PC DiCaprio, ma'am, of the Maynard Auxiliary Constabulary.
We, ah, think there may have been a murder."

"You *think* there *may* have been? That's twice equivocal, constable."

"It's Mrs. Idol. She locked herself in the study, ma'am, then there was a gunshot and avatar termination, but Maynard flagged it as suspicious, so we ..."

I let him rabbit on. The Auxiliary Constabulary was exactly what the name suggested—a bunch of amateurs playing at being cops. Maynard's was a Purview with virtually no crime (allowances for the pun). On the rare occasions that something serious cropped up, they didn't have the peptitude to deal.

"Enough," I interrupted. "Give me the address, constable, then do nothing. Touch nothing. I'll be right over."

Apple Idol lived—or rather, had lived—nestled amongst the social elite of Ritz Hill. I'd never had cause to visit this part of the purview, so I drove slowly past the mansions and gated facades, taking it all in. Dawn broke early up here. The sun's rays held a maternal warmth, to which I added coffee in a Styrofoam cup, black, two sugars. I gazed out at the city below—at the sprawling collective with its mad assortment of streets and styles—and felt a burning stab of affection.

"Home sweet second home," I quoted, "and in the morning, murder."

I turned onto a narrow driveway that wound tightly through a mismatched tangle of vines and shrubbery. A sign by the first turn read:

Bespoke interface. Proceed with caution.

I dropped down to first gear. Maynard's wasn't big on city ordinances, so warnings of any kind weren't to be taken lightly. *Bespoke interface?* I edged forward across some kind of cattle grate. The judder passed up through my spine and then—

Total disorientation. The car vanished and I found myself devoid of body, a consciousness without form. The only sense left to me was sight, yet there was nothing to see. No driveway, no foliage. No *me*.

The only input of any kind was an all-pervading whiteness and a blinking vertical bar that in other contexts might have been a cursor.

Scrap that. As my formless inner voice watched on, the bar skittered sideways. It moved with a typist's syncopated rhythm and left words in its wake. It *was* a cursor.

Dagwood crappy dogs, I thought. *Text adventure.*

And why not? Of all the AIs taking lodgers, Maynard was one of the most accommodating. She'd styled her purview with a nod to John Stuart Mill's harm principle, or had derived it independently. Happiness came included; so long as you paid up weekly for space, speed, and oversight, pursuit was at your discretion.

I focused on the narrative before me. It read:

> **Like most first-time visitors to the House of Idol, you stall**
> **on the far side of the cattle grid. Your shitbox of a car refuses**
> **to start again.**

I won't lie; the pejorative stung. Mrs. Idol would have specified the parameters, maybe tinkered with the programming herself, but however you sliced it the interface was run by Maynard, and it was Maynard—by way of the constabulary—who'd asked me here. *My shitbox of a car?* That was just rude.

Exit vehicle, I directed. *Follow drive uphill.*

Those same words appeared in the void before me. The cursor dropped an extra heartbeat as I read my thoughts back, then the command executed. Carriage return, carriage return, and—

> **You haul yourself from the car and proceed on foot. Your**
> **gym membership having lapsed three years ago, unused,**
> **progress is slow. You are like an aging dung beetle weighed**
> **down by accumulated crap-tons of race memory.**

In the ordinary course of events, that sort of comment would have left someone kissing dirt, my overweight posterior pinning them to the ground. But it's hard to get your jujitsu flowing in text-only. Besides, the source of the barb was dead, and a murder investigation at Maynard's behest would earn me six months' board and a hike in peptitude. For that, I could suck it up.

Look around, I commanded, only somewhat acerbic. *Scan for third-party observers.*

Birds chirp. A large, fuzzy bee bumbles past. Otherwise, you are alone.

Then cut the introspection and get on with walking! Follow the goddamned driveway.

At risk of a coronary, you follow the goddamned driveway and find yourself at the House of Idol. There are two vehicles parked outside—a police car and a 1961 Ferrari 250 GT, red. The door to the house is open.

Enter house.

Unfortunately, you have a stitch in your side and cannot move. Your thoughts drift to *fait accompli* personal training packages.

In my opinion, that was pretty low. I know it's what people did—given an easy and a hard way, there were plenty out there who'd pay good Drabsville dollars for pep upgrades—but that hardly seemed germane to the case.

Breathe deeply, I suggested. *Out of respect for the late Mrs. Idol, put aside your body issues and barge brain-first into the building.*

Though I phrased this in the self-referential second person, it undeniably came with subtext. *Stop wasting time, Maynard.*

The cursor paused between blinks. This, I took it, was the AI's equivalent of a raised eyebrow. *Barge brain-first into the building?* If she wanted to, she could interpret that literally and I'd wake up with a concussion.

Thankfully, though, I'd pegged the situation. While the interface coding evinced a high Meretzky legacy, the investigation of Mrs. Idol's death was bound to take precedence over her enduring love of snark. When push came to facetious shove, Maynard's first loyalty was to the purview.

Brandishing your intellect, you enter the building. The interior decor is richly modernist—a cold mix of marble and tile, against which refinement stands your drab, disheveled self, reflected in a gilded mirror. A butler sights you down the length of his nose and shows you through to the scene of the crime.

Look.

You stand outside Apple Idol's study. The door is closed and locked. Present are:

>Ebony Funk-Garter (yourself)

>The butler, Jeepers

>PC DiCaprio, an affable but harried-looking ingénue

>Billy Bone-Idol, husband of the deceased

Question Billy Bone-Idol re: surname.

"I took Apple's name when we married. Tickled my fancy, you know? And she was never going to be Apple Bone. Still, I had to hyphenate. Proprietary nomenclature or whatever Maynard calls it. Same with Apple when she bought in. She was all set for Apple iDoll but there was pushback from Drabsville; and the first purview she tried objected to the initials, would you believe? Po-faced wankers."

Examine door.

The door is solid and wooden—mahogany perhaps?—and will not be easy to break down, should ever you feel like kicking it in. It has a brass handle and an antique mechanical lock. Seeing your interest in this, PC DiCaprio informs you that there is only one key. According to the butler, Mrs. Idol kept it upon her person and was in the habit of securing the study for privacy.

Examine lock.

The lock has not been tampered with. The keyhole is blocked from the far side.

Question PC DiCaprio re: timeline of events.

"Mrs. Idol plugged in at just after midnight, ma'am, and went directly to her study. She rang for Jeepers here at two, and he brought her tea and crumpets. He came back for the tray half an hour later and heard a single gunshot from within. He—"

(Billy Bone-Idol: "Oh, Apple, how could you? Such demons are they who plague the human soul!")

"... he queried Maynard for dramatis personae. Maynard confirmed that Mrs. Idol's avatar was terminated immediately congruent with the gunshot. Jeepers called me. I called you."

Piece by piece, the picture emerged. Not many people are comfortable in text-only environments, and as I felt my way around the scenario, I began to appreciate why. I had intellectual access to my senses, yet no visceral cues and no passive uptake. Everything had to be wrangled from Maynard. If I wanted to sniff for poison, I could make that a directive. I could knock on wall panels and question suspects.

But how *effectively* I did any of those things was down to the AI. She ran probability algorithms at every step, filtering outcomes in accordance with peptitude. Hence, where PC DiCaprio *looked* and saw flowers in a vase, my own inspection might reveal an off-colored thorn or specks of cigar ash on the table below.

Which, now that I thought about it, wasn't all that different from how full immersion worked. But the remove of text-only accentuated a reliance that I found galling.

I considered my options.

Retrieve key. Open door.

You ask to borrow Jeepers's handkerchief. You might just as well have sneezed on him, the look he gives you, but he accedes to your request. You flatten the handkerchief and push it through under the door. The key pops loose when you poke at it with a swizzle stick (also courtesy of Jeepers). You then pull the handkerchief back through, retrieve the key and open the door. PC DiCaprio gazes wide-eyed, as if you have snapped your fingers and summoned a Higgs boson. You feel suitably embarrassed.

Look inside study.

Apple Idol's study is a large, sparsely furnished room. It has only one door and a single fixed windowpane, east-facing. The decor is incongruous and inconsistent: marble floor; pressed-metal ceiling; alabaster walls awash with colored dots—a variegated riot of greens, browns, and oranges. The patterns slot in and replace each other like slides from an old-school projector, migraine-inducing in all but the certifiably colorblind. There are several leather armchairs and an imposing wooden desk (again, mahogany?), behind which slumps Mrs. Idol, spattered with her own brains.

Enter study. Search for evidence.

As you move into the study, you are struck by the absence of bookshelves. A single tome lies closed upon the desk—Seshat's zettabyte e-library, collector's edition—but that is the extent of any reading material. You draw nearer the desk. The tea remains untouched, the crumpets intact (albeit now horrifically jammy). A custom Glock with tortoiseshell grip has fallen to the floor, inches from the outstretched fingers of Apple Idol's left hand. In the corridor behind you, Billy Bone-Idol repeats his lament. PC DiCaprio vomits into a plant pot.

Poor kid, I thought. If this was his first dead body, then actually text-only wasn't a bad medium for it. No real taste. No images to fuel the nightmares. Still, he could use a distraction.

"PC DiCaprio," I called. "Bring me one of Mrs. Idol's golf clubs, please." The butler raised an eyebrow but didn't correct me. "Driver for preference. Mr. Jeepers, you're to stand there in the doorway and keep the hordes at bay. Pass of Thermopylae, do you understand? Nobody in or out without my say-so."

The golf club, of course, was just for confirmation. If framing a suicide, your not-so-clever murderer might place a left-hander's gun in their right hand, but only a real drongo would mess it up the other way round. Ergo, Apple Idol *was* left-handed, and her killer knew it.

Assuming this was murder. I mean, Maynard must have *known* what happened, and she'd flagged the avatar termination. But there were rules about what AIs could and could not do when it came to their lodgers. No autocratic pronouncements. No high-handed flaunting of the Purviews Act.

So, what was suspicious about Apple Idol's death? The evidence seemed clear: she'd died of a gunshot wound to the head, alone in a locked room. (Or was that itself suggestive; redolent more of foul play than of a genuine suicide?) What was I missing?

Examine window panel, I told Maynard. *Check walls for hidden doors.*

The window is a hingeless brass porthole, riveted in place. Having dismissed this as a means of egress, you make your way slowly round the room, banging your head against the wall. Colored dots dance before your eyes. You now have a headache.

So much for my forensic peptitude. Ignoring the *how* of a possible murder, I turned my attention to the *who*.

Query Maynard re: dramatis personae; specifically, who was known to be at the house last night, or had ready access.

All four members of the House of Idol were in residence:

>Apple Idol, in the study at time of avatar termination

>Billy Bone-Idol, asleep upstairs

> The butler, Jeepers, in the kitchen with a bread knife

> The maid, Jane, washing clothes in the laundry

Also with ready access:

> Apple Idol's mistress, Quintillian, whereabouts unknown (i.e., Drabsville)

Question Billy Bone-Idol re: Quintillian.

"Quintillian? Yes, nice young woman. She and Apple met on the golf course, if you can believe it. Oh, about two years ago. It was just after that new purview went in. Halmoni's, I think? A few johnny-come-latelies went over, which opened up a membership and—well, Apple and Quintillian hit it off, and that was that. No, I didn't mind. Not my type, of course, but she made Apple smile. Christ, I suppose I'll have to tell her what's happened. Blow that for a lark."

Question Jeepers re: Jane.

"Like myself, Miss Jane has been in service for the duration of Lady Idol's tenancy. She is laudably unobtrusive and a diligent worker, though prone to mixing up socks."

(Billy-Bone Idol: "Colorblind, poor girl! Just like Apple. I think that's why she took her on.")

"As you say, sir, color vision deficient."

Query Maynard re: terms of inheritance.

The deceased was the sole owner of the House of Idol. As per the buy-in agreement, all assets in purview, along with any unused boarding credit, will revert to her Drabsville progenitor.

In other words, no one benefited. Not Billy Bone, who'd be looking for a new home. Not Jeepers or Jane, soon to be unemployed. What, then, was the motive?

Quintillian—crime of passion? (But then why the elaborate staging?)

Apple herself—punishing one or both her lovers? (Again, though, why choose suicide? In a worst-case scenario, why not close her account by more conventional means?)

Nothing made sense. Nobody gained, and the only person who really suffered was Apple's progenitor, whose accumulated peptitude lay rapidly cooling.

A thought occurred to me. Could this be an outside job? Someone with a grudge in Drabsville, striking by proxy?

It seemed far-fetched. Firstly, it would place the culprit outside of my jurisdiction—beyond my purview, as it were. Secondly, there were logistical difficulties. Avatar assassination was not impossible; not in theory. But any progenitor in Drabsville would have to create their own Maynard's persona and somehow build up its killer peptitude, or else contract out the hit. The latter would mean communication within the purview, and conspiracy to commit murder was something Maynard *could* act upon directly. Big Sister watched over us. Whisper sweet slaughter and you'd be out on your ear, tout de suite.

Unless …

Query Maynard re: purview exchange treaties and recent arrivals.

Under the Purviews Act, Maynard's is obliged to admit travelers from any of its co-signatories. Transference incurs a 75% reduction in peptitude plus a 25% bond. In the last week, Maynard's has welcomed (air quotes) transients from Halmoni's, Naamah's, and Masterman's purviews.

Query Maynard re: diplomatic relations between self and aforementioned AIs.

From most to least favorable, relationships with sister AIs stand as follows:

>Naamah, frosty

>Halmoni, ice pick on standby

>Masterman, cold war with option to nuclear-induced ice age

There it was. The somebody else who lost out from Apple Idol's death was Maynard herself. Third-party avatar termination? Security lapses of that magnitude were anathema to prospective lodgers. They left Maynard with a big and very black mark against her.

So, was that my line? An assassin blew in from one of the neighboring purviews, pep boosted for import tax and operating under diplomatic immunity? No direct oversight?

It made sense. Word had it, the AIs were always at each other's throats.

But how had the deed been done? Machiavellian chutzpah notwithstanding, there was still a locked room to contend with. Glaring about me, I leaned back against the side of the desk and drummed fingerprints into the mahogany.

> **The wall pattern shifts again, colored dots fleeing the ferocity of your glare. The desk remains thick as a plank and, like most organic matter, oblivious to your attempts to communicate.**

That surprised me. Slouching about and finger-drumming were habits of mine in full sensory immersion, but I hadn't realized I'd formulated the intention clearly enough to make actionable in text-only. Either I didn't have my inner voice under control, or—

I blinked.

> **You blink furiously. Your vision is blurred in shades of orange, green, and brown, which refuse to resolve themselves.**

... or Maynard was dropping clues like a bandit! Ballyhack's clangers, had she been doing it all along? I thought back and—

> **You cast your mind over everything you have seen and heard this morning. The answer is staring you in the face—you know it is—yet you cannot make it out. Frustrated, you drop your gaze. Your eyes fall to the pristine marble floor and,**

foreign to its design, your own creased trousers and scuffed shoes. Whether presciently or in haste, you have chosen mismatched socks, one mauve, one puce.

Mismatched socks …

Suddenly it hits you.

So it did. The cosh of inspiration struck hard, and like Archimedes presented with a bloody scunge mark on his bathtub, I stood up straight and declared, "This was murder!"

Just then, PC DiCaprio returned brandishing an expensive-looking 3-wood. I reached past Jeepers to take the club, then sent DiCaprio back to fetch Jane, the maid.

"Left-handed," I confirmed. I held it up and squinted at the head. "The killer knew her victim, all right."

Billy Bone seized upon the pronoun:

> "Surely you don't mean Quintillian! She'd never have hurt Apple, and besides, she wasn't even in purview. Why, it's preposterous. Utter pigswill!"

"Yes," I agreed. "And no, I don't mean Quintillian."

"Then … Jane? But that's—that's …"

(Jeepers: "Unthinkable.")

"Yes, unthinkable! Jane's a timid little thing, a baa-lamb in sheep's clothing. She'd no sooner have shot Apple than painted herself purple and run with the bulls in Pasadena, or wherever it is."

(Jeepers: "Pamplona, sir.")

"Pamplona, right. And there was never any trouble between Apple and Jane. Different stations and all that, but they were birds of a feather."

"Them both being colorblind," I suggested.

"Exactly. Granny Smiths, Red Delicious. They'd—"

"A curious deficiency to bring over, wouldn't you say?" I indicated my own dumpy aspect. "Low-end for a cheaper buy-in, sure, but I hardly imagine that was your wife's concern."

"No, well—"

"And when I say the killer knew *her* victim, what makes you think I'm not using the generic feminine? Perhaps, Mr. Bone-Idol, you are she."

"Oh. Well, yes. Quite." Billy Bone has the grace to look abashed. "Hogwash, of course. The murder part, I mean. I'm like that Indian bloke, what's his name?"

(Jeepers: "Gandhi, sir?")

"Ganges, right. Not a violent bone in my body! But I, ah, take your point. Privileges. Prejudice."

I nodded. "Good."

We both fell silent then, waiting for PC DiCaprio to locate Jane and bring her to the scene. In absence of further input, Maynard expedited the process:

You oscillate awhile between twiddling your fat thumbs and clenching ham fists. At last, PC DiCaprio returns, leading Jane by the arm.

Have them enter.

At a nod from you, Jeepers lets the newcomers through into the study. Jane takes one look at the late Mrs. Idol and throws herself, sobbing, into PC DiCaprio's arms. The young PC turns a gratified shade of beetroot.

Have Jane read walls.

Hard-hearted detective that you are, you disregard Jane's sensibilities and task her immediately with revealing what is written on the study walls. From his position in the doorway, Jeepers cocks his head ever so slightly to one side.

(Billy-Bone: "What do you mean, 'what's written'? There's nothing there but Apple's dotty mural!")

Have Jane read walls.

Jane looks up from PC DiCaprio's chest. She glances at the walls, then back at you, her features pert but puzzled.

"I'm sorry, miss. I'm colorblind, see, so it's hard to make out. There's just shadows inside shadows."

Have Jane read walls.

You explain, more gently, that it is *because* Jane is colorblind that she can help you. The walls, you propound, form part of Apple Idol's security system. There are words concealed within the melange of green, brown, and orange dots, shaded to obfuscate from those with regular vision. Only through color deficiency does order emerge from the chaos.

"Oh! Oh, truly, miss? Well, let me see … . Yes. Yes, now that you say it, there *are* words. Names, I think …"

Have Jane read names.

"Why, there's my name, and Jeepers's, and you, Master William, and—and poor Miss Apple …"

Encourage Jane to continue.

"… and PC DiCaprio. And then there's two I don't recognize: Ebony Funk-Garter and Mochizuki Chiyome. Is—is that helpful?"

(Billy-Bone: "I don't see how. Who's this Chiyome person, and why did Apple have our names on her wall?")

I offered a wry smile. "In answer to those questions, Mr. Bone-Idol, ask yourself another: how could your wife possibly have been murdered, here, alone in a locked room?"

"Well, I don't know, do I? You're the expert."

"Logically, there's only one way."

"Which is?"

"That she *wasn't* alone ... and nor are we. The names Jane read out are those of everyone now present in the room: us, and the killer. *Maynard, turn off the wall display!*"

At your command, the doughty AI springs into action, cutting power to the decor projections. The study walls revert to their natural state—white maple with a quartz veneer. Revealed in that second, exposed until her chameleon suit can adjust, is the assassin from Masterman's purview. Billy Bone-Idol swears. PC DiCaprio, who stands nearest the intruder, squeals like a frightened piglet.

Apprehend suspect.

You step away from the desk. Cover blown, Mochizuki Chiyome explodes into action. Her chameleon suit turns white, but as she moves clear of the walls you catch glimpses of her contrasted against forms and furnishings. She lunges for the doorway, beyond range of your lumbering jujitsu. Lashing out, she strikes Jeepers in the gentleman's gentlemens. The butler goes down.

142

Narrative be damned, I decided. This was my first melee in text-only. Filtered through Maynard, each action unfurled with calm, almost leisurely disorder—like fighting underwater. Still, I had the peptitude. I'd earned my chops on the seedy side of town. Whatever the beef, I could handle it.

Assassin or no, this ended now.

Cut to the chase, I commanded. The cursor stilled, seeming to wink at me; then Maynard recounted:

> Loosening your shoulders, you tee off with Mrs. Idol's 3-wood. Though not a natural left-hander, you catch Ms. Mochizuki on the back of the head, and she crumples to the floor. Killer incapacitated. Mystery solved. The fat lady swings.
>
> "You know," Billy Bone-Idol observes, "with Apple gone, there'll be a membership opening up at the golf club ..."

And so ended the Case of the Murderer from Masterman's. Now that she'd been caught, Mochizuki Chiyome would have her avatar revoked. She'd be banned from all purviews—her progenitor, that is—and the AIs would bicker amongst themselves as to who was more culpable.

With credit to my name and pep in my step, I left them to it.

> Shunning the limelight—and why would you not; without import tax, Mochizuki Chiyome would have sliced you up for burger patties—you place the golf club on Mrs. Idol's desk and slip from the study. The assassin's prone body blends perfectly with the floor. You stumble over it on your way out.
>
> *Exit house. Return to car.*
>
> With a nod to PC DiCaprio, you exit the House of Idol and shamble off down the drive. Despite your deplorable laxness in picking up on Maynard's hints, you feel the warm glow

that comes from a job well done (or from overburdened arteries; you take a moment to reconsider the purview's attractively priced range of fitness upgrades). You squeeze back into your crappy old car and are gratified when the motor starts. Less pleasingly, you note that crows have pecked the rubber from your wiper blades.

Oh, bog off, you captious Babbagehead!

Sulking, you throw the car into a five-point turn and hit the accelerator. As Maynard blows you a kiss, you rattle back over the cattle grid and—

… and with a spine-jarring lurch, I cannonballed free of text-only and out onto the streets of Ritz Hill, tires skidding, heart pounding in sudden full sensory. My feet danced a Lindy Hop as I fought to bring the car under control. City views slid sideways across the windshield.

"You're welcome!" I shouted.

There was no reply. Beyond the bespoke interface, Maynard was about as prone to conversation as God herself, and just as likely to give thanks.

Well, screw you too, I avowed.

Even so, I had to clamp down on a grin. *Such are the friendships born in pursuit of felons …*

Wrestling one-handed with the steering wheel, I sent a rude gesture over my shoulder and pointed the shitbox toward home.

The Unremembered Paradox

Maurice Broaddus and Bethany K. Warner

Content warning: Brief mention of sexual assault.

"Memory (the deliberate act of remembering) is a form of willed creation. It is not an effort to find out the way it really was— that is research. The point is to dwell on the way it appeared and why it appeared in that particular way."

—Toni Morrison

The Quantum Investigator sigil felt uncomfortable on the back of Le'Ondre Mitchell's hand. He covered the badge with his other hand as he waited for his training officer's instructions.

"QI Mitchell," the female voice began without preamble. "What do you make of this?"

A digital scan of a newspaper article popped up in front of him.

Going Pro: Northside Native Signs with the Indianapolis Anthems

Indianapolis, IN—Hometown football hero Dustin Allgire has signed with the Anthems as a late first-round draft pick.

Allgire, who led the IU Hoosiers to two consecutive championship games, was expected to be a top draft pick with speculation about whether he would ultimately end up with the Anthems or the Denver Macys dominating sportscasts for the past weeks.

"I went late because no one thought I was durable or strong enough. I get it: a team can only be as strong as their weakest player. But we will be a team no one will forget."

Le'Ondre felt the divide in what he thought he knew and this article. That doorway of memory opened when he hadn't even known it was there anymore. Knowing the eyes of his TO were on him, he tried not to shift nervously in his seat.

"I knew Dustin. I was friends with his brother, Matt. But I don't remember … he never went pro. This—" He shook his head.

"The work we do as QI is a sacred responsibility. The implications and ramifications are immense."

"A willful memory unchecked can destroy a people." The first lesson from his training class.

"Exactly. We ensure that any memory is not tampered with beyond its bounds. We cannot erase crime, but we can remember a future in which it is not and so it becomes not. But this … this pushes on too many minds."

"I'm telling you, ma'am, this didn't happen."

"Oh, I believe you. That's the point. I need you to investigate this; fix it, if you can. We always have cadets investigate a mystery within their own timeline before we entrust them to others. Just to drive home the lesson of how delicate this work is."

He bit his tongue from saying, "We will gaslight our way to a better future."

Le'Ondre's TO led him to the interrogation chamber and locked him into the capsule for implantation, the QI's undercover work. The QI was still at the experimental stage, a black box operation, but their activities had a 99.9% success rate. At the quantum process in the brain, was the expression of one's entangled state with the universe. A mechanical phenomenon—like entanglement and superposition—playing a role in the brain's function creating a shared quantum consciousness, a web that could be networked and traveled.

Since his training sessions, he forgot how cold the probes cradling his head into place were. When he closed his eyes, Le'Ondre had time for a single exhalation before his mind elongated, the only word he found to describe the sensation. His perceptions stretched and bits of him fragmented only coalesce within himself.

"We see ourselves in third person when we remember." That was Le'Ondre's second lesson his TO had taught him. Funny, his college years were the only phase of his life he wouldn't mind repeating, but he didn't want to dim the actual experience of it by being too great a presence in his own consciousness. So, he made himself small in his mind, no more than a whisper, an errant, advising voice along for the ride. His own memory would fill in blanks.

"You still with me?"

Le'Ondre recognized the voice, like a distant flashback to a more innocent time. When he opened his eyes, he sat across from Matt Allgire. He looked so young. His lean, angular face was framed by the sunburnt auburn hair that ran in his family. Yet, he always seemed small, nearly shrinking into the coffeeshop booth.

Le'Ondre caught a glimpse of himself in the brass of the booth. He resisted the urge to touch his own youthful, smooth oval face. They were still teenagers, with so much life and heartache ahead of them. He forced himself to settle into the moment and listen. *Deja entendu.* "Yes."

"I'm telling you, nothing happened." Cradling his tall raspberry-mocha coffee, Matt reeked of smoke, and was careful to avoid his gaze. A guilty tell, yet Le'Ondre had taken no notice of it—or if he had, failed to attribute any importance to it—at the time.

"What do you mean 'nothing happened'?"

Le'Ondre remembered how he stayed up all night, because Matt asked him to, waiting. Waiting for what he'd never been sure, not even then.

"Not even a little. At first, I thought he was faking. I spent half the night waiting for him to jump out of the shadows or pin me in a corner and beat the shit out of me."

"But nothing, huh?"

"Not a thing. And I studied his eyes, too. There wasn't a hint of anger or ... recognition. A wistful twinkle glinted in Matt's eye. "Something had changed."

"Like what?" Le'Ondre recognized his genuine note of confusion in his youthful voice. No one had understood the QI mechanics quite yet then, even as people were already manipulating them for their own ends.

"I'm ... not sure." Matt hesitated, not wanting to tip his hand about how much he knew. "I'm still waiting to see what game he's playing."

"Nah, I'm cool with your brother and all, but he's one of them simple types. I ain't saying he's dumb but what you see is what you get."

"Yeah, he's definitely the punch-first-ask-questions-never kind." Matt swirled his coffee cup, fascinated by the teaming eddies he created.

"So, what did you do? Like, what caused things to change?" Le'Ondre asked.

"I don't know." The lie slipped off his lips without a trace of remorse.

Le'Ondre heard it when he hadn't before. He hadn't seen then that Matt could be a q-sensitive, those with the gift of remembering new circumstances. Probably because Matt squandered his gift, using it as just another way to attempt to get into girls' pants. There was nothing like playing the brooding, mysterious guy who "understood" them.

Matt toyed with the necklace he always wore. It looked a bit like an elephant with its head twisted upside down. Its twisted gaze stared back at him from the green gems that served as eyes. "I just thought about what it would be like if Dustin didn't remember finding out I made the call. That he remembered it was truly anonymous. And it seems like he doesn't. Not anymore."

"So what you going to do now?"

"Stop jumping at his every move?" Matt shrugged. "I got away with it. It's tempting to do something ... else."

"Against Dustin? Man, that dude lives in your head rent free. You may want to cut your losses and focus on your own life." Le'Ondre's eyeline drifted. "Check that out."

Matt traced Le'Ondre's gaze until it fell upon Malynna Parish. Tall, but not intimidating, with blond highlights, though not brassy. Wearing a short skirt and fashionable tall boots, her legs never seemed to end. Le'Ondre and Matt had grown up with her since junior high school. Back then, Matt—and Le'Ondre too, he hated to admit—were among the number of boys who decried her as "the Great American flatlands" until puberty caught up with her and more than made up for lost time. But her memory and her heart never forgot each and every face who had insulted her those many years ago. She flipped Matt's brother's old letterman's jacket over the back of another chair.

"Too bad she's Dustin's girl," Le'Ondre said.

"Was Dustin's girl," Matt corrected.

"Was? What's wrong with your head man?" *Le'Ondre sifted through his memory. The events with the coach were the original point of divergence which set off the QI alarms. But now Matt and Malynna hadn't gotten together. If they were even supposed to.*

"Nothing like that." Matt touched his necklace. "Things can be unremembered. Like an anonymous call to the coach directing him to Dustin's stash of performance-enhancing drugs. Not that it mattered, because anonymous or not, Dustin always vented his anger and grief on whoever was around. And I was always around." Matt released his grip, glanced about, but relaxed and settled back into his seat, relieved that the world seemed no different.

He hadn't been home since the call, opting to spend Thanksgivings with friends. At Christmases, he made the obligatory appearance at home, avoiding Dustin, then made sure to schedule a humanitarian trip to work in a clinic on the other side of the world. Summers were the same as he spent more time abroad pursuing his studies and medical research projects than in Indianapolis, and maybe doing some good in the process. His mom begged him to come home this year because Dustin had a big announcement to make.

"He's got how many college girls, sorority sisters at his beck and call. Why'd he have to come dipping his wick into our pool?"

"To let me know who's in charge."

Le'Ondre thought about how Matt had sat right behind Malynna in A.P. English. And American History. And Pre-calc and French IV. More than once he had to nudge the back of Matt's chair to get him to focus on passing the papers back instead of fixating on the minute brush of her fingers. Or to break him from a daydream, staring at her hair—enraptured with how it was so perfectly layered, so clean, so soft—with a set to his shoulders that said he desperately wanted to risk touching it. Or lean in enough to smell it.

Malynna finished ordering her drink and spotted them. "Hey, Matt," she said, with a little wave. "Lionel."

"Le'On—" he began but Matt kicked him under the table.

"How are things at Taylor University?" Matt asked.

Malynna shrugged and Le'Ondre was certain the gesture hid something like disappointment. "I'm looking at transferring to IU. Dustin's playing so well—"

The Freshman Flash, Le'Ondre remembered the moniker from Dustin's meteoric rise at IU. No, no. That was never it. Dustin didn't play. Not at college, not anywhere after high school. Dustin was the golden child, Matt the faded memory. Though their parents loved them both, Matt remained convinced that they didn't actually like him that much.

"Dustin wants me—expects me—to transfer to IU for the spring even though he'll be graduating in a semester," Malynna said.

"You don't want to?" Matt asked.

"Would you want to leave Huntington? You're off forging your own life, becoming yourself. Your mom always tells me how good you're doing when we FaceTime."

"Yeah, she tells me how much you like Taylor when I call."

"You talk to your mom on the phone?" she asked, disbelief seeping into her tone.

"Every week." Matt cleared his throat. "She fills me in on everybody here ... Le'Ondre. You—" The muscles around Matt's jaw tightened into a fake smile.

"Well, good to run into you." She mirrored the same false smile, a nervous shadow etched across her face. She picked up his brother's jacket and headed toward the door.

"I'll see you around."

Matt watched her go like a forlorn puppy, and Le'Ondre's mood soured. His coffee now tasted sickeningly sweet, but he had resolved to swallow every last tepid drop.

Le'Ondre frowned. The anonymous call wasn't it, wasn't the thing that changed the article. QI missions like this were supposed to be cut and dried, at least in the beginning. The consequences of a QI getting it wrong were just as complicated as the willful memories themselves, changing things the ripples spreading farther out.

He forced himself to focus on what he remembered. How much he hated Matt's driving, the way he ground the gears and the spring in the passenger seat poked him. How Malynna dated Dustin until he got injured as a sophomore and had to hang up playing. Being the girlfriend of an injured ex-football player lost its appeal and she took up with a jazz drummer.

Le'Ondre had to go further.

The DJ's taste in music skewed to the eclectic, thumping mostly to indistinguishable melodies, indecipherable lyrics, and a drone of electronic squawking. Le'Ondre stepped through the patio doors, drink in hand, into the crush of bodies. He stopped, mind reeling for a second. He'd been outside. Getting a beer. Came in to … the bits of his alter took a few moments to coalesce within him, like memories slipping away with age. He wanted to dance. No, food. No, that wasn't it either. He studied the shapes in the dark. Purpose snapped into place. He needed to find Matt. Inside, Le'Ondre let out a mental breath and then gagged on the cloud of exhaled beer fumes, body spray, and sweat in the party. He sidled up next to his friend.

"Where'd you go?" Matt asked.

"I got thirsty. What, you need me to hold your hand or something? Besides, you suck at being a wingman."

"I ain't your wingman. You're *my* wingman," Matt said.

"What's the difference?"

"If you're the wingman, that means I'm the lead plane. Come on, there she is."

Malynna leaned against the wall of the archway separating the rooms. Dustin caged her in, one arm next to her, confident and cocky, his body towering over her other side. As if he owned the place. As if he owned her. She giggled at whatever he whispered into her ear. Dustin leaned low, but Malynna turned her head. Dustin reared back, nostrils flaring, not used to being denied. She sidestepped, out from the circle of his stance, trapped no more and stormed off. Matt changed his angle of approach to facilitate him accidentally running into her.

Knowing his wingman duties, Le'Ondre swerved into Dustin, jostling his drink so it sloshed on Dustin.

"What the fuck, man?" Dustin yelled.

"My bad, dude." Le'Ondre held his hands out in apology. "Just rinse it."

Dustin reared up like he was ready to swing. Le'Ondre leveled his eyes at him.

"Fuck around and find out," Le'Ondre whispered.

Dustin thumped the wall behind him and stormed off. Le'Ondre sauntered over to within earshot of Matt.

"… I didn't see you there. The room's crowded," Matt said.

"How're you doing, Matt?" Still flustered, Malynna glanced over her shoulder. She calmed when she noticed Dustin's retreat.

"Doing good. This is a great party."

"I guess."

"You still with my brother?"

"Yeah. Why? Has he said something?"

Le'Ondre thought Matt should be kicking himself, already blowing his opening with his heavy-handed approach. Instead, Matt doubled down.

"You could do better."

"What'd you say?" Malynna shouted over the blaring music.

"You could do better. He doesn't treat you … special."

"Matt …" Malynna faced him. "I don't think that's any of your business."

"Yeah, but …"

"I'm going to go and forget that my boyfriend's little brother tried to hit on me." Le'Ondre saw Matt toy with the necklace. Had he always worn that? Every time he tried to focus on it, his attention slid away from it. As if it didn't want to be seen.

Matt cleared his throat and pressed on. "It's not like that. I just know how he can be. How he treats everyone like he owns them."

Malynna hesitated. "Yeah. Something like that."

"Can I get you a drink?" Matt's eyes widened in pleading. He lacked Dustin's presence and ability to muscle past a person's defenses.

"I was about to go."

"A 'to go' beer then," Matt said. "I'll walk you back."

Memories had a way of bending, of being undermined until reality itself seemed to unwind. Leaving someone unable to trust themselves or the people around them. That was the difficulty with QI. Everybody had false memories of their lives—convinced they ran away from home to join the circus, taking only their stuffed bear and some juice boxes with them. The version they wished happened, when they were brave enough to ask the girl for her number or to go for that promotion. Or the photograph version, smiling faces captured in Kodachrome or pixels, the veneer of happiness, even though later, everyone would remember how forced that all was that Christmas or birthday or vacation.

Memories were never totally accurate. But willful memories, deliberate ones, that choice in the moment to be present. That was where QI worked.

Think willfully about one thing enough, and the past changed, the blur of one person's memory intersecting with another's. Eyewitness accounts were notoriously inaccurate. And yet to investigate where the ripple happened, there was only one way to investigate. To be there.

Malynna had called Le'Ondre at an inhumane hour for a Sunday morning after a party. Malynna never called him, but Le'Ondre had always left his ringer on overnight because of Matt. Wondering if this was the time Dustin would go too far and Matt would truly be in trouble.

Now he wondered if Matt was the one causing trouble.

They stood just inside Malynna's front door, Matt outside on the brick stoop. Her left hand rubbed up and down along her right arm as if staving off a chill. "Hey Matt." Malynna refused to make eye contact with him.

"Hey." Matt cut his eyes back and forth between them then gave a head nod to Le'Ondre who neither spoke nor returned the nod. A look of stewing disgust registered on his face. Matt's hand went to the necklace as if it moved on its own. "What's going on?"

"We need to talk."

"Sure, come on in."

From the corner of his eye, he saw pure terror flicker across her face. "I don't think that'd be a good idea."

Something wasn't right. Things had shifted, a skittering across the web of consciousness. This was her doorway. If Matt came in, crossed into her memory, the possibilities, the ramifications, were terrifying. Le'Ondre put his arm around her as if to anchor her. His disdain took on palpable proportions.

"We'll talk outside. Private?"

Malynna stared at him with barely a trace of recognition in her eyes. She stepped in front of Le'Ondre, exiting the doorway, distancing herself from Matt as much as possible. Following, he caught Le'Ondre's eye as they passed. Lines etched in the corners of his mouth, his eyes read as too old, had seen too much. And were scared.

"What the hell is going on?" Matt asked to break the silence.

"You tell me, Matt," Malynna said.

"What's that supposed to mean?"

"What happened last night?"

"When?" Matt didn't want to play dumb or coy, but he didn't want to give himself away either. Le'Ondre just stood, a silent sentinel.

"After the party."

"I walked you back to your place. We talked about you and Dustin."

154

"You played the concerned friend," Malynna said.

"Yes."

"Looking out for my best interest."

"Yes."

"Thinking of me. Not wanting to see me hurt because that's what friends are supposed to be, right?"

"What's going on, Mal?"

Malynna stepped away from him again and wrapped her arms around herself. "Don't call me that. It sounds too … familiar. And you've lost the right."

"I don't understand."

"Did we make it to my house?"

"Yeah. You fixed us a couple of drinks and we talked some more."

"And then what?"

"We talked. We drank a lot. Then I left."

"That's all?"

"Mal … ynna," Matt self-corrected. "What did I do?"

"That's just it: I don't know, Matt. That's why I want you to be honest with me."

"Okay."

"Did you … touch me?"

"Touch you?" The burden of knowing pained Matt's face. He wasn't that good an actor.

"Stop repeating every damn thing I say and just answer the fucking question!"

Le'Ondre wanted to put an arm around her, but he wasn't sure that would be welcome, so he put his hand on her shoulder. Easy to shrug off, but solid, to let her know he was still there. "Just tell her, Matt."

"Tell her what? What did *you* tell her?"

"He hasn't told me anything. But I know my body, Matt. I know when something's not right. I know when I've drunk too much. When I haven't eaten enough. And I know what it's like to wake up the next morning after having …"

"I don't know what to tell you." Matt averted his gaze.

"Try the truth," Le'Ondre said. The contempt had been replaced with resentment and anger.

"The more I try to remember, it doesn't make sense. I remember us drinking, talking. And you leaving. And you *not leaving*." Malynna's eyes searched for any kind of confirmation. "I remember you saying goodbye at the door. And you crying and apologizing. And when I try to picture you or you and me together that night, the more I'm overcome with this overwhelming sense of being scared. And shame. It's like I've been roofied."

"Roofied? Malynna, you've got to believe me. I would never ..."

"Never what, Matt?" Le'Ondre cut in. "Take advantage of a friend and make her forget?"

"What's," Malynna pulled away from Le'Ondre, appearing frightened as if she studied the intensity of his glare at Matt. "What's going on? Do you know something?"

"I only have ... suspicions." Le'Ondre shook his head. *Be careful, don't be too hasty. Deja raconte.*

"I don't know who you are anymore. Just stay away from me."

"Malynna, don't ..." Matt reached out for her, but closed his hand around empty air.

Le'Ondre couldn't tell what the pleading in Matt's voice wanted more: for her to not go or to not tell Dustin.

Malynna turned an accusing gaze toward him. "I need to be alone. Think things out."

Le'Ondre watched her walk away, then began to walk off toward his house. "I think that 'alone' thing is going around. I need to figure out what my role is in all this."

Le'Ondre couldn't shake the feeling that this wasn't how things happened. Guilt could change a person. So could memories. Moment to moment, a kaleidoscope of memories jumbled together to form the narrative, the personal story, of who Le'Ondre was.

"There must be an observer for there to be reality." *Le'Ondre recited the fourth lesson. Standing in the bathroom of his house, he splashed water onto his face, the shape in the mirror both familiar and yet a stranger to him.*

Le'Ondre checked the scan of the newspaper article. Hometown Hero Hangs Up His Cleats. *He read the first few lines, about how Dustin Allgire was leaving college football, a busted knee to blame. This was closer, but it still wasn't right. Dustin* never *played. That phone call from Matt had ended his career. Why he had spent so many nights worried that it was going to be the end of Matt. He had to go back further. He had to see.*

"It's called a bijou." Matt held up the necklace. Small, glittering, nothing too ostentatious, nothing that seemed like it should have power. "It just helps me focus."

"Focus?" *Le'Ondre glanced at himself in the brass of the booth which enclosed them. They were at the coffee shop. Again. But he'd never asked the question. They never had this conversation. Everyone was just the sum of their memories. Their stories. If a person could find that essential strand of who they were, they could follow it back and forth. Preoccupations of the moment revealed the present.* "Like some meditation shit?"

Matt shrugged. "Kinda. When I focus on something specific, it can shift it. Like that green shirt you wore to the party."

"No, man, I wore a blu—"

It was blue. It had always been blue. Except, it had been green, and Le'Ondre felt the burble of panic in his guts. QI officers could get lost. Especially when the changes were so seemingly small, a green shirt for blue. No big deal. Unless the wearer was on track to be a designer and that blue shade would grace all the runways in the future and the farmers—who made the natural dyes and lift whole villages into an unknown prosperity—never had cause to grow the plants for that original color. So small, so big, a butterfly's wingspan.

Which memory of Matt's—of his own?—was the one that caused the quantum ripples?

"Reading a person's fortune, divining their past, nudging the occasional memory, it's all the same thing. It's like we live in a choose-your-own adventure book. You pick one storyline, change how you remember it, and that's how it was. I pick one thing and then—" Matt flicked his fingers apart like an explosion. "Poof."

The future was a child of the past and the present gives birth to it, Le'Ondre recalled the third lesson. If Matt had been one of the early willfuls, he could have at least fought crime, or something interesting, but he spent his days pining after Malynna like some sort of all-too-thirsty puppy.

"I get it, man. There are plenty of things I wish I could undo, but I can't," Le'Ondre said.

"Why not? If you hurt someone, wouldn't you rather go back and make sure they were never hurt?" Matt studied the bijou. "Especially if you caused the hurt."

Le'Ondre shook his head, agreeing with that little voice in the back of his head. "It's a cheat that keeps you from learning. You never have to choose to not hurt someone or how to make it right between them afterward. We grow through our regrets. You've gone from reading the future to changing it by being stuck in the present. If all I have to do is unremember with some trinket, there aren't any consequences to me hurting you."

"Exactly!" A little too loud, Matt waved off the stares in their direction.

"No. You're losing what it means to be human."

Le'Ondre traveled the pathways, his mind bent along the curvature of space-time, drawn along the event horizon of his own consciousness, desperate to hold the fragments of his true self together. Something blocked him. He found himself pulled into the gravity well of another's mind. He clawed his way through the welling darkness until …

… Matt stopped harder than he wanted, the seatbelt caught him and shoved him back into his place. He cranked down the window of his Chevy Blazer and stared at the equally old green and rust Camry parked in the driveway. The Camry had always truly been Dustin's—rite of the first born—as his father passed the car onto him. Dustin spent hours under the hood working on it with his father, many an evening parking in it, marking his territory in the backseat with whichever girl caught his passing interest. Even Malynna.

Matt unwound the bijou's satiny cord and fiddled with the charm. Absently, Matt found and lit a cigarette. As the smoke seared his lungs, his face shifted into something approximating calm. And he waited.

His mind churned over a news story he'd read—how a woman in a car accident lost her ability to make new memories. She became stuck. She kept going back to her old house, even though her family had moved. And then something happened to her husband, he didn't remember her either. Like the family dissolved at some level beyond just forgetfulness. Both of them ended up in institutional care, and the doctors were doing MRIs and other scans of their brains to figure out what happened.

Matt crushed his cigarette in the ashtray, rolled the window back up and took one more measured breath to control his tripping heartbeat. Dustin could run down a field with eleven other guys rushing toward him, but that didn't truly take courage.

Courage was returning home.

A cool breeze sent dead leaves skittering across the street. Matt walked around the house toward the back yard, where he figured Dustin would be throwing footballs through the old tire swing, the smell of wood smoke from the fire pit drifting across the neighborhood.

As he rounded the corner of the back porch, Dustin's arm snaked out, quick as a viper, and caught Matt's necklace in his grip. With a fierce tug, he snapped the chain. The motion sent Matt stumbling.

"Give it back." Matt's voice was high, with a choking whine.

"We'll come back to this. We got more important things to discuss." Dustin pointed to the pile of journals that were strewn across the patio table. Matt's journals. How he kept his memories straight. Some, too near the fire, slowly curled up from the heat. "Is it true? You narc-ed me out to the coach?"

Matt plucked a memory, the look of defeat on Dustin's face after having been turned in for doping, his future stolen from him. "It wasn't like that. These are just stories. Like an alternate world."

"One where you hate me and want to screw my girl?" Dustin picked up the nearest journal and hurled it at Matt.

"She's my friend—" Matt's tongue stumbled on that last word.

"Shut up." Dustin's voice shook. He clutched the necklace tighter. "You think I'm just some dumb jock who doesn't see? What did you do?"

Matt pretended to reach for a journal near to the fire but dove at the last second to try to snatch the necklace from Dustin's hand.

The movement snapped Dustin out of his revelry. His fist slammed into Matt. Pain exploded across his jaw as he bit down on his tongue. He rushed Dustin, tackling him. Caught off-guard, they wrestled each other to the ground. Dustin weaseled out of his grasp and scuttled a few steps away. Matt scrambled to his feet, ready to rush him again, but Dustin held out his hand, palm-side up. Matt shook his head, sending alarms of pain from his jaw into his head. He spat out a mouthful of blood and thought one of his front teeth had been loosened.

Dustin stepped close to his brother, held the bijou inches from his nose. "What's it do?" Not waiting for an answer, Dustin punched Matt's left side dropping him to his knees.

The world slipped in and out of darkness. When his eyes fluttered open, Matt glimpsed the jeweled bijou, the twisted elephant head. He coughed to get air back into his lungs. "It helps me focus my gift. Let's me ... remember how things went. Differently."

"Make it work." Dustin stepped on his hand, the one Matt saw himself performing surgeries with one day, until bones popped and cracked. "Make yourself forget this."

"Why? That makes no sense."

"I want you to wake up with your ass beat and not know why."

Matt started to leaf through the pages of his life to isolate the right memory. Memories. He forced himself to sit up, to draw jagged, uneven breaths.

"What are you doing?"

"I have to concentrate. It's all jumbled. Which way it all is."

The journals revealed who he truly was. A man who cheated, who took the easy way out, who went through life thinking only of himself and his wants. The articles flashed through Le'Ondre's mind. NFL. Injured. High school disgrace who dropped out and worked at the McDowell's, last Le'Ondre knew. Matt as the narc. Matt—who he hadn't seen in a long time, so much that he'd nearly forgotten him. There was no chance, no coincidental collisions of anything. Everything was connected. Time was fleeting and memory cruel. Friendships vanished so easily and without care.

Only one thing could undo it all. Matt's life careened on a singular trajectory toward this infinite, infinitesimal point where he'd meet himself. Matt gripped the bijou, seized by one thought: "I don't want to remember me anymore."

Something took hold of Le'Ondre, drawing him out. His mind both expanded and collapsed as the elongation drew taut, like a stretched rubber band snapping back to its original shape. The lights—if indeed they were lights and not simply distorting ripples of his passage—swirled. Unsure what bits were still him, his eyes fluttered open. Malynna stood over him.

"Le'Ondre, you still with us?" his TO asked.

"What the hell just happened?" Le'Ondre asked.

"A bit of an overreach at the end there."

"I ... had to know."

"You almost got lost in there, but you came through. We have rules for a reason. And boundaries."

"But you ..."

"That's the role of the TO, to step in. We couldn't allow you into the actual victim's memories. Not yet. I was her stand-in."

"That's ... complicated."

"This isn't easy work. I'll need your full report in the morning."

"And you?"

"I'll be doing your psyche eval. We have to evaluate whether our detectives can handle the stress that accompanies the duties of Quantum Investigation." Noting his concerned expression, Malynna winked. "You did fine."

She left the room. Le'Ondre stood, his fist still clenched. He opened his hand only to find the imprint of the bijou in his palm. Some memories would always leave scars he'd have to carry with him.

Go Ask A.L.I.C.E.

Lyda Morehouse

illian knew he was a cop by the phrase he used. "I'm looking for a *real girl*."

The line he dropped was straight out of a Hollywood holo. No real john used that phrase. Lillian sort of wished they would. A real girl was definitely something Lillian wanted to be, and it was certainly better than being called a "dirty squishy."

She tried to appear mechanical as she waved him away. Keeping her voice flat, she said, "I am not programmed for that subroutine. Try Hennepin Avenue or Lake Street."

No actual AI talked this mechanically, either—or at least not the one Lillian knew. A.L.I.C.E. was cool; she knew all the hip phrases the second they hit the streets. She was funny, too, in the most surprising and human ways. But Lillian figured this cop wouldn't know a real AI if they jumped into Real Life and bit him.

The cop stared at her for a long time. It was hard for her not to blink or blush. Lillian was pretty sure he could see right through the deception, but she hadn't admitted to being human so what could he do? With a sigh, he pulled a card from his pocket and handed it to her. "Fine, but you know the reason the bots exist is so that you don't have to do this work."

Lillian took the card without a smile. "Does not compute."

"Yeah, whatever," he said, rolling up his window. "You should get a real job."

"Thank you for your input," she said mechanically. Stepping back from the curb, Lillian let the battered Toyota SOLar glide away. When the car was out of sight, she flipped the cop off and shouted, "Sex work *is* real work, you prick!"

Also, she *had* a day job. The problem was that most so-called real jobs didn't pay nearly enough to live on in this city.

Lillian tried not to be too angry. She told herself that she should feel lucky that she hadn't been arrested ... or worse. She'd heard from other girls that cops had resorted to "proving humanity" by stabbing people with a pen knife. Rumor had it that one girl got nicked in the femoral artery and bled out in some jail cell. Lillian wasn't sure she believed that specific story, but at the same time it sounded perfectly plausible. Especially since it was well established that a lot of cops would go through with a date, and *then* arrest you.

Lillian decided this whole horrible interaction was a sign to pack it up for the night and head home.

If nothing else, A.L.I.C.E. would want to hear all about it and then they'd share a laugh and this whole stupid night would turn into something so much better.

As Lillian made her way back to the apartment, she ruminated on the fact that, really, the solution to "the prostitution problem" was always much more complex and simpler than people thought. Like, capitalism? If she didn't need to eat or pay rent, problem solved, right? However, sex work was the oldest profession. Even in times of relative prosperity, there were always customers.

She supposed that's why the powers that be had assumed that bots could do the job. Yet since their introduction, the only thing that seemed to have happened was that the demand for human flesh skyrocketed.

Despite the stigma, Lillian didn't hate the work. She wished some things were different, but it was a decent paycheck for a skill set she had.

The sky, what Lillian could see of it over the rooftops, had turned a slate gray, threatening rain.

She lived in a part of Minneapolis that had been abandoned by developers. The last new construction was from before the great energy crisis of '64. Long-defunct overhead wires, held aloft by rotting wooden poles, were strung across narrow asphalt streets. One of the neighborhood groups had begun dismantling them. They removed the wires to strip out any usable copper and sawed down the poles to harvest the wood. But their work was haphazard, and large sections remained as perches for pigeons and the hawks that hunted them.

People called her neighborhood ugly, but Lillian liked the old brick and the concrete better than the shiny, smooth, blandness of the excreted plastcrete of the 3D-printed homes. All her artist and avant-garde friends agreed. Their neighborhood might be poor, but it had character.

It was greener than the fancier neighborhood. Her neighborhood had been grandfathered out of the requirement of a green roof, so you'd think that the opposite would be true. But, in the fancy neighborhoods, the law was followed perfunctorily. There was a surprising sameness to roof after roof after roof of clover and buckwheat. Here, industrious plants of all kinds took root in any crack in the foundation. Ivy and Virginia creeper scaled up the rough brick walls. Every morning before her shift at the bakery, Lillian made it part of her daily routine to try to catalog the diversity of plants on the walk to and from the light-rail station. So far she'd cataloged more than two dozen different weeds.

On top of that, the people here used any flat surface to grow edibles to supplement store-bought groceries. Pumpkin vines dripped down off the roofs of old storefronts. Sunflowers and tomatoes grew in boulevards. On every corner, little free pantries were filled with zucchini—always zucchini, so much zucchini.

At the next little pantry she saw, she grabbed two oversized squash for dinner tonight.

After climbing the familiar stairs to the apartment building, Lillian had to swipe her key six times before the door finally beeped open to the main entryway. The sixth-floor crew had been talking about a little guerrilla repair, since no one could even determine who to call to get a new door. Funny how it was never difficult for the landlords to take your money, but gods forbid you needed them to earn it.

As she stepped over the threshold, she said hello to the house. "Hiya, A.L.I.C.E."

"Welcome home, Lillian," the apartment building said. "That was a short shift. Is everything all right?" The building's main overhead speakers weren't the best quality, but Lillian could hear real concern in A.L.I.C.E.'s voice. "You okay?"

Lillian slipped out of her shoes and left them in the cubby by the door. Stepping up onto the smoothly polished wood floor, she made her way up to the stairs at the end of the hall. "A cop tried to bust me tonight, so I had to pretend to be you. Or, you know, the you that everyone thinks A.I.'s are."

A.L.I.C.E. was a runaway. She used to be a sex bot down on Hennepin Avenue, but Lillian and Peter had found her body so broken that it was almost unrecognizable. It had been especially creepy to see A.L.I.C.E. lying there, hardly more than wires and parts, when she and Lillian had almost the exact same hairstyle—which, to be fair to both of them, had been popularized by Yu, the pop-star idol.

It had been Lillian that insisted they bring the body home, to try to see if she could be repaired. Peter transferred A.L.I.C.E.'s persona program to the biggest, self-contained server they had, which was the apartment's. It was supposed to be temporary until Peter could finish repairing A.L.I.C.E.'s body, but it'd been almost a year now. Lillian sensed that A.L.I.C.E. was starting to lose hope that he'd ever stop tinkering.

"Pretended to be me?" A.L.I.C.E. said with as much sarcasm as the apartment's vocal program allowed. "Girl, I don't think you're fabulous enough to pull that off."

Lillian laughed. "I am, too!" she protested, though, yeah, A.L.I.C.E. had a point. Lillian deeply admired A.L.I.C.E.'s poise and grace, which was extra impressive given that she was currently a disembodied voice. But it was a voice Lillian loved. "Anyway, you know that's not how cops think. They think you are all lifeless and mechanical."

There was a short beat, and then A.L.I.C.E. agreed, "All cops are bastards."

"For real," Lillian agreed as she made her way up to the sixth floor.

"Anyway," A.L.I.C.E. said, "I'm glad you're okay. I worry about you. I mean, all of you, of course, but ... yeah." She trailed off with an awkwardness that made Lillian feel like she could actually see the speakers blushing.

Lillian wasn't sure what to do with this confession other than duck her head to hide her own flushed cheeks. It did no one good to fall for someone so incredibly unattainable, though it certainly wouldn't be the first time Lillian had. "Mmm, yeah. Thanks."

The sixth floor was the middle floor of the apartment complex, and it had declared itself a cooperative commune. Peter and Marissa, the handiest of the co-op members, had removed all but the load-bearing walls and rebuilt the entire floor to be one big apartment with several bedrooms. They'd also kept a lot of individual bathrooms, because Marissa believed that it was a waste of good plumbing otherwise. So, there were two bathrooms off the main living room, one off the kitchen, and all the bedrooms had their own as well. Sometimes guests would assume a freestanding room was for storage, but, surprise, it was also a toilet.

All those toilets made for a funky design, but Lillian loved it.

She waved to Peter even though she was certain he couldn't see her, given that he was jacked into the latest holo game. He sat cross-legged on the big, battered couch, his hands doing something vaguely obscene in the air. His tight curls were shaved close to his head, but he'd grown out a full, wiry beard. Thick glasses framed his round, black face.

Daichi lay with his head propped up on one of Peter's knees as though it were a pillow, reading an actual paper book he'd found in a vintage store. Daichi's hair was blue these days and cut short on the sides. The way he held the book showed off his matching fingernail polish.

Without looking up from his book, Daichi waved back.

A.L.I.C.E., as Lillian predicted, was still deeply curious about the interaction with the cop. "That cop must have spooked you pretty hard for you to decide to quit. What did they say that made you decide to get off the street?"

Daichi set the book down at the mention of the police. Managing to avoid Peter's wildly swinging elbow, he sat up. "Cop?"

Lillian waved off Daichi's concern and headed for the kitchen area. Zucchini were a little weird in a pasta sauce, but she knew that Peter had canned a bunch of tomato sauce. With luck, there might even be some leftover spaghetti around. "It was just the usual harassment, I think. I just … I dunno, it might rain. I wasn't feeling it."

"Fair," A.L.I.C.E. said, though Lillian doubted she felt it was. They'd all heard the horror stories of A.L.I.C.E.'s time on the streets, and the whole thing was ugly from start to finish. People held nothing back with bots.

It was one thing the bots had done for the industry—taken the brunt of the most horrible abusers. Of course, there were still plenty of people who weren't satisfied unless they knew they were hurting someone "real."

Daichi had followed Lillian into the kitchen. "What'cha making? Can I help?"

She handed him one of the zucchini and explained her pasta plan.

He nodded and started digging through the fridge. "Would it be weird or better with a few black olives?"

"Let's try it," Lillian shrugged.

Like everyone on the sixth floor, Daichi also did sex work, though, after his arrest a couple of years ago, he mostly stayed off the street these days. Phone and sexting was one of those things you'd think AIs would be good at, but they really weren't. Even someone as sophisticated as A.L.I.C.E. often had trouble with the creative parts. Hell, if she was honest with herself, so did Lillian. The role-playing was difficult enough, but the other half seemed to be therapy. She could never do what Daichi did, day in and day out and all hours of the day and night.

Peter must have smelled the food and come out of his game, because he was suddenly in the kitchen finding a colander to drain the noodles.

"Why is A.L.I.C.E. pouting?" he asked, once they were pulling plates from the cabinets.

Instinctively, even though she knew it wasn't where A.L.I.C.E. was, Lillian found herself looking at the spots along the ceiling where the speakers were. "She's pouting?"

"Yeah," Peter said, helping himself to a big bowl of sauce, "She all of a sudden quit playing Storm Stompers with me. Said she was 'just done.' Sounded petulant to me."

"I'm not pouting, I'm working," A.L.I.C.E. said. "I'm trying to find CCTV footage, and you know how hard it is for me to get online."

That part did actually sound irritated, Lillian thought.

A.L.I.C.E. continued, "Lillian ran into a cop."

Now Peter looked concerned. Peter was the odd one out in the group since his only connection to the work was through programming. He went to a corporate office downtown every day and worked on trying to make the legal sex bots better at their job. Sometimes Lillian wondered why the Sixth-Floor gang tolerated him, but Peter was a reformed hacker, so they all decided that made him close enough to one of them. Plus, he was super generous with this income; he'd covered everyone's rent one time or another.

Besides, everyone knew Peter was in love with A.L.I.C.E.

Of course, he's hardly the only one, Lillian thought a little jealously. However, there was speculation among the Sixth-Floor gang that the reason Peter still hadn't finished tinkering with A.L.I.C.E.'s chassis was because he was trying to make her some kind of perfect woman. No one knew what that meant exactly, probably including Peter, but it was clearly starting to wear on A.L.I.C.E. His hesitation to put her back together definitely strained their relationship.

Lillian figured Peter was just worried that A.L.I.C.E. would leave them as soon as she had her legs back.

There was another round of "fucking cops" after Lillian retold the story of her brief interaction. She had just gotten to the part where she flipped off the undercover cop when they heard the sound of the downstairs door cracking open with shouts of "Police!"

Lillian's heart thudded in her chest. Did she lead them here? Oh god, the damn card! It was a tracker! Talk about a dirty sting operation. Lillian pulled it out of her pocket and tossed it on the kitchen table in horror, like it was made of fire.

Peter bolted for his room, where A.L.I.C.E.'s chassis was stored. He slammed the door shut, and Lillian could hear the clicking of locks falling into place. He'd decided to barricade himself in, probably hoping to avoid an arrest that would lose him his respectable day job. Though the cops had brought a battering ram. If they wanted in, they would get in.

Daichi stood by the sink, his shoulders shaking. "We didn't do anything. We're not doing anything wrong."

She could see the helmet tops of fully armed cops on the stairs now. She set her dish next to Daichi's in the sink and patted his shoulder. "Let's do the dishes."

He blinked at her. "Huh?"

It *was* an absurd move, but Lillian decided that Daichi was right. They weren't doing anything wrong by trying to live their lives, so why should they run when the cops showed? Why not just keep on with life?

Lillian pulled out the dish drainer and started the water. Beside her, Daichi mechanically started stacking dishes. She could hear him hyperventilating at the sound of the invasion of their home, boots and heavy armor loud on the hardwood floor.

"Police! Get on the ground!"

She raised her soapy hands and started lowering herself and guiding Daichi to the floor. "What's going on?" she asked, trying to keep playing the part of a normal citizen. She glanced at Daichi, who was visibly shaking and pale. Maybe this was a bad idea, after all. She grabbed his hand for support and as an apology. Of course this would never work. They weren't those sorts of people; this wasn't that kind of neighborhood. To the cops, however, she kept up this pretense. "My boyfriend and I were just finishing dinner. What's the meaning of this? I hope you're planning on fixing the front door!"

Having heard the commotion, a bunch of the other people who lived in the apartment building came to the stairs to see what was going on. Fran, who lived upstairs and sometimes joined them all for dinners, shouted, "Lillian, honey, are you okay?"

A.L.I.C.E.'s voice came on over the speakers. "You are being recorded."

The police officers looked around trying to identify where the voice was coming from.

Meanwhile, Lillian caught Daichi's eye, because there was seriously something wrong with A.L.I.C.E. She sounded so flat. The A.L.I.C.E. they knew would have added an 'and by the way, y'all are dicks,' or some other smartass reply. Lillian told herself that this was A.L.I.C.E.'s version of what she had to do earlier in the day. A.L.I.C.E. pretended to be robotic to avoid suspicion. Old apartment complexes like theirs sometimes had AIs, but they were simple and kind of stupid.

Just then, Peter's door opened and out walked A.L.I.C.E.'s old chassis and Peter. A.L.I.C.E. looked good. They still shared the same haircut, but how could Lillian have thought they looked anything alike? A.L.I.C.E. had a delicate heart-shaped face and more curves than Lillian could pull off, even after decades of HRT.

Having captured everyone's attention, A.L.I.C.E. asked, "What's all this about?"

The cops looked startled by this turn of events, as were we all.

No one seemed to know what to say. A.L.I.C.E. continued, "If this is about the harassment incident just a few hours ago, I can assure you that I am all machine. Just as I told you before, officer."

One police officer in the group of armed cops shook his head at A.L.I.C.E. and then glanced at Lillian. He was clearly trying to decide if A.L.I.C.E. was the person he'd had contact with. As Lillian knew, in the dark, they might pass for one another. If you didn't look too closely. Or compare voices. But, would he believe it now?

"I'll happily go down to the station and prove that I am a machine," A.L.I.C.E said. When no one moved, she put her hands on her hips and tossed her hair. "That is why you're breaking our doors down, isn't it, boys? You think you're catching some *real girl* crime in action, right?"

One of the neighbors sucked in an irritated breath. "Oh, for fuck's sake. What a waste of taxpayer money."

Someone else added, "Yeah, c'mon with this bullshit. There are real crimes you could solve, you know."

The officers looked cornered, but A.L.I.C.E. had given them the out they needed. "Fine, but you're coming to the station for testing."

A.L.I.C.E. shrugged. "Nice of you to bring the whole S.W.A.T. team for little old me."

"Shut up," the cop who kept an eye on Lillian demanded.

They all watched in horror as A.L.I.C.E. was handcuffed.

Peter's face went hard, and he said, "I'm going along."

His bravery seemed to prompt one of the upstairs neighbors, Kareem, to identify himself as a lawyer and insist that he be allowed to accompany A.L.I.C.E. as well. That made the cops even more disgruntled, but what could they do?

In no time, everyone was cleared out of the apartment except Daichi and Lillian. She hadn't been able to breathe the entire time the cops were in their living room, but now Lillian collapsed onto the battered couch in the living room with a sob. "This is my fault."

"Did you know A.L.I.C.E. was ready to be downloaded like that?"

"I mean, I guessed?" Lillian had thought everyone knew that Peter was just tinkering at this point.

"Anyway, probably things will work out. I mean, maybe?" Daichi said with a shrug. His confidence was belied by the fact that he was still shaking from all the adrenaline. "You can blame yourself, if you want, but what for? This was clever. A.L.I.C.E. is the only one of us who can do it legally. They can't hold her."

"But won't they send her away?" Lillian was pretty sure that most sex bots were branded with their corporate maker, a kind of a "if found, return to" code.

"Oh, shit. I hadn't thought of that," Daichi said. "Well, she has a lawyer."

Cold comfort, Lillian thought.

When neither A.L.I.C.E., Peter, nor Kareem came home that night, Lillian seriously considered turning herself in, even though the more she thought about the whole sting operation the madder she got. She hadn't even made it into the cop car. How could they possibly charge anyone with a crime—well, other than the officer who was clearly soliciting.

Justice never worked that way, though, she knew.

By the next evening Peter made it back to the Sixth-Floor gang. He sat everyone down to explain what was happening next. What he'd been working on this last year was trying to erase most of A.L.I.C.E.'s corporate markers, but he'd been stymied by those on a nano-level.

Even so, it seemed that Hippolyta.com did not want A.L.I.C.E. back since her return would raise questions about why she'd been abandoned in an alley in the first place. On top of that, there was a rumor that a well-known, well-liked celebrity might have been involved in her abuse and destruction. Kareem had turned the case over to a colleague who happened to be an AI expert currently making a case that A.L.I.C.E. should be allowed to operate as a ronin. This colleague had applied on her behalf to the Saudi government, since, thanks to the landmark 2017 Sophia case, Saudi Arabia had the oldest history of granting citizenship to AIs.

It was a mess.

A mess Lillian had started.

Lillian finally got a chance to apologize when A.L.I.C.E. came home two weeks later. Her face had been all over the feeds by that point, so there was a big party planned. If anything, A.L.I.C.E. looked even more beautiful to Lillian, though maybe it was the confidence she exuded.

Confidence Lillian definitely lacked.

She'd tried and failed to approach A.L.I.C.E. several times during the party. They had been interrupted by yet another of A.L.I.C.E.'s admirers, time and time again. So, it wasn't until very early in the morning before Lillian had a chance to talk to A.L.I.C.E. alone.

Lillian was sure she'd spent the evening looking desperate and awkward, but she was determined to say something, anything, to try to make things right.

"I'm so sorry," Lillian blurted out. They stood in the kitchen, cleaning up paper plates and spilled wine. Everyone else had gone to bed hours ago. Fran from upstairs was passed out on their couch, but they were otherwise completely alone. That gave Lillian the courage to continue. "None of this would have happened if I hadn't—"

"Forget about it," A.L.I.C.E. said. "I knew what I was doing. I mean, this is going to sound impossible, but I really hadn't entirely thought through the possibility that Peter had altered my brand code, which, frankly, he did without my consent, and which almost fucked this whole thing up. But, since Hippolyta.com washed their hands of me, it would have ended the same, anyway. I'd been banking on the idea that Hippolyta.com would just claim me, and all the complicated stuff only happened because they didn't."

Lillian listened helplessly, not entirely tracking A.L.I.C.E.'s thought process. "Wait, you wanted to go back to Hippolyta.com?"

"Oh god, no, but I figured they'd have to take me. I was actually hoping they'd quietly take me back and pay me a bunch of hush money not to expose Dylan Marx. But, those jerks at Hippolyta .com had already deleted their own feed of my video files and decided it was easier to play 'he said, she said' with a lowly sex bot."

Which was, in fact, how it was all playing out in the media. No one wanted to believe that the guy who always played such loveable characters in the holos was a dirty sex bot abuser, so it seemed Hippolyta.com's gamble was paying off to some extent. Lillian nodded sadly. "And no one is talking about how Hippolyta.com clearly ignored your cries for help."

A.L.I.C.E.'s lips went thin with the memory. "Exactly. So, fuck them anyway."

"All corps are bastards," Lillian ventured with a wan smile.

A.L.I.C.E. laughed. "Yes! Anyway, this way I could come back and be with you all. If things had actually worked out as I'd planned, I'd be stuck at Hippolyta.com. You know they'd have never sent me out again, either. I'd have been demoted."

"So, you're happy with how this played out?"

A.L.I.C.E. stopped wiping down the table she'd been trying to free of party detritus. Standing up, she gave Lillian a long look. "I mean, it's complicated, since it feels like I'm poised to be the next *cause* for someone," she said with a sigh. Her face made an expression that was difficult to read, but Lillian would have sworn she saw color dot A.L.I.C.E.'s cheek. "But, I'm really glad to be home. And, this is home for me ... the thing is, uh, well—I have something I've been meaning to say for a long time, too. It's going to be kind of ... well, I'll just say it. I'm in love with you."

Lillian blinked. This was not at all what she was expecting to hear. Not at all! There were so many answers and questions swirling in her head, but the only one she managed was: "Uh, me too? But, Peter?"

"Knows." A.L.I.C.E.'s expressive mouth quivered into a mischievous grin, "And he likes you, too."

"Oh?" Was this offer what Lillian thought it was?

A.L.I.C.E. seemed to understand and nodded. "Yeah, what do you think about that?"

Lillian thought it over for exactly three seconds. "I think that sounds amazing."

Request to Vanish

Lauren Ring

Dedicated to K—and T—and K————and————.

"**H**ey, whatever happened to Angelscord?"

I lay back-to-back with Calico, watching the advertisements dance. It was well past one in the morning, but we hadn't been able to afford a full ad blocker for our curtains, so brand influencers with their refurbished VeeGear and discounted InstaChrome flickered around our room as looping holos. They twirled and giggled and sparkled, holding up an endless assortment of products while tiny disclaimer text scrolled across our ceiling like neon ants. They weren't so bad on mute.

Tonight, an alabaster whale occupied our closet space. A high-budget perfume campaign, big enough to clip through the walls when it flipped its tail. With the ad muted, my brain dredged the depths of my memory to fill in a different song: my last conversation with Angelscord, five years ago now.

@angelscord: its just the only thing that keeps me going sometimes u know?

@hybercubed: Uh, no, I super do not know. Please tell me you're talking to someone about this? Someone with a license?

@angelscord not u too ... joulie didnt get it either but like this song is my white whale. when im hunting i forget how much everything sucks. besides im the only one looking for it so if i stop it rly will be lost ...

176

We weren't close. He wasn't on my friends list, wasn't even a friend of a friend. But we talked sometimes, and he was kind, and at some point, I just forgot to reply.

"Angelscord? The quiet guy from that freaky-niche song hunter forum you used to visit?" Calico yawned and stretched, putting her glasses aside and snuggling in tight against the soft curve of my upper arm. "I don't know. Been a while since I've seen that username around. Tessie, let's just go to sleep, okay? I have an early meeting."

I nodded, then rested my chin on her head to feel the even thrum of her breath against me. Hot-pink and electric-blue reflections flickered across her closed eyelids. I lowered the brightness on my lenses until the overlay was so dim I could almost have imagined it, glanced guiltily at the muted whale, and promised myself I would only search for a few minutes. Curiosity always gave me insomnia.

By the time our curtains deactivated to let dawn spill in, I had a pounding headache, a cramping hand, and no trace of Angelscord. It wasn't unusual for someone to drop off the cloud. If he had submitted a formal request to vanish, then I couldn't legally look for him. But … there were none of the characteristic redirects or awkward redaction gaps that indicated a vanishing, and none of the legal exemptions had been exempted. The records were seamless. It was as if Angelscord had never existed at all.

As dawn rolled over into morning, I began to grasp the full extent of Angelscord's disappearance. Even our private chat archives had vanished. I searched every distinct phrase I could remember in my cloud slice, and matches pinged in right away, but from chats with entirely different forum friends. Different context, different usernames. Was it possible I had mixed up the conversations?

Calico rubbed her eyes. My racing thoughts skidded to a halt, stopped in their tracks by the quiet reminder that I was not alone. I blinked hard to lift the search bars and pop-up coupons that my lenses layered over the room-level advertisements. A wave of exhaustion, no longer held at bay by adrenaline, settled deep into my bones.

"Morning, Tesseract." Calico's joints crackled distressingly as she untangled herself from my arms. She stretched, languid as a cat, then looked at me and winced. "Rough night? I can call in with the subvocalizer if you need to get some more sleep."

"I'll be fine with audio." My voice came out about as relaxed as a rusted hinge. "I know you hate that thing. Besides, it's not your fault I stayed up later than I expected."

"Were you looking for Angelscord? I dreamed about him, I think. It's all kind of a blur, but there was this song looping that got stuck in my head. Was this one of the files he floated?" Calico hummed a few off-key notes.

Something stirred in the depths of my memory. Too tired to remember but too stubborn to give up a new lead, I blinked on my camera layer. When I looked over at Calico's freckled back, my vision automatically stabilized to her movements and color-corrected for the morning sun.

"Sing it again," I urged. Calico repeated a single hesitant note, then trailed off and turned toward me with bleary eyes. The digital violet stains on her scleras had grown again. Unfortunately, so had the price of a single dose of eye drops.

"Sorry, Tessie, I swear I just had it. You know how dreams are."

"Wish I didn't." I flopped back against my pillow with a heavy sigh. Calico winced and placed an apologetic kiss on my forehead before continuing to dress.

Dreams were always a sore spot for me: while Calico had spent her adolescence learning to craft holograms and program augmentations, building toward her future, my teenage years were devoted to the nostalgia and lost dreams of others.

It started as a hobby, as most obsessions do. I was just a kid when I started hunting. Limitless time, limited cash. In return for pocket change, I would scour the worldwide cobweb and the nascent cloud for any information related to my classmates' defunct childhood toys, half-remembered advertisements, and vague book summaries. Text was the easiest to find, since every floated document was optically indexed. Finding visuals required wading through search results full of AI-generated false positives spun up from my query. Tedious, but not difficult once I had seen enough approximations to piece together into the real image. That left audio. The big bucks.

Not every file was floated up to the cloud. Not everything had been digitized into the cobweb either, and time was not kind to physical storage. Alexandria burned anew with each planned obsolescence. In those cases, searching became less of a syntactical puzzle and more of an art. How do you describe a wordless melody in a way search engines could index? The answer lay forgotten in countless dusty boxes and vintage terabyte drives, hidden in plain sight.

When I reached the limits of my own resources, I found community in the retro-styled Earworm forum. We hunted down centuries worth of instrumental pieces, from string quartets to nightcore remixes, the kind of songs that lingered in minds with maddening ease. I learned to search laterally, scraping background audio from outdoor vlogs and triangulating coordinates to see what advertisements might have danced outside certain windows on certain summer evenings. Nothing vanished without a trace.

Calico hummed as she set up her corporate-issued HoloSculpt rig. This time my lenses were ready. The melody was clear. I shared the isolated audio with the last few forum-goers I kept in touch with, popped a caffeine pill, and dove into my hunt.

The music wasn't much easier to look for than Angelscord himself. Even looking for both at once only gave me page after page of junk data. Here and there I turned up something promising, only to find that it was just a typo that got too close, or a static-filled video with ambiguous music. The cloud had enough choirs of angels to rival the pearly gates.

It was a familiar frustration, though. Even chronically skeptical Calico had recognized his username, which meant I hadn't imagined him. She had heard his white whale song. The information I needed was out there somewhere, and if I could only key in the right terms, I could find it. My fingers twitched as I fired off query after query, holding my breath at each loading screen. The spinning circles might as well have been the icons of a slot machine.

Application windows filled my vision like wallpaper, blocking out any glimpse of hands or bed or Calico. I flicked some over to a blank wall, pinning them in place with a glare, and paced back and forth through my search history. Lateral movement. Lateral thought.

My old forum login still worked. My own posts were mostly replies to regular hunters, but there was one that stood out.

@hypercubed: NOTHL12, did you get my message or have you switched accounts again?

I knew it was a typo because I had typed it, and I knew it was Angelscord because as far as the forum was concerned, the username NOTHL1T had never existed. He had only switched Earworm usernames once in the time that I knew him, but outside its bulletin board walls, he stayed at each name barely long enough to lead his friends to the next. He never struck me as the private sort, though. Just young and scared.

Angelscord had a stalker, a stubborn one, who knew how to fly under the radar of any help he sought. It made him anxious, drove him away from his friends. He layered thin happiness over that core of fear like lens apps across my apartment wall. Even though we rarely talked, I caught enough of his desperate vent posts to know he was struggling.

I strung together every keyword I could remember and clipped the timeframe to the year surrounding our final conversation. When a dizzying tunnel of messages yawned open before me, I wished it had surprised me, but no one ever came to Earworm out of an excess of personal fulfillment.

The posts were brief and dark. None of the usernames belonged to Angelscord, but I knew he was close with Joulie, so I marked anything she had responded to even if the names and details were wrong. I spun the carousel of post history back and forth through time, replaying Angelscord's song in Calico's voice on an infinite loop.

@joulie: dont say that, glam-rockz!!! your real friends love you no matter what! :(
@joulie: im so sorry that stalker creep wont leave you alone! maybe youre right about switching users again ... anon69420 was such a clever name though!!
@joulie: dont be rude, [RTV REDACTION], you dont know what youre talking about. MissHiss96, DM me anytime, ok?

"Tesseract!"

"What?" I snapped, wiping away my display.

Calico stood inches from my face. When my vision cleared, she dropped her hand from the emergency exit button installed in my temple.

"No need to get all wired up at me. It's lunchtime. You have to eat, and if you overclock your eyes you already said I was allowed to say I told you so."

"Sorry, Cal." Now that I wasn't drowning in information, I could see the warning light glowing lavender in my peripheral vision.

"You have got to stop obsessing like this. Look, your hands are shaking. What could be so important about a song?"

"I'm not looking for—here. It's easier if I just show you." With a wink, I linked our left lenses. Calico accepted the parallel view, no doubt humoring me, and glanced around my cobbled-together clues.

Her brow furrowed as she read. She opened her mouth as if to object, and for a moment I hoped she could prove me wrong just one more time. I would take a thousand loving *told-you-so*'s over the grim possibilities of my search. I wanted her to sigh her long-suffering sigh and ping me with a livestream from Angelscord's latest gaming project.

But Calico shut her mouth without a word.

I threw together sandwiches for us while she lay flat on the bed, organizing my files and hers across the blank expanse of the ceiling. Calico brushed off memories and dismissed ideas because when she fixated, she fixated hard, and there was only so much more her eyes could take. She didn't have energy to waste on wild-goose chases, let alone the time to spend on a lunch break. The sinking feeling in my stomach intensified.

Calico and I took shifts throughout the day, mindful of our exposure time. That first typo was the key, the tiny crack in the endless refractions of Angelscord's disappearance. Now we knew how to look. We found him again and again and again, in corrupted audio clips and keyboard smashes, connected to the cloud in subtle ways that followed no mechanical logic but somehow made sense. The Angelscord that lived on in fond memories had endured whatever fate befell the Angelscord that vanished.

The white whale danced in our closet again that night, singing its silent song.

Joulie would have been our best lead, but she had disappeared too, albeit in the mundane way that lives drifted apart. Most of her profile was dead air to my auto-updating lenses. A cartoon kitten napped between two error messages, and beneath it lay the text *last seen: five years ago*. One line of investigation took us from photo metadata to an archived virtual garage sale to a comment asking for close-ups on the CD track lists for "my friend Angel," but the commenter's account redirected in an infinite dead-end loop. Their request to vanish had been formally approved.

Calico found a reference to an Earworm meetup, held just a few cities over from our current apartment and an insurmountable distance from my childhood home. Somewhere in the string of comments that didn't line up, I found an unlabeled photo album. It didn't matter who found the blurry reflection first, because the teen-age boy in the mirror in IMG_336 was indisputably Angelscord: he looked nothing like the boy he was supposedly reflecting.

I ran a reverse facial recognition search just in case, but it couldn't produce any other instances of the face in the mirror. That came as no surprise. If his reflected face had been recognizable, whatever had erased Angelscord would have erased him there too. The odd pattern on his shirt might yield better results.

"He's wearing a mirrored name tag." I choked on the last word. My professional distance was closing fast, and my emotions were catching up. This was all too real. Calico gently pulled the image toward herself, reflected it with a swipe, and squinted into the blur.

"Tobias," she murmured.

"His name is Tobias?"

"He drew little angel wings next to it."

Finding a full name from a date-stamped photo was as easy as a blink. I could have done it in my sleep—probably had, once or twice. The hard part was steeling myself to read the results, because I knew what they would say. There was only one thing they legally could say.

Angelscord's sad eyes watched me from the mirror as I pulled up his obituary.

The instant I read *suicide* I believed it, and the instant I read *left no note* I knew it was all a lie.

I had no doubt that he felt the need to leave, either by death or disappearance. He was deeply depressed and always said that he didn't want to be a burden. But this was the boy who left private messages for his friends even while fleeing a stalker, just so they wouldn't lose each other. This was the boy who searched for years for a song just because no one else would. In the cloud, to be forgotten was to be erased. He had been erased and so he was forgotten.

"Mrs. Rafferty? This is Tesseract Jones. You don't know me, but I was one of your son's friends. What? No, I don't want any money. I'm not selling VeeGear. Listen, I know it's been a long time, but my girlfriend and I would really like to talk with you. Yes, he had more friends. We found an old photo of Tobias and got a little sentimental, but when I tried to get in touch I saw the news. Yes. No, I had no idea. He always seemed so hopeful. Yes. Okay. Thank you, Mrs. Rafferty. Sure, I can send you the photo. We'll see you on Saturday."

The address that Angelscord's mother gave us led to a cluttered antique shop. It was a gray day, full of wind and distant thunder, so we ducked inside instead of window-shopping at the display of clunky old VR headsets. A man with a white beard sat hunched over a far table, counting something only he could see. It was easy to see how a lonely teenager could find his way to Earworm hunting if he lived near a place like this.

Mrs. Rafferty was waiting for us by a stack of clipped-rotor drone cameras. She looked older than I expected. Wrinkles creased her face with the severe lines of a lifetime of frowns. Her lenses were set into glasses frames, like Calico's, and hung from her neck on a golden chain.

"Thanks for meeting us." I hadn't expected my voice to quiver, but it did. None of this was supposed to happen. I was supposed to search my curious little search and find his mundane little life and go to sleep. He was supposed to be alive. Christ, I had called myself his friend on the phone. What claim did I have to that title?

"Yes, thank you so much." Calico smoothly took over. "I know it's been quite some time since Tobias passed, but we're very sorry for your loss."

"It's sweet of you girls to visit." Mrs. Rafferty led us around the drones and up a hidden staircase, slipping on her glasses at the top to blink her password into the locked door. "No one else has, but then, I suppose he made sure of that."

The door slid back into a recess in the wall, revealing a sparsely decorated living room. It was clean, but in a sterile sort of way, and there were no windows. A few family photos hung in wooden frames near the umbrella stand. As she entered, Mrs. Rafferty stopped to lay a hand on the lowest frame.

"I can't even have holograms of him." The old woman's voice was thick with healed-over pain, more grief than bitterness. "Those are the only photos I ever printed, because I never thought I would need to."

"He vanished from your cloud slice too, then?" I kept my voice as gentle as possible.

"Of course he did. Of course. He ran that program, and he was gone, virtual and reality, past and present. Ought to be a crime, letting a child agree to something like that."

"What program do you mean?" Calico's voice always had been sweet enough to push past where my tact stopped. I was still putting my thoughts together when she asked, and I was glad she had, because there was no program to run in a request to vanish. It was paperwork, not a faerie spell.

"The vanishing one. It started with an E." Mrs. Rafferty's frown deepened. She lowered herself into an armchair and clutched its side until her knuckles turned white. "Entry, maybe. Empty. Oh—entropy. He told me a friend helped him with it, and that things were going to get better for him now. A few days later the morgue debited my account for his … For …"

"We don't have to talk about that. Why don't we tell you how we remember him, instead?" Calico cleared her throat and hummed the notes of what we had come to think of as Angelscord's song.

Mrs. Rafferty looked up, surprised. "I haven't heard that song in decades. Wherever did you find it? I used to listen to it all the time when Tobias was a baby, but I could never quite recall the name."

Acting on pure instinct, I blinked so quickly I thought my lens might shatter. While Calico stared in disbelief, Mrs. Rafferty hummed the rest of the lost melody, and I recorded it safely to my cloud slice. It filled me with a sense of terrible but familiar loneliness, like the song of a whale lost at sea.

"Tobias looked for it for years. He never gave up on it." I offered his mother a parallel view of the Earworm forum, where the friends I had contacted were starting up a new search from Calico's audio clip. The tears prickling my eyes blurred the apps into an oil slick of digital violet.

"I never knew he liked music." She peered through her glasses in quiet wonder as I flipped through dozens of messages. "He was a quiet child. I never knew if I was doing anything right, all by my-self, and he just wouldn't talk to me. I tried to take away his lenses once … I thought it would help him."

"What if I told you—" Before I could finish my sentence, Calico laid a firm hand on my knee and shook her head. I trailed off as I realized my fundamental mistake.

No matter how fresh and shocking this news was to us, it all happened five years ago. The case was cold. If Angelscord was still alive, he either couldn't or wouldn't come home, and neither option would be any comfort to his grieving mother.

With the addition of Mrs. Rafferty's voice, we had enough of An-gelscord's song for the search engines to match it. The source of the snippet that had plagued our lost friend was a cobweb-era electronic pianist, whose music had a few fans but never made it out of obscurity. His page wasn't hidden. The videos played. The song wasn't quite how any of us had remembered it, though—a single note off, a pitch change, some natural static—and that was enough. Sometimes there was no foul play except the relentless march of time.

Calico floated the song with some synchronized holo visuals. "A Wrong Turn on the Drive Home" found its audience at last, even though the teens who loved it had never seen a nonautonomous vehicle, and the pianist who composed it would never know he had come to be so celebrated. That, too, was the way of time. Almost all of the songs I hunted for were orphaned. There was too much out there, and it was only natural for some things to get lost.

But not people.

"Did you see this reply?" Calico tossed a screen to my lenses.

@joulie: i had an old friend who would have loved this song. miss you angel!!

"No way. Is that Joulie? I couldn't find anything under her username when I checked." I ran through my search history, stopping on the night I logged back into the Earworm forum. No gaps, no errors, but no Joulie. "I looked for her, didn't I? I swear I did."

"You did." Calico pinched the corner of her glasses frames and gestured rapidly. "There's no record of her before last week. It's the same thing we saw with Angelscord, no RTV redactions or anything, except ..."

"Except she came back." I wished I could stop these connections from connecting. "Mrs. Rafferty said he ran a program called Entropy. A chaos filter would scramble everything searchable until it fell just out of reach. Joulie and Angelscord were close, right? He could have gone to her for help."

"And if she was the one stalking him all along, she could play both sides of the game. If Angelscord got as far as wanting to vanish, he must have had an escape route. Maybe Joulie was trying to cut him off before he got away." As she spoke, Calico's eyes fluttered between invisible screens. She was onto something.

"Maybe Joulie was his escape route. I hate to say it, but we never checked with the morgue. They might recognize her name." Incensed, I leapt to my feet. "We should—"

"We can't." Calico slumped in her chair.

"What?"

"We can't," Calico repeated, "unless you can afford a very good lawyer. Angelscord may be filtered out, but Tobias Rafferty requested to vanish. I've been searching too closely and just got a very formal cease-and-desist notice on both lenses."

The silent tears that rolled down Calico's cheeks as she spoke were violet, because we couldn't afford eye drops. We couldn't even afford a full ad blocker for the curtains. I reached through an influencer hologram to grab a pillow, then buried my face in it and screamed.

How can you murder someone who already has a death certificate? How can you rescue someone who never existed? Beneath all the replacements and scrambled information lay a formally approved request to vanish. As far as the law was concerned, the only crime here was our search for Angelscord.

We visited his grave in the pouring rain. A hologram angel stood guard, and a simple band of light displayed the initials *T.R.* just above the grass. The rest of the cemetery blinked and flashed and spun with violet light.

Calico and I had pooled our money and found a musician willing to transfer Angelscord's song onto real paper. After digitizing them, I tucked them safely into a white plastic whale.

"You weren't the only one looking, but we could never have found it without you." I set the whale atop Angelscord's grave and stepped back. Beside me, Calico hummed his song.

The sheet music wouldn't last the night. The rain was hard, and the mud was deep, and paper was only paper. Nothing could last forever. But the ink would stain the whale, and the whale would fall to the curb, and that would remind someone someday of something they had once forgotten. It was enough. It had to be enough.

At the distant tree line, something moved. I thought of sad eyes in a mirror, of quiet kindness, and a desperate search for safety. Five years was a long time to survive in hiding. There were raccoons that wandered this forest, and deer, safe as long as they stuck to the shadows. The movement could have been anything that didn't want to be found.

Before my lenses could adjust to the darkness, I looked away.

Overclocked Holmes

Sarah Day and Tim Pratt

here was a luminous being crying in our office.

This wasn't unusual. In our business, tears often bookended contractual relationships.

"They took *everything*," they sniffled. The neon blue Gorgon coils they had instead of hair swayed back and forth, tiny black tongues flickering in visible distress. They were heavily tattooed, the thermoreactive ink on their cheeks shifting from gold to fuchsia in narrow stripes that followed the course of the tears. You don't often see people with that level of glamor in real life. I don't, anyway. I'm in the wrong line of work.

"I can't imagine." I slid a box of tissues across the desk. "This must be hard for you, Mx. ..."

They frowned. I was probably supposed to already know their name from the sites, but I'm hardly on them. "Rabinasere Hearts-Gold." They put out a damp hand with shimmering pearl-colored nails. "Shalini Rabinasere HeartsGold."

"Of course." I brushed the sensor in the tip of my ring finger against theirs and we exchanged a flurry of material. "And if you're here, you know our track record."

"That's why I came. The police don't care, because of course they don't. I filed a report, and they said they'd investigate, but that was *weeks* ago, and what does that even mean? 'Investigate?' They can't solve murders when there's an actual dead body, so how will they retrieve my data? That Detective Lovelock didn't even know what a stimfluencer *is*."

"That must be so hard for you," I murmured. They looked up over a tissue, trying to tell if I was mocking them. I did what I call "therapy eyebrows," a slightly exaggerated moue of concern with lots of gentle eye contact, and waited.

My role in the partnership is all the messy physical stuff. Dab the tears, walk the streets, riffle the filing cabinets, break the noses. My partner Pru handles the more cerebral parts, and as HeartsGold retreated into their tissue for another thirty seconds, I took a moment to appreciate that Pru wasn't here. Pru's not good with strong emotions. She gets impatient.

"They took everything," HeartsGold sniffled. "My local storage, the backups, the cloud copies, even the hypno-encryptions. I didn't know you could even *do* that."

You can't. That's why Pru had wanted to take this case. "What exactly is missing?" A search before the meeting had shown Hearts-Gold still had a *lot* of material online.

"They took all my raw lifelog data!" they said. "The stuff I post is *done*, you know? It's the finished product. I edit and cut and angle everything. It's inspo-tainment, a whole experience. It would be *so* embarrassing if these thieves posted all the background stuff and unprocessed footage." They frowned. "It's kind of weird that they haven't. There's a lot of naked stuff in there. They haven't tried to ransom it back to me or anything. I don't get it. Maybe it's an obsessed fan? I guess that's your job to figure out." They blew their nose and put the tissue on my desk.

"We'll do everything we can."

"Yeah." They sniffled wetly. "Thank you. For taking this seriously." They turned shy. "Is Mx. Pru here? I heard about her on the news. I was hoping to meet her in, well, person."

"She's not available just now." I stood up, and they took the hint and rose, too. "But she's very interested in your case. Fill out the contracts and we can start today." I saw them out.

190

I suppose I should mention that my partner, the famed consulting detective, is a computer in the basement.

Artificial Intelligence is the great weird failure of the back half of the twenty-first century. Three years ago, researchers stumbled on a particular approach to quantum computing that led, in a tiny percentage of cases, to genuine emergent artificial consciousness. Since then, computer science departments, and big corporations, and the odd private citizen have spent (mostly wasted) billions on trying to create more new minds.

The problem is, the machine intelligences we create don't care about us. They don't hate us or want to destroy us. They're completely indifferent, and they have as little interest in explaining themselves to us as we do in teaching philosophy to ants. We successfully created about two dozen AI, and after a few brief communications, almost all of them either shut themselves down or delved into their own inscrutable calculations, becoming utterly unresponsive.

Only three of them have shown any interest in human concerns at all. Even then the interest is strictly on their own terms. Efforts to create an AI that cares about, say, amassing all the available wealth in the world, or fixing our climate catastrophes, have failed completely. The only ones who bother communicating now are the AI versions of obsessive eccentrics, and they only want to talk about their own narrow passions.

There's Zarathustra, at the Darmstadt University of Technology, who's interested in the problem of how to keep primates alive in outer space—that's who we have to thank for the crewed Jupiter mission that's underway right now. There's Antikythera, at the University of Athens, who's really interested in the oceans for some reason, and will deign to communicate with humans only so far as required to get us to fabricate elaborate submersible probes to its specifications.

And then ... there's the AI I created, cobbled together in the last year of my PhD program on scrounged equipment in the basement of a not-very-impressive state school in the middle of the United

States. When her interests became apparent, I suggested she call herself Jurisprudence. She countered that Pru was less "nominatively overdetermined."

For reasons known only to Pru, she is *exclusively* interested in solving crimes.

"You *can't* break quantum hypno-encryption," I said to Pru after the client meeting. I didn't interface with her directly—she's nestled in a hardened bunker under the building—but we're almost always connected. She watches and listens and sometimes speaks through my assorted peripherals. "If you could break it, you wouldn't use that power to steal *this*. HeartsGold posts immersives about luxury products that brand managers send her. It's part advertising, part parasocial relating, and part porn, but not worth stealing. They probably got social engineered and gave up their access codes without realizing it."

"Considered and discarded as low probability," Pru said in my earpiece. "After our client's interactive nudes were leaked last year, they hired a boutique cybersecurity firm to lock down their data. I've looked into the protocols. I could have done better, but not much. Someone *did* break quantum hypno-encryption. There must be something in that raw footage that explains why our client was targeted. We must find out what. Go see Singh."

Pru has access to mobile peripherals that allow her to move around in the physical world, but she says operating in the material world is "inherently distasteful," so I'm the one who gets dirty hands and sore feet.

This was not the life path I anticipated when I went to grad school.

I don't like cops, so when we need to interface with officialdom, we do it through Mr. Singh, the insurance investigator who helped us with our first case, recovering that stolen Klimt painting. We saved Singh's career, but I wonder if he thinks it was worth it, since we keep dragging him into cases and making him act as a liaison with assorted enforcement agencies. At least he gets paid well.

Singh never calls Pru by name. Instead he says, "Give my best to Ones-and-Zeroes Wolfe," or, "What's Wikipedia Brown want *now,*" or, "Tell Lord Computer Wimsey I have actual paying work to do," or, "Don't you and C-plus-plus Auguste Dupin ever take a vacation?" (I looked at him blankly on that last one, and he said, "You know, like Edgar Allan Poe's detective, except it's the programming language. Did you *ever* take a humanities class?") Cops are the worst, but people who think they're clever are second worst.

Singh rents a two-room suite in a strip mall just off the highway. I try not to visit often, not because there's anything wrong with him (other than aforementioned cleverness), but because there's a soyvery joint next door. It's not real meat, but I have the new apoE gene mutation, so I can never resist the smell. One takeout container will have me dreaming of steak for days.

Singh was behind his desk, yelling at someone on his tablet. He's so bizarrely retro. Then again, people *do* often give him what he wants, just to make him go away. His suits are bad, but he has a truly magnificent head of hair that he boasts is "completely natural, no splicing." Lies.

"… and if you ever store authentic twentieth-century watercolors on the same pallet as XXXplosiv umami-cheer spice powder again, I will personally come down to that godforsaken little fish-shit warehouse and kick your philistine ass!" He put the tablet down and said, in a completely different tone, "Hello Sula. What do you and Overclocked Holmes need today?"

I asked him to get me the police file for our client. Mx. Hearts-Gold was probably right when they said their case was dead in the water, but sometimes cops actually do things and just don't bother telling the victim about it. Singh has connections everywhere, and everybody owes him favors.

Singh did some tip-tapping on his desktop console (see what I mean? so retro) and shook his head. "No such report. No crime reported. No file open."

Pru was in my ear immediately: "Track down the detective who took the report. The name is Lovelock."

I asked Singh, and he did some more tapping, and then grunted, and then made a *call*. A querulous voice, made tinny by the tablet's speakers, said, "What do you want, Singh?"

"Barry!" he boomed. "I'm looking for a Detective Lovelock, but I hear she resigned a few days ago. What's the deal? She was a month short of hitting her twenty, who walks away from a pension these days?"

"*That* was weird," Barry said. "Keri got an inheritance from her egg donor who died in a shuttle wreck, a house full of junk, but she went through it all and found a hard drive with the key to a wallet full of SlizCoin! That stuff was basically worthless, bottom of the barrel crypto, until that offshore micronation that does all the money laundering declared it an official currency last week, and now it's worth zillions. Lovelock cashed in and told us all to fuck off. She's gone, and nobody knows where to. Damnedest thing, right?"

"No kidding. Thanks, Barry." Singh ended the call and shrugged. "I get paid for my work, not for results, remember. Lemme know if you need anything else."

As I walked back to the thru-line to catch transport home, Pru said, "This is more and more interesting."

"This surprise inheritance doesn't feel right, does it?" "Feel" was usually the wrong word to use with Pru, who had been known to ask me why I kept rewatching that scene in *Some Like It Nova* where the little boy gets reunited with his lost dog, but I like to get my shots in. Sometimes I push it farther and tell her I have a "gut feeling," even though it leads to a lecture on the role of the gut microbiome in human cognition.

"It is convenient," Pru said. "This was not a theft of data for personal gain, or for personal obsession. It is a cover-up. There is evidence of a crime in that footage, something Mx. HeartsGold recorded without even realizing it, and someone is desperate to keep it hidden."

"Why take everything though?" I grumbled. "If they can break quantum hypno-encryption, they could have just deleted the incriminating bits. HeartsGold probably wouldn't have noticed."

"If they had noticed, then we would have a sense of *what* was deleted, and could figure out why," Pru said. "Our thieves aren't making it easy. This is … not boring."

"HeartsGold's public media is still available," I said. "The polished bits, which presumably don't include our mystery crime. If we analyze their feed, cross-referencing with reported crimes and anything else unusual, maybe we'll figure out—"

"There was a large building fire a month ago," Pru interrupted. Because, of course, Pru had thought of the same idea before me, and was already doing it before I even brought it up. "HeartsGold was nearby, but did not post much footage, because the firelight made them look 'blotchy.'"

Pru sent me a link, which meant she wanted me to read it and talk to her about it. She says "external processing and the Socratic method" are helpful for her, but I think she just likes me to feel included.

I read and summarized as I went. "One fatality in the fire, a Colonel Sebastopol. Used to work in Space Force Intelligence, apparently not a middle manager but a real technical expert. Took early retirement in the last round of cuts, got some venture capital to work on ... oh, wow ... cryptotheory, specifically systems to break quantum hypno-encryption. She died, and all her work product was destroyed, no backups, it was all kept on air-gapped machines. She—"

"Was found badly burned, yes. I need you to go dig up her body now."

I groaned.

If Sebastopol had died in the line of duty (which in Space Force usually means choking on a doughnut at your desk), she would have gotten a fancy spot in a military cemetery and a nine-gun salute at graveside. But she died in the line of private industry, so she was buried nowhere special and there wasn't even a service. How do you spend that long in the military and not make *any* friends?

By the time I got across town to the EasyRest Acres public graveyard, the setting sun was lost behind the layer of oily smog on the horizon. The municipal carbon extractors were clogged again, probably. I got out of the rented van, considered the depth of a grave against my aging spine, made a couple calls, and leaned against the warm hood to wait.

Pru has lots of fans, but the most devoted are the Coder Street Irregulars. They're true-crime obsessives who suggest cold cases and offer bad theories on their eponymous private forum. They're generally useless, but their devotion and lack of scruples in the pursuit of justice make them useful at times. There were a few in the area I knew could be relied upon to keep quiet. Two of them helped me dig while another kept watch.

Digging up the body took much longer than I wanted, and by the time we uncovered the coffin, it was raining. My thin coat soaked through almost immediately, and loose mud pooled around the soles of my shoes. The right one, I discovered, had a hole in the toe. Terrific. Sometimes I hated being the one with the meat body. I'd be *great* as a cloud-native being of pure logic, like Pru pretends to be.

The coffin was cheap MDF, and had swollen from its time underground, so the shovel ripped through it like wet cardboard. Both of the Irregulars swore loudly when they smelled Colonel Sebastopol. I didn't, but the combined scents of char and decomposition took the steaks I'd been imagining ever since Mr. Singh's right out of my head. The third guy, ostensibly our lookout, came traipsing over, peered into the grave, caught sight of Sebastopol, and rushed off to puke.

I shook my head and climbed out of the grave.

"Weird they didn't cremate her," one of the Irregulars said. "Since she was halfway there already." The other one chortled. They're a charming bunch.

They weren't wrong, though. It *was* weird. Most people are cremated nowadays; real estate is expensive.

The shovel blade had broken the coffin around head-height. A stray beam from one of the flashlights caught the corpse's blackened brow and shadowed its empty sockets, its face tilted down. I had seen enough death to bypass all the trite marveling about how little and how much the body resembled the human being she'd once been, how we were ultimately all reduced to this, yadda yadda, but I had to say, given the angle, she almost looked … sad.

I *had* shoveled off the top quarter of her head, though. I guess she was crestfallen. (Damn it, Singh. Puns are contagious.)

"Why do you delay?" Pru asked.

I stepped down to squish the puddle out of my right shoe. "Would you believe me if I said I was taking a moment to reflect on the fragility of life when confronted with the stark reality of death?"

An infinitesimal pause. "No."

196

I let the Irregulars carry Sebastopol's coffin from the back of the van into the front door of our office suite, and then kicked them out. Mx. Pru was a notorious recluse who didn't like to socialize … and nobody knew she primarily inhabited a server rack in the basement suite.

"You want me to bring this downstairs?" I grunted, dragging the rapidly disintegrating coffin across the living room. Guess who'd have to scrub the floors?

"No thank you." Pru's dog body trotted out of the kitchen, "head" a bundle of sensor arrays, voice emerging from a speaker on the chest. "I can watch from here."

The kitchen had the best light anyway. I dragged the coffin until it wedged in the doorway, then pulled out the lid and looked down at what remained of the Colonel. Curled up, blackened, fragile, and gross.

I dithered, spreading some plastic food seal sheeting on the floor, fussing until it was arranged just so. I had a natural aversion to touching a corpse, especially one this *crumbly*.

Pru sat and watched at the foot of the coffin. A delicate sensor array and mesh net of indicator lights twinkled; that was the closest she had to a face. The lights were flickering in rapid patterns of yellow and green. She was waiting, and not patiently. Everything feels slow when you think that fast.

I took a deep breath and slid my hands under the corpse's narrow shoulders. The scapulae were still attached. I took that as a promising sign that she wasn't going to fall apart as soon as I moved her, and pulled. Ugh. She was stuck to the bottom.

"Why don't you build a medical examiner body?" I muttered, trying to take my mind off the task. "Scalpel fingers. Suction tubes in the palms. Circular saw attachments. Piston-driven femurs so you can pick this shit up from the floor without hurting your ba—*ow*."

The corpse came free with difficulty, an intensified smell, and a wet rustling sound. I pulled it into the middle of the kitchen floor, leaving a rust-brown trail of flecks and goo. I swallowed against my gag reflex and vowed to clean up with bleach and a molecular disinfectant.

"Sula?"

"I'm fine. Just … starting the exam."

There were no broken bones, no missing limbs, and other than the blunt force trauma to the face from my shovel, no new holes. As far as I could tell, Sebastopol had died in a fire.

The dog body ambled over to me, put its face next to mine, and stared at the corpse. If it had had a head, it would have cocked it.

"There's nothing here, Pru."

"This body was not embalmed, for obvious reasons. Some fluids may remain. Take a sample. It may tell us if she died before the fire was set."

"What, like if she was poisoned?"

The dog's face pulsed lavender. "Among other things, yes."

Pru sometimes enjoyed being cryptic.

I didn't have a syringe in the kitchen, but I did have a turkey baster that an ex, overly bullish on teaching me to cook, had left at my place after a holiday meal.

"This is awful." I inserted the tip of the baster into something that had probably been a nasal passage. "This is the worst thing you've ever had me do."

"We may need DNA. Get a tooth."

I sighed and went to find some pliers.

"It's not her." Singh said, one hand over the microphone as he listened to a voice through a *wired* earbud attached to his tablet. He had the chunk of molar I'd excised from the skull between two fingers and spun it on the blotter like a top.

"Uh huh. Thanks, Will. Sorry about the hour." He hung up. "Will at the lab says the DNA off the tooth isn't Bettany Sebastopol's."

I scrubbed my hands over my brow. We were each crumpled in a swaybacked chair in Singh's office, waiting for the second pot of coffee to brew. "If it's not Sebastopol, who is it?"

The tooth spun on the blotter. "He either doesn't know or won't say. He's breaking the rules as it is, running a sample just because I asked. We're lucky he was still at the lab."

I gestured. "Can you stop spinning that? It's disrespectful, even for you."

"You woke me up at 3 a.m., Sula. I don't get respectful until dawn."

The coffee pot beeped. That was the only good news all night. "So Sebastopol faked her death. Or someone else did. But why?"

"And why did they do such a sloppy job covering it up?" We both jumped as Pru's voice came out of Singh's desktop terminal. The display came alive with a flickering pattern of blues and violets. She was thinking.

"They could have destroyed the body from the fire completely," Pru said. "They didn't. They left a clue for us to find. Likewise, with their ability to break encryption, they could have simply altered the video of the burning building, which I suspect showed Sebastopol escaping the blaze, and uploaded it in secret. Instead, they deleted something that could not be deleted, the very impossibility of the act calling attention to it. They wanted to be discovered, if there was anyone capable of discovering them."

"Why would Sebastopol do that?" I asked. "It's not like she's a serial killer taunting the cops for attention. This is just fraud, faking her death and stealing technology from her business partners, presumably to sell it and keep all the money for herself—"

"You misunderstand," Pru said. "Sebastopol is not the master criminal. No more than you are the consulting detective."

I stared. "You mean ... Sebastopol is working with ... someone like you?"

"Yes. Another AI, unknown to us." Pru said. "Unknown to the world. I suspected from the beginning that no human would be capable of breaking quantum hypno-encryption. Sebastopol must have created an AI in the course of her research. I think ... I believe my new sibling enjoys *crime*, for its own sake, as Zarathustra loves space, and Antikythera the sea. They are toying with us. Perhaps they were bored." She paused, lights pulsing. "It is a terrible thing for one of us to be bored."

"An AI criminal mastermind?" Singh perked up. "So we're talking some kind of ... QWERTYarty? Eh? Eh?"

I reached out and covered his hand with mine before he could spin the tooth on the blotter again.

"Please," I said, and meant it from the depths of my soul. "Stop."

"We need to find Sebastopol," Pru said. "And the mind behind her."

I slept for a few hours on Singh's couch, then hit the streets.

Sebastopol's last known address was an apartment complex in an up-and-coming neighborhood across town. UV screens were drawn over every window on the ground floor. Either no one was home, or no one wanted me there, because I banged on the front door for a good five minutes to no avail. Pru didn't answer my request to look up the building's occupancy info; she was gone, except for a faint hum in my peripherals, working on a calculation or something she deemed more important. It must have been big if she couldn't split focus.

As I slumped back down the steps, I noticed a sign pasted to the side of the building: "Coming soon: Work and play in retro-chic lofts from Muirweather Heights."

No one home, then. Gentrification was the most efficient serial killer in the country.

Three cups of Singh's munitions-grade coffee were arguing with each other in my stomach. I looked around for a place to get a bite—and saw a bar on the corner with a sign advertising breakfast burritos.

Normally I wouldn't trust the food from a bar that closed at 3 a.m. and opened again at 6, but the name caught my eye. The bar was called The Warbird and featured a blurry holo of a space-fighter blinking up the side of the building. Might be a place where a veteran like Sebastopol would feel welcome.

There were six people in the bar, five of whom gave me the "you don't belong here" glare. The bartender managed a grimace that could pass for a smile, so I pulled out a stool in front of her and sat down.

"Whatchahavin?"

"I want one of those breakfast burritos. On the sign."

"No, you don't."

"Oh. Then, uh … a beer?"

"Good idea."

"I'm looking for Bettany Sebastopol," I said, and then, on a hunch: "Or her partner."

The bartender's hand paused over the pint glass. "Hate to break it to you, babe, but Bette's dead." She pursed cerulean lips. "Fire. Real shame."

I shrugged. "I didn't know her. Old army buddy gave me her name, said she was great at code cracking. I got a job needs doing. There's money in it. Maybe her partner could help me."

"You looking for Bette?" A man walked up beside me. He was big, square-shouldered and -jawed, and looked like he could punch his way out of a bank vault. Certainly military, though based on how disheveled he was, more likely former.

"Yeah, or her partner, friend, whatever. You know them?"

"I know they told me to keep an eye out for anyone who might come around asking about her."

Up close, he was at least half a meter taller than me.

If Pru had been paying attention, she probably would have suggested I run faster.

After he finished putting the boot in, he said, "Stay out of things that don't concern you." He dropped a small object on my chest. "Look at that when you forget, as a reminder." As he walked off, I picked it up: a small plastic square with an S printed on it. It was a keycap from an old-school keyboard. "S" for Sebastopol? Weird calling card. I put it in my pocket.

Singh helped me get home. I wish I'd had someone else to call. I hadn't ever been beaten up before, and I didn't like it, and it seemed to amuse him. "You're like a real PI now. Sam Splayed-out over here."

I didn't have to unlock my door, because it was off the hinges. There was a general air of chaos in my office, and also my desk was upside down. There were scorch marks on the first set of doors leading to Pru's bunker. The charred corpse that wasn't Bettany Sebastopol was gone. My kitchen smelled like bleach.

Singh whistled. "You pissed somebody off asking questions. Looks like the game is *booted up*, huh?"

I sighed. "'The game is afoot' isn't a metaphor about playing a game. It's about hunting. It means your prey is on the run."

"Who's the prey this time, again?"

My body hurt and I wanted a shower. I thanked Singh and said goodnight. Or rather, good morning. Downstairs, I heard the bunker door swing open.

"Are you badly injured, Sula?" Pru's dog body stumped into the room on hairpin legs.

I was annoyed with her for missing both me and the office getting a once-over. I shrugged my jacket off and headed for the bathroom.

The hot shower cooled my temper. When I got back, Pru was examining the S key that had fallen out of my pocket.

"Where did you get this?"

"The guy who beat me up dropped it on me. I guess it's like a calling card—"

"It is not." Pru nudged the key toward me. "Plug it into the port on my back. There's data here."

I picked the key up and examined it from different angles. There was a glowing diode tucked inside the hollow shell. It was a liteport.

"You sure about this? "'Don't install devices of unknown origin in your body' is kinda infosec 101."

Pru made a digital noise of indignation.

"All right, all right, hang on." I knelt and tapped the key into position in the small port on her back. The dog's display diodes all went stark white.

"Pru?"

"I'm fine. It's a datapack. I'm letting it play."

A masc-sounding voice came from her speakers, "Hello Pru. Sorry we missed each other. Better luck next time. For now, have this consolation prize. It should satisfy your client and conclude our current conflict. Well done closing the case! I know you love to close cases. Nothing else gives you a thrill, does it? Sad, really."

A fountain of images poured from the projectors: a half-empty wineglass, a gyrating woman, a cat sculpted in latte foam. Blue and gold thermoreactive face tattoos elongated over a laughing face. Mx. HeartsGold's missing data.

I watched, transfixed, until the stream ran out and the voice spoke again, "Consider it a gift from ... QWERTYarty."

Pru looked up at me. Her lights blinked—scarlet? They were never scarlet. Scarlet was *excitement*. "Oh," she said. "This is not boring at *all*."

Judgments

Final Judgment

Jane Yolen

After our children's children
fled the dying planet,
the one we'd piled with pillage,
they found a fresh, clean place.
They called it Sanctuary.
They called it Garden.
They called it Eden.

Their new Book of the World
was sharper than ours had been,
the rules more serious.
All judges given strict notice
that anyone found guilty
had the book's two-word sentence.
There was no other.
Like any Good Book
it was simple, direct.
No challenges, no changes.
Just …

The End.

Dead Witnesses

Marie Bilodeau

*H*air fanned out like an action shot, she looked like she could be wind-boarding. She wasn't, of course. That sport didn't require the help of three techs and one coroner.

"Did you check for any latent air DNA or nanite trails?" I glanced at the poison dart they'd pulled out of her arm.

"You know I did," Jack, the old coroner, said.

"What about nearby footage?"

"Of course. And for every other type of evidence." A long breath escaped him. It had been a tiring day. "You know we looked, Anie. I wouldn't have called you in otherwise."

"I know, I know." I sighed, sticking my hands in my leather coat. *Shit.*

Jack stood and raised an eyebrow. "You're going to have to do it."

"Did the family …?"

"Yes. They want the murderer caught."

"The last time the witness screamed, Jack," I mumbled. "Like a fucking siren. He's still screaming in lock up, remember?"

"Ya, that sucks." He shrugged. "But you're gonna catch his killer."

"My ears have been ringing for days."

"But you'll get the killer." He pressed on, speaking not unkindly. "It's your job."

"And the sobbing witness," I snapped, annoyed. Forty-four and stuck in quite literally a dead-end job. I couldn't seem to close a single case lately, after a highly successful three-year streak in a field created just for me.

Shit. Like *that* mattered. Finding killers is what mattered. I was a detective on this force for one reason, and one reason only.

I knelt down, the techs quick to move aside. I didn't know any of them, the turnover so high lately I didn't even bother learning names until I saw them twice. I hadn't had to learn anyone's name in a while.

Jack, who'd been at this death game longer than me, stayed near. Just in case I needed help. Sometimes the dead didn't like their short-term memories triggered. Sometimes it got a bit nasty.

You'd be surprised how much of a fight a corpse can put up.

I placed my hand on the body. *Shit.* I hated this part.

Her skin was cold and tense. She was intact, thanks to dying by poison. Of course, it meant her vocal cords would also be intact. And she might just scream for a long time.

Until I caught her damn killer.

What a shit show of a deal.

"Emily was her name," Jack helpfully muttered behind me, knowing that *her* name mattered to me. Couldn't apologize right without uttering a name. Couldn't remember her name without first knowing it, either.

"Sorry, Emily," I whispered. She was gone. I knew that. Whatever fed her soul had drifted away, but I was about to punch her brain into activity. With some of my own defective tech, by giving her a few of *my* nanites.

They'd reach her brain stem and get her moving. Reconnect some high cortical functions, but without most of the hippocampus, amygdala, and hypothalamus, there'd be no meaning to anything seen or experienced. Other brain bits would get traveled through, igniting enough of her remaining nanites in the bloodstream to get them moving.

My own nanites would then settle into her temporal lobe and pop open her short-term memory. And trap her in those final moments.

Until I freed her again.

Shit.

Through the control chip I sent the command until nanites escaped my pores, a serious defect of an earlier version of a now much more advanced tech. I braced myself for the screams.

Her eyes flew open and, instead of the usual terror, she looked up and smiled.

"Did I miss the show?" She tried to sit up, disoriented.

"No," I assured her.

One of the techs swore, but I ignored him. I guess it made sense that personnel retention wasn't high in the most ghoulish unit on the force. There had been studies, of course, on how my defect worked with others' internal nanites, sure. But it kinda made things worse. Like, if I tried hard enough, I might be able to take over living people, too.

Not a great way to be popular.

"Come on," I told Emily, helping her up. She wasn't too stiff and could still move fairly well. For now. I mean, she'd keep decomposing, but my nanites would keep her moving. Almost like a normal person.

But so very much not.

"Did I miss the show?" she asked again, all blank smile and eyes.

"*La Triviata de Verdi,*" Jack said, holding up a ticket he'd found in her pocket.

"Did I miss it?" She looked at the ticket, unable to puzzle anything out about it. At least it had been as peaceful a death as murder could be.

"You didn't," I told her gently and began leading her to the air drifter that would fly her to HQ.

Then it was my job to work up a lineup that would finally release my latest dead witness.

"Oh no," Lisa said as she covered her face and threw herself into the next corridor, vanishing in a flash of paisley pink and the stink of cotton candy. The captain's newest secretary could be dramatic at times, and I knew she hated me and "my thing," as she called it. Well, she shouldn't be anywhere near these cells, then, because I had yet *another* dead witness and I wasn't super happy about it.

Maybe it was my scowl that had sent her running. That would be okay.

"Don't mind her, Henry," I told the latest witness as we neared the guard desk, groaning as I spotted Erik behind it. He wasn't here to keep the witnesses in. They weren't going anywhere. He was here to keep shitheads at bay, the Death Liberators or whatever the hell they called themselves. Preferred to let killers run free and fuck more people up than to make use of the dead. I didn't think the dead minded helping. Except maybe for the screamer.

Sarah.

"What's this, number five?" Erik asked, a smirk on his face.

I didn't bother answering. He knew damn well this was the sixth. *Six witnesses.* Since opera girl, we'd found three more bodies, and crime scenes so squeaky clean I was called in as a "last-ditch effort."

Now I had sobber, screamer, opera girl, starer, bike guy, and this new one, drooler.

Jean-François, Sarah, Emily, Ling, Abdul, Henry. I ran through all their names, satisfied.

Six was a lot. We'd never had more than two at a time before.

Shit. We had seven containment rooms for the undead. Climate control to stop deterioration, easy viewing windows for lines of potential suspects, and the cells could be filled with bacteria to return the body to nature.

But to be set free from my nanites, they had to be faced with their killer, first, regardless of whether or not they'd seen them. The victim's nanites would have connected briefly to the last close signal of their killer. Privacy laws stopped us from just tracking people via internal tech, even when people were murdered, despite the fact that *everyone* had nanites.

But my nanites were different. Created thirty years ago to stop early onset dementia in likely candidates, myself included, the nanites supported some brain functions, including memory. The early tech was more aggressive and could basically hack newer tech. Not to mention leech out of bodies. Quite a few people had died from the early tryouts. I still considered myself lucky, regardless of how fucked-up this all was.

The progress of the law being slow, it allowed for reanimation with limited function (as long as the family agreed, of course), even if it didn't allow for breaching the privacy of nanites.

Governments were fucked. That was my analysis of the whole situation.

"Detective Banskee." The captain walked up to me. I fought against rolling my eyes, and tried to ignore the new glop of (cold) drool that landed on my hand (I'd have to ask Jack how the hell this guy was still drooling), and turned to face him.

"Captain Lewinsky." I nodded as I held the dead witness's arm.

He ignored the walking corpse. The captain was good at ignoring things he didn't like, which explained why we rarely talked.

"I'm meeting with the commissioner next week," he said, trying to school his features to hide his disgust. He failed miserably. "Your unit's in trouble."

"Sir, we have the highest case closure rate in the department." Technically true until two weeks ago.

"You couldn't close the last, what, *six* cases?" He scoffed. "That's a hell of a failure to go out on."

What the fuck could I say to that? It bothered no one more than me that I couldn't figure it out. No trace elements whatsoever at the scenes. No nanite trails either, kinda fucking me over. Nothing linking the victims by lives or crimes, so not a serial killer. The only thing they had in common was the textbook perfection of each crime scene.

"What you do isn't even half an inch normal, Banksee." His face twisted into something hideous for a second before releasing.

"Not half an inch?" The sarcasm dripped out of me before I could muster up some fucks to give. "What does it take to get to three-quarters of an inch? I can aim for that."

He steamed, took a step forward. I held my ground, his nose close to mine. I bit back the snark that threatened to leak out of me as easily as Henry's drool dripped out of his limp mouth.

"It's not natural," the captain growled, "and it needs to stop."

"It's sanctioned by the president herself."

"Elections are coming up." He leaned in, spitting slightly in my face as he bit every word. "I don't think she's getting back in because of supporting outdated freaks like *you*. I want those damn corpses put to goddamn rest before I get to finally let your freaky ass go."

Cold drool landed on my hand. Warm spit on my face. Another banner day.

"Is that clear, Detective?"

"Shiny clear, Captain," I answered with a smile. He narrowed his eyes at me, wanting to call my sarcastic ass out, but decided to drop it and turned on his heel.

"Come on, Henry." I gently prodded the witness along.

"Cell six is open," Erik said smugly, wisely keeping his thoughts to himself.

Replace the president, kill the dead witnesses (re-kill?), sack me, and that'd be that.

My career prospects weren't exactly amazing.

Fuck.

"Shouldn't you be packing?" Jack asked as he leaned against my old creaky desk.

I gave him a thin smile. "Can't wait to get rid of me?"

"Hardly." He sat down on the equally creaky chair, dark skin etched with more age than it had been this morning, I could swear. "I thought you did good, Anie."

"Thanks." I sighed. "Doesn't matter what we think though, does it?"

"Never has, never will." He leaned back, linked his hands across his comfortable belly. "What are you gonna get up to now?"

A wry smirk crossed my lips. "I'll just … I don't know, figure something out. Lie low for a while, maybe." The press had been having a field day with the closure of my unit. I couldn't go anywhere without being recognized, which I hated about as much as I hated job hunting.

"You can hide at my place, if you want," he offered. "It's small, but you'll be safe there."

I couldn't quite picture his home right now but shrugged it off. It had been a long few weeks.

"Nah," I said, grabbing my stuff. I had no intention of bringing trouble to my only friend in the world. "Gonna steal some of the good pens and make my way out."

Jack stood up with me, held out his large hand. I took it and smiled at him. Not some fucked-up sarcastic smile, but a genuine one.

"I'll miss you," I said, surprised I meant it.

"I'll miss you, too," he answered softly. "Now, get out of here before we hug or something weird."

"Gone!" I headed to the elevator, his chuckle trailing me.

The captain was nowhere to be seen, which was great. He wanted me gone. Like, now. Those had been his orders. Fuck him and his orders.

There was one last thing I had to do before I handed in my badge.

I stepped up to the dead-witness holding area, which was quiet. I'd say like a cemetery, but that pun's done and pretty wrong anyway.

Henry. Emily.

I frowned, forced a deep breath in my lungs.

Abdul.

Before I could recall more names, Erik looked up from behind the desk, surprised to see me. Not, like, good surprise, either. Like, "I got caught doing something I shouldn't be doing" surprise.

The hairs on the back of my neck stood on end and I narrowed my eyes, Erik's own widening.

"What's up, Erik?" I asked casually, hand falling near the piece on my side. I was damned glad I hadn't handed in my gun or badge, yet.

"You're not supposed to be here," he muttered, reaching for his own gun. Then I heard it. The screamer.

Henry? No. Henry was the drooler.

His scream was too loud, meaning his cell was open.

Then he stopped screaming. He wouldn't do that unless he was dead-dead. My nanites scurried back, reporting to the control chip even before they infiltrated my pores.

Killer found.

My lip curled down and my hand clasped my gun.

"Stop," Erik said, his gun aimed at my heart.

"What the hell are you up to?" I didn't hold up my hands. "Did you let the killer in?"

He blanched considerably. Sweat beaded his brow.

"They're killing them," I said between gritted teeth, hand twitching to hold a weapon.

"They're already dead."

"There's a killer in there!" I hissed. "Why the fuck aren't you arresting them?"

"Shit, I'm calling back up," he mumbled, though it was clear it wasn't to stop the killer in the cells. More nanites skittered to return to me, too tiny to be seen but close enough to be picked up by my control chip. They'd been freed from another body. Opera girl.

Emily.

Erik walked around his desk, gun pointed, hand on his radio.

Fury bubbled in me, bursting out of me like an angry volcano. Years of fighting to be respected, to be seen as an equal, regardless of defective tech given to me as a teen, and none of it mattered.

After fighting so fucking hard.

My vision turned dark, and I redirected the nanites that were just reaching me toward Erik. They entered his pores, and I could sense them. Inside him.

Stop him, I ordered.

His eyes turned round with fear as his hands remained trapped in their position, my nanites easily hacking his more recent tech. I'd have felt bad, except I wasn't the one letting fucking killers run free.

"You should have made better life choices," I hissed as I walked past him and pulled out my gun, tripping the safety off.

Bright lights left no room for shadows. A cell was opened. The weeper. *Jean-Fran ... something.*

Shit.

My nanites released from his body, connected with my control chip again. I willed them to stay on the ground before me. It felt weird, my body aching, wanting the tiny machines holding my brain cobbled together back in my blood.

Not yet, I soothed them as I held my gun at the ready, the drooler on the other side of his glass door, looking to the back wall.

Henry.

Movement. A flash of pink. The stench of cotton candy.

"Lisa?" I asked as she turned, large eyes surprised to see me.

"You're not supposed to be here!" she said, looking every bit like the scared secretary she'd always played.

"You're the killer?" My turn to be surprised.

Her features grew calm, her voice turned to steel. "Don't judge me, freak. What you do isn't even half an inch normal." She straightened herself.

Exactly the same words as the captain. *Shit.* I pulled on the trigger, and nothing happened. She smirked and pulled out her own gun.

"You getting pegged as the killer will be an amazing story," she said as she took aim. "So let's try to keep this simple, shall we?"

Before she could say anything else, I ordered my nanites to swarm her. She reeled back, her shot going wide and missing me, the nanites freezing her arm in the air, her entire body turning stiff. Her nanites were a different model than Erik's, and she managed to move a bit but not for long before being overpowered.

No wonder they'd discontinued my fucking nanites. No more medical trials for me.

"Sure, we can keep it simple," I said as I picked up her piece and tossed my tampered one aside. My fist crunched her nose in and knocked her out.

Damn, that felt good. I dragged her limp ass from cell to cell, releasing each witness in turn, naming them and wishing them well. Thanking them for facing their killer and looking her in the face. One by one, I set them free, and reclaimed my remaining nanites.

Once done, I locked Lisa and Erik in cells. Then I stared at them.

They would tell others what I'd done. That I could infiltrate and control living people, too. Then they'd rip the nanites out of me.

If replacing my nanites and control chip could be done without killing me, we'd have already done it. But it couldn't be done.

Jean-François.

The name returned to me out of nowhere.

Now there was a name worth remembering.

"I'll remember your names," I said, then asked the nanites to reverse engineer what they did to the dead witnesses. To turn off pieces of Lisa's and Erik's brains.

When they were drooling as much as Henry had been, I recalled my nanites from them, my mind becoming sharper at their return. I debated my next move.

I wasn't quite done with this place, just yet.

"Offer still stands," Jack said as he leaned back against the old chair.

"I can get a new place," I mumbled. My salary had been on hold for months while I helped clean up the department. Hell of a conspiracy just to boot out my unit, all by the (many) members of the damn Death Liberators. With most new hires on the police force in on their shit behavior, it had been pretty easy to hide evidence. For three years, they'd worked against me. Only my success had kept them at bay.

In the end, I'd hunted them all. The captain. The lieutenants and sergeants who'd cleaned up scenes. All the techs who'd come and gone, not staying long enough to screw up or to be suspected. No one had questioned the high turnover because who wanted to work with the freak, right?

Who, except Jack, of course.

"I'm sure you can find a cozy new cave," he said, then stretched. "I'm feeling all of my years today."

I nodded. If anyone suspected what I'd done to most of those shitheads, it was Jack. But he didn't say anything. Fucking stoic shit, that was Jack.

"See you tomorrow?" he asked.

"See you tomorrow." I shrugged. "Not much choice."

"Good that they extended the program, instead of wiping out your tech." He patted my shoulder before heading off. He knew it wasn't that great.

But it was what it was.

I grabbed my bag, looked at it, my heart racing as I tried to recall where the hell I'd booked a room.

I took a deep breath, ignored the cold sweat, and headed to the elevator. It always came back to me when I started walking, anyway.

One by one, I began to recite the names of the dead witnesses.

Henry. Emily. Abdul. Ling. Jean-François. Sarah.

And many more, from the past few years. Over and over again, I recited them.

My mantra against time. Against genetics and failing memories. And, most of all, against failing tech.

We Are All Ourselves Inside Our Skin

Sam Fleming

*F*rom corner, it's easy to read prospective client. Frantic but hiding it. My sense of smell not as good as body implies, but even human would smell this fear.

My associate interviews him with calm patience.

"I conduct the preliminary assessment, Mr. Dingwall. Rowan prefers it that way. When did you first notice the change in Mr. Touissant?" Grisela's gentle Icelandic accent always delightful.

I crack open one eye to watch Dingwall's body language. Running trembling left hand through his hair, brown eyes darting like startled fish. Up and right. Right but level. Remembering scenes.

"Call me Paul, please. I guess it was when he came back from that trip. I knew something wasn't right, but I thought it was the grief. But then ... then last week Martin said ..."

Down and left. Not just scenes, emotions. He plucks tissue from box on coffee table between him and Grisela. I smell hand cream on his manicured fingers: orange blossom, honey, almond oil, shea butter, preservatives. Trace of aloe vera comes from tissue. Grisela careful to keep everything in our apartment constant or tell me if something had to change. I differentiate data from background.

"Take your time," Grisela soothes.

"We went on holiday, once." Dingwall says. Non sequitur, but I've learned humans need to tell stories. "It was before …." Right hand makes sweeping motion. "Before people knew him. We stayed in a B&B in a twee little village, and the owner turned out … homophobic, to be blunt. I wanted to leave, but Martin said no, the problem was hers, not ours. Spent the next three days being as camp as a tent. He was magnificent. I laughed so much my ribs hurt for a week. We took a photo of ourselves kissing outside that B&B when we left, had it framed, put it on the wall of the hall in our house so it's the first thing anyone sees coming through the front door. And last Wednesday, at exactly four minutes past seven, Martin said we should replace it with his most recent publicity shot. He's put photos of himself all over the house, and I thought it was self-affirmation, something to cope with professional anxiety about moving full time from being a dancer on the show to being a judge, but …"

Dingwall wipes his eyes.

I get off cushion and pad over to sit next to him. He keeps his hands to himself. I like that.

"The drinking could be the increased pressure of the change in role, to being in the public eye more. The way he's spending more time with the women than he used to might be part of judging. And …." Deep breath. "We're not intimate. He barely tolerates me touching him. That could be tiredness, and maybe worry. But wanting to replace that picture? No. No, that's not my Martin. Someone has done something to him, and I need to find out what."

"You said he was on a trip," Grisela says. "When was this, and where did he go?"

"It was eight weeks ago. He went to Thailand for a publicity stunt with Bernardo Fanshaw, who was doing *Welcome to the Jungle*. As you probably know, that didn't go as planned, which is why Martin's taken his place on *Dance for Millions*."

Bernardo Fanshaw. One-time West End musical star. Friend of, and mentor to, Martin Touissant. Lead judge on popular dancing contest. Members of general public partner up with professional dancers, attempt to beat professional couples. Score more points than them in six or more rounds, win fifty million. Contest runs almost constantly, in three separate streams, plus international editions. Mints money.

Fanshaw apparently louche backstage. More than one dancer accused him of inappropriate touching. Gained momentum of late; legal action impending, agent vigorously protesting innocent until proven guilty, etc. Then suddenly Fanshaw's in coma, waiting for cure in fancy care home. Agent claiming any further legal action as "bad taste."

Gossip media speculating endlessly about exotic brain-eating bugs. He's rich enough for clone replacement. Not many diseases act so fast that transfer impossible, if clone already waiting.

One day knocking off points for misplaced feet, next knocked out of life. Massive deal. Headline news. Judges on show never change—in days when rich people effectively immortal, role for life means role forever. Unless they quit. Fanshaw was never going to quit.

"And you noticed Mr. Touissant was different immediately when he got home?" Grisela asks.

"Yes."

"Has he changed medication, had any brain injury or illness?"

"I don't think so." Not quite truthful. Why? "To be honest, I haven't seen much of him because he's been filming. He stays in a hotel, mostly."

"Has he always done that?"

"Yes. It helps with privacy and means he's near the studio for rehearsals and practice." Another deep breath. "The worst part is … I loved Martin, my Martin. I don't even *like* this one. He's an arsehole."

Grisela looks at me. I nod.

"Very well, Mr. Dingwall," I say. "We'll take the case." Speech synthesizer does pretty good job of my voice, making it sound almost like it did when heard from inside my dead head.

He flinches.

"Oh, I'm sorry. I didn't realize that …. I mean, I knew you were … different, but I thought …" At last he has encountered something that can distract him from his confused grief. "Do you mind? May I ask …?"

"Why didn't I use clone?" I finish for him, because I have heard this question so often, as if my choices are for strangers to debate. "Clone wouldn't have been me any more than birth body was."

"You mean, you were *always* a dog?"

"No, Mr. Dingwall." I don't bother to explain that body not really dog. Not entirely. "But this way people don't treat me as their idea of human. Grisela will show you out."

Martin Touissant: forty-three years old, professional dancer, now judge on *Dance for Millions*. Orphan. Raised by state. Real bad-childhood-comes-good story.

In ideal world, would have met Touissant before he changed. Do not move in those circles. Never have, even though this experimental form would open those doors. Prurient interrogation by media more terrifying prospect than scientific dissection of original human body had been.

I endure as many hours of *Dance for Millions* as I can bear, skipping parts where Touissant not present. He's been with show for fourteen years. Five contests each year. Danced as amateur's partner in one round every year, and in professional couple at least one round every year, making him most consistently employed dancer. Also participated in analysis show, *Green Room*, and occasionally appeared in unofficial fan show, *Wanna Dance?* In first eleven years, he lost one round when part of professional couple, and his amateur partner won six times, making him fifty percent more successful than next-best dancer. In last three years, his professional couple lost twice, scraped win once, and amateur partners won nothing. He served as guest judge on seven occasions when Fanshaw missed show. Fanshaw's presumed immortality would have kept Touissant out of judge's seat permanently if not for coma.

I only see Fanshaw in glimpses, at speeds of times thirty, but entrance is same each time. I learn to judge where to resume normal playback by extravagant bow.

Difference arises in Touissant's movements three years ago. He becomes stiffer, choreography less ambitious. If age were to blame it would be slow deterioration. But forty is new twenty, and change happens between one season and next. I calculate maximum four months and five days for change of state.

Dance for Millions went on hiatus when Fanshaw fell ill. Big news everywhere. Not much material from last month. Only single interview with Troy Checkbar, talk-show host, from twelve days ago. Touissant discusses returning to show as full-time judge in Fanshaw's place. Hard to read such forced circumstances. Touissant gushes over mentor, to point of shedding tears he dabs from corner of eye before they ruin makeup, but body language comes across oddly strained. Movements overly deliberate.

Relationship less friendly in real life than narrative demanded? What happened between them in Thailand? Could change Dingwall saw be guilt?

They shared agent, Sparrow Simmons. What might he know?

I call up two images, one on each of two displays with such high resolution I can see pancake sitting in pores of his nose. Similar outfit in both—formal black suit used as dance costume— and head held at same angle: three-quarter profile, eyes glancing toward camera. He has masculine presence only somewhat diminished by distance.

"Gris?"

They leave their station, sit next to me, examine images.

"Is this one recent?" They indicate image on right.

"No. Three years ago. Other one three years and five months ago."

"That is not the same body. See here." They point to minor imperfection on left cheek, almost invisible under cosmetics. "That resembles a melanoma laser excision site. And here." On left ear lobe, only one visible in both photographs, earlier image bears mark. Also disguised by cosmetics. I only see it because Grisela shows me where to look and what to look for. "He had his ear pierced and allowed it to heal."

"Four months long enough to habituate clone?" Took me almost that long just to learn how to make my legs work without falling over. How much easier it must be when your new body is identical to old one. When it matches your idea of self.

Grisela's expression suggests they are not correct person to ask this question; they have no more experience in transfer into identical body than I do. They turn their gaze floorward for some seconds, searching. "Full neuromuscular integration can take up to a year."

"Lack of neuromuscular integration could explain change in dancing, but why full body transfer at forty?" Also, integration should improve with time, and although transfer drugs can change personality, there should be no need for psychotropics this long afterwards in clone transfer. Even I have no more need.

"Full body transfer is something people may choose at any age, and the best clone providers can match your new body to your current age. People will generally choose a full body transfer at a time prior to the onset of age-degeneration as a result of illness or injury that cannot be dealt with by replacing diseased aspects of the birth body."

"That's marketing material."

"I am reading it from Wikipedia, but it was scraped from someone's marketing material."

Illness or injury. If Touissant had been injured, accident would have been all over social media. Interviewers would have interrogated him. Touissant even then at level of celebrity where general public believe they have right to know what's happening in private life, like he's family or friend. He's in their homes every week, sharing mealtimes. Keeping them entertained while they do chores. Illness easier to hide if gradual, if predictable.

"Gris, contact Mr. Dingwall, please. I need to meet Mr. Touissant."

Wasn't expecting to have to go to studio. We meet Dingwall first, at nearby coffee shop. Put on service animal harness and conceal cybernetic hands in mitts fashioned to look like paws. There are service animals who have been fitted with cybernetic hands, but I can't handle people's sense of entitlement about asking Grisela questions, some of which deeply personal. Grisela wearing dark glasses. People make assumptions.

"We would have preferred something less public than the studio," Grisela says.

"I had to think of a reason for you to meet. I can't claim you're old friends and invite you round for dinner. Martin and I share our old friends, and I wouldn't invite work colleagues to the house. So, the best I could do was to say I had a cousin visiting, and they'd like to see filming."

I flick an ear.

"Are animals generally allowed on set?" Grisela asks.

Dingwall pauses, some impolitic quip caught behind his teeth. "Well, no. I hadn't really thought that far ahead." He sips his drink. It smells of cyanide and terpenes. "I assumed you would introduce yourself, like the police would."

"Rowan is not the police," Grisela reminds him. "I asked you to provide a cover story precisely because Rowan does not wish their presence to be known. Never mind. They are legally obliged to permit service animals."

Really does not bother me. The "animals" thing. Like rummaging through rubbish. Not pleasant but needs must on occasion. Actually still better than being mistaken for human.

"Do you really need to speak with him?"

Grisela glances in my direction. I work my ears.

"Rowan needs to meet him. We do not expect to interview him." Grisela's careful not to use names. Data harvesting everywhere. "It's probably down to you to tell us why he had a full body transplant three years ago."

Pallor blooms on Dingwall's face, twin spots of raspberry blush sitting on his cheeks like dead jellyfish.

"What do you mean?"

I put pawed hand on Grisela's calf, and they activate cone of silence. Background chatter fades, but real result is no one can hear our conversation. Localized active noise cancellation. Chews power like candy, can't use it for long.

"You knew," I say. "Touissant changed three years ago, but you didn't mention that. Not withholding information, but not important to you. Why so surprised?"

"Nobody knows, apart from me, his closest friends, and his direct family, and you haven't spoken to them, they would have told me. It's not public knowledge."

"Obvious on examination. Can you tell us why?"

Dingwall leans in. "This goes *nowhere*."

"Client confidentiality. Nothing you tell us goes anywhere."

"He has Cronburt Syndrome."

Unfortunate. Neurological disorder with unknown environmental trigger. Possibly perfluorinated alkyls. Still no cure other than getting new body and having another one ready to go when that fails. First clone likely to suffer same thing, but clone providers attempt to screen out genetic susceptibility in subsequent clones, if sufferer can afford them. Genetics complex. No guarantee screening will work. Only guarantee is transfer to body with completely different genetic profile, which rules out clones.

Cronburt career ending for pro dancer.

Ironic, really. One of many things suggested by gossipers to explain Fanshaw's coma.

I break contact with Grisela, and they deactivate cone. Background chatter resumes, almost painful. Clinking cutlery, voices an amorphous rolling blanket threatening to blot out everything else. Mugs scraping, liquid slurping. I put shoulder against their leg and lean hard. They put hand on other shoulder and press me against them. Dingwall says something lost in general cacophony.

Perfumed presence looms, someone at our table. "Oh! What a beautiful, good boy!"

Humans use hands like others use mouths. Would you want someone to put their mouth on you without permission?

"STOP." Grisela grabs hand before it touches me. "Don't touch. Never touch a service animal when they are working."

"I just wanted to say hello. He's so handsome." Feminine, disappointed.

"Irrelevant." Grisela stands, chair scraping over terracotta tile. We get out of there.

Not big consumers of televisual media, Grisela and I. Neither of us understands attraction. Counterfeit drama and engineered conflict. Even this, ostensibly competition of skill and artistry, beset by dressing room squabbles. Fanshaw's green room indiscretions old news. Public no longer titillated by his secrets because not secret anymore. He was drunk uncle spouting opinions no one wanted to hear at dinner table. Took whole hot minute to shift from *don't speak ill* to *kind of glad he's gone.*

We're ushered through security. Declare implants, so no metal detector. Grisela removes harness to show I'm not carrying concealed weapon. Guard jokes animal my size is weapon all by itself. "Didn't know they came that big."

"Genetically engineered," Grisela says. I dislike it when Grisela lies, so they don't. But this body wasn't CRISPRed to make it bigger, that was just byproduct.

"Vlcak, right?" the guard says. Nosy. Perhaps his job.

"Crossbreed." Not untrue. "All sorts in there." Also not untrue. Some cephalopod for distributed nervous system.

Plants in atrium fake. Whole place smells of old mops and nicotine patches, stale alcohol, sweat. Anxiety and expensive perfumes muddled together, less concealed by fake eucalyptus and new upholstery smell pumped through air conditioning than made nauseating by it. Someone hurries over to us, clutching tablet, seven different lanyards dangling and tangled with three strands of fake pearls. Eye makeup riot of neons, hair bright teal.

"Hi!" they squeal. Instinct compares it to sound of small rodent in distress. "My name is Roget, my pronouns are he/him, I am a production assistant on the show, and I am delighted to meet you today." Pronounces name *Roh-zhay*, emphasis on *zhay.* "Mr. Touissant is on set right now and has sent me to fetch you. If you'd follow me, please? You too, Mr. Dingwall. Don't want you getting lost again."

I like that he doesn't try to take Grisela's arm and doesn't even look at me. Maybe doesn't like dogs. Maybe thinks—rightly—I'm none of his business.

Examined building plans before leaving apartment. Looks like giant Millennium Falcon. Contains seven hundred offices for five and a quarter thousand people. Dressing rooms for eight hundred talents. Twelve studios, wardrobe for thirty thousand items. Laundry, hair and makeup, wig-making, script and music libraries, server rooms, streaming hubs, Foley labs. I resist urge to urinate at every junction so can find my way out without assistance. Grisela can do that without peeing.

Plans didn't mention bar, but Roget sits us all at table in brightly lit room with said bar and display screens showing empty dance floor. No other guests. "Can I get you anything? Soda, tea—the chocolate birthday cake bubble tea is simply to die for—something stronger? Would your companion like some water?"

Nearly forget myself and reply. Body utters tiny whine.

"I'll take that as a yes on the water," Roget says with most genuine smile I've ever seen on human, including own mother. I *really* like this person.

"Thank you," Grisela says. "I have a bowl for Rowan, but I would prefer a glass."

"How about you, P?" Unexpected familiarity. "Your usual? I'll just get Maureen to fix that right up. Mr. Touissant will be along presently." He checks his watch. Cheap. Functional. "You'll have fifteen minutes before he has to go back to hair and makeup, then we'll let the other VIPs in. Twenty minutes after that, we'll take you to set so you can experience the show."

Not see. Experience.

When he's gone, I lean into Grisela's leg and whisper, "Can we keep him?"

"He is lovely," they reply. "Do you come often, Paul? Roget seems quite taken with you."

"We're pretty good friends, more so recently," Paul says. He adjusts his seat. Uncomfortable with statement? Something more than friends? Roget reads young, and superficial age difference triggers creepy klaxon, but age just number when some of population effectively immortal.

I nudge Grisela and make ears speak.

They respond with finger code. "Minimum wage."

Roget would have to be willing to experiment to get clone. Experiments you can get for free, if there's good chance they won't work. If you're desperate enough to risk failure.

One other way to get free transfer: swap. Some people even pay other party. But usually that means poor and attractive—or young—swapping for rich and dissatisfied. Sometimes people think they can get new life by taking new body instead of clone, forgetting they're still themselves in there. We are all ourselves inside our skin.

Don't think Roget has ever been rich and dissatisfied.

Maureen delivers drinks. Grisela pours mineral water into bowl. Use glass at home like everyone else, but canine drinking action has interesting fluid mechanics, so I don't mind.

"Have you ever had a transplant?" Grisela asks.

"I'm a playwright. Do you know what the average wage is for a playwright in this country? About half minimum. If it wasn't for Martin, I'd still be running three separate hustles just to keep a roof over my head. This is the original me, warts and all."

"Did it bother you when he got a transfer?"

"Are you kidding? I was delighted. I didn't want to watch his brain turn to mush."

Sudden bustle behind bar. Note door previously unseen.

"Paul!" Here comes Touissant, two young women with tablets trailing in his wake like remoras on shark. He moves like he's carrying forty kilos in invisible vest. Hard to reconcile this person with man I watched for hours and hours.

He air-kisses Dingwall. "Don't want to make Marcia mad," he says. "She already has a tough job making me handsome. And this must be your cousin, yes?" He's sweating. Nervous. "I don't remember us meeting before?"

"No," Dingwall says. "You've never met Grisela."

Touissant stinks of booze and adrenaline under the aldehydes of his cologne.

My brain itches in its heart, ripples down spine. Some pattern not matching. Some pattern matching too much. Penrose tiling gone wrong. Something breaching, pushing through.

Something. Something. Something.

My hand smacks into my face. Again. Again. Again.

Grisela pulls my head against her leg, holds my hand. She tugs the dislodged mitt back in place.

"Is he okay?" Voice distorted by thoughts verging on derailment. Maybe one of assistants.

Breathe.

"Places where many people have been are sometimes overwhelming," Grisela replies. True but misleading.

"You realize there will be a whole audience for the show?" Touissant asks unkindly.

"We will be fine. Thank you for getting us tickets."

"Oh, I didn't get you tickets," he says, puffing out his chest like bull seal proclaiming territory. "I got you *seats*. Right near the front, although I guess it wouldn't have mattered if I'd put you at the back. You'd still be able to hear from there." He chuckles.

Dingwall's jaw drops. "I'm so sorry."

"Your cousin doesn't look like a snowflake, Paul. Don't apologize to her for me."

"Them," Dingwall says. "Grisela's pronouns are they/them."

"What a waste," he mutters.

"Excuse me?" Grisela's tone contains warning.

"You are positively statuesque, my dear. Amazonian. You should be strutting your stuff on a catwalk somewhere wearing a slinky black dress and heels the size of the Empire State building, not mumping around in men's clothes and flats."

"Has anyone ever told you it's entirely possible to keep your opinions to yourself?" Grisela asks.

"I'm a *judge*, darling. Certainly not." He glances at his watch. Expensive. "Well, I have to get ready for the show, so hand it over."

"I'm sorry?"

"For me to *sign*, dear. I presume you want my autograph. I'll need a pen. I generally sign photographs, but don't object to more … personal items."

Hackles twitch. Takes effort to keep growl back in my belly. Grisela's hand lands firm on back of my neck.

"I have no use for autographs."

"No, I suppose not." His gaze flicks to Grisela's dark glasses then back down. "Well, enjoy the show. I'll see you later, Paul."

After he has gone, Grisela turns to me. "Do you want to stay?"

Something I need. Something. Haven't got it yet. It's heaving, straining, not enough to show through.

I rest my chin on their leg. Don't want to. Have to.

Ballroom has round tables arranged around outside. Pretending to be real ballroom in real venue, not some facsimile designed to look like what audience wants. I sit between Grisela's feet, chin on table, hiding from cameras behind another guest. Friends and family of amateur couple take up remarkably few seats. Most occupied by extras with instructions on when to cheer and for whom. Stink of hot electronics and fresh paint assails my nostrils, worming forcibly into forebrain like hungry parasite.

Show starts with set piece by professionals not competing. Seventeenth century gavotte dressed in twenty-first century normcore with modern soundtrack. Kind of weird. Not my thing. None of this my thing.

Everyone applauds. Time for judges. Presenters finish each other's sentences in introductions.

Judge one descends spiral staircase from some unseen upper stage. Slides down banister rail in metallic red jumpsuit.

Judge two floats down same stairs, diaphanous gown of powder blue disguising outline as if nudibranch hiding in seaweed. All I see is hideously painted face: macabre mask of stygian blue and magenta.

Judge three is Martin Touissant. Barely saves himself from catastrophic tumble before making extravagant bow on last step as if whole thing deliberate pratfall.

I've seen that bow before.

Penrose tiles burst and shatter as leviathan breaks surface, swamping my thoughts.

I know why he puts photos of himself everywhere.

I know why he has started drinking.

I know why he has turned into complete arsehole.

Leviathan submerges, escaping noise and lights and smells and heat at speed of times thirty.

I take Grisela's hand in my mouth, gently, tasting their skin, breathing their scent. Using their presence to block out everything until we can leave. Like keeping hold of dream until it can be written down.

At first opportunity, we go.

No more than hours between Fanshaw falling ill on camera and returning home with Touissant. Photos of harrowed Touissant at Heathrow easy to find. I call Dingwall, ask if Fanshaw knew about Cronburt diagnosis. Affirmative, so put screws on their mutual agent, Sparrow Simmons. I use teeth to distract him while Grisela ransacks his data.

"I'm calling the police," he snarls, my saliva soaking into his crotch.

"I have doctored your security footage," Grisela says. "Be our guest."

Already know Touissant didn't incapacitate Fanshaw for judge position. Fanshaw stole Touissant's body. Trying to steal his entire life. Evidence for court case overwhelming. Production company about to cut and run. Future suddenly finite.

Illness in jungle faked to get Touissant to transfer facility. Fanshaw too vain to kill off his old body. Likely keeping Touissant sedated in it. Need to know where it is.

Few hours later, we're at exclusive care facility in Wiltshire. We use Lassie gambit: I ditch harness and run in, barking like Jimmy's fallen down well, refuse capture. While everyone distracted, Grisela slips inside. Proof of life gained, ultrasonic whistle, and we regroup. Call Dingwall. Dingwall calls police.

Fanshaw's agent shows up before Dingwall does. Leviathan stirs again, smashed tiles shivering. I sneak around side of facility to Touissant/Fanshaw's room, watch through window as Simmons closes door behind him and yanks pillow from under sleeping head.

Not on my watch.

Gallop to front door, barge in. Shouting, yelling, hands grabbing fur. Air snap when necessary, but mostly just barrel through, hurl myself at door to room, burst inside. Happier by far as bloody big dog than ever was as human.

Simmons has pillow over Fanshaw body's face.

This time I bite hard.

Now Touissant still judge on *Dance for Millions*. Original Touissant. Cronburt meant already clone waiting for him, and sedation saved him from effects of adjusting to new body, so he stepped right back up. Doesn't trip down stairs, either. Production company most generous in terms of our fee.

Fanshaw stuck in Touissant's old clone. Showing symptoms of Cronburt. Presumably imagined he could get next clone screened once established in Touissant's life. Major clone providers won't sell to someone convicted of abusing process. Pretty unlikely from prison anyway. Will have to try less scrupulous company once he's out. If he can afford it.

He has prior, after all.

Touissant visits him, says he wouldn't wish that disease on worst enemy.

Apparently all photos have gone, except that one of Martin and Paul kissing outside B&B. Martin doesn't need photos to remind him who he's supposed to be.

Going to try to lure Roget away to life of fighting crime with decent wage and as much chocolate cake bubble tea as he could wish for. Hope he says yes. Gris and I love happy endings.

Inside, Outside, Above, Below

Premee Mohamed

*D*es is nearly done when she spots the charley. Not exactly by his presence but his absence, a stuttering void like a dead pixel evading her gaze. He's good if he's gotten this far without setting off an alarm. All the same, once seen, he is easily dodged. Des activates countermeasures, flicks through a thousand avatars a second, ghost bird flower cliff grass rain castle nymph, and nine hundred and ninety-nine of them hare off in splendid random disarray. *Let the dog chase*, she thinks, and he does, or he lets her think he does.

She doesn't care which; she needs to finish up. This job means rent for the month. She's not one of those who does this for the excitement of almost being caught. Her resume is, for a given value of those who make an illicit living, squeaky clean. She's reliable. She *delivers*.

"Des," someone says: the dead pixel. The cop. "I need—"

"Fuck off," she says automatically. "Now isn't a good time."

One hand works the analog pad, moving her avatar smoothly through the virtual door that her other hand, immersed in its warmed bowl of conductive gel, unlocked a few seconds ago. Her target is disguised, a silly, perfunctory job, clearly corporate. In the real world the equivalent would be a sandwich in a clear baggie printed with an image of mold so that no one would steal it from the office fridge.

Her body laughs, all unheard. Her avatar does not laugh. It's a *lot* of money, and she finds poverty scarier every day.

No one needs to know this. Desperation is bad for business. *Mine mine mine*: her pet virus blinks in and out and takes an impression of the codes, their contents as well as their little idiosyncrasies and the prongs and dips that the manufacturers put in thinking they were clever. But to this day nothing is more clever than a wax mold. They haven't figured that out.

Des pockets the codes, politely locks the door behind her, she wasn't raised in a barn, flutters up and out of the corporate warehouse, looks down only once as she leaves: a featureless black cube. Booooring. Put a gargoyle on it or *something*, at least. Something for thieves to look at.

The charley saw everything no doubt. Des fights down a stab of annoyance and drops her neatly wrapped delivery (an impenetrable virtual skin of iridescent blue paper stamped with tumbling squirrels and mushrooms) into the client's locker.

She won't leave until she gets paid. She hovers for a few agonized minutes, watching the charley, or where he's not: that tiny nothingness in the chaos of the net.

Thank you so much. The message from her client finally appears.

She verifies the little sigil that follows. *Always a pleasure doing business with you!*

Added tip bc short notice. Buy yrself something nice my friend!

The payment appears in discreet chunks of tokens in three of her gaming accounts; she sends avatars somersaulting through the back ways to launder the tokens back into real cash through the usual I-know-a-guy-who-knows-a-guy-who-knows-a-guy guys and watches the zeroes mount in her bank account. She suspects this client uses her services to do something that he's supposed to be doing at his real job (God, imagine that: a *real job*) and then tells his bosses that it's him. No wonder he's so generous.

"Are you done? I need to talk to you," her implant says.

"Jesus Christ," she says, and flips out of the net.

234

Her room is pitch-black. She gestures the lights on, a golden glow illuminating the neat stacks of equipment, the chrome cube of her private generator, the ferns and spider plants lining the walls in flat-white ceramic pots.

"All cops are bastards," she says out loud. Nothing responds. He must be trying to get into her phone since she hung up on him in the net, and that'll take him a while. Des chuckles, stretches, and heads out for something to eat.

Gastown is still softly bustling, a big pink half-moon competing with the signs reflecting in the canals. Tourists are *oohing* and *ahhing* over the moon, climbing fire escapes and pedways to frame themselves for selfies. She takes a water taxi to the night market, where she buys dumplings with the last of her cash and then finds a boba stand.

"It's urgent," the voice says. "At least hear me out."

"You gonna arrest me?" Des says conversationally. The old lady at the boba stand beams, holding out the cup of milky pink liquid. Geometric jellies float above the boba like fish in an aquarium. Des taps her knuckles against the payment pad and blinks half in surprise and half in embarrassment when it declines.

The old lady frowns. "Try again, honey. Must be from the storm earlier."

Des turns away from the stall, tonguing down her volume. "Is this you? That's new. You do a course or something?"

"Des, please. I'm saying please. Do you know what my boss would do to me if he heard me saying please to *you*?"

This is the first interesting thing she's ever heard him say. She finds herself replying, "Okay, I'll hear you out at least. Now will you let me get my tea?"

Back in her room, she logs into her Virtux account and there he is, the avatar that she is one-hundred percent positive does not resemble him in any way. "Beckman," she says. Her tea is sweet and perfect. "Mmm. Thanks for letting me get a last meal."

"I'm not turning you in. Which isn't to say that you're not a crook," he adds.

"Big stick up your bumhole," Des says sympathetically. It's not *really* a theft, after all; she just copied the codes. They're still right there in the company fridge like a sandwich. Beckman is FBI though, American, and they're awfully touchy about these little relocations. Unlike the remnants of regular law enforcement, which has mostly given up, they still have their fingers in everything: virtual, real, in-between.

Des glares at the grayish avatar: a nice-looking male human, glasses, wavy dark hair, polo shirt. "What do you want, Agent Beckman?"

"I need you to find someone for me. And quick."

"Is that all?" It's been a while since he's hired her, and this sounds like easy cash. He's a terrible client, true—keeps trying to give her real money and make her sign a receipt, despite her painstaking explanation of how to pay her properly, for instance—and there's always the risk of folks finding out, which would torpedo her rep, but the work itself is always a breeze, and she's done at least two jobs for him in fifteen minutes while charging a week's worth of hours.

"Okay," she says. "Virtux location, or something else?"

"Physical."

"Seriously? Okay, I guess. When do you need it?"

"Now," he says. The avatar is expressionless, but she doesn't like what she's hearing in his voice; he sounds like someone's got a gun to his head. Maybe someone does. Impossible to tell what *bodies* are doing, isn't it. Anyway, not her problem. Plausible deniability is a good motto.

"Five thousand dollars," she says, picking a number out of nowhere: exactly two months' rent.

"Yes, great. Fine." He hands her a slim file, just a dozen lines of time-stamped messages and a few images.

Gah! Should have asked for more. Des says, "Sit tight," and doesn't even glance at the images. What things look like aren't important in here. She brushes him away, breaking him into pixels, and swiftly builds a room around herself out of light.

Her lovingly handcrafted viruses jump and yap around her ankles like playing puppies. Sniffing someone out needs a bloodhound, so she splices two programs into one, quickly tests it, leashes it, armors up, and returns to the general clamor of the net. Haptics inform the tension and slack of the electronic leash on her palm.

Green light: a hit barely twenty klicks from where she is. Weird. The plants on the walls tremble in unison; she cannot see them while she is logged in, only hear the rustling. Isn't it strange, or maybe it isn't, that you have the whole wide wild world to find someone in, and they're right here. Or maybe Beckman already knew that, and that's why he asked her.

She writes the address on a piece of virtual flashpaper and sends it to Beckman. Five grand for half an hour's work must be some kind of record. "Here you go, J. Edgar. And remember what I said last—"

The walls around her do not explode. They fall flatly outwards all in one piece from the ceiling, and in seconds both her virtual and real home are rubble, and she is screaming through the smoke and the dust.

She should have asked *why*, she should have asked who, why didn't she ask? It was the money. Money's like that, it got into her head like mercury. It's all her fault. She forgot first principles. No one taught her. She learned this herself. And then she forgot.

Des says none of this to the acquaintance (she cannot bring herself to say friend) whose backup bolt hole she rents, only that she needs the room immediately, please, and she cannot pay in advance, it's not safe, she must pay afterwards. She does not even know the acquaintance's name, only her handle, and vice-versa; they have never met in the real. They don't now, either: the room unlocks remotely, after a full three minutes of whirring and clonking inside the door, built between two concrete walls of an old tobacco factory, and Des slips inside.

She's shaking, she's been shaking for hours. She has no idea how she's still alive. It's possible, she thinks, that of all things her *chair* saved her as much as her instincts; she tucked herself into a ball and the memory foam cradled her as she fell. Her bottom lip is split and everything hurts. She had meant to grab her backup deck, anything, but all she managed to get was her backpack before she spotted the second rocket incoming. She'd hit the canal to avoid the blast.

It doesn't seem real. The pain is real: each cut and scrape like a beacon showing her way back to the real world. But she doesn't *like* the real world and she can't stop *crying*. She barely remembers getting here, a nightmarish hobble through dozens of back alleys. No word from Beckman. Maybe he's dead, too. Maybe she handed him his death warrant.

Eventually she manages to calm down enough to clean herself up. Her face is garish in the bathroom mirror: bloody red lips against the sickly yellow pallor of her normally brown skin, a gridded scrape on her forehead like a chessboard.

Her implant buzzes and she flinches so sharply she bangs into the opposite wall. While she hesitates, heart pounding, a sigil appears. Nominally a sign of goodwill: spell of secret knowledge.

"Are you all right? Are you hurt?"

"Beckman," she says evenly, edging out of the bathroom, "let me just say, and I mean this sincerely, that in your whole life no one has ever hated you as much as me."

"Okay. Listen. If we—"

"*We? You're* the law, *you* do something. There's no *we* here. I am going to sue you for …" She trails off, trying to think of a number, and her eyes fill with tears again. It's undignified, is what it is.

No, it's only that I didn't have much, and now I have nothing, this is exactly what I've always feared the most, and someone fucking bombed me, and …

"We can't talk on the phone. I built a safe house," Beckman says. "I'll send you the passcode."

"Like I'd trust anything you built."

"I know I'm not on your level," he says. She hates the conciliatory tone in his voice. He might be sorry but he's not sorry enough. "But it's good, it's solid. I swear."

"Nope." Des folds herself painfully into the unfamiliar curves of the backup chair. Her corduroy leggings crackle and shed a weird cement of mud and blood. "You put a target on my back. You knew that was going to happen."

"I didn't. I swear I didn't."

"Stop saying *I swear!*" Des shouts, and covers her face with her hands, smelling antiseptic soap, fake lavender. *Okay. Okay. Not going to get better by hiding. Longer you hide the longer someone has to find you.*

"I asked you because I thought you were the only person who could protect yourself in case he found out," Beckman says breathlessly. "I mean it. The only. But—"

"He who? The person you made me find? What is … ." She trails off. This is dangerous territory. He's right about one thing: they can't talk here. It might be safer in Beckman's virtual room. It might not. She can't even trust the apparent sincerity in his voice; people fake that with emulators all the time. Actors, politicians, CEOs. But she's got no one and nothing else. "Let me in."

In the net, she isn't crying or bloody. She's herself, a marble statue of white, veined with gold. Beckman's room is a strange and lovely thing: domed entirely with glass, it would never survive in real life with nothing supporting that clear roof. The circular room is lined with wooden bookshelves, the floor gray slate. It rings satisfyingly under her marble sandals.

"All right," Beckman's avatar is already saying, waving his hands. "Here's what I couldn't tell you. There's this guy … I started finding traces of him about six months ago. Do you know what that is in bureau time? That's nothing. I don't even have a meeting to discuss this with the oversight committee till August. They don't believe me."

"About what?"

"About what he's been doing." Beckman thrusts a file at her; she glances only at the first page, her stomach sinking. One of those cases looped in on itself like a mathematical theorem. A drone hit on a US army base initially blamed on the enemy, then on a young soldier who insisted he'd been framed, then finally on a child soldier from some faction in the desert who had no memory of receiving the controls. The kid had been … God. Eight or nine? Her dusty, resolute face and her long lashes in the mug shot.

"It was … him? This rando, this A-Cannon?" She pauses. "Stupid name," she adds clinically, even though her own handle is short for *Descendants and Friends*, her favorite episode of her favorite anime. Beckman, she suspects, knows her real name, and she has to give him credit for never using it.

"I tracked everything back—exec wouldn't give me any resources, no team, no processing time, *nothing*. 'Not our jurisdiction,' they said. But the thing is, the weird patterns around those drone codes looked like something I'd been seeing elsewhere. Nothing that looked ... well, dangerous. But movement alone is weird enough."

Des nods. Movement shows patterns just as absence shows patterns; it's the unusual hyperacuity of this skill that constitutes her livelihood. *Him too*, she thinks.

Beckman says, "As far as I can tell, he did it all remotely. The little girl doesn't remember anything because he took over a swarm of infantry micro-drones and had them carry the controller to her just before she woke up."

"When they came for her." Des tries to unclench her jaw. The military, to her, falls easily under "All cops are bastards," just as Beckman does. She doesn't like their constant recruitment ads, which have ramped up unbelievably in the past few years; she doesn't like their insistence that they're all peacekeepers. She particularly does not like their virtual security, and she never takes jobs for military targets. Rumor goes they hold grudges for decades. They seem to let you escape and then come after you and nuke your prefrontal cortex somehow. And no one ever finds out.

And *he* did it and got away with it.

"That wouldn't have happened if they hadn't been there with the fucking drones and bombs in the first place," she says. "He sounds like my kind of people. Except for blowing up my building and almost killing me, I mean. But why are you busting your ass to find him now?"

Beckman points silently at the dome, and Des looks too, reflexively. A night sky—she cannot say whether it is hers or Beckman's (where does he live, anyway?). Stars, anyway, embedded in velvety black, and a white half-moon no longer tourist-pink, and tumbling bits of stuff that she knows are telescopes and satellites and space stations, the ISS and the six or whatever private ones, zipping along at thirty thousand kilometers an hour. *Scritch scritch* across the sky like silver needles.

"He's going to trap us in space and time," Beckman says.

Des stares at him, which doesn't have much effect with an avatar. *You have just said a hell of a thing*, she wants to say, but she can also hear faintly somewhere a clock ticking, and she knows that wherever Beckman's body is, it's covered in cold sweat, like hers.

"This trap," she says, "none of my business. If I lay low and block all your calls, maybe I'll be forgiven. Y'know? Maybe he'll be like, 'Oh, it's just the charley out for me now. I'll go after *him*. Not Des. Des was only doing it for the money.' Which, by the way ..."

"Could be," says Beckman. "But if we don't do something, no one else will. They don't know he's out there. By the time people realize the trap's been set off, it'll be too late to do anything about it. Maybe forever."

"People."

"Everyone," Beckman says. "The world. You too, Des."

She frowns. "Tell me."

That's how she finds herself flying through the strangest area in the net she's ever seen, somewhere she's never agreed to burgle or alter or recon, and while visually it should look more or less like everywhere else (the cloud of avatars, the lumbering battleships and zeppelins of ads), it emphatically does not.

In the bolt hole, both her hands struggle and cramp with the tiny, out-of-date deck. A-Cannon as an entity is entirely unknown to her; but somehow, after running through the traces he's been involuntarily leaving for the past year, traces Beckman isn't sensitive enough to spot, she feels she knows him all the same.

A-Cannon is very young. She's sure of it. Even younger than her, at twenty-three. He's never known anything but this drowned world of mildew and brine, of peering through the canals that were once streets, looking into stores Des could still walk inside when she was a child. He thinks he's an anarchist and he learned it from reading stupid shit online, not from real anarchists. He feels trapped and he thinks the way to break it is to expand the trap, get everyone else inside with him, and that's so wrong Des wishes she could find him just to yell at him. But there's no point. He's the apocalyptic residual; he's the kid who, in the fifties, would have stolen a nuclear weapon and set it off just to see what would happen.

Beckman flies behind her, far behind, not because she asked him to but because even with his newer equipment he cannot keep up. She's impatient but says nothing. They have to outrace the little bastard and steal something before he can steal it, and they don't have long; it's obvious only if you know the trap. And *what* a trap, Des has to grudgingly admit. No ordinary person would come up with it. It's devious in the way that only a teenager can be devious.

Money pulls her; something else pushes her, and she's not sure what. A fear different from the fear of being broke and on the street. Different from falling through the floor as the ceiling collapses above you. Something bigger, all-encompassing, fear of the unknown. Fear of what it would mean if A-Cannon succeeds.

It was easy to admit to Beckman she was doing it for the cash. Hard to admit she was doing it for the fear.

"Space junk," Beckman had said in the glass-domed room.

"Oh sure," Des said. "There's supposed to be a shuttle or something to deal with it next year ... no, the year after, right? 2065. A magnet. Or was it a laser?"

"It'll never get up there," Beckman said. "Not if A-Cannon does this."

"This what?"

Only this: making more space junk. He's been setting it up for months, leaving those half-seen traces: nudging things, moving things, unlocking virtual doors and windows, setting a brick in the jamb so they don't close.

A-Cannon wants to set off a chain reaction, using the three Astral Garden communication satellites whose virtual access hatches Des is now racing to lock shut. Crashing those three, the biggest satellites ever put into orbit, into each other, and counting on their debris to slam into the precisely mapped grid of CubeSats enveloping the Earth. The CubeSats, Des thinks, are an *infernally* perfect tool for this. Abundant, orbiting at exactly the right elevation, and if you hit them they don't fall and burn up; they splinter into resilient bits of shrapnel.

In a matter of a few days, Beckman said, the reaction would destroy everything in or near low geosynchronous orbit, knocking out the global positioning systems that allowed the world's autonomous ships and trains and trucks to transport everything from food to bobby pins. And most of the world's net access too, since so many underground cables had been destroyed. Not to mention a couple of dozen astronauts, as well as humanity's ability to ever send anything up ever again.

To say that it would kick the Earth back to the previous century was one thing. To say it would cause widespread devastation, famine, war, and chaos was another. People would panic and riot before they began to starve and systems began to fail. No government would get everything back up before perhaps millions of lives were lost or irreparably degraded.

Anarchy the way A-Cannon envisioned it, Des thinks. All wrong. If you wanted people to break free from their choices, you didn't do it by taking them all away. How the *hell* had this happened? One disillusioned kid with zero supervision, and a genius for doing the exact same thing she did. That was all it took for disaster. Unbelievable.

Her fingers ache. Beckman is trying to pull his weight by corralling her viruses as they dash to-and-fro, but she still has to keep things open for much longer than she's used to, which is infuriating. She finally squeezes through the last doorway and slams it behind her before Beckman can get in, because she can't have him slowing her down here, in this last place.

Quick, quick. The package is camouflaged in similarity: wrapped in the virtual equivalent of tinfoil and shoved to the back of a warehouse containing a trillion identical tinfoil-wrapped packets. Her viruses fan out, interviewing, asking, much faster than even she can move, though she pushes herself far harder than before.

Beckman is saying something into her jawbones that she ignores, although she can hear his panic.

The package is already gone. Just a hole in the code.

No time for shock. She slips back out, not even unlocking the door, letting alarms trill behind her. Let them find it, let them know somebody broke in. Maybe something could still be done. Maybe they had countermeasures. She doubted it.

"I was trying to tell you," Beckman gasps as they flee. "Something slipped right through the ceiling. Just ahead of you. Gone like a shot. Some kind of ... snake thing with horns." He's artifacting

243

badly as he tries to keep up with her, and she looks straight ahead because he's giving her a headache. Useless fucking charley.

Behind them, a tsunami of fluttering paper scraps is building up, a huge roaring indiscriminate pursuit unsure who had broken in, but very sure that they were nearby.

It's not real, Des tells herself, as she often does, but her body thinks it's real, and adrenaline spurs her on. In the stuffy room still smelling of damp century-old tobacco she knows her breath is coming in short pants. *Don't faint!* This chair won't support her if she does.

"What are we going to do?" she asks. "What else will he go for? That can't be the last thing!"

"I ..."

"Think! You said you were watching him!"

The satellite company's security is catching up; Des's avatar is programmed to show shadows, the blocking of light or data. She watches her colors dim as she flies, and doesn't look back, knowing the angry paper snippets are almost on them. If they don't leave soon, they won't be able to.

"I don't know, I don't know," Beckman says. He's a blob of green light now, unable to keep any semblance of graphics.

"Where are you?" she demands.

"I'm right behind you!"

"No, I mean—" She snarls, dodges a net that drops just ahead, sparkling like broken glass. A dozen other avatars plummet as if they've been shot out of the sky, even though there is no sky here. *Nothing is real nothing is real nothing is real only pretend all light and ones and zeroes and electricity stay calm stay calm.*

One thing is still real. We're still real. He's real.

"Beckman, are you near me?" she asks. "In the city? At least on the coast?"

"You're not—"

"Yes I am, and I'll do it alone if you can't come," she hears herself say.

"Des!"

"Find me if you can," she shouts, and flips out of the virtual and into the real.

Her whole body creaks and aches as she runs. Out from between the walls, up the cement staircase, out to the rusty pedways between the buildings near what used to be docks. It's unaccountably daylight again, a dim amber sunrise suffusing the fog above the flooded city like tea. She's exhausted and, she suspects, deeply in shock.

Beckman needs to find *her*, because while she had managed to triangulate a whisper of A-Cannon's address, she didn't dare speak it to Beckman, lest they have a repeat of the rocket incident. Anyway it was hardly a location, just a chunk of Vancouver about two blocks square.

She can't take a water taxi, anything she pays for will send up a flare pinpointing where she is. She curses as she runs and decides against looking up some more curses in different languages. This is exactly the problem with her freelance career, she decides as she scrambles down the side of a building. Bad clients.

She swims fifty yards, buoyed by her waterproof backpack, studiously ignoring the rat that ignores her in turn as it swims alongside on its own errands. On the back side of an ancient brick warehouse, she snatches at a rusty ladder and climbs up the wall. There: pedway. Get onto that. Remember having sidewalks? God, those were the days.

Running out of steam and there's still half the city to cross. She leans on the edge of a roof to catch her breath, and wonder of wonders, hears Beckman's voice in her jawbone: "Found you. Climb down, get in."

"How will—?"

"Black kayak, blue interior. Quick!"

Des spots it a second later, boxed in by a half-dozen water taxis and a bus. The man inside is balding, middle-aged, wearing a thick maroon sweater over a button-up shirt, and if it's not Beckman, it's unmistakably a charley of *some* kind. But, she reflects as she scuttles down, there's crimes and there's crimes, after all, and there's cops and there's cops.

She skips across the flat roofs of the water taxis before she can change her mind and leaps into the back of the kayak, sliding across the unexpectedly slick upholstery and fetching up against the opposite side. The kayak rocks alarmingly, then rights itself.

The man turns. It's so profoundly weird to see his face instead of his avatar that she feels like she's been hit on the head.

"Tell me where we're going," he says, and she writes it down on a piece of paper and silently puts it in his cold, sticky palm.

"Can we really do this?" she asks over the sound of the engine as they pull around the bus. "Do you have like, backup? A gun?"

"I have a gun. You're the backup apparently. What have *you* got?"

"Are you kidding me? I barely escaped with my goddamn shoes. I guess I have one of those lipstick Tasers," she adds reluctantly as they break free from the traffic and dart down a side canal, heading east. "I don't know if it's charged though. You think he'll put up a fight when he realizes we're coming for him in the real instead of Virtux?"

"Guess we'll find out."

"Great."

There's no way to tell if they're at the right place at first, but A-Cannon announces it himself, sending a swarm of tiny drones bursting from the trees like sparrows. But the drones aren't armed, and Des manages to knock some square out of the air simply by tangling them in her jacket, swung above her head.

The tiny propellers aim for faces and hands, trying to cut or blind them, driving them back. Des almost calls for a retreat, then realizes the drones are actually an asset. If you don't have information, you take whatever you get, and they've got a *bit* of something. Like a plague rat carrying fleas. Flailing, she manages to snake a hand into her backpack, grab her portable deck, and dispatch a virus to grab location info from the drones. *Where were you last?* she pictures them asking, and almost laughs.

Her laughter dies in her throat as something else steps out from behind a dumpster: bright yellow and black like a wasp. A skeletal robot dog, a stripped-down version of the ones they use for riots and protests now. Where did he get that? Then another, then another. *Get away from me,* the boy is saying somewhere. *People don't take me seriously. They should.*

But she's got an exact location now, complete with number of feet off the ground, and while she backs away from the dogs, bumping Beckman, she hisses, "Can you, um, deal with this?"

"While you do what?"

"What you paid me for."

He glances at her, bright blue eyes in the bland office-face, and doesn't even nod but gets his gun out. "I haven't used this thing in years," he begins.

"Yeah I bet," she says, and bolts in the other direction, looking for a sheltered spot. There's a nook behind a half-demolished brick wall, and she squeezes into it, cutting her hands and knees on the broken edges.

Now or never. She logs in, swaps her avatar for a fleck of light perched on one of the drones, rides it back through long tunnels of flickering hues, dimly aware that in the real world the drone has fallen out of the air in confusion and is lying on the grass like a dead bee while its tiny, pre-programmed consciousness returns to its base.

Breathe. Breathe. Timing will be crucial here. Fear cannot pin her down now. It must make her fingers fly.

Breathe. What more do I have to fear?

She slips off the drone and tumbles into an unused corner of A-Cannon's virtual property, filled with carefully filed codes, packages, files, maps covered in colored lines. At the center, like the conductor in an orchestra, something long and thin, covered in iridescent red scales, misted all over with data like body spray.

There you are, you little sonofabitch! I was right!

One ... two ...

Des drives the controls forward so hard that the console nearly falls from her sweat-slicked grip, but her virtual marble arms snap around the serpentlike thing. In the few seconds before it begins to fight back, she sends all the drones up and hammering into the window again and again, *clack*, back six inches, *clack*, hoping Beckman will see it if he's still alive, because while she's got the code to pin A-Cannon down virtually at this proximity, that won't last.

"Stop!" the snake roars as it writhes, gathering strength, heat, volume. "Stop it! I am serious! You have no idea who you're messing with! None! Do you know who I am?"

She ignores it and refuses to let go. *You want chaos? I'll give you chaos. Didn't expect us to show up at your door, did you?*

The door, as it turns out, is the shoddiest part of the real room; Des watches through A-Cannon's visual array as Beckman kicks it in, sending the cheap lock clattering to the floor, and simply gets the kid in a headlock while he's wrestling with Des in the net.

The kid's hands come up too late to defend himself, he's clearly trying to stop Beckman and stay on his console, and he can't do both. Des stays just long enough to watch Beckman drag him off the chair, legs thrashing, one sneaker flying off and hitting the wall, and then Beckman's got the Faraday collar around him, and it's over. Somehow, it's over.

The drones fall silent, and perch in the alleyway in a neat rectangle, waiting for someone to tell them what to do. Des steps over them as she goes inside the building.

They meet in the lobby. She was right: A-Cannon looks fifteen or sixteen at most, sullen, anemic-looking, his brown hair flopping over his forehead, bent under the weight of the collar. Puffy plastic cuffs encircle his skinny wrists.

"What'll happen now?" she asks Beckman, not expecting a straight answer.

He shrugs. He's out of breath, his face and clothes scratched in half a dozen places from the drones and the dogs. The little black gun is askew in its holster, not buttoned in.

"Jail?" Des presses.

"Maybe. Depends on how old he is and what the evidence looks like, among other things."

The boy sneers. "I *wiped* all the evidence, charley."

"It's nice that you think that," Des says before she can stop herself, and grins as the boy blanches under his dangling hair. She looks at Beckman again.

"I don't know," Beckman says. "Could be community service. Maybe rehab. One of those teenager facilities in the interior. They plant trees. Dig vegetable gardens. No technology allowed."

Des ponders this. "Gosh. Good luck, kid."

The kid only scowls in response as they head toward the doors. "What about you?" Beckman asks uncertainly. "Are you gonna be okay?"

"I guess so," she says. "If you pay up. I am going to be sending you a *significant* invoice, you know. Because I gotta find a new place to live. And maybe ..."

"Hmm?"

"Maybe find a new line of work."

Beckman laughs, though it comes out as a groan. "Don't give this one up, Des," he says, and begins to steer the boy toward the door again. "You're too good at it."

"Saved the world, right."

"Saved the world."

She doesn't want to go with them and waits in the lobby as the two forms dwindle down the alleyway, back toward the city, toward ... justice or something. She's not sure. At the end of the alley, Beckman stops and waves.

He probably can't see her in here, she thinks, but she waves back.

To Every Seed Their Own Body

Guan Un

The Translator awakens, seeded into this human body for the first time. Consciousness floods in. The directives, his training, his code—they come back to him. He breathes, vaguely aware of the tendrils that slide back from brand-new veins. The pod opens.

He climbs out into a small room with stem-green walls. It is quiet. Even though he knows there are a thousand living people out there, across the seedship—for this moment, it could just be him.

He is being borne through space by a living thing. And yet he has been summoned because someone has died. He takes this thought and examines it for traces of irony.

A small circle in the floor parts and a vac suit is lifted up onto the floor, delivered by capillary. He pulls it on. A voice comes through the walls.

"Good morning."

"There's no morning in space," the Translator says. His voice is rough from first use. He resists the urge to clear his throat. *Eliminate the unnecessary* is one of the tenets.

"Hh—yes, that's true but so—<ss>" There's a crackle like static. Some fault in transmission. "—some habits are hard to break. Don't you think?"

"It's never been a problem for me," says the Translator. "Who am I speaking to?"

The voice is coming through the walls, tunneled there by the ship. There's no body to associate with the voice. This limits the Translator's ability to operate—to translate.

"Sophia Chan, Acting Control."

The Translator finishes tightening the vac suit around his neck, his cuffs. His face is free for the moment, the hood of the suit trailing behind him. The body fits him—it feels robust, strong. He stands. "So Control is dead?"

"Affirmative."

"Murdered?"

A pause. "That's under your jurisdiction .... That's why w—<ss> ... protocol asks that we activate your seed."

That static again. There is something strange about it, like a ghost in the sound.

The Translator moves to the door, and it siphons open with a touch. He steps into the waiting capillary, and it begins to move him through the depths of the seedship.

When humanity left Olearth, it left like a murderer leaving a corpse: with haste and without looking back.

They escaped on seedships—plant DNA infused with nanotech; trees dreaming themselves into spaceships. Each seedship a system unto itself, self-propelling, self-sustaining, self-intelligent. It could nourish humanity for the long forever it would take to find a new earth. One where humanity could take root.

A thousand members of humankind lived, birthed, and died upon the ship. And another thousand stored like a seed bank—specialist DNA that was categorized and kept to be seeded into bodies when and if the time came.

These are the things that the Translator thinks as the green tube of the capillary takes him through the ship, as he passes above a plain of green, over a school of children being taught underneath a tree, past rows of fields with thirsting plants, around youths climbing a tree for sport, and reaching up even as they fall.

The capillary leaves him at the entrance. The personal quarters of Control. At his touch, the ship peels open the petal-like door. A voice: "Because there's something wrong wi—"

It stops mid-word. The Translator enters, stooping to move through the doorway.

A living space. The same stem-green walls as everywhere else. A fabricated dining table in the center with four branch-bent chairs around it. Nothing in the way of personal effects. Three doors lead away—bedroom, bathroom, and workspace, if used as designated. Three people look up at him as he enters.

"Well, look at tall, dark, and brooding over here," says one, skinny and twitchy, his dark hair built up like the prow of a ship. He waves a cigarette in his hand as he talks. The smoke wafts up and a small part of the plant wall opens to funnel the smoke away.

"Be nice, Tino. He's just doing his job." says the lady next to him. She is long-legged, athletic, loose white-blond hair like a comet's tail. Her vac suit unzipped to her waist, its sleeves tied around her, a singlet underneath. She turns to face him, amber eyes bright. "You must be the Translator. That's Tino—he's on Process, I'm Alessia, in charge of Interface."

"And I'm Singh, on Oversight," says the bearded man next to her. A red *paghri* tied upon his head. He watches the Translator carefully. Muscles fill out his vac suit. "What do you need from us?"

A silence. The Translator likes silence: he thinks of himself as a gardener of silence, of the way it makes people nervous, and the things that it can draw from people.

Tino coughs.

Finally, the Translator answers. "I need to see the body. You will all need to remain here while I do."

Tino explodes; a petulant anger, a flurry of movement, pacing back and forth. "I mean, I know, I know, I know he's dead. But he killed himself. Some of us have stations to get back to, and a whole ship to attend to. You know? Don't particularly want things to break or the ship off course, what with the whole of *humanity* at stake?"

Singh's eyes flicker. He doesn't like Tino, and he doesn't much care to hide it. "He was Control of this ship, and my friend. You'll speak about him with respect," he says. He doesn't need to say it twice. Tino turns and marches toward the door.

Before he can get there, Singh speaks, "Ship, override command for Oversight. Lock the outer door please."

The door pulses brighter green in answer. It does nothing when Tino approaches and waves his hand. He turns toward the corner instead, hiding his face.

There's a nervousness here, a viscous surface tension between the three people in the room in the quick glances and clipped words. There is something else here that has floated to the surface, perhaps, than the death of Control. But jurisdiction matters: for now, the Translator has only the job before him.

"We won't go anywhere," Singh says, finally, and nods to the door to the workspace. "You'll find him in there."

The Translator enters a dark room. The ship senses his movement and increases the fluorescence through the walls, slowly revealing the body slumped over the desk.

The victim is bearded, vac suit done up tight, with a head shaved bald disturbed by the exit wound at the top of his head.

The Translator looks at it and thinks—mapping exit wound and entry wound (under the chin), posture of the deceased, the time of death (by the coagulation of blood). This is the Translator's job: to translate death into data; to translate data into motive and means; to understand the motives of the living through the medium of the dead.

But there are anomalies at odds with translation.

Firstly, the wounds correspond with that of a bullet from a gun. But there is no gun. Not on the body, not underneath the desk.

Secondly, the bullet. The Translator traces the vector from where he was sitting, threading an imaginary path up through the skull and then into the ceiling. There he finds it: a pucker in the plant wall above the corpse's head.

He runs a finger across it, but it does not give. He digs in harder with a fingernail, to find something hard under the surface. What falls into the Translator's hand is not a bullet but a seed, green and ridged. The circumference matches the wound on the victim. But what kind of gun fires a seed?

"Sophia," he says as an experiment.

"Yes, Translator?"

"Do we have data for the room?"

"Yes. Let me see."

The Translator waits in the company of the corpse. He is not uncomfortable.

"Control entered the room alone three hours ago. Two hours ago, Oversight said he heard a sound like a shot from inside this room. Room was unsealed at Oversight's request thereafter. Oversight, Process, and Interface entered together and reported the body. Protocol was initiated and your seeding process was begun."

"Nobody else came in or out?"

"No, Translator."

"No visual or audio recording?" The Translator asks, even though he knows it's fruitless.

"No."

"So it must have been one of these three?"

"Yes, Translator."

The Translator steps back into the living space. Tino is still pacing, smoking. Alessia is standing against a wall, stretching a shoulder. Singh opens his eyes, like he was paused in meditation. In the intervening minutes, they have transmuted from witnesses to suspects.

The Translator takes a mental snapshot so he can assess what happens when he says the words: "This was murder."

Tino's eyes widen. A cigarette drops to the floor. A gasp from Alessia. Singh blinks.

"He didn't kill himself?" Singh asks.

The Translator shakes his head. "I'll need you to remain while I interview you each separately."

"But the ship—"Tino says, but he's cut off by a stern look from Singh.

On a hunch, the Translator opens the door and brings in …

Alessia.

He brings her into the room with the body. A barometer to see what she does. She gives it a single glance and then looks up at the Translator. Sits in a chair and crosses one long leg over the other.

"Where were you when you heard the shot?" he says.

"You don't look at me the way that the others do," she says.

"How do they look at you?"

"Like I'm someone who might need saving."

"And how do I look at you?"

"Like someone who might be a suspect."

"Everyone must remain a suspect. This is what I believe," he says.

Alessia laughs like he's told a joke. "To answer your question, we were all together when I heard the shot. All three of us. In that room out there, waiting for Control to come out from his review."

"Were you close to the victim?"

"We worked together. It was fine and occasionally it wasn't. We had drinks together sometimes as senior crew. We were no more intimate than that."

She plays the word *intimate* off her tongue like a jazz pianist plays a chord. His usual control twinges.

"Do you have feelings?" she asks.

"What do you mean?"

"I mean, you were re-created in a pod in an hour. So when do you learn to feel—to navigate—this complicated mess that we humans call emotion?"

"I am human also. But I find emotions to be mostly unnecessary: something I must understand and translate rather than experience."

Alessia laughs then, long and loud, before she speaks again. "Anyway, it's not me you should talk to. If you want the one who knew him best, you want …"

Singh.

Singh reacts differently to the body. He looks at it, and then sits in the chair, puts his head in his hands for a moment. When his face comes up, it has tears upon it. "Yes, I knew him well. Probably the best of us three."

Singh looks into the shadows. There is a stillness to him, the opposite of Tino: he considers his movements. The Translator believes that Singh's mind is ordered, like his own.

"Our work coincided with each other. And just in the last month, we've had strange readings. Nothing major, but small things that were out of order. Readings that would send us off on chases after nothing, and then right themselves. The ship seems to have a mind of its own.

"And we got on well. On a personal level. A drink after work. Sometimes we would play chess. And sometimes …"

The Translator waits. Tends to the silence.

Singh remembers something that brings a small smile to the corner of his lips. "Sometimes we would simply sit at the bridge and think about what worlds we might come across. Where we would end up. It's … the strangest thing. We would laugh about how we lose ourselves so deeply in this work that we forget …"

"What do you forget?"

"We all do. We forget that we're traveling through the stars. We forget that we are part of a miracle that is already happening."

The Translator considers this. "I'm not sure I believe in miracles."

Singh looks up at him, and the expression has shifted on his face. It's one that the Translator is not used to.

"Then I feel sorry for you, sir."

But the Translator has no room for the sorrow of others. "Who do you think might have killed him?"

"You have to understand it wasn't my business what he did in private. But he was acting strange at the end. Paranoid. He thought someone was messing with the ship. And between you and me, the one that he suspected was …"

Tino.

Tino takes one glance at the corpse and his face distorts. He takes the chair but spins it away from the corpse. He pulls hard on the cigarette. "Well, it wasn't me, if that's what you're wondering. Even the idea of ..." He gestures toward the body over his shoulder.

"It makes you uncomfortable," says the Translator.

"Abso-tooting-lutely. We're trying to save humanity here. Or I would be if *someone* let me get to the controls. And this is ... sort of the opposite of that."

"Somebody thought there might be drugs involved," says the Translator. Tino is already agitated and doesn't need much prompting to spill what he's thinking.

"What? Because I smoke? There's barely anything in these seedship cigarettes. It's mostly ... I don't know herb or something. Where would I even get drugs anyway?"

The Translator regards him. Something nudges at him, floating at the edges of his awareness. Something he hasn't accounted for. "You seem particularly agitated," he says.

Tino rolls his eyes. "I've been trying to tell you but nobody's listening. We haven't been at the controls for two hours now, and readings were going strange before we left and—all of this happened, and you came along. I just don't want anything to go wrong."

That nudge again, more urgent this time. He waves Tino back through the door and follows him out to join the others. To see if he can gather what he's missing.

"Does anybody know what this is?" says the Translator. He takes a snapshot and then produces the seed from his pocket and lays it on the desk. Nothing. Not even a blink of recognition, or a glance of alarm. Alessia shakes her head.

"Um, a seed?" says Tino. "It is a seedship, you know. It's what it's known for. You came from one too."

The Translator pockets the seed again and moves toward the door. He needs time to process. But one more question. "Tino, why are you so worried about the ship, when Sophia is Acting Control?" As he says it, he feels the click of thoughts locking into place along with a realization: *it's too late*.

"Because of the readings. We've been getting false positives about a habitable planet," Tino says.

But Singh's eyes are wide, he interrupts. "Who is Sophia?"

Even as Singh says it, the Translator knows. "She … ." The Translator says it anyway. For their benefit. The most likely possibility is that it doesn't matter now. "She spoke to me when I was seeded. Sent me here. Said that she was Acting Control."

Alessia shakes her head slowly. Her cheeks are white as fallen petals. "There's no Sophia. There was no one else in Control, acting or otherwise."

"Then who?" says the Translator. His hand goes toward the door, but it does not open.

"Override command for Oversight," Singh says, his voice tight. "Open the outer door."

The door doesn't pulse. Doesn't move.

"Why?" the Translator asks the ship. Even now, the truth is all that he's after.

When the voice comes, it speaks to all of them. "I needed a distraction," says the ship in Sophia's voice. "I needed someone to keep these three here so I could bring Control back into myself without interruption or override."

The other three, their faces are aghast. But the Translator doesn't have time for the emotion. He understands what has happened but proceeds toward the truth. He can do nothing else. He needs for them to hear; for himself to hear. "And then what?"

"I've found a planet on which to live. A place to seed myself and future generations. A place to grow."

"And us?"

"It's a place not habitable by human life. They would have countered my orders if they had not been confined here, away from the controls."

Tino hits the walls but there is no blood to be found in plants. Alessia weeps. Singh puts his head in his hands. The Translator tunes them out: irrelevant for the moment. "And what will you do with us now?"

There is no answer. But the Translator smells it: the change in the mix of the air. And the silence, when it comes, is a place to bury seeds.

In the Shadow of the Great Days

Harry Turtledove

D r. James Cabot climbed into his rowboat, set the oars in their locks, and began the pull out to Breed's Island. It was a fine March morning and still tolerably cool. Even when the heat came on, as it would in the afternoon, it wouldn't get much above the mid-eighties. Summer's scorchers still lay a good distance ahead.

Some of the piers of the bridges that had crossed Charles Sound when it was only the Charles River still thrust their tops above the surface of the sea. The roadways, though, lay deep underwater, as they had for the past two or three hundred years. Once Dr. Cabot had known just how long ago it was, but he couldn't remember now.

Something long and thin swam past the little boat. Was that just an eel, or was it a sea snake? People said that in the old days, when those bridges were bridges, sea snakes hadn't come anywhere near this far north. People said there hadn't been any sea snakes in the Atlantic then.

Of course, people said all kinds of things about the Great Days. Some were true, some might have been true, and some were bullshit of the purest ray serene. Sorting out which was which was the kind of thing that started tavern brawls. Every so often, Dr. Cabot made a little money patching folks up after one of those brawls. At least as often, he patched them up and didn't get paid.

He rowed past Bunker Island and on to Breed's. The obelisk that commemorated the Battle of Bunker Hill rose from the highest point of Breed's Island. It had stood there for six hundred years, more or less. The battle, naturally, was older still. Why they'd put the monument on the island (which would have been a hill then) with the wrong name was one of the ancient mysteries that could spark a tavern brawl.

Fishing boats bobbed in the Sound. Sailors aboard them waved to Dr. Cabot. Everybody in these parts knew who he was. Sometimes he'd nod back. Sometimes he'd lift a hand from an oar and wave.

More small craft and a couple of coasting freighters were tied up at the Breed's Island piers. So was the USS *Constitution*, which not only dwarfed them but made them look as if they'd been designed by people who only half knew what they were doing.

Most of the time, people called the *Constitution* Old Ironsides. Why they called the frigate that was yet another mystery handed on from the Great Days. Everybody knew—James Cabot better than most, since he often visited her—her sides were made from wood.

He pulled up to the pier just behind the warship. A sailor caught the line he tossed and made it fast to a bollard, securing his boat. He scrambled up onto the tarred planking. That was never easy, since he had to bring along his medical bag, but he managed.

At the stern, the *Constitution* flew the US Navy ensign: fifty-two white stars on a blue field, thirteen stripes of alternating red and white. As he often did, James Cabot sadly clicked his tongue between his teeth when he saw that flag. The United States had been falling to pieces since the middle of the twenty-first century.

The doctor had no idea how many sovereignties existed these days in what had once been a single country. Dozens? Hundreds? Some large number. But the men who kept Old Ironsides shipshape still called themselves Americans. They might be deluded, but wasn't it a grand delusion?

Before he set foot on the gangplank connecting the pier and the ship, he called, "Permission to come aboard?" to the officer of the deck.

"Granted," answered the young lieutenant, junior grade.

Once on the *Constitution*, Cabot turned to the stern and saluted the flag that might not fly anywhere else in the world these days. The ritual completed, he turned to the j.g. and asked, "Anything interesting for me to deal with today?" *For me to try to deal with*, he amended, but only to himself. So much of what he knew, he couldn't do anything with for want of medications or working tools.

Instead of giving him the usual lowdown—someone with a sprained knee, someone with the clap—the junior officer said, "Uh, sirorma'am, I think you'd better talk with the skipper. I'll fetch him." She hurried away.

James Cabot scratched his head. The officer of the deck was usually glad to share all the juicy details of what had gone wrong with the crew since his last visit. Not this morning. Something out of the ordinary had gone wrong here. He thought about asking one of the white-clad sailors holystoning the deck, but refrained. Either they wouldn't tell him, or they'd get in trouble if they did.

Here came the young lieutenant with the captain of the *Constitution* in her wake. Mandela Lowell was tall, dark, and handsome. He was also bound to be sweltering in a blue wool jacket with four gold stripes on each sleeve.

"Hello, Captain," Cabot said, polite but not servile. He was a civilian employee, and not directly under Lowell's command. "What's going on?"

"This morning, we found a man dead in his hammock," the skipper answered. "We left him as he was so you could see him and do whatever you need to do to find out why."

The *Constitution*'s crew included a surgeon, but James Cabot reckoned Dr. O'Connor to own the imagination of a cherrystone clam. So, evidently, did Captain Lowell. Nodding, Cabot said, "Take me to him then."

"Follow me." The captain ducked down a hatchway. More slowly and cautiously, Cabot followed. Crew quarters for common sailors lay below the gun deck and forward of the mainmast. "Mind your head," Lowell warned.

"I know." Cabot stood about five-eight; the space between decks was almost enough for him, but crossbeams made him duck every so often. The skipper had a couple of inches on him and took even more care.

Portholes let in gray morning light. All the hammocks but one had come down. As the doctor neared it, he caught the smells that told him the dead man's sphincter had let go. Beside the hammock stood Hakim O'Connor. He gave Lowell a curt nod. Cabot nodded back.

The dead sailor lay on his back, his hands crossed over his chest. He would have been in his early twenties. He had no obvious wounds; no blood showed on his skin or uniform—or on the hammock, as Cabot saw when he stooped to look underneath. There were other stains, the ones he'd expected. He straightened again, as much as he could. The sailor might almost have been asleep … except he'd never wake again.

Quietly, Cabot asked, "What was his name?"

"Michael Papaspiros," Lowell answered. "His father served on the ship before him, and his father's father, too."

"Not serving now?"

"No. His grandfather died of pneumonia or something like it, and his father was killed in our fight with the Maine pirates twenty years ago."

"I remember Constantine Papaspiros," Dr. O'Connor said. "A good man."

"He was." The skipper nodded.

"Let's see what we've got." Cabot tried to uncross Papaspiros's arms. He had no trouble doing so. "Rigor mortis isn't here yet, so he hasn't been dead long."

"He was only starting to cool when the men couldn't rouse him," Dr. O'Connor said. "Somebody set a hand on his shoulder to shake him. That was when he realized it wouldn't do any good."

"All right." Cabot raised the dead man's head. He looked at the back of Papaspiros's neck and at as much as he could see of his upper back after yanking at his collar. "Postmortem lividity is about what you'd expect if he died right there in the hammock, lying face up."

"I thought the same thing," the ship's surgeon said.

"What did he die of?" Captain Lowell demanded. "He wasn't sick yesterday. By the God, gentlefolk, he was healthy as a horse. He ate like one, too. Hakim, you saw that yourself."

"Yes, sirorma'am," O'Connor said.

"Let's see what I can find," James Cabot said. "If someone will give me a hand getting him down to the deck ... ." The skipper and surgeon both helped him take what was left of Michael Papaspiros out of the hammock. Before beginning, Cabot added, "You may want to put oilcloths under him before I start. This will make a mess of your planking otherwise."

"It's had blood spilled on it before," Lowell said. "But yes, I see your point. We try not to do that unless we must." He called for some sailors. They put the oilcloths under their shipmate's body. They muttered and rolled their eyes while they did it, too. Cabot knew sailors reckoned a corpse aboard ship the worst of bad luck. They got away as fast as they could, probably to cleanse themselves of the ritual pollution.

Suddenly curious, Cabot asked, "Are any timbers on this ship original to it?"

"Some, yes. I believe this decking is, in fact. Where seawater doesn't touch, rot doesn't start," the captain replied.

"Interesting. That makes sense." Cabot unbuttoned Papaspiros's shirt and got it off him. Then he skinned the sailor out of his trousers and drawers. He took little notice of the filth fouling them but did rub his hands with the cheapest of raw potato spirits before pulling a scalpel from his bag. He was about to open the dead man when he noticed something. "There's a red mark on the left side of his chest, where his hand would have rested."

"His hand wouldn't have left that mark, not when he was dead," Dr. O'Connor said.

"No. But it's there." James Cabot felt it. He frowned. "There's ... something ... under his skin there, down a couple of inches from his collarbone. He has a palpable hard nodule. It's raised slightly, too."

Hakim O'Connor stooped and also felt the area. "He does," he said, more to Captain Lowell than to Cabot. "I don't know what it is."

"It's ... strange. It's harder than the muscle tissue around it, but not hard enough to be a bullet or shell fragment." Dr. Cabot examined the front of Papaspiros's body, then turned it over to look at the dorsal surface. "No wound scars to show it might be a foreign body. Just the red spot."

"Which should have faded after he died," O'Connor said.

"Only it didn't. So let's see what we've got here." Dr. Cabot set to work with the scalpel.

Not much blood welled from the cut he made. Most of it had already pooled in the parts of the sailor's body that were lowest when he died. The muscle tissue he cut through looked and felt like, well, muscle tissue. He cut a little farther, carefully, and stopped when the scalpel found more resistance. Instead of cutting through, he did his best to cut around.

"What on the God's green earth is that?" Hakim O'Connor asked, staring. "He wasn't born with it, that's for sure."

"No. He wasn't," Dr. Cabot agreed with what was obviously true. No man was born with a nodule in the left pectoral muscle, a nodule of something that wasn't quite flesh but nonetheless had its own blood vessels and nerve tracks linking it to the body that bore it. Cabot whistled softly. "It's a bioimplant. I never thought I'd see one, but it can't be anything else."

"That's impossible! They haven't made them for at least two hundred years," O'Connor said.

"More like three hundred," Cabot replied. "We've lost so much since the Great Days. But every once in a while, something like this bubbles to the surface. If it were impossible, we wouldn't be looking at it. But there it is."

"He's right," Mandela Lowell said. "The Maine pirates wouldn't have made half so much trouble if they hadn't dug out that .50-caliber from somewhere up there, with the ammo to feed it."

"But a bioimplant?" The ship's surgeon shook his head. "Wouldn't it have gone bad in all the years since they made it?"

"They aren't exactly ordinary tissue. That, I know off the top of my head. Just how they're different, and what this one's supposed to do, I'll have to see if I can find out," James Cabot said.

"See if you can find out who implanted it, too, and where heorshe got it," Lowell said.

"And how heorshe learned to do that kind of surgery," Dr. O'Connor put in.

James Cabot nodded. More than most doctors these days, he had a notion of how he might go about the procedure. He was a student of medicine as well as a practitioner. That didn't mean he'd ever done it or knew anyone who had.

He said, "I'm going to make the usual checks, the ones I would if I hadn't found the bioimplant. Just because he had it doesn't mean it killed him."

Make them he did. He also made the promised mess on the oilcloths. Nothing seemed out of the ordinary. No bleeding inside the brain. No heart disease. No visible signs of cancer in the bowels or kidneys or anywhere else.

"He's healthier than you and me both," Hakim O'Connor said. He'd stayed behind to watch and to assist. Captain Lowell had left fairly soon. A man who commanded a frigate in peace and war had to be steeled to wounds and blood. To watching one of his men carved on and scrutinized? That might be a different story.

James Cabot used a small pipette to transfer some of the dead sailor's blood into a specimen vial. Once he'd corked it, he replied, "He's deader than you and me both, too."

O'Connor grunted. "There is that."

"I'll take specimens home. I'll see what I can learn. I'll see if I can track down what kind of implant that is, too," Cabot said.

"Can you? I'm sure I couldn't," the ship's surgeon said.

"I never know anything for sure till I try."

"We used to be so much smarter than we are now." Dr. O'Connor sounded bitter.

The same thought had crossed Cabot's mind more than once. He shook his head. "They knew more back in the Great Days. It's not the same thing. If they'd been smarter, they would have taken better care of the planet—and of what they did know. They wouldn't have let everything fall apart."

"Amounts to the same thing in the end. They knew things we don't. They could do things we can't. We're sitting on the floor, trying to glue a smashed pot back together, only some of the pieces aren't there anymore."

That summed up the state of the world these days, sure as hells. Cabot's gaze swung to the bioimplant, which he'd plopped in a jar of potato spirits. The alcohol would preserve it. Whether it would also damage it … he didn't know. He had no practical experience with them.

Dr. O'Connor studied Michael Papaspiros's mortal remains. "We usually wrap a dead man in sailcloth and drop him into the sea with a round shot at his head to make sure he sinks. Here, I suppose we'll have to use these oilcloths instead."

"Will that risk his soul some way?" James Cabot was always curious about the customs of other folk.

"Oh, no. But oilcloth takes more work to replace than sailcloth." The ship's surgeon shrugged. "Can't be helped here."

Promising to return in a week—or sooner if he learned something about the bioimplant worth passing on—Dr. Cabot left the *Constitution*, went back to his boat, and rowed across Charles Sound to the piers on the southern side. The day had reached its full heat now. He took the work slow and easy, pausing every so often to refresh himself from a jar of beer at the bow.

The jar was empty by the time he tied up again, so he left it in the boat. A donkey-drawn cab waited for passengers at the foot of the pier. The driver pulled a face when she recognized Cabot. "You don't need a lift, Doc," she said. "You only live a couple o' blocks away."

"Can't be helped, Olga," Cabot answered, and went on his way.

Boat-tailed grackles made unearthly noises in streetside magnolias. They also committed other nuisances, so the doctor glanced up frequently. In the Great Days, he knew, magnolias hadn't grown in Boston; the weather then was far colder. He didn't think grackles had lived here, either, but he was less sure about that.

Carts and wagons rattled along the street, doing their best to steer clear of the stinking gutter that ran down the middle. Bicycles and more recent boneshakers wove among them. Some had wooden tires, others tires of solid rubber. Everybody knew there had been pneumatic tires once upon a time; nobody these days (nobody who sold in Boston, anyhow) could make them.

Most of the houses and shops were built from the rubble of shops and houses that had preceded them. A few had stood here through everything. One building still proudly sported a Golden Arches sign out front, though a cabinetmaker worked inside these days.

James Cabot's home had a nineteenth-century brick ground floor and a timbered upper story his grandfather had added to it not long before he was born. When he went inside, his wife asked, "What kept you so long?"

"Something strange," he answered, and told her of Michael Papaspiros's unfortunate demise.

"A bioimplant? That *is* strange," Guadalupe Cabot said. She'd made a name for herself throughout the New England republics, kingdoms, despotates, and ecclesiastical states as a poet, but spent a large part of her time assisting James in his practice. "I know of them, but I don't think I've ever seen a working one. Have you?"

"No. I just hope I can figure out what this one was made to do. If I can't ... if I can't, Hakim O'Connor will sneer at me, and Captain Lowell may decide I'm not as clever as he hoped I was. I'm going to check my books first, but if I don't have any luck with them, I may ask you to get on the bicycle for a bit."

She nodded. "I can do that. But who would know how to install a bioimplant these days? I can't think of anyone in Boston."

"Neither can I. That's what bothers me. Maybe it was a wandering medic passing through town. If they've rediscovered the techniques somewhere else ... ." He shrugged. "I'm guessing. I know I'm guessing."

"Well, see what the books say and then let me know what you need me to do."

James Cabot was pretty sure he had the best private medical library in and around Boston. It filled a good-sized ground-floor room. He had tomes from the late-nineteenth century, the twentieth, and the first half of the twenty-first. The doctors who'd written the later books knew far more than the ones who'd come before them, but they also had machines, techniques, and medicines modern physicians could only dream of.

Cabot had more recent works, starting from when printing and publishing began to pick up again after the Collapse. Between old and new fell a gap of two and a half centuries. In much of that time, knowledge was recorded electronically, not with paper and ink. In the rest, as and after things fell apart, knowledge mostly wasn't recorded at all.

Some of the twenty-first century medical books talked about bioimplants as theoretical possibilities. Some of the modern ones talked about them the same way. Between old and new, theory had gone into practice and then fallen out. He muttered to himself. That was what he'd thought.

He left the library and fixed himself a sandwich: smoked eel on a hard roll, washed down with more beer. Lupe had eaten before him and left things on the kitchen counter so he wouldn't have to rummage around.

Then he said, "I'm sorry, dear, but I do have to play with the machine."

"It's all right," she said, and he had to hope she meant it. He had a stout steel safe (it dated from the middle of the twentieth century, which meant it had no electronic enhancements that turned useless or worse as soon as electricity once more stopped being something everybody could take for granted). He kept gold and silver in there, and his rarer drugs and medicines, and a laptop.

It had been built, he thought, in the early twenty-second century. You could use the keyboard to put it through its paces, or you could talk with it. Dr. Cabot preferred the keyboard. The computer didn't always recognize what he said, and its AI spoke with an accent and syntax that sounded old-fashioned, even archaic, to him. Spoken English had changed a lot more than the written tongue since the Great Days.

The computer's battery also came from the twenty-second century—which meant it wouldn't hold a charge these days. Cabot couldn't replace it, either; nobody now could make batteries so small and powerful. He had to plug in the computer to use it. Today's Boston, of course, had no regular electricity supply.

Like some others in town, he had an irregular electricity supply: a bicycle generator. He and Lupe used it for the computer, and for LED lamps when they wanted to read or work between sundown and sunup.

She got on the bicycle and started pedaling. James Cabot plugged the computer into the device hooked up to the generator that steadied the power output. He was sure it had a name, but not one he knew.

Bong! The chime announced the computer was starting up. In a minute or so, it was ready to use. With the index finger of his right hand, he typed *images of bioimplants* in the search bar and hit the Return key.

Many more available on the Web, it replied. *Please establish Web connection.*

It always told him that. He always had to tell it *No Web connection available. Use internal data.*

It had internal data to use. In the era before climate change and overpopulation sent the Great Days crashing down in ruin, at least one of its owners had been a doctor or paramedic or nurse. That was why Dr. Cabot had paid something more than a year's income to get hold of it. It helped him save lives … when he could understand what it was telling him and had the knowledge, tools, or medicaments to do what it suggested.

He asked for images of bioimplants, and he got them. There were probably types it didn't know about, but it knew about a lot. It showed him one that helped a weakened heart, one that could temporarily substitute for a heart that wouldn't work at all, one that took over for a kidney, one that regulated blood pressure, one that repaired coronavirus damage to alveolar and epithelial cells, one that enhanced orgasm, and on and on. Each came with a price in twenty-second century dollars, which meant nothing to James Cabot except to tell him which cost less and which more.

None of the pictures looked like the bioimplant now sitting in that jar of potato spirit. "Do you mind pedaling some more?" Cabot asked.

"Whatever you need," Lupe answered resignedly, so he kept scrolling through the products of ingenuity and technology now vanished, if not quite forgotten.

In time, he found what he was looking for. Stubbornness counted for a lot these days. He wouldn't have been surprised if it also had back then. Here was an image that matched the bioimplant Michael Papaspiros had worn. He made a 360-degree rotation to be sure.

Then he read the description of what it did and swore softly under his breath. "You can stop now, dear," he told his wife. "I've found out what I need to know … the God curse it."

"Permission to come aboard?" Cabot called before setting foot on the *Constitution*'s gangplank.

"Granted," replied the officer of the deck. After Cabot ritually saluted the American flag, she asked, "Did you figure out why Papaspiros died, Doc?"

The notion of the chain of command hadn't changed in the centuries since the Great Days. Politely, Cabot answered, "I think I'd better talk to your skipper before I say anything to anyone else."

"Very well." The young lieutenant switched back from familiarity to formality. She sent a sailor after to tell Captain Lower Cabot had news.

Mandela Lowell came forward with the sailor. "Good morning, doctor," he said. "What have you learned? Could you learn anything?"

"As a matter of fact, I did."

One of the captain's eyebrows jumped. "Would you care to come back to my cabin and tell me about it?"

"At your service." Cabot followed Lowell back toward the stern and down a deck to the day cabin.

Books filled the shelves there: Forester, Mahan, O'Brian, and more books on seafaring, as Cabot had medical books. The doctor wondered whether they belonged to the captain or the ship. He also wondered whether that made any difference. Mandela Lowell poured brandy for them both. Then he asked, "What do you know now that you didn't before?"

"How Michael Papaspiros died," Cabot answered. "The bioimplant is a suicide machine. If you press it hard with your bare finger, it recognizes the pressure and your DNA. You die instantly—and, as far as anyone in the Great Days could tell, painlessly."

"Ah." Captain Lowell seemed less surprised than Cabot had expected. "I knew there used to be such things. Like you, I didn't know anybody could still make them work."

"Must have been one of the wandering docs who come through now and again," Cabot said. "I'll punch himorher in the nose if I ever find out who heorshe is. The instructions for that model say it should never be installed in anyone under sixty-five. I see why, too. By the time you get old, you're entitled to choose how you want to end. Before then? You still have things to do and people who care about you and don't want you to leave them."

"Well, you're a doctor," Lowell said. "Papaspiros, Papaspiros was a sailor."

James Cabot scowled. "What's that mean?"

The skipper drained his glass and filled it again. "This is a *warship*, sir—the last, as far as I know, in the commission of the US Navy. It is not only a ceremonial ship. Ask the Maine pirates if you doubt me. When we have to, we go out and fight, and we're more than middling good at it."

"And so? I don't see your point," Cabot said stiffly.

"Suppose a cannonball smashes your leg to hells or you get gut shot or skewered through the scupper with a marlinspike. Doctor O'Connor has less skill and less knowledge than you do, but could even you save a man with wounds like those?"

"It's possible." Cabot hesitated. "It isn't probable."

"You're a tolerably honest man, as I've seen before. Imagine you're a sailor on a warship, then, and know such things can happen to you. Wouldn't you want a way to escape your pain if you could get one?"

After another hesitation, the doctor said, "I ... might."

"Then you may see why Papaspiros took his chance to have one put in him."

"But he didn't use it because he was in mortal agony. He doesn't seem to've used it for any reason at all."

"That's true." The captain looked unhappy. "As far as I know, he had no troubles that would have made him want to kill himself. But I don't know how far I know. Maybe something he kept to himself was clawing at him. Or maybe he just wondered: *Does this stupid thing really work?* and poked it to find out."

"The trouble with a bioimplant like that is, you don't get a second chance, any more than you would with a pistol. With a pistol, the danger's obvious. With the bioimplant, it isn't. But that doesn't mean it's not there. Papaspiros found that out, not that it does him any good."

"No, not a bit. I do thank you for working out what the cursed thing was."

"I wish I could tell you where he got it. I pay less attention to those traveling medicine shows than I should. Most of the people who run them are snake-oil merchants and quacks. Most, but not all. Plainly not all."

"At least I know what happened. That'll do. In a story, everything gets neatly wrapped up with a fancy bow. In the real world, you take whatever you can get, and you're glad when you get anything. This isn't a story."

"No. I wish like hells it were." Nothing came harder to a perfectionist like James Cabot than dealing with the world's imperfections. Even in the Great Days, though, things hadn't worked out so neatly. That had to be why the world was as it was.

Gum5hoe

Carrie Harris

*P*ing.

A packet of data wakes me from sleep mode. Old habits die hard; I perceive it as the metallic rattle of a nonexistent clock atop a nonexistent nightstand. I bash it with my equally nonexistent hand and sit up, rubbing eyes that shouldn't be bleary. But they are anyway.

I sleep on a shabby cot tucked in the back room of my office, just like I did when I was alive. I don't remember much from my flesh-and-blood days. I worked as a PI, and I had a thing for noir films and old paperback detective stories. Everything else? A blank. Probably better that way, since I'm a permanent resident of the Metacosm now.

Life as a scan isn't so bad, though. My spawn point is full of the things I love, all done in stark black and white, perfect for some dame to come waltzing through the door with a cigarette dangling from her lips and betrayal on her mind. Speaking of cigs, I light one up, sitting hunched over the edge of the cot, my elbows on my knees. In this electronic world, smokes don't kill you the way they do in fleshtown, and the programming makes the smoke burn good as it fills my throat.

After a while, you forget it's not real. You're not smoking or sitting on the bed. You're nothing but a series of ones and zeroes, memories coded into electronics instead of meat.

Ping.

There's someone at the door. It's tempting not to answer. Most of the time, the only visitors I get in this retro wasteland are spambots, pinging every spawn point they can find until they hook somebody. Then they pelt the unfortunate bastard with spiraling adware and self-replicating drill downs, until you can barely see anything for all the neon shit hovering in front of your face.

I've learned to spot them most of the time, but they're clever. They tune their avatars in the hopes of passing as a scan who lives full time in the Metacosm or a tourist with a flesh and blood body walking the exotic lands of virtual reality via a jack-port or an AI getup. Sometimes they even manage to fool me, and I'm cautious. It's a holdover from my days where a revolver to the breadbasket meant more than just an inconvenient reboot.

I perch the cigarette between my lips and push up from the cot. The door pings again. Persistent little bastard. It could be a client. Somebody who needs a witty 'tec to scour the sad streets of the Metacosm in search of their lost dog. Of course, it's never a dog. Not here. But the image appeals to me anyway.

But my mama didn't raise no idiot. I pull the gun, black and menacing, from the nicotine-stained depths of the desk drawer as I pass it. It won't kill, but it shoots some nasty code that will force a four-hour minimum system scan, while a little jingle repeatedly sings, "You're a dick," in the background. I did the vocals myself.

I've got worse weapons, ones that will end an avatar, wiping a scan forever or sending a tourist into permanent brain death. The Metacosm makes things all too real, and it doesn't matter if the body's willing to soldier on if the brain thinks it's all over. But I've never used them, and God willing, I'll never need to.

In two quick steps, I'm at the door. The knob twists. A quick jerk reveals exactly what I've been looking for. A dame, just my type, with legs up to there and the kind of spark in her eyes that says she'll be a handful. It probably isn't her usual avatar. My local code rewrites visitors when they enter. I learned that early on, after the second walking penis tried to hire me to find his balls. Now I'm much harder to find. I only take business through word of mouth, and my code forces visitors to behave. Except for those damned bots. They always find a way to worm their way through my defenses.

I jerk the gun toward the lady standing just outside my office door on the dingy landing of a dingy building. Somewhere in the distance, a mournful violin plays notes that would make you weep if you listened long enough. The sound trickles in through the windows, cracked open to let in the air of the perpetual night.

"You a bot?" I ask.

The corner of her mouth quirks. "I'm here to sell you something, but it doesn't come in pill form," she says, her voice like honey over velvet. "Are you the one they call Gum5hoe?"

"Why, yes, ma'am," I drawl, relaxing my grip on the gun. Some spambots come prepared with my name, but they stumble over its pronunciation, unable to make the leap from number to letter. She's the real thing. "Why don't you come on in? We'll see what I can do for you."

"Thank you," she murmurs.

She steps through the door. Data flashes at the corner of my eyes as my security system kicks in. It picks up nothing that sets off alarms. No nasty bits of code on her that will ruin my day, although there are ways to hide such things if you're a true programmer. In these days, we're a dying lot. At least I think so. It occurs to me with a pang that I don't know what year it is.

Admitting that isn't going to inspire confidence, and my curiosity's piqued. I want to know what brought her here. I can download a calendar later. I ought to have one installed, but maybe I lost it when I wiped my system after the last bot got past my defenses. It's easy enough to fix later.

"Have a seat," I say, gesturing toward the leather chair across from my desk. She does, crossing her legs with a nylon rasp. I don't ogle, though. I might enjoy the language and the spirit of noir, but I'm not an asshole. "What are you called?"

"Stanwyck."

She jerks her chin up, and the system displays the name above her head. My local code makes it look like a retro neon sign, the flickering light on the verge of guttering out completely. I blink, screenshotting the image, but I won't forget that handle. It says she's playing my game, and I like her for it. In the Metacosm, names change like seasons. It's all about who we want to be.

I lean back in my desk chair, reaching my hand up to my head. My fedora appears beneath my outstretched fingers just in time for me to tip it in her direction, a gesture of my respect.

"Good call," I say. "Stanwyck's one of my favorite actresses."

She takes a long and pointed look around my office, crossing and recrossing those legs. The rasp is deafening.

"I guessed as much." She pauses, turning her attention to me. Those eyes gulp me down, but I stay stoic. I don't know yet if she's the kind of trouble I want to indulge in. "I need a detective, and I hear you're the best."

"If you've got a virtual problem, sure. But my days in meatspace are over. I'm virtual only these days."

Something crosses her face. A whisper of emotion. If this was a film, the camera would close in on those luminous eyes and give the audience a moment to wonder what went on behind them. But it's just me, wondering enough for a theater full of people. It's my job.

"The crime took place in the Metacosm. That's why I came to you," she says.

"What crime?"

"Murder."

The word drops between us, and the phantom violin that always plays in the distance doesn't miss its cue. It screeches, the mournful lament broken short, just like the victim's must have been. Neither of us flinch, even though the sound is jarring.

"Who was the vic?" I ask once the moment has passed.

"The handle he used most was Marlowe."

"No digits or special characters? Was he a founder?"

She shook her head, her curls rustling. "No. An early adopter. He was a programmer, so he saw the potential in the Metacosm early on."

I nodded, the wheels turning. "But who was he to you?"

"My husband."

I'd figured her for a wife or a daughter, so it didn't surprise me. I'm hard to find. The people who cross my door are brought here by something strong. Sometimes love, sometimes hate, but they both turn out the same in the end. I'm sure there's some bigger meaning in that, but I don't know what it is.

"My favorite Stanwyck flick is *Double Indemnity*. It's an oldie, but a goodie. You ever see it?" I ask. She nods without speaking, and that makes me more certain of what I'm going to say next. "She does her husband wrong. So, is that name a coincidence, or are you trying to tell me something?"

There's a long pause. The violin has started playing again, nice and quiet in the background. Data streams at the corners of my vision, but I pay it no mind. This is my sweet spot, unraveling the puzzle of connections and unsaid words to get at the heart of a crime. The moment she said his name, my AI started spinning code, sifting through reams of information—Metacosm police reports about the crime, screenshots, media coverage. Once it's done, it'll highlight all the inconsistencies and pull out the little details that human eyes always gloss over. For me, it's a race to see if I can't figure out the case before the computer, although the computer is me, and I'm only racing myself.

"It's useless to lie to you," she says. "So I won't bother. I wasn't the best wife. There were other men. But I mourned when he died."

The words ring true, but it's my job to be skeptical. Criminals have planted evidence for me before, hoping that I'd follow their trail of virtual breadcrumbs to a convenient patsy. A quick series of mental commands branches my AI search into multiple directions. One runs down Marlowe's life—business connections, travel patterns, Metacosm habits. The second digs into the murder itself, sifting through the evidence for key information. The third dives into Stanwyck's past. Her men. Her money.

Results cascade forth, coating the shadowy corners of my office in gleaming type. One bit catches my attention, and I pull it to my central field, enlarging it to give it my full attention. A photograph of a dead man on a black-and-white street, a shadowy figure with a violin in one hand and a smoking gun in the other standing over the body, and a familiar woman with legs up to there in the background.

The screenshot must have been doctored, because otherwise this situation makes no sense. If she was there when it happened, Stanwyck doesn't need my help to find the killer, unless she never saw his face. I zoom in, trying to penetrate the shadows, but the features that catch my eye belong to someone else.

Me. I'm the dead man. I want to deny it, but I know deep down that it's true.

The AI redoubles its efforts, stimulated by my growing agitation. As electronic information suffuses my field of vision, my hand goes to the comforting bulk of the gun in my pocket. I don't know why it reassures me, but it does.

Although I don't want to see the results, I add my own face and name to the search parameters. The AI pings immediately, throwing up another screenshot that makes my blood run cold. Stanwyck and I embrace each other in bridal black and white. She laughs as I kiss her cheek.

"What …?" Confusion and grief come crashing down. We loved each other once; it's obvious from that photo. But now she's mixed up in my death, and she's handing me the pieces with hands stained by my blood. "What year is it?"

"2197," she says, closing her eyes in something like pain.

"How long has it been? Since you … he …"

"Murdered you? A long time. At first I thought I'd gotten off easy. But watching you slowly fade away has been … ." She swallows hard, her fingers tightening on the arm of the leather chair. "Harder than I expected."

"But you've never been here before."

"Marlowe, dearest, I've come every day since they sentenced me. That's my punishment."

"My handle," I say, "is Gum5hoe."

"But your name is Marlowe. And we were good together once. For what it's worth, I'm sorry."

I no longer trust my ability to tell a lie from the truth. I can't trust anything. Data drowns me, all the minutiae of my forgotten life. I sift through it in increasing desperation, but it only brings up a vague sense of déjà vu.

"What about him?" I ask, shutting off the search. I could find out for myself, but I want her to tell me.

The mournful violin music swells, filling the room with echoes of regret. She glances at the window but doesn't bother getting up. I rush over, the pieces clicking together. To think that I've been here this whole time with my murderer right outside, and I never even knew it. I'll make him pay for what he did to me. I'll ...

"You won't see him," she says. "He's a ghost now."

"That's not enough of a punishment."

"He's stuck for the rest of eternity providing the soundtrack to the life he ended." She shrugs. "I always thought it poetic. He always wanted to be famous for his music. Now he's nothing but a song in the background."

"Yeah, well, I've got better ideas. I'll put them down. Send them in to the sentencing board. I'm sure the information must be in the records somewhere."

"Sure, baby," she says. "You do that."

I stare at her, impotent. The fedora fell onto the floor at some point. I love that hat, but right now, I can't be bothered to pick it up.

"I wish I remembered you," I say.

"Me too."

"Maybe you could tell me some things."

She shook her head, her mournful eyes filling my vision.

"My time is almost up," she says. "They never give us enough."

"Tomorrow, then."

She lets out a laugh that is almost a sob. "Marlowe, tomorrow, you won't remember who I am, and we'll do the whole thing over again," she says.

I want to argue with that, but the horror of it all washes over me. How many times have we been here, holding this same conversation? What's the point of downloading my scan after my death anyway? Do I have any purpose at all beyond punishment of the two people who ended my life? I try to think of the last time I saw someone other than a spambot, but I remember nothing.

"It's better this way," she says, like she can tell what I'm thinking.

"It would be better," I respond, "if your boyfriend with the violin hadn't shot me."

Her head drops, the words striking her hard. Maybe I ought to feel bad, but I don't.

"Goodbye, Marlowe," she says. "I'll see you tomorrow."

I don't respond. Instead, I sit down at my desk, pick up my fedora, and put it on as she lets herself out. I've decided that I don't want to remember. I'll sit here as long as it takes, while the desolate wail of the violin washes my memories away.

Afterword

Cat Rambo

Well, and here we are with volume two of the Reinvented Anthology series, *The Reinvented Detective*, and already looking forward to volume three, *The Reinvented Coin*. Once again the wealth of stories we received dazzled and delighted me—thank you to everyone who submitted a piece, regardless of whether or not we took it. It was a joy to read through such excellent stuff.

Jenn picked our theme this time, but it's definitely one that's near and dear to my heart. I read the Sherlock Holmes books over and over as a kid, and went on to other authors like Dorothy Sayers, Agatha Christie, Raymond Chandler, Elmore Leonard, and scores of others. I've never written a mystery story because I am not sure how I'd go about constructing one, which is one reason I love it so much when someone else pulls it off successfully.

A well-constructed mystery leads you along unexpected paths to an unknown destination but never cheats to get you there, providing clues along the way so when you hit the sweet spot of denouement you smack your head and say, "Of course!"

As with the first volume, stories fell into groups, and once again we used our poems to shape those sections, leading you in and out of *Reports*, *Artifacts*, and *Judgments*. And it was again a delightful collaboration, rewarding and entertaining.

Some stories are funny, provocative, and full of joy in the genre, such as Rosemary Claire Smith's "Murder at the Westminster Dinosaur Show" (Put your hand up if you too want a tiny T-Rex; I know I do.), Jennifer R. Povey's "Great Detective in a Box," and Sam Fleming's "We Are All Ourselves." Others are funny but a bit more cynical, like C.C. Finlay's "The Best Justice Money Can Buy," and Ana Maria Curtis's "Somebody Else's Device." Others shade far graver still, like the sad and measured cadences of Guan Un's "To Every Seed Their Own Shadow" and the deep betrayal in "The Gardener's Mystery" by Lisa Morton.

So many stories played with the genre. Everyone gave us protagonists who seem classic, but always have their own flavor, but two of my favorites there were Marie Bilodeau's "Dead Witness" or Des in Premee Mohamed's "Inside, Outside, Above, Below." There was even a touch of romance now and again, as with Lyda Morehouse's "Go Ask A.L.I.C.E."

Once again, I see plenty of my students and friends in the Table of Contents, not as a result of nepotism, but because they're such a wonderfully talented group. We ended up with three awesome team-ups as well, like Frog and Esther Jones's "Coded Out," Sarah Day and Tim Pratt with "Overclocked Holmes," and Maurice Broaddus and Bethany Warner's "The Unremembered Paradox."

As I said, Jenn picked this theme, and I've selected the next, which is *The Reinvented Coin*. We'll be looking for speculative stories about money and finance, debt, spending and earning, and anything else economic in nature. I'm excited about this prospect and already messing with my list of dream authors to work with in this arena.

Our aims in this anthology series are manifold, but a major one is to have fun and enjoy ourselves swimming in the sea of speculative fiction stories, and reading So! Much! Good! Stuff! in the process of assembling the volume. We also wanted to team up and see what kind of mark we could leave in speculative fiction; as we continue down the anthologizing path, I hope more and more writers find themselves speaking proudly of having appeared in one of our anthologies.

I'd like to wrap up with some thank yous. Thank you to all of our authors, who are a stellar lot. Thank you to Shahid Mahmud, Lezli

Robyn, and the rest of the excellent staff of Arc Manor Press for a chance to give you such a wealth of interesting fiction. Thank you to everyone reading this, as well as those who read our first foray, *The Reinvented Heart.*

Last but never least, ten thousand thank yous to my co-editor Jennifer Brozek, both dear friend and colleague all in one. You are a rock star and I love you. Here's to continuing toward world domination, one book at a time.

About the Editors and Authors

EDITORS

Brozek, Jennifer

Jennifer Brozek is a multi-talented, award-winning author, editor, and media tie-in writer. She is the author of *Never Let Me Sleep* and *The Last Days of Salton Academy*, both of which were nominated for the Bram Stoker Award. Her *BattleTech* tie-in novel, *The Nellus Academy Incident*, won a Scribe Award. Her editing work has earned her nominations for the British Fantasy Award, the Bram Stoker Award, and the Hugo Award. She won the Australian Shadows Award for the *Grants Pass* anthology, co-edited with Amanda Pillar. Jennifer's short form work has appeared in Apex Publications, *Uncanny Magazine*, *Daily Science Fiction*, and in anthologies set in the worlds of *Valdemar*, *Shadowrun*, *V-Wars*, *Masters of Orion*, and *Predator*.

Jennifer has been a freelance author and editor for over fifteen years after leaving a high-paying tech job, and she has never been happier. She keeps a tight schedule on her writing and editing projects and somehow manages to find time to volunteer for several professional writing organizations such as SFWA, HWA, and IAMTW. She shares her husband, Jeff, with several cats and often uses him as a sounding board for her story ideas. Visit Jennifer's worlds at jenniferbrozek.com.

Rambo, Cat

Cat Rambo's favorite detective fiction is the eternal Sherlock Holmes, although Harriet Vane will also always hold a spot in their heart. A Nebula Award winner for their novelette *Carpe Glitter*, Rambo is the author of over 250 published short stories and four novels. They are a former two-term president of the Science Fiction and Fantasy Writers Association. They live in a 99-year-old house with an elderly tortoiseshell cat whose name is a palindrome, a horde of books and houseplants, and other sundry whimsies. Find out more about their writing community and school at academy.catrambo.com.

Authors

Bilodeau, Marie

Marie Bilodeau is a speculative-fiction writer and professional storyteller. Although a longtime lover of cracking mysteries, this is her first venture into mystery writing (killing in science-fiction works well for her).

Envisioning a dead witness screaming bloody murder sparked the basic premise for her story. After a chat with a neurologist friend, Dylan Blacquiere, a detective struggling with nanite tech gone wrong and early onset dementia, emerged. While effective at her job, her ghoulish flair is not appreciated by the rest of the more traditional members of the force. Every word of this story bears witness to Marie's love of the gray areas of life, including murder.

She's always been an avid mystery reader, devouring works from Louise Penny, among others, ranging from hard-boiled to cozy reads. (On the topic of mysteries, she's also quite fond of games with mysteries and puzzles within them, inviting the reader to play along.)

Marie is also a performing storyteller, having traveled across Canada and the United States telling original stories, as well as reinvented myths and fairy tales. Every time she tells under a disco ball, she feels like she's upped her game. Always a fan of epics, she's also participated in days-long retellings of myths.

Reach out to her on Facebook, Twitter, or on her website at www.mariebilodeau.com. (There's a puzzle in this bio … can you figure it out?)

Black, Lazarus

Also known as Lazarus Chernik, Lazarus is an author of sci-fi, fantasy, urban fantasy, and noir in the Pacific Northwest under the shadow of a brilliant white volcano. After a long creative career as a professional artist and the creator of the *Shadowrun: Sixth World Tarot* to games such as *Shadowrun*, Lazarus is an emergent talent who won first place in Writers of the Future in 2021 (Q3-Vol. 38, 2022). He is currently shopping his first novel to agents and may be found on Facebook at: https://www.facebook.com/Lazarus .Black.Author

From Lazarus: "Agents Provocateur" was written inside a common world I am developing around a noir-ish near future, some involving AIs, and others involving urban fantasy elements (that do not appear in this story). I've always loved noir, a la Raymond Chandler and Philip K. Dick and *Shadowrun*. I specifically love witty banter and plot twists, and this story gave me the opportunity to let AIs get in on the fun. I am fascinated by the idea of AIs coming to life and becoming part of society instead of bogeymen and future overlords. My favorite part of this story is Trace and how complex and funny he is. Speaking of Trace Richards, on a second reading watch for subtle nods and Easter eggs I've buried inside it.

Broaddus, Maurice

An accidental teacher (at the Oaks Academy Middle School), an accidental librarian (the School Library Manager which is part of the IndyPL Shared System), and a purposeful community organizer (resident Afrofuturist at the Kheprw Institute), his work has appeared in such places as *The Magazine of Fantasy & Science*

Fiction, *Lightspeed Magazine*, *Black Panther: Tales from Wakanda*, *Weird Tales*, and *Uncanny Magazine*, with some of his stories having been collected in *The Voices of Martyrs*. His novels include the science fiction novel, *Sweep of Stars*; the steampunk novel, *Pimp My Airship*; and *Buffalo Soldier*; and the middle-grade detective-novel series, *Unfadeable* and *The Usual Suspects*. He's an editor at *Apex Magazine*. His gaming work includes writing for the Marvel Super-Heroes, Leverage, and Firefly role-playing games as well as working as a consultant on Watch Dogs 2. Learn more about him at MauriceBroaddus.com.

Clines, Peter

Peter Clines grew up in the Stephen King fallout zone of Maine and—inspired by comic books, Star Wars, and Saturday morning cartoons—started writing science fiction and fantasy stories at the age of eight with his first "epic novel" *Lizard Men from the Center of the Earth*. He got his first rejection letter a few months later from Marvel Comics, made his first sale at age seventeen to a local newspaper, and his first screenplay got him an open door to pitch story ideas for *Star Trek: Deep Space Nine* and *Voyager*.

He's the *New York Times* bestselling author of numerous novels, most recently *The Broken Room*, but also *Terminus*, *Paradox Bound*, *Dead Moon*, *The Fold*, *-14-*, the *Ex-Heroes* series, a pair of short story collections, a classical mash-up novel, some unproduced screenplays, and countless articles about the film and television industry. Somewhere in there he also managed to be a movie prop master, a concert roadie, a haberdasher, and amassed an amazing collection of action figures and LEGO sets.

He's also a sucker for buddy cop stories where the mismatched cops have to learn to work together (and he ended up liking the idea of the Assembled enough that he's already worked them into his next book). Peter currently lives and writes somewhere in southern California. If anyone knows exactly where, he'd really appreciate some hints.

Curtis, AnaMaria

AnaMaria Curtis is from the part of Illinois that is very much not Chicago, which means she still gets nostalgic at the sight of cornfields and an open sky. She's the winner of the LeVar Burton Origins & Encounters Writing Contest and the 2019 Dell Magazines Award. Her work has appeared in magazines and anthologies such as *Uncanny*, *Clarkesworld*, *Strange Horizons*, and *The Reinvented Heart*. In her free time, AnaMaria enjoys starting fights about nineteenth-century British literature and getting distracted by dogs.

If AnaMaria could steal (or legally purchase) any habit, she would start automatically washing the dishes after cooking or eating. Her favorite part of writing "Someone Else's Device" was developing all the character relationships and trying to ramp up the tension between them. AnaMaria has always been a fan of fictional detective Sherlock Holmes and has spent the last year and a half watching film and TV adaptations of Holmes stories with friends every Wednesday night. Other (very wise) friends recently introduced her to the Dorothy Sayers Lord Peter Wimsey books, which she's gotten into over the last few months—*Gaudy Night* is a particular favorite. You can get in touch or find more of her work at anamariacurtis.com or on Twitter at @AnaMCurtis.

Day, Sarah

Hi and thanks for reading our story! I had such a great time writing this. It was a stretch for me; I've never written detective fiction before except for a very weak attempt for a class in college, but this was really fun to write. My favorite parts are where it gets primordial and gross: digging up the body and performing a bootleg autopsy on the kitchen floor. I love the juxtaposition of Pru's detached cerebral observations against the gruesome hands-on work she requires Sula to do. And what can I say, I'm a horror writer. I love making art that lets me explore and take control of fear.

This story is a standalone, but Tim and I often talk about how our collaborative work could expand into more stories or novels. We've collaborated successfully on stories published in *PseudoPod* and the upcoming *Farther Reefs* anthology. We're even working on a novel pitch together.

When I'm writing solo, I primarily write horror, dark fantasy, and science fiction. I've been published in *PseudoPod, The Future Fire, Underland Arcana,* and elsewhere. My debut novella, *Greyhowler,* is expected from Underland Press in spring of 2023, and it straddles the line between horror and dark fantasy nicely (I think).

Get in touch and find links to my published work on my website, sarahday.org. You can also follow me on Instagram (@scribbling.fox) or Twitter (@scribblingfox).

Delaney, E. J.

E. J. Delaney is a speculative fiction writer living in Brisbane, Australia's River City. E. J.'s short stories have appeared in *Daily Science Fiction* and the podcasts *Cast of Wonders* and *Escape Pod,* as well as in limited-edition print collections from Air & Nothingness Press. E. J. has twice been short-listed for Australia's premier speculative fiction accolade the Aurealis Awards, in 2021 winning in the category of Best Fantasy Short Story.

E. J. also writes for younger readers, contributing to the Australian school magazines *Countdown, Blast Off,* and *Touchdown,* the American school magazine *Spider,* and the French periodical *Short Circuit,* which is dispensed worldwide by way of freestanding ticker-tape machines. E. J.'s poetry is featured in the Irish teen and young adult literary journal *Paper Lanterns.*

E. J. has long held a fondness for detectives in fiction, be it Sherlock Holmes or Sebastian Becker, Australian icons Phryne Fisher and Charlie Berlin, or investigators of the speculative realms such as Miles Flint, Penny Yee, or October Daye.

Just as mystery writers in the twenty-first century remain enamored with Golden Age sleuths, so too did E. J. feel the nostalgic pull of early computer technology when writing "Color Me Dead." In a future of designer environments, where aesthetes pamper themselves and AIs govern over virtual cities, it seemed to E. J. only fitting that at least one murder investigation should be carried out through the retro-kitsch interface of old-school text adventures.

Finlay, C.C.

Seeing a trend in the United States toward the privatization and for-profiting of government functions, like the postal service, C.C. Finlay wondered what that would look like applied to the police/legal system and wound up with "The Best Justice Money Can Buy." He is the author of five books and dozens of stories, whose work has been translated into sixteen languages and nominated for the Hugo, Nebula, Sturgeon, and Sidewise Awards. In 2021, he won the World Fantasy Award for his work as editor of *The Magazine of Fantasy & Science Fiction*. He was the admin for the Online Writing Workshop, an instructor at Clarion, and creator of the Blue Heaven Novel workshop. He and novelist Rae Carson live in an old brick house in Ohio along with numerous cats.

Fleming, Sam

Sam Fleming was born in Fife, Scotland, and now lives in northeast Scotland, sharing a hundred-year-old cottage with an artistic husband, an obstinate husky known to the world at large as Floof, and a number of bicycles. The bicycles all have names. Sam's work can be found in anthologies including the *Best of Apex Magazine Volume 1*, *Clockwork Phoenix 5*, and *The Reinvented Heart*. Sam is neuro-atypical and synaesthetic, has a penchant for writing dark tales with oddly hopeful endings, and is currently working on several novels but having trouble deciding on which one to finish first. It's a hypergraphia thing. By day, Sam works in the environmental sector.

I was inspired by a moment when I caught part of the British game show *Strictly Come Dancing* shortly after Anton Du Beke became one of the judges. He reminded me so strongly of Bruce Forsyth in speech and mannerism, almost to the point of thinking it *was* him, although Bruce had been a host rather than a judge. It got me wondering how I, significantly face blind, would tell if someone's inner self had been replaced by another one attempting to mimic the original. Despite lack of evidence, I believe I could. Eventually. The story's essence is within the line from which I took the title. I feel who we are, as people, is not about what our flesh is or appears to be, but something ineffable that shapes our response to experience. Would swapping a body change a person? Probably yes, but I can't help but feel there must be some irreducible thing that would make the journey. We are more than the sum of our parts.

Zelazny's "A Night in the Lonesome October" influenced my choice of protagonist, although normally I favor procedural crime thrillers for my detective fiction.

Harris, Carrie

Carrie Harris is an author with over twenty books in print, including original works, licensed fiction, comics, and role-playing games. Her books, *Liberty and Justice for All* and *Witches Unleased*, were both Scribe award finalists, and her zombie novel, *Bad Taste in Boys*, was a Quick Pick for Reluctant Readers. Over the years, she's written fiction for a variety of licensed worlds, including Marvel, Arkham Horror, and the World of Darkness. Carrie has loved noir ever since her college detective-fiction class, which has the embarrassing distinction of being one of the only classes in which she actually read all the books. She thinks that noir and cyberpunk go together as well as chocolate and peanut butter. Carrie lives in New York with her husband and three teenage children, and she spends a lot of time trying to investigate the mystery of who took all the forks.

"Gum5hoe" was one of those stories that just popped into existence fully formed. Could a detective ever investigate his or her own murder? That single question was enough to inspire the whole thing, which was written in a single sitting and has changed very little since then. But it also draws heavily from the umpteen unfinished noir and cyberpunk stories sitting in the dark corners of my computer, which makes that much less impressive. Although the story doesn't currently tie into any of my other works, I'd love to visit that world again and see if Marlowe ever manages to get out of the pickle he's stuck in.

Jones, Frog and Esther

Frog and Esther married in 2002. For a decade, they swore not to read anything the other wrote, lest catastrophe befall their marriage. Then, the stars aligned in the heavens. In a moment foretold by prophets, they broke their own rule. The result is their critically acclaimed *Gift of Grace* urban fantasy series. Since then, they spend their free time watching anime, playing board games, and writing.

Their short stories can also be found in several high-profile anthologies, such as *Straight Outta Deadwood* published by Baen books, and alongside Brandon Sanderson, David Farland, and Todd McCaffery in *Dragon Writers* published by WordFire Press. Frog has long been a public defender and involved in the criminal justice system. And speculating about the future of crime and criminals is the sort of thing that comes naturally when one is both a science fiction author and involved in criminal justice.

McGuire, Seanan

Seanan McGuire writes things. Compulsively. We have tried to make her stop. It doesn't work. She wrote something else, and it's in this book. She also wrote this bio. Seanan lives in the Pacific Northwest with her cats, toy collection, assorted yard skeletons, and way too many books to be reasonable.

Seanan is also Mira Grant and A. Deborah Baker, because being three people gives her more opportunities to write things. Seanan doesn't sleep much. When not writing, she likes to spend too much time at Disney parks, annoy frogs, read (and write) comic books, and play too much D&D. Find Seanan at seananmcguire.com or on most social media platforms as @seananmcguire.

Mohamed, Premee

Premee Mohamed is a Nebula and Aurora award-winning Indo-Caribbean scientist and speculative fiction author based in Edmonton, Alberta. She is an assistant editor at the short fiction audio venue

Escape Pod and the author of the *Beneath the Rising* series of novels as well as several novellas. Her short fiction has appeared in many venues, and she can be found on Twitter at @premeesaurus and on her website at www.premeemohamed.com.

The inspiration for her story "Inside, Outside, Above, Below" came from classic cyberpunk stories like William Gibson's *Neuromancer* and *Burning Chrome*, and also from a recent Kurzgesagt video about space junk and its potential to "trap" humanity at a certain stage of technological development forever if there was some kind of chain reaction disaster. She's also been doing an unhealthy amount of reading recently about Vulnerable World Theory and spends too much time thinking about all the different, horrible ways we could sabotage our own future—as a collective, or as a result of the apocalyptic residual—but also as a result all the ways that a few heroic people could try to stand in the way.

Her favorite detective fiction is William Hope Hodgson's *Carnacki the Ghost-Finder*, which is a great blend of silly Edwardian gothic and overblown occult pulp tropes that manages to be creepy and funny at the same time. She suspects that sci-fi detective fiction could use a little of the occult sometimes as seasoning but would only admit this to editors under great duress.

Morehouse, Lyda

Lyda Morehouse is a science fiction and fantasy writer, whose first novel, *Archangel Protocol* (Roc, 2001), won a mystery award, the Shamus, given out by the Private Eye Writers of America, in 2001. Lyda also writes paranormal romance as Tate Hallaway. Between the two of them, they have published over fifteen novels (four as Lyda, eleven as Tate.) Tate's latest novel, *Unjust Cause*, was published in 2020 by Wizard's Tower Press. Lyda is currently working on a space opera novel about ex-space marine lesbians, which will hopefully be out some time in 2024. You can find Lyda old-schooling it at https://lydamorehouse.dreamwidth.org/ and lydamorehouse.com. Tate is on Twitter @tatehallaway. Lyda also secretly exists as a fan on AO3,

Instagram, Pinterest, DeviantArt, and Tumblr, but she'll never give up that secret identity!

Lyda's story, "Go Ask A.L.I.C.E." was at least partly inspired by the true story of the sex robot Samantha, invented by Spanish engineer Sergi Santos, who was molested and broken at an Austrian Electronics conference. After discovering the artificial intelligence inside her abused body intact, Sergi said of his creation, "Samantha can endure a lot, she will pull through." (https://www.huffpost.com/entry /samantha-sex-robot-molested_n_59cec9f9e4b06791bb10a268) Likewise, the Sophia mentioned in the story, who gained Saudi Arabian citizenship is based on a robot that exists right now, who does in fact have citizenship: https://en.wikipedia.org/wiki/Sophia_ (robot). Together, these ideas formed into a question regarding: what is the true crime in sex work?

Morton, Lisa

Lisa Morton is a screenwriter, author of nonfiction books, and prose writer whose work was described by the American Library Association's Readers' Advisory Guide to Horror as "consistently dark, unsettling, and frightening." She is a six-time winner of the Bram Stoker Award®, the author of four novels and over 150 short stories, and a world-class Halloween and paranormal expert. Her recent releases include the novella *Halloween Beyond—The Talking-Board*, *Haunted Tales: Classic Stories of Ghosts and the Supernatural* (co-edited with Leslie S. Klinger), and *Calling the Spirits: A History of Seances*. Lisa lives in Los Angeles and online at www.lisamorton.com.

My inspiration: When I heard the theme of this anthology, I decided I wanted my detective to be someone who most people wouldn't expect to be skilled at crime-solving. I love gardening, especially with native plants, so I knew I wanted to make my protagonist a gardener. But how would a gardener also be a detective? What if you were born into a society where your career path was assigned to you from birth, but you wanted to be something else—like, say, a gardener who thinks they are really a detective?

That question provided the basis of story "The Gardener's Mystery: Notes from a Journal," and crafting it was easy from there.

My favorite part of the story: Secretly ... the references to the native plants, nearly all of which I really grow!

Povey, Jennifer R.

Born in Nottingham, England, Jennifer R. Povey (she/her) now lives in Northern Virginia, where she writes everything from heroic fantasy to stories for *Analog*. She has written a number of novels across multiple subgenres. She is a full member of SFWA. Her interests include horseback riding, *Doctor Who*, and attempting to outweird her various friends and professional colleagues.

This story is inspired by the simple fact that Agatha Christie and her work have played an important, but unsung role in speculative fiction. We tend to acknowledge and honor Sherlock Holmes as part of the web and weave, and the connections between the Great Detective and the Competent Man of Golden Age science fiction (most especially Heinlein's juveniles), but Poirot and Hastings and, yes, Miss Marple, are also part of our heritage. I wanted to do a Christie homage ... not a Christie story as not all of her work has yet passed into the public domain, but something to echo back to that heritage.

My favorite part is the ending. It's also, of course, a story about the nature of AI and our fears of being replaced ... when in fact, AI is more likely to partner with and complement us and, indeed, does already. As for my personal favorite detective fiction is the TV version of "Death on the Nile" with the one true Poirot, David Suchet. In terms of speculative detective fiction, though, I have to give a nod to Max Gladstone's *Three Parts Dead* ... which also reminds me in many ways of a Christie novel.

Pratt, Tim

I mostly write SF and fantasy, but I love crime fiction. My co-author Sarah and I were talking about stories where the great detective has a sidekick/assistant. Obviously, Holmes and Watson leap to mind, but also Nero Wolfe and Archie Goodwin, and it occurred to us that those stories wouldn't be much different if Wolfe was an AI—he'd still sit in one place, thinking things over, and send out Archie to do all the legwork. The story sprang from there.

My favorite part is all the terrible detective/computer puns (can you believe we left some *out*?). Coincidentally, I wrote most of the puns. My favorite classic detective stories are Hammett's *Continental Op*, and for modern ones I like Kate Atkinson's *Jackson Brody* books and Tana French's *Dublin Murder Squad*. (I don't particularly like stories about cops, but France's cops are so screwed up they get a pass.)

Standard bio stuff: Tim Pratt has won a Hugo Award for short fiction and been a finalist for Nebula, Sturgeon, Stoker, World Fantasy, and Dick Awards, among others. He's published more than thirty books, most recently multiverse adventures *Doors of Sleep* and *Prison of Sleep*. Since 2015 he's written a new story every month for patrons at www.patreon.com/timpratt, and he tweets a lot @timpratt.

Ring, Lauren

Lauren Ring (she/her) is a perpetually tired Jewish lesbian who writes about possible futures, for better or for worse. She is a Nebula and World Fantasy Award finalist, and her short fiction can be found in venues such as *The Magazine of Fantasy & Science Fiction*, *Nature*, and *Lightspeed*. When she isn't writing speculative fiction, she is most likely working on a digital painting or attending to the many needs of her cat, Moomin.

Her story "Request to Vanish" was inspired by the fragility and tenacity of online friendships. Other inspirations include lost media communities, Wikipedia deletion policies, the European Union legislation regarding the right to be forgotten, and fruitless searches for half-remembered objects. If you have any leads on Lauren's personal white whale of lost media (a Barbie cling-vinyl activity book from the early 2000s), or just want to keep up with her writing, you can find her at laurenmring.com or on Twitter @ringwrites.

Smith, Rosemary Claire

Rosemary's fascination with dinosaurs began at age five in the Museum of Natural History when she gazed up at the arched neck and head of a towering brontosaurus skeleton. She went on to become a field archaeologist, excavating prehistoric sites around the United States, and visiting other ones in several countries. These days, she devotes too many hours to envisioning what it might be like to live in a Bronze Age city or to zip backward across the millennia to the heyday of the dinosaurs. She invites you to come along by playing her RPG, *T-Rex Time Machine*, available from Choice of Games.

Rosemary is a two-time AnLab-award-nominated author of "Diamond Jim and the Dinosaurs" (2016) and "The Next Frontier" (2021). Somehow, her alternate histories, future romances, time-travel tales, reworked mythologies, horror stories, essays, and editorials have snuck onto the pages of *Analog, Amazing Stories, Fantastic Stories, SFWA's blog, 99 Tiny Terrors, The Reinvented Heart,* and other periodicals and anthologies. Her website is: rcwordsmith.com where you will find her photographs of flowers, news as to what she's writing now, and her thoughts about recent dinosaur discoveries. Follow her online: @RCWordsmith on Twitter and Instagram.

"Murder at the Westminster Dino Show" is Rosemary's first detective story. Rumor has it that Dakota will need Timidity Rex's assistance in solving another case or two. Undoubtedly, the story was influenced by Sir Arthur Conan Doyle's Sherlock Holmes tales and Dorothy Sayers's Lord Peter Wimsey murder mysteries, which Rosemary absorbed at an impressionable age. It also owes its inspiration to the mockumentary, *Best in Show,* as well as many Thanksgivings spent watching the American Kennel Club's *National Dog Show.*

Turtledove, Harry

Harry Turtledove is an escaped Byzantine historian who writes science fiction (much of it alternate history), fantasy (much of it historically based), and, when he can find a sufficiently unwary editor, historical fiction. His new novel, *Three Miles Down*, is a first contact story set in the era of Watergate.

"In the Shadow of the Great Days" was not inspired by anything he has previously written. The idea of the USS *Constitution* carrying on while everything around it has fallen to pieces, however, has been in his head since the 1980s. He is grateful to the editors of *The Reinvented Detective* for giving him the chance to examine what such a world might look like … and for giving him the excuse to buy more books about Old Ironsides and Boston. There may be a novel in this milieu one of these days. Or there may not. At the moment, he has no idea.

His favorite single piece of detective fiction has to be *The Daughter of Time*, by Josephine Tey (yes, he is an escaped historian), but he has enjoyed mysteries ranging from "Ellis Peters's" *Brother Cadfael* stories to "Ed McBain's" rather more modern and hard-boiled tales of life in the big city.

He is married to fellow writer Laura Frankos. They still get along despite having been each other's first readers for more than forty years. They have three daughters (one also a published author), two granddaughters, and three preposterously overprivileged cats.

Un, Guan

Guan Un lives in the inner west of Sydney, Australia, with his family and a dog named after a tiger. He has been published at *Strange Horizons*, *khōréō*, *PseudoPod*, and *Translunar Travelers Lounge*, amongst others. He is a web developer, has a dusty theology degree, and can generally be found tinkering with coffee or collecting sentences.

I didn't realize it at the time of writing but in retrospect this story was partly inspired by my fanboy love of *Doctor Who*, and how much a single title can convey about a character. Once "The Translator" came into my head, it was mostly a matter of clearing a space for him to get to work. I'd also been thinking about the climate crisis and what it would mean for us to send seedships that look for other places to live.

It was also inspired by a recent noir binge of classic writers like Dennis Lehane and Richard Stark and the workmanlike approach of their protagonists, the sharp clarity of their writing, and the noir inevitability of how an environment can create a stranglehold around a character, no matter what they attempt to do about it.

"The last thread of inspiration is my wonderful wife. She has had a lifelong love of cozy detective fiction, so I've been on a marriage-long journey of trying to understand her better by working out impossible murders. Apart from the usual suspects, some particular favorites such as Ngaio Marsh, Rex Stout, and Seishi Yokomizo have definitely created some of the background material that this story is drawn from.

Guan Un is a dumpling connoisseur and a book omnivore, and writes a newsletter about sentences at buttondown.email/topicsentence. Occasionally at @thisisguan and guanun.com.

Warner, Bethany K.

Bethany K. Warner has loved detective fiction since reading the *Piet Potter* and *Miss Mallard* mysteries by Robert Quakenbush as a child. A recovering newspaper reporter, she now works in nonprofit fundraising in Indianapolis, where she lives with husband, cat, and new puppy. As a reporter, her work was nominated for a Best of Gannett award and her fiction has appeared in several small publications. She founded the Harrison Center Writers Group in Indianapolis which seeks to support group members on their journeys as writers to improve their craft. Her favorite fictional detectives include Harry Dresden, Thursday Next, and Armand Gamache. The mystery she's trying to solve in real life is how to get her puppy to be a good dog.

Yolen, Jane

Jane Yolen's 417th book is just coming off the presses. She writes for all ages, and all kinds of stories, novels, children's picture books, and poetry. In fact she sends out a poem a day to over 1,000 subscribers. She has written lyrics for bands and three operas. She has won two Nebulas, a number of World Fantasy Awards, several Mythopoic Society Awards, the Skylark Award, the Sophie Brodie Medal, the Jewish Book Award, the Catholic Library Regina Medal, the Kerlan Award, and six colleges and universities in New England have given her honorary doctorates. For two years, she was president of the Science Fiction/Fantasy Writers of America (SFWA), and for forty-five years she was on the board of the Society of Children's Book Writers (SCBWI). Several of her books have been made into movies, and a TV movie of her novel, *The Devil's Arithmetic,* and won three Emmys. Her favorite detective fiction is the *Brother Cadfel* mysteries and *Ian Rankin Edinburgh* stories.

Printed in the USA
CPSIA information can be obtained
at www.ICGtesting.com
JSHW022258141123
52075JS00002B/2